ALSO BY ADRIANA TRIGIANI

Big Stone Gap
Big Cherry Holler
Milk Glass Moon

LUCIA, LUCIA

LUCIA, LUCIA

A NOVEL

Adriana Trigiani

RANDOM HOUSE

NEW YORK

Copyright © 2003 by the Glory of Everything Company

All rights reserved under International and Pan-American Copyright Conventions. Published in the United States by Random House, an imprint of The Random House Publishing Group, a division of Random House, Inc., New York, and simultaneously in Canada by Random House of Canada Limited, Toronto.

RANDOM HOUSE and colophon are registered trademarks of Random House, Inc.

ISBN 1-4000-6005-2

Printed in the United States of America

Book design by Victoria Wong

For my sisters,
Mary Yolanda, Lucia Anna,
Antonia, and Francesca,
and my brothers,
Michael and Carlo

LUCIA, LUCIA

*F*rom her window Kit Zanetti can see absolutely everything that happens on Commerce Street. The name doesn't really suit the street; it should be called Winding Trail, or Lavender Lane, or Rue de Gem. Greenwich Village doesn't get any more enchanting than this at night, with the puddles of blue light around the roots of old trees that grow a few feet apart on either side of the street; or any lovelier by day, when the sun bakes the connecting row houses, none more than four stories high, some festooned in ivy, a few white clapboard with black-licorice trim, and one storefront so old that the brick façade has faded from maroon to pale orange. The brownstone stoops are hemmed with old terra-cotta pots containing whatever flowers grow in the shade, usually pink and white impatiens. The sidewalks are uneven, the concrete squares like slabs of layer cake. The shutters that swing from the windows are painted mottled shades of cream and Mamie pink, a powdery peach tone not seen since the Eisenhower administration (it appears the shutters have not been painted since then, either).

This is the ideal home for a playwright, clusters of buildings filled with stories and people whose quirks play out with small-town regularity. Every morning Kit sits in the window while her coffee brews, and witnesses the same scene. A petite woman with shocking red hair walks a Great Dane as tall as she is, and as they turn the corner, she yanks the leash, and he leaps into the air, setting off the car alarm in the Chevy Nova. On the opposite corner, a bald accountant in a suit the color of a Tootsie Roll emerges from his basement apartment, looks up at the sky, takes a deep breath, and hails a cab. Finally, the superintendent from the apartment building across the street comes out of the foyer, hops on his stripped-down bike (essentially two wheels connected by a coat hanger), throws a broom over his shoulder, and rides off, looking very World War II Italy.

There is a loud knock at the door. Kit is expecting her landlord and super, Tony Sartori, to stop by and unclog her sink for the tenth time this year. The tenants have never seen a professional anybody (plumber, electrician, painter) with actual tools work in the building. Everything in this building, from the wiring to the gas to the pipes, is fixed by Tony with duct tape. The tape thing became so funny that Kit cut out a magazine article about how Miss America contestants create cleavage under their evening gowns by hoisting their breasts with duct tape, and put it in her rent envelope. Mr. Sartori never mentioned receiving the article, but he began addressing Kit as Miss Pennsylvania.

"I'm coming," Kit calls out sweetly in the high-pitched, grateful tone of a renter who doesn't want to be any trouble. She opens the door. "Oh, Aunt Lu." Lu is not actually Kit's aunt, but everyone in the building calls her "aunt," so Kit does, too. Sometimes Lu leaves gifts for Kit outside the door—a small bag of expensive coffee beans, a bar of lilac soap, a sample box of tiny perfume bottles—with a note that says, "Enjoy!" in big, cursive handwriting. The stationery, small ecru cards with a gold "L" engraved on them, is uptown tasteful.

Lu smiles warmly. "How are you?" She lives upstairs in the back apartment and is the only other single woman in Kit's building. She's in her seventies, but she has the chic look of New York's older ladies who stay in the moment. Her hair is done, her lipstick applied in the latest shade of fiery fuchsia, and she wears a vintage Hermès scarf wrapped around her neck and anchored by a sparkly brooch. Aunt Lu is trim and small. Her perfume is spicy and youthful, not flowery like a grandmother's.

"I thought you were Mr. Sartori," Kit says.

"What happened?" Lu peers into the apartment, expecting to see water gushing from the ceiling or worse.

"The sink. It's clogged again. And it won't open up no matter what I do. I plunged. I prayed. I used enough Drano to blow up Brooklyn."

"If I see Tony, I'll tell him to get up here and fix it immediately."

"Thanks." If anybody has an in with the landlord, it's Aunt Lu. After all, she is a blood relative.

Aunt Lu pulls on her gloves. "I was wondering if you were busy this afternoon. I'd love to have you up for tea."

She has never invited Kit up to her place. They both know and live by the unwritten rules of apartment dwelling. It's best to keep a distance from neighbors in a small building; cordial greetings by the mailbox are acceptable, but beyond that it gets dicey, since there is nothing worse than a fellow tenant who stops by too much, chats too long, and borrows things. Kit says, "Thanks, but I'm writing. Maybe we can do it another time."

"Sure, whenever you can, you let me know. I've been cleaning out my apartment, and I have lots of things I think you might like"—Lu looks around the apartment—"or could use."

Kit reconsiders. Nothing is more alluring than a free indoor flea market without other customers to beat to the prizes. And Aunt Lu reminds Kit of her own grandmother. She also seems self-sufficient and has an air of discernment, something Kit would like to cultivate. How many women can wear an enormous enamel dragonfly brooch and pull it off? "Maybe I can make it around four."

"I would love that!" Lu says, smiling. "See you then."

"How ya doin', Aunt Lu?" Tony Sartori asks as he climbs the stairs to Kit's apartment.

"I'm fine, but Kit's drain has seen better days." Aunt Lu winks at Kit as Mr. Sartori enters the apartment.

"Yeah, yeah, it's always something around here," he grouses.

Lu grabs the hand railing and makes her way down the narrow stairwell. It's early October and not too chilly outside, maybe fifty degrees, but Lu is already wearing her full-length mink coat, which drags the stairs behind her like the cape of a duchess. No matter the temperature, from September to June, Aunt Lu wears that mink coat.

"Come on in." Kit need not invite him, since he's already in the bathroom. "Aunt Lu's a pretty lady," she tells him, hoping to score some points.

"You kiddin' me? In her day, she was a looker. They say she was the most bee-yoo-tee-ful gal in the Village."

"Really?"

"Yep. You said you had a leak."

"A clog. In the bathroom sink," Kit corrects him.

"Again?" he says in a tone that implies it's Kit's fault. Tony Sartori is a small man with white hair and black eyebrows that look like thick hedges. He looks enough like Gepetto, the gentle cobbler in *Pinocchio*, to make Kit feel safe, but his vocal tone is pure New York rasp, which scares her a little.

Kit laughs nervously. "Sorry. You know I spend my nights stuffing the drain with olive pits so you have to spend your days fixing it."

Tony Sartori looks as though he may yell, but he smiles instead. "Remain calm, Miss Pennsylvania. I'll fix it."

Kit grins weakly but knows better. He'll plunge the sink and then wrap some crappy tape around the hole in the pipe and return in two weeks when the sticky stuff comes undone and she has another flood.

"We might have to get a plumber this time," he says from under the sink.

"Hallelujah!" Kit claps her hands together joyfully.

Sartori grips the sink and pulls himself to a standing position. Kit's bathroom is wallpapered floor to ceiling with rejection letters from every regional theater in the nation, from Alaska Rep to the Wyoming Traveling Players. They are all variations of the same message: good characters, good dialogue, but "you don't know how to tell a story, Ms. Zanetti." Tony Sartori reads one and shakes his head. "Don't you ever want to give up? I mean, with letters like these, what's the point?"

"I'm getting better," Kit tells him.

"Maybe you are. But evidently there aren't a lot of people out there in the theater world who think you can write a play." Sartori shrugs. "Besides, what *is* the theater anymore? It's not like it was. It used to be cheap and wholesome, dancing girls and good music. Now it's too damn expensive. They herd you in like cows, and then the seats are so small, you get a blood clot in your leg before the first song is over. My wife loves that *Phantom of the Opera* show. I thought it was all right. To me it's just a guy in a mask scaring a girl with a good figure and then singing about it."

"The reviews are in!" Kit says cheerfully. She is used to the barbs, criticisms, and comparisons that come with her chosen profession. Playwriting as a career is pathetic. A writer can't make a living, and in this culture, plays are about as relevant as glassblowing or whittling forks out of wood. Kit will keep these thoughts to herself, since the last thing she needs is an artistic standoff with Tony Sartori.

"That's just my opinion." Mr. Sartori spins the roll of duct tape on his index finger and goes to the door. "Can you hold off using the sink for a while?"

"How long? You know I do an intense beauty treatment each night, and it requires running water to make the thick paste that I trowel on to prevent premature wrinkles."

"That must be quite a sight. Use the kitchen sink for now."

"Yes, sir." Kit smiles. "Mr. Sartori?"

"Yeah?"

"Do you ever think anything I say is funny? Even just a little?"

"Not really."

Tony Sartori closes the door behind him, and Kit hears him chuckle from the other side.

The Pink Teacup on Grove Street has the best coconut cake in the city. Made from scratch, it's a yellow cake so moist, for a moment it seems like it may not have cooked through. The batter is full of tiny pineapple chips, and the icing is butter cream whipped so light that the coconut curls sink into it. Juanita, the cook, likes Kit because she raved about the cake in an online magazine piece. Whenever Kit passes by, Juanita cuts her a slab for free. Today Kit takes two slices, one for herself and one for Aunt Lu. As she walks back toward home, she makes a mental note to add some dishes to the article she is writing for *Time Out*, "Best Food in the Village." The articles don't pay much, but the perks are fabulous—free food in her favorite restaurants. So far her list includes:

Best Breakfast: the weekender at Pastis, on Ninth Avenue—includes a basket of sticky buns, chocolate pané, cocoa bread, and nut loaf followed by scrambled eggs with crispy home fries made with onions and butter.

Best Lunch: the hamburger at Grange Hall, on the corner of Commerce and Barrow, with a glass of robust red wine.

Best Sandwich: the tuna salad with a delicate paste of avocado and sliced tomato at Elephant and Castle on Greenwich Avenue.

Best Dinner: Stefano's spaghetti pomodoro at Valdino West on Hudson Street.

Best Comfort Food: garlic mashed potatoes at Nadine's on Bank Street.

Kit's neighborhood is often host to small literary tour groups who wander around with their guidebooks, pointing out the brownstones where Bret Harte and e. e. cummings lived, and the bar where Dylan Thomas raised his last glass before passing out in a booth and meeting his maker. Kit imagines creating an Eating Tour of the Village. Literature vs. a good sandwich. She has a hunch her tour would draw larger crowds.

Back home, Kit places the slices of cake in a Tupperware container and settles down to work. It takes all of her willpower not to eat the coconut cake before her four o'clock tea with Aunt Lu. She knows she will spend most of the afternoon circling it like a lonely hawk hovering over a platter of steak tartare in the desert. Of course, this is what writers do when they're not writing: they walk in circles around food and decide whether or not to eat it, as if taking a bite will somehow make a bit of dialogue work or help create a missing scene (it never does). This is why the Weight Watchers meetings at Fourteenth Street and Ninth Avenue are packed with women writers, including Kit, who has reached her goal weight twice in the last year. Eating and writing are the husband and wife of creativity.

Promptly at four o'clock Kit climbs the stairs to Aunt Lu's apartment, feeling triumphant about her two gorgeous uneaten slices of coconut cake. She hopes hot tea and something sweet will get them through the visit, since she can't imagine what she and Aunt Lu will talk about.

Like most New Yorkers who live in walk-ups, Kit has never gone above her own floor. Lu's fifth-floor landing has charm, and there's a small skylight over a metal ladder that leads to the roof, resembling a periscope on a submarine. Kit has always wanted to check out the view, but the lease forbids tenants to go on the roof. The more Kit thinks about it, the more she realizes that Tony Sartori is stricter than her parents ever were. But it is worth a little suffering to live on Commerce Street.

"Aunt Lu?" Kit calls out. The door is propped open with a black iron kitten.

"Come in, darling."

Kit eases the door open slowly. "I brought . . ." She looks around the chintz wonderland in awe. Every corner, nook, cranny, and wall is filled with stuff.

"What, dear?" Lu says from the kitchen.

"Cake," Kit blurts. "From the Pink Teacup. It's really good. I wrote about it. It's fresh daily. I hope you like it."

"I've been there many times. The food is excellent."

Aunt Lu answers the whistling teakettle in her tiny kitchen while Kit does a full turn and takes in the expanse. The walls are high, and much of the ceiling is covered by a large skylight that slants down, making an eave to a door that leads to the terrace. It has begun to rain, and as the drops hit the glass, they tinkle like music. Aunt Lu's canopy bed is covered by a chenille bedspread, white with shaggy violets on scalloped trim. The furniture is precious and frilly: a pale blue velvet love seat and two chintz slipper chairs with a pattern of irises. The coffee table holds a collection of silver mint-julep cups filled with tiny silk flowers.

"I have a lot of stuff, don't I?" Aunt Lu says from the kitchen, chuckling.

"Yes, but it's all . . ." Kit struggles to describe what she sees. "Interesting. Like you've lived—I mean, live—an interesting life."

"Look around. Enjoy."

Kit skirts the furniture carefully. Every flat surface is covered with knickknacks—two pink ceramic poodles with a gold chain connecting them, tiny vases of Venetian glass, a jeweled letter opener, years of collected clutter, bad gifts, inherited bric-a-brac, and sale items too cheap to resist. Even the wallpaper says, "Old lady lives here," with its fat cabbage roses on a crisscross trellis. Kit feels overwhelmed, as though she is standing in the middle of someone's hope chest, among layers and layers of stuff that has meaning but no purpose.

Kit turns and faces the long wall of the apartment. It is lined with red and white department-store gift boxes, each one with swirly letters that say, "B. Altman's." The boxes at the top have been faded by the sun, so their red is more brown than the boxes stacked underneath.

In the corner next to the wall of boxes is a small end table dressed with a lace doily. Arranged atop are several photographs in ornate silver frames. In the center is an eight-by-ten color photograph of a beautiful girl in a strapless gold lamé gown. The color in the photo is intense and saturated, like that of an old movie still. The young woman in the picture is around twenty-five, her heart-shaped face creamy pink, her full lips in a light pink pout. Her almond-shaped eyes are set off by long black eyelashes and perfectly sculpted eyebrows, making her seem Egyptian or Italian. Something exotic. "Who's the knockout?" Kit asks.

"That's me," Aunt Lu tells her. "When I was about your age."

"Really?" Kit says, then immediately apologizes for her tone. "I didn't mean that like it sounded. Of course it's you. That's your face, for sure."

"No, no, I'm an old lady now, and that's over. It took awhile for me to accept that. It's not easy to let go of your youth, believe me."

"You would be on magazine covers today with your face. And that body! I write for magazines sometimes, and they look for models who have that."

"Have what, dear?"

"That quality. That golden kind of beauty, where each feature is perfect and it adds up to something original. Your eyes are a color of blue I've never seen before. And your lips, they're a cupid's bow. And I don't mean to sound funny, but your nose is the best I've ever seen; it's straight, and the tip goes up a little. That's a feat for us Italian girls. Sometimes we end up with real honkers."

Aunt Lu laughs. "Well, thank you."

"No, no, it's true."

Lu takes the photograph from Kit and looks at it. "What a night that was. New Year's Eve at the Waldorf. The McGuire Sisters rang in 1951 with me, my boss, Delmarr, and my mother and father at a front table at the foot of the stage. That was one of the best nights of my life."

"You're breathtaking," Kit says.

"I was just lucky," Lu says, then adds, "You're a pretty girl, too."

"Thanks. But my grandmother always says it doesn't matter what a woman does to look young, when we hit seventy, we all wind up looking like Mrs. Santa Claus."

Aunt Lu laughs. "It sounds like I'd get along fine with your grandmother. Come sit down." She places a silver tray with the cake, the teacups, a small pot of tea, sugar, and creamer on a side table.

Kit leans back in the chair, which is so soft, the cushions must be filled with down. She pours cream in her tea while she tries to think of what to say next. "Is your real name Lucy?"

"No. Lucia." Aunt Lu says her name softly, with a perfect Italian accent.

"Loo-chee-uh," Kit repeats. "Like the opera?"

Aunt Lu smiles, and Kit notices a deep dimple in her right cheek. "Papa called me Lucia di Lammermoor."

"What did he do?"

"He owned the Groceria."

"On Sixth Avenue?" Kit leans forward in amazement. The Groceria is revered as an authentic Italian market and is therefore one of the biggest tourist traps in the city. It features all the best imported staples, including Tuscan olive oil, fresh pastas, and hanging salamis from every region. It sells cheeses from around the globe, and mozzarella cheese made fresh daily that floats in tubs of clear water like golf balls. The store is known for its elaborate displays of breads, meats, and fish.

"Do you still own it?"

Aunt Lu frowns. "No, dear. It was sold about twenty years ago. The family business is now centered around managing apartment buildings."

"Tony Sartori owns *other* buildings?" Kit can't believe that the king of duct tape would have other properties.

"He and his brothers. Tony is a real piece of work. So impatient. That temper. The boys today are nothing like my father. Sometimes they remind me of my brothers, but my brothers had respect for the family. Today I'm lucky if they remember I live up here. I know old people aren't terribly interesting to young people, but I am, after all, their aunt, and their only connection to their father's people."

Kit nods, feeling a little guilty. She hadn't been too excited about spending any time up here, either.

Aunt Lu continues, "Tony is the eldest son of my eldest brother, Roberto. Of course, my brother has been dead for many years."

"So, how many of you were there growing up?"

"I had four older brothers. I was the baby."

"What happened to them?"

"They're all gone. I'm the last of the original Sartoris. I miss them, too. Roberto, Angelo, Orlando, and Exodus."

"Great names. Exodus. Were you all named after opera characters?"

"Just two of us." Aunt Lu smiles. "Do you like the opera?"

"My grandmother does, and she passed it along to me. I've offered to burn CDs of her record albums, and she won't let me. She likes to stack them on her record player and let them drop and play through, scratches and all. Gram thinks the scratches make the music better."

Aunt Lu refills Kit's teacup. "You know, Kit, when you're old, you like to hold on to all the little things that meant something to you. It feels comfortable and right. Let her have her old ways. They're *her* ways, you understand?"

"Yes, I do. Is that why you live in your nephew's building? Or is the Sartori family holding out to make a big sale on the building, and then you'll cash out and move uptown with a view of Central Park?"

"Sure, sure. I'm holding out for my view of the park." Aunt Lu smiles.

"I don't blame you. You should get something out of living here. The place isn't exactly maintained, but I don't like to complain. I'm afraid Mr. Sartori would throw me out."

"I know the feeling," Aunt Lu says quietly.

"Of course, my place is in worse shape than yours. My bathroom wall is ready to cave in."

"How should they know how to take care of these properties when everything they have was handed to them? I worked my whole life, so I know the value of things."

"When did you stop working?"

"I retired in 1989 when B. Altman's closed. Of all the employees, I had been there the longest, since 1945. They even gave me an award." Lucia picks up an engraved crystal paperweight off the coffee table and hands it to Kit.

"This is kind of like a perfect-attendance certificate in high school."

"That's exactly right."

Kit returns the award to its place on the table. "You were there so long. You must have liked your job."

"Oh, I loved it." As Aunt Lu remembers, her face is transformed. Beneath the distinguished older woman she is now, Kit can see the young woman with moxie and beauty. Kit is ashamed that she tried to come up with an excuse to avoid this cup of tea. After all, Lucia

Sartori is no Greenwich Village kook like the guy on Fourteenth Street who dresses up like Shakespeare and walks through Washington Square Park broadcasting sonnets. Kit looks over into the alcove where Lucia's mink coat hangs on a dress mannequin. The sleek black fur looks almost new in what little light is coming through the windows. The rain has stopped and left behind a late-afternoon sky the color of a gray pearl.

"Aunt Lu? May I call you Lucia?"

"Absolutely."

"I've always wondered, since you wear it a lot, what's the deal with the mink coat?"

Lucia looks off into the alcove. "The mink coat is the story of my life."

"Well, Lucia, if it's not too much trouble, can you tell me the story?" Kit picks up her cup of tea and settles back in her chair as Lucia begins.

CHAPTER TWO

"*L*oo-chee-uh! Loo—"

"Mama, I'm coming!" I shout from the top of the stairs.

"*Andiamo!* Papa needs the envelope!"

"I know, I know, I'm on my way." Quickly, I grab my purse and throw in lipstick, keys, my small leather datebook, a bottle of clear nail polish, and my felt pincushion in the shape of a small red tomato with the elastic wristband. I've chosen a simple navy-blue dress with a full skirt, deep tiered pockets, and a button-down bodice with a stand-up white collar, mist-blue stockings, and blue high-heeled shoes with a single strap and beige button. I throw open my everyday hatbox and pull out a small turquoise velvet cloche that swoops over one eye, keeping my side part flat and neat. I take my short white gloves, slam my bedroom door, and click down the stairs so fast, I'm in the vestibule in under a minute.

"Tell Papa I want him home at six." When Mama issues an order, I obey. She pushes a loose curl back into place, tucking it into her chignon. The strands of white in her black hair are becoming more pronounced, but her skin is still smooth as a girl's. Her high cheekbones are flushed with pink, and her jawline is strong.

"Remember," she says as she tucks the envelope into my purse, "we have our big dinner tonight."

"What are you making?"

"Bracciole. Papa is cutting the tenderloin himself. The meat will be so *delicato*, it will fall off of Claudia DeMartino's fork."

"Good. I really want to impress her."

"And we will. Make sure you're on time." Mama kisses my cheek and pushes me out the door. What a perfect autumn day. The sun is so bright on Commerce Street, I close my left eye to let the pupil in the right adjust, then open both.

"*Bellissima* Lucia!" our neighbor Mr. McIntyre comments as I pass.

"Why can't I find a good Irish boy with that brand of blarney?" I ask him.

He laughs heartily, chomping down on the end of his cigar. "I'm too old. Anyhow, you're destined for a nice Italian boy."

"So they say." He knows, and I know that from the moment my brothers and I were born, Mama had the same wish for us. Bring home an Italian. Mama's sermons about "marrying our people" can be re-created by my brother Exodus, down to the praying-hands gesture she makes when invoking God, begging Him to have us use our heads. We may laugh when Ex imitates her, but we know she means business. Papa is no problem. He always says, "*Stai contento.*" If we're happy, he's happy.

The schoolboys on Seventh Avenue South whistle as I pass. "Lucia!" one of the boys calls out. When I don't respond, he hollers again, "Lucia! Lucia!" Sometimes I turn and wink; after all, they're just boys.

My brother Angelo hoses down the sidewalk in front of Sartori's Groceria, Greenwich Village's only Italian fresh market. My brother has opened the wall-size display windows and rolled back the awnings to let the sun dry the terra-cotta floor.

Angelo has a classic, angular face; wide-set brown eyes; full, even lips; and a small nose. At five foot eight, he's the shortest of my brothers, but many people believe he's the best-looking. Mama thinks he should have been a priest, because he's the peacemaker in the family. Angelo spritzes the Halloween pumpkins stacked neatly near the entrance and makes a motion as if to spray me with the hose.

"Don't you dare!"

Angelo laughs. He's twenty-nine, a full four years older than me, but he'll never be too old to tease me.

"Where's Papa?" I ask.

"Can't you hear him?"

I lean in the door and hear the voices of Roberto and Papa raised in an argument. "They're fighting again?"

"As usual. I serve two masters. One wants everything as it was in the old country, and the other wants it like the A&P up the street. Nobody wins."

"Not yet, anyway," I tell him.

The door is propped open with a giant can of crushed tomatoes. Papa and Roberto are nose to nose before crates full of ruby-red apples.

"I buy the apples where I buy the apples!" Papa yells.

"You pay too much!" Roberto counters.

"I know the farmer for thirty-two years! He grows the apples just for me! I don't buy produce off a truck. Who knows where it comes from?"

"From an apple tree! An apple tree, Pop. They're all the same! And who cares where they come from when they're fifty cents less a bushel?"

"I care! I care a lot! Half the fruit on those trucks is rotten! I won't sell old and rotten in my shop!"

"I give up! You hear me? I give up, Pop!" Roberto grabs his clipboard.

"Don't yell at Papa!" I shout at my brother.

Roberto, at six foot one, is much taller than our father, but he shrinks a bit at the sound of my voice. "It's none of your business. Stick to your sewing," he says petulantly, then turns and goes to the stockroom. Roberto looks like our mother's people: black hair and brown eyes, long, straight nose, and thick, expressive eyebrows. He acts like them, too; he has a terrible temper. When I was little, he always seemed to be shouting, and his anger frightened me. Now I yell back.

"Here's the envelope from Mama." I give Papa the envelope filled with cash.

"*Grazie.*" Papa takes the money to the register and places the bills neatly under the metal catch. "How's my girl?" he asks in a serious tone.

"Papa, why do you worry about me?" I ask, but I know the answer. He worries about everything, his family, his business, and the world that is changing too fast for him. Since the war, business has doubled, his daughter has become a career girl, and his sons have developed big mouths and lots of opinions.

"I can't help it." Papa shrugs and dumps the coins into the register. "I want you to be happy."

"Papa. I *am* happy," I promise him.

Everything about my father exudes warmth and humor; the room fills when he enters. Papa has curly salt-and-pepper hair and blue eyes. I'm the only one of his children who inherited his blue eyes, and this is one of the many things that seem to bind us in a special way. When Papa laughs, which is often, his eyes crinkle shut. He has broad shoulders and a thick waist like a dockworker's, but his hands are like a musician's, with long, tapered fingers.

"What's happiness, anyway, Pop?" I throw my arms around him and give him a big hug. On my way out, I shout toward the stockroom, "Now I have to go to work. Lots of sewing to do!" and to my father, "See you later, Pop."

When I'm out on the sidewalk, I hear Papa holler, "Lucia di Lammermoor!" I turn back. "Be careful!" he calls after me.

I throw him a kiss and walk to the bus stop.

Every morning when I hop off the bus at Thirty-fifth Street and Fifth Avenue, I am still awed by the fact that I have a job at the best department store in New York City. I never take it for granted. My favorite moment is when the passengers exiting the Thirty-fourth Street subway station merge with the crowd on the sidewalk and, like a great wave, we walk up a hilly portion of the street that suddenly dips down and reveals B. Altman & Company, so grand it covers an entire city block.

When the store opened at this location in 1906, it was called the Palace of Trade, and the name still fits. On Fifth Avenue, where most of the buildings stand out as architectural wonders, this one is special. The style is Italian Renaissance, six sprawling floors with twenty-foot ceilings, immense and spectacular. The majestic storefront has a series of colonnades made of French limestone that reach up to the second floor. Over each giant window is a half-shell awning of smoky green glass; from the opposite corner they look like a series of elegant Tiffany lamp shades.

The interior is filled with the highest-quality goods from every corner of the world, each item carefully selected and displayed to fill the customer with longing, just like Papa's store. Each time I walk through the main entrance, and it's been this way every day of my working life, I feel a rush of excitement followed by a jolt of self-confidence. I look up at the twinkling chandeliers, inhale the fine perfumes—sweet notes of delicate freesia, woodsy musk, and fresh roses—and believe anything is possible.

I still can't believe that this is where I work, that every second Friday I receive a paycheck printed on pale blue paper with my name typed neatly in black. PAY TO THE ORDER OF: MISS LUCIA SARTORI. The bottom right corner bears the official stamp of R. Prescott, Vice President, and in the bottom left corner, "Custom Department" is neatly handwritten.

I never take the elevators to our offices on the third floor. I prefer the escalators, because I don't want to miss a single display. They're changed monthly by the window dressers, who are renowned for their realistic tableaus. Last winter they built an ice-skating pond with mirrors on the floor, surrounded by evergreen trees with clumps of artificial snow, and set out mannequins skating à deux with glass stars swinging over their heads. The male mannequin wore a navy-blue and white Nordic wool sweater. The display was so popular that every daughter in New York City, including me, bought her father that sweater for Christmas.

As I pass the display cases, deep glass boxes lined in velvet and trimmed in polished cherry wood, I do a quick inventory of new arrivals. The latest Austrian crystal brooches, sleek leather gloves from Spain, and beaded evening bags twinkle under the soft white lights. Everywhere you look, a treasure. Thank heaven for layaway!

My route never changes. Each morning I walk across the main floor through Men's Furnishings, past Custom Shirts, through the Silk Department, past the Camera Department, around Engraving and Stationery to the escalator, up to the second floor, through Infants' and Children's to Misses' Wearing Apparel, and then up to the third floor, through Furs, Stoles, and Coats. By now I've removed my gloves, and I touch the sumptuous mink and fox coats as I pass. The luxurious sable! Regal ermine! Chic leopard! A girl could get lost in here forever and never tire of the glamour.

By the time I push through the double doors marked SPECIAL ORDER DEPARTMENT FOR DRESSMAKING AND TAILORING into the Hub, a large workroom with a long cutting table, drawing boards, sewing machines, and steam presses, I'm ready to work. My boss and chief designer, Delmarr (no last name, how avant-garde!), pours himself a cup of coffee from a black-and-white-checked herringbone thermos. He looks as though he posed for the "Seen Around Town" article in the *Herald*, in his gray tweed jacket with the black suede elbow patches and black cashmere slacks. "Half the battle is looking the part," Delmarr has told us. He is tall and lean, with feet so large that he has his tasseled suede loafers custom-made. "Navy subs," he calls them. "A good cobbler is a genius. Making a stylish and comfortable pair of shoes takes artistry and architecture."

Delmarr has an open face with wide cheekbones, deep dimples, and a strong chin. It's a handsome face, but there is substance and wisdom in his intelligent eyes and graying temples. Delmarr is a "sophisticate," my best friend, Ruth, would say. When he isn't working long hours, he's out on the town with one of a long line of society girls. Delmarr is the quintessential ladies' man, tall and handsome, with no intention of ever settling down. Now and then his name shows up in the society pages. Delmarr knows everybody, it seems. When a new client walks in for a consultation, he doesn't rest until he figures out some connection to her. And when it comes to design, he knows what will be fashionable before the pack. Delmarr has a talent for the moment.

"Hey, kid," he says now with a big grin. "What's the word from Greenwich Village?" He pulls a silver case from his jacket pocket, removes a cigarette, and lights it.

"Well, it's the first week of October, so the apples are in."

He throws his head back and laughs. Nobody laughs like Delmarr; it's from the gut. "With news like that, we might as well be in Ohio. What's next? A hayride through Central Park?"

"You never know."

"So, your father will spend the day stacking apples into a pyramid, crafting a perfect display. Sometime I'd like to watch him," Delmarr says sincerely. "You know that's a talent. Presentation. That's a *real* talent."

"I told you, I come from artistic farmers." I steal a cup of coffee from Delmarr's thermos and head over to my desk.

Ruth Kaspian, my fellow seamstress, looks up from her drawing table. "What's with the navy blue? It's positively funereal. Somebody die?"

"Not that I know of."

"It's so severe. You're too pretty for severe. The dress has got to go."

"It was a gift."

"Give it back." Ruth takes a stub of pink chalk and gently rubs it along the hem of the dress she has drawn.

"I can't. It came from family. My future mother-in-law."

"Ick." Ruth makes a face, slides off her stool, and stretches. She is tiny; compact, really, maybe five foot one. We're both twenty-five, but she could pass for much younger. She has beautiful dark curls that frame her face in neat ruffles. Her pale skin and brown eyes are offset by her bright red lipstick. "I get it. You're wearing it to impress Mrs. DeMartino. The old soft soap. Let me know if it works. My future mother-in-law gave me an umbrella. Maybe I should open it indoors and scare the devil out of her. She's superstitious, you know. Russian."

"Mrs. DeMartino has been nice to me. I don't have any complaints."

"Lucky you. Mrs. Goldfarb is helping to plan our engagement party. She wants to do it at the Latin Quarter."

"Could you try to sound a little more excited?"

"No," Ruth says flatly. Her tone makes me laugh. "I'm too practical to get all hepped up, you know that. I don't want to go to the Latin Quarter with either my relatives or Harvey's. They'll sit there like stumps. Like a bad breeze from Brooklyn."

"Give them a chance."

"Well, I guess I should just be honest. I don't want to be a Goldfarb." Ruth rolls up her sketch and stuffs it in a tube. She hands it to me, and I place it in the bin behind my desk. Later we'll lay out all the drawings for Delmarr, and he'll choose a few to show our customers for next spring.

"But you love Harvey," I remind her.

"I love him. Yes, I do. Since I was fourteen and he was fifteen and I danced with him at Morrie's Acres in the Poconos after he bought me a hot dog. But I've always hated his name. I can't believe I have to trade Kaspian, a name I love, for . . . Goldfarb."

"Don't," Delmarr says as he drops work orders into the bin. He takes a final drag off his cigarette and tosses the butt out the window. "It's 1950. There are plenty of women who don't change their surnames."

"Sure, they're called spinsters," Ruth says.

"No, married women. Particularly in art and design. Actresses. Women in the public eye who had a life before meeting their future husbands."

"Who?" Ruth wants to know.

"You've heard of Lunt and Fontanne?"

"Sure."

"They're not Lunt and Lunt, are they?" Delmarr shrugs and takes the paperwork into his office.

Ruth lowers her voice so Delmarr can't hear. "Harvey is not going to go for Kaspian and Goldfarb, I promise you. It sounds like a fish market on the Lower East Side."

"Maybe you should ask him what he thinks. He might let you keep your name."

"Fat chance. I could never even bring up the subject. I'm his girl, and I'm going to take his name, end of story. Harvey makes decisions ten years before he has to. He's already named our kids: Michael, for his grandfather Myron; and Susan, after his grandmother Sadie."

Suddenly I feel claustrophobic, listening to Ruth talking about children and names and what Harvey wants and what Harvey doesn't want. Ruth is a brilliant artist, she can draw anything, she has excellent taste and an eye for what works. Delmarr believes she'll be a great designer someday. All this talk of Harvey and babies makes that seem like a faraway dream. Can't Ruth hear what she is saying?

"What, you don't like Susan?" Ruth looks at me.

"No, no, it's a nice name."

"What's the matter?" Ruth looks at me intently. She knows what I'm thinking, but I don't want to get into an argument. I love her too much to force my opinions on her. So I smile and say, "Nothing."

"Faker." Ruth breaks off a piece of black chalk and begins sketching. "You have nothing to complain about. DeMartino is as nice a name as Sartori. You're lucky."

I look down at my engagement ring, one round carat nestled in a circle of gold on my left hand. I guess I am lucky. I'm engaged to a nice Italian fellow whom I've known all my life. My parents like him. Even my brothers don't mind him.

"Dante's the kind of guy who would let you keep your name. He'd do anything you ask. I don't know how you did it, Lu. You ended up with a looker who has a good heart. Not many of those to go around."

"Lucia, Ruth, I need to see you in my office," Delmarr says from his doorway. Ruth and I look at each other. Delmarr's tone sounds official, and official usually means bad news.

"Okay, what did we do wrong?" Ruth asks as we take our seats in Delmarr's office. "Mrs. Fissé hated the collar on her opera coat?"

"There's no problem, which is why I went to Hilda Cramer and asked her to give you gals a raise."

"A raise!" I look at Ruth.

"What did she say?" Ruth asks evenly.

Delmarr smiles. "You got it. You go from forty-six seventy-five a week to forty-eight dollars and fifty cents."

"Thank you!" I clap my hands together.

"Thank you," Ruth says solemnly, letting the good news sink in slowly.

"You two make my life pleasant around here. You work hard, you take on extra assignments when I ask, you even work weekends once in a while. You're professional, smart, and can actually carry on a conversation. I'm glad Hilda Beast bit on my request. It makes me very happy."

Ruth looks at me, I look at her. We stand to embrace Delmarr to show our gratitude and realize that's a line we've never crossed. She knows what I'm thinking, and I know what she's thinking, so we cross the line anyway and throw ourselves on Delmarr. He pushes us away like eager puppies.

"That's enough, kids. We got work to do. Sartori, let's go. We got a date in B."

I go to my desk, pull the pincushion over my wrist, grab the seamstress chalk, and follow him into the fitting room. Our favorite model, Irene Oblonsky, a six-foot blond Russian beauty, all neck and legs and angular edges, stands in her slip on a pine block. From every angle in the three-way mirror, she looks like a rose, one lean line with a bloom at the top. The only curve on her body is the round descent of her shoulders into her long, slender arms. A cigarette dangles from her mouth. She looks bored. She is bored.

Delmarr gently takes the cigarette from Irene's mouth and places it in an ashtray. "Scissors." He holds out his hand. I place the scissor handles in his palm, like Kay Francis when she played a surgical nurse in one of her melodramas. I watch as Delmarr drapes white cotton muslin tightly over Irene's frame and begins cutting. Where he cuts, I pin. I follow his every movement, across her back, under the arms, over the décolletage, nipping in the waist, draping the skirt, closing the seams. Soon Irene is totally covered in a muslin that looks like a strapless gown.

"Take it in at the knee. Jacques Fath is showing the mermaid," Ruth says from the doorway. "Make it so tight that she walks in short steps." Delmarr nods in agreement, and I pin the gown closely around the knees like a second neckline.

"Needs interest over the bust, or we're looking at another dull strapless." With his scissors, Delmarr creates giant petals from the muslin, handing them to me to hold. Then he takes a large runner of muslin and ties a giant bow over her bust. He anchors the petals of fabric under the bow, creating a stiff base over the bodice. I pin them quickly. The slim silhouette works. It is bolder than the New Look, already passé with its circle skirts and tight waistlines. This is much more dramatic and modern.

"Done." Delmarr steps back, and I finish pinning.

"Now, that's interesting," Ruth says.

Irene lifts and extends her arms, slowly turning. She stops and looks at herself in the mirror. "Goot." She shrugs.

"Let's do it in satin. Ruby red. Not cherry. Not garnet. Ruby. And make me a wide belt, let's say four inches, with a simple square closure. The belt should ride over her natural waistline. Cover all of it in satin, I don't want to break the line. I don't want to see a black grommet, nothing but red from bosom to floor. Make one, complete and finished. By Friday."

"Yes, sir."

"Helen, Violet!" Delmarr calls, never taking his eyes off Irene.

Helen Gannon, the pattern cutter, a lanky redhead so lean she could be a model herself, breezes in. She stops when she sees the gown, and complains, "Uh-huh. Big bow the size of Jersey City. Nice,

Delmarr. Didn't your mother teach you simple is better? This thing has more layers than a tulip."

"It's called au courant," Delmarr tells her. "Violet, where are you?"

Violet Peters, a small brownette in charge of assembly, comes running. "I'm here. I'm here," she says nervously. Violet worries about everything, but she needn't worry about her job. Delmarr trained her himself, so they have a shorthand. Violet looks at Irene. "Whoa." Then she says to Delmarr, "This is labor-intensive."

Delmarr disregards her. "Uh-huh."

Helen and Violet hover around Irene like bees and remove the pieces of muslin one at a time, placing them neatly on a long table off to the side.

I go directly to the fabric room next door to check our stock. As I flip through the tall tubes, bolts of velvet, wool, silk, and gabardine, the only satin I find is a sheer beige, left over from a trousseau we built for a Greek girl from Queens (there's lots of money in those diners).

"Why the rush?" I ask Delmarr on the way back to my station.

"The McGuire Sisters have a new show at the Carlyle. And they want Paris runway."

"The McGuire Sisters!" Wait until I tell Ruth.

"Deliver a fabulous gown, and there may be some ringside tickets in it for you."

"Please. My dad loves them!" I say.

"What about your fiancé?"

"What about him?"

"I was thinking a romantic evening, just you and Dante."

"He's not the nightclub type. Bakers are in bed by eight. The dough has risen by three A.M., so that's when they get up to make the bread."

"I'll remember that the next time I order ham on a roll. I'll think of your Dante, who gave up all fun so that I might have fresh bread for lunch."

"You do that," I tell him.

After a day of hemming black satin opera coats with Ruth (the Philharmonic's fall schedule resumes this weekend), I am ready for a good meal and a glass of wine. This is the first time the DeMartinos and Sartoris have had dinner together since Dante and I announced our engagement. We see so much of the DeMartinos in the neighborhood, since they supply the Groceria with bread and pastries, that an official dinner about wedding details seems a little much. But Mama, who wants to do things right, insisted we sit down and discuss all the plans with both sets of parents. "Respect," Mama says. "You'll find out it's more important than food on the table once you are married."

Dante and I have been engaged for six months, so it's time to start planning in earnest. It's not easy when Dante works around the clock with little time off. At least Papa closes the Groceria on holidays. My future father-in-law challenged me when I suggested that he close the bakery once in a while. He said, "What day of the year don't people eat bread?"

After waiting a few minutes for the bus, I decide to walk home. I love my long walks in the city. Nature itself doesn't change as much as the store windows on Fifth Avenue, where there is always something new to see. The streets empty out after work hours. For several blocks it's actually quiet enough to think.

I take a right turn on Ninth Street toward Sixth Avenue, passing stately brownstones with wide stoops and bay windows bedecked with elaborate silk draperies. There are a couple of large apartment buildings with green and white canvas awnings stretched over the sidewalk on polished brass rods. I've wondered all my life what it would be like to live in one of those buildings, to have an elegant uniformed doorman hail cabs and help with boxes after a day of shopping uptown.

The most beautiful homes in New York City are always situated near the parks, in this case Washington Square. The doormen wink at me as I pass, and sometimes I wink back. Some days I get more winks than others, usually when I'm wearing this hat. There's something about blue velvet. As I wait to cross Sixth Avenue, a truck comes to an abrupt halt in front of me.

"Get in."

"Exodus, for crying out loud!"

"Move it, sis."

I climb into the delivery truck with Exodus, the most rugged of my brothers and the one who's usually in trouble for one thing or another. Exodus has light brown hair with some red in it. His face is shaped like Papa's, and he has Mama's eyes. He's often mistaken for one of those tall, broad-shouldered Irish boys, but once you hear him curse in Italian (which he does often), you know he's one of us. I've always admired his bravado; he's honest, and couldn't care less what anyone thinks of him. He can also keep a secret, which is a plus in a large family.

"Ma's tearing her hair out. The DeMartinos are sitting there like marble statues. I just dropped off a case of soda, so it's an eyewitness account."

"They're already there?" I should have known to get home sooner. The DeMartinos are always early. When Dante and I once went to the movies with his mother, she arrived so early that she saw the end of the show before ours and ruined it for herself.

"Yep. I hope when you have a girl, it don't look like the old lady. *Faccia de* Bowwow."

"She's not that bad," I tell him.

"Here's how I see things. A beauty like you marries into a tribe like that, you have a baby girl, and the beauty gets half canceled by his mother automatically, no questions asked."

"Thank you for pointing out that our children—your future nieces and nephews—won't get a fair shake in the beauty department. It gives me great comfort."

"Why you wanna marry him, anyway?"

"I thought you liked Dante."

"He's a dolt. They're all dolts. They work in dough, for Christsakes. Yeast rises, and how? It's full of air. How smart can they be?"

"They run a very successful bakery."

"Who can't make cookies and make a living? That's nothin'. I hope you know what you're doing, Lucia."

"I absolutely do. Besides, nobody asked you."

"Yeah, well. You should. I know you're gettin' old and all, but it doesn't mean you got to rush."

"I'm not rushing." If only Exodus knew how slowly I have taken things with Dante. I love my fiancé, but I wish I could stay engaged another year or two. I like how things are.

When Exodus pulls up to our house to drop me off, Papa is waiting on the sidewalk.

"You're late." My father opens the door for me.

"Sorry, Papa. They weren't supposed to be here until seven." I jump out of the truck. "I have news. You'll never believe it. I got a raise!"

Papa claps his hands together joyfully, just as I did, and smiles broadly. "That's my girl!" he says with pride. "You deserve it. My mother would be so proud. See, all those sewing lessons she gave you paid off."

"I wish she could see me put up a hem now. I hardly miss a stitch!"

"She sees you. She knows." Papa puts his arm around me as we go up the steps. I am happy about the raise, but the best part is making my father happy. His approval means everything to me. As we enter the house, I hear Perry Como on the phonograph. The sweet smell of sage, roasted onions, and basil greets me in the hall. I don't bother going to my room to freshen up. I open the door and walk into the front parlor.

"Mrs. DeMartino, you look lovely." I kiss my future mother-in-law on the cheek. She smiles at me. Exodus is right; this is a plain face with a touch of the bulldog. "I like your hair."

"I went to the beauty parlor." She fluffs the curls in her jet-black hair. "Why so late, Lu?"

"I walked home."

"O Dio. Alone?" Mrs. DeMartino looks at her husband.

"Yes. But don't worry about me. I stick to a safe route. I know all the doormen." As soon as I say this, I realize I shouldn't have. I sound cheap, as if I collect doormen like racing stubs. Mrs. DeMartino leans over and mutters something to her husband in Italian that I don't catch.

"Mr. DeMartino, it's wonderful to see you." I extend my hand.

"How are you?" Mr. DeMartino is wearing wool slacks and a shirt and tie. I've never seen him out of his white apron.

"Where's Dante?"

"He's locking up the store. Your brothers went to pick him up." Mrs. DeMartino looks at my dress intently.

"Oh, thank you for this lovely dress."

"My cousin brought several back from Italy, my girls picked theirs, and I thought you might like one. I know you're fussy about clothes, but I figured this one would do." She smiles.

"I like it very much. If you'll excuse me, I should go and help Mama."

I go into the kitchen, where Mama is ladling tomato sauce over the braciole, small bundles of tender beef stuffed with basil. "They got here so early!" she whispers.

"I see."

"I'm going to give you some advice. You're young. You can bend. Never argue with Claudia DeMartino. She will kill you."

I laugh loudly. Mama shushes me. I say, "It's not like when you were a young bride and Nonna lived here and you were practically her maid. Times have changed. I don't have to take orders from my mother-in-law. I'll do my fair share because I want to, not because I have to."

"Have to, want to, doesn't matter. She's the padrone," Mama whispers.

"Lucia?" Dante stands in the doorway. He looks so handsome in his suit, and his smile is so warm, I am reminded why I love him. Dante bears a strong resemblance to the movie star Don Ameche, with black eyes, thick brown hair, a strong nose, and a full mouth; and my Dante definitely has his broad shoulders. When I was a girl, I made a scrapbook of newspaper clippings about all of Don Ameche's movies, and when I saw Dante for the first time, I thought it was fate that a boy from the East Village looked like my favorite movie star.

I throw my arms around my fiancé and kiss him on the cheek. "Sorry I kept your parents waiting," I apologize.

"It's okay. Mama's been waiting all day to taste your mother's bracciole."

Mama grunts softly at the competition. We ignore it.

"Dante, I got a raise!" I tell him proudly.

"Good for you!" Dante kisses me. "You work so hard. I'm glad they noticed."

"Lovebirds? I need a hand here." Mama hands a platter to me and a gravy boat to Dante. "Congratulations, Lucia. I'm happy for you. Now help me." She kisses me on the cheek, then calls the DeMartinos to dinner. As we take our seats, I look out into the backyard. Right now it's not much of a garden, a small patch of brown grass with a gray marble birdbath in the center. At Christmastime Mama fills the basin with fresh greens and a ceramic baby Jesus in his crib. Today there's only an inch of black water. I wish Mama had scrubbed it out; it looks creepy. But she makes up for it indoors. She has set a beautiful table with a cluster of small white candles in the center, which Papa lights as we sit down. Even Mrs. DeMartino looks softer in the candlelight. Papa says grace. I help Mama serve the food.

"Where are your sons tonight?" Mrs. DeMartino asks.

"They're unloading a truck at the store," Papa tells her.

"We thought it would be nice if it was just us tonight," I tell her as I smile at Dante, who looks as happy as I have ever seen him.

"Signore Sartori, are you aware your daughter walks home alone after work?" Mrs. DeMartino ladles gravy onto her meat.

"I don't like it, but she's a grown woman and can walk wherever she pleases." Papa says this pleasantly as he passes her the bread. "Thank you for the bread, Peter," he says to my future father-in-law.

"It's fresh," Mrs. DeMartino says.

As we begin to eat, the chatter is warm and friendly. This is the best part of marrying an Italian boy. There are no surprises. Our families are similar, our traditions are the same, the meal is delicious, and the conversation, peppered with neighborhood news and gossip, is a lot of fun. This could not be going any better.

"So, should we get down to business?" Dante says. He puts his arm across the back of my chair and looks at me.

I begin. "I was thinking Saturday, May first, at Our Lady of Pompeii Church—"

Mrs. DeMartino cuts me off. "No, no, Saint Joseph's on Sixth Avenue is better."

"But it's not my home parish," I say politely.

"It will be. When you come and live with us, you'll go to our church. It's tradition." Mrs. DeMartino looks to my parents for support.

"I know that, but until I'm married, I live here on Commerce Street, and this is the church I was baptized in, confirmed in, and attend every Sunday. It's where I met Dante. I know you had a falling-out with the old priest, but that was many years ago—"

"Father Kilcullen hated the Italians," Mrs. DeMartino says.

Mama shrugs. "I thought he was all right."

"We're getting off track. Ma, Pop, it's Lady of Pompeii," Dante says firmly.

Mrs. DeMartino looks at her husband. "I think it's okay," he says.

"So, good. May first. Our Lady of Pompeii." Dante pats my hand. I don't know why, but the way he does it irritates me. Dante goes on to tell a long story about the bakery truck getting lost in the Bronx, and how when the truck was returned to them, the driver had eaten his way through a dozen rolls. Mrs. DeMartino laughs too hard at every detail. It occurs to me that I should be laughing at my fiancé's story, but somehow it doesn't seem particularly funny to me.

"I'll have to get used to the trains on your side of town. Since you live farther east, I'll have to take the El to get to Thirty-fifth and First, leaving early enough to walk over so I'm at work on time," I say casually. A deep silence follows; I try to fill it up. "Ruth Kaspian is designing my gown, which should be very convenient, since—"

Mrs. DeMartino interrupts me. "You're not going to work at the department store."

"I'm sorry?" I pretend I didn't hear what she said, but the truth is, I can't believe what she said.

"No, you'll be a housewife. You marry my Dante, and you live with us, and you help me at home. We're giving you the street-level apartment. We put in a new kitchen, and it's very nice. You'll be very happy there."

"But I have a job." I look at Dante, who looks down at his food.

"You can sew from our house," Mrs. DeMartino says.

I look at my mother, who blinks at me as if she's trying to communicate something, but I don't know what.

"I don't take in sewing. That's not what I do. I'm a seamstress at B. Altman's in the Custom Department. I've been there for six years, and someday I hope to run the department, if I'm lucky and they choose me. Am I expected to resign?" I look around the table, but no one is looking at me. I pat Dante's hand, but not as gently. "Dante?"

"Honey, we'll talk about this later," he says in an authoritative tone I've never heard before.

"Why? We can talk about this now. I don't believe your mother should be misled. I intend to keep working." I remember my grandmother telling me the story of her betrothal and marriage, arranged by her parents in Italy. There was no mention of love or romance, only obligation and duty. Chores! Take in sewing? Not in 1950! Not in New York City! Claudia DeMartino is crazy if she thinks I'm going to put up hems at a pittance for the women on Avenue A. No, thank you!

The only sound in the room is my father wrestling to remove the cork from another bottle of Chianti. The tiny squeaks fill up the silence. "Let's not talk about work and jobs. Let's iron out the details of the wedding," Papa says nicely.

Mrs. DeMartino ignores him. "What about when you have a baby?" She puts her fork down and lines it up next to the knife and spoon.

"We'll be happy when that happens," I tell her. Who isn't happy to have a baby?

"I am not raising your children while you're off at the store!" Mrs. DeMartino bellows.

"Who is asking you to?" my mother wants to know. Evidently Mama intends that I make nice with Mrs. DeMartino; she, however, can fight with her. Mama takes a deep breath and speaks slowly.

"Claudia, my daughter is a career girl. That doesn't mean she can't take care of a home." She looks at me. "That doesn't mean she *won't* take care of a home. These are skills she has had from an early age. She cooks, she irons, she cleans. She has been a full partner helping me here at home."

"Thank you, Mama," I say.

"She has been trained." Mama pushes her plate aside and smoothes her napkin. "But she isn't like me, and she isn't like you. I have tried to make her realize that a woman has enough to do at home without running to a job. In time, I believe she will come to understand this and make the necessary adjustments in her life."

"This is all well and good *if* that is her intention," Mrs. DeMartino fires back. "But this is not your daughter's intention! If she works, then she is not home, and if she is not home, then who takes care of the children?" Mrs. DeMartino slides her chair back and angles it toward my mother. "You see my point, don't you?"

"That is not your business. Or mine. That is *their* business." My mother points to Dante and me.

"Mama, I think Mrs. DeMartino has a point."

"See there. She knows! She knows that it's not right for a woman to work when she has children at home."

"Mrs. DeMartino, I didn't say that. And that's not what I mean. Let me be clear." But I don't feel clear. I feel overwhelmed. Claudia DeMartino *is* a nightmare, like Mama said, and she will only get worse. "Let me explain."

"I wish you would," Mama says, wearily resting her face on her hand.

"I was hoping to take things one step at a time. To be married for a while, and then discuss the possibility of children—"

"Possibility? You spit in the face of God with talk like that. God sends babies when He sends babies, not when you want Him to send babies. You can't tell God when to send you a baby!" The tip of Mrs. DeMartino's nose turns bright pink as her eyes fill with tears. "I don't understand you. Do you love my son?"

"Yes, of course I do."

"Then how can you put him after your job at a department store? It doesn't make any sense. A man needs to know that his wife puts him in first place. Otherwise she does not deserve him."

"Mrs. DeMartino, I know it wasn't that long ago that marriages were arranged—" Dante kicks me under the table. I see why. His parents' faces drain of all color. They must have had an arranged marriage. No wonder she sees me as a selfish modern girl. Compared to her, I am. "And that was a system that worked—"

"System? What system?" Mr. DeMartino speaks up.

"But things have changed. We want to determine our future. We want a partnership, not a dictatorship."

"I am not a dictator!" Mr. DeMartino slams his hand on the table. The silverware jumps off the tablecloth with a jolt. "I am the head of my household! I am the leader! The man is the leader!"

Mr. DeMartino looks as though he may have a heart attack, so I take a deep breath and turn to Dante. He loves me and would take me under any circumstances. Looking at him, I realize that I love him, too, but I want things my way. If I join this family, it will be a disaster. I won't put my dreams behind those of my husband, mother-in-law, and father-in-law. And why should I? I make my own living. I have always known that if I walked out of my parents' home, I could get my own apartment and live a good life. I stay here because I love my room with the window overlooking Commerce Street. And I love my mother and father, and until I marry, I want to be with them. "I'm sorry. I can't do this." The words tumble out of my mouth so quickly, I don't know where they came from.

"What do you mean?" Dante is stunned.

This is one moment when I wish I didn't have to be honest, but I look at his face and know that I cannot lie. "I can't marry you. I'm sorry. I just can't." I begin to cry, then swallow hard to stop.

"Lucia, don't say that." Dante looks devastated. "We'll do whatever you want. You can work, I don't care."

"You say that, but you don't mean it. Once we're married and I'm living in your parents' home, they will have total say over our lives. I was kidding myself to think that we would marry and I would move into your parents' house and keep my job and keep my life." The buttons on the bodice of my dress feel like carpet tacks punched into my chest. "I'm very good at what I do. I got a raise today. A raise!"

"What is wrong with you?" Mrs. DeMartino demands. "Look at my son. He is a duke! How could you throw him off for nothing, for a job?" She says "job" like it's the filthiest word in the world. "How could you do that?" She stands and holds the wall behind her as though without it, she would fall.

"I'm not doing anything. This is how I feel." The tears are making my face itch. Papa gives me his handkerchief.

"You should feel ashamed! That's what you should feel!"

"*Basta*, Claudia, *basta*. Can't you see Lucia is upset?" Papa says quietly.

"You do not have control of your home, signore," she says to Papa. Mama looks at Papa and almost starts to laugh; no one speaks to Papa in this manner. Then Mrs. DeMartino turns to me.

"Lucia Sartori, you are young now, and all the boys pursue you. You! The great beauty of Greenwich Village! All I ever heard was 'Lucia Sartori. *Bellissima!* You won't believe the face when you see it. Every good Italian son would give his eyes to marry such a girl.' But you won't be a good wife! You are stubborn!" Mrs. DeMartino shouts.

My father stands and faces Mrs. DeMartino. He says calmly, "No one says a word against my daughter in this house."

I look at my mother, who shakes her head from side to side.

"Get the ring!" Mrs. DeMartino says to her son.

"You want the ring?" I say in disbelief.

"You don't want Dante, you don't want the ring." Mrs. DeMartino extends her hand and holds it there steadily, waiting for me to drop the ring into it.

I look at Dante, who turns to his mother. "Mama. Please."

"She," Claudia DeMartino sneers, "loves her job more than she loves you."

"That's not true," Dante says softly.

"You may have the ring." I twist it off my finger and turn to Dante. "I thought this was yours?" Then I turn to his mother. "Or does it belong to you?"

"It belongs to me." Mr. DeMartino stands and takes the ring. "I bought it."

Mr. and Mrs. DeMartino head for the foyer and grab their coats.

"Lucia, this is crazy," Dante pleads with me. "Talk to me."

"Oh, Dante." I know I should reassure him, put myself in the path of his parents' exit, and beg their forgiveness. I'd like to throw my arms around Dante and tell him that we can go away, elope, come home, get our own apartment, and start anew. How did this dinner party derail? How did such a wonderful day turn into this?

"Lucia? I'll call you later." Dante follows his parents out the front door. Once they're gone, I feel sick to my stomach.

Exodus comes in the front door, followed by Angelo, Orlando, and Roberto. "We're here for dessert," Exodus announces. "Where are they going?"

"Home," Mama says weakly.

"They seemed angry," Angelo says.

"Mrs. DeMartino stomped the sidewalk so hard it looked like she was putting out cigarettes all the way to her car," Orlando chimes in.

"What did you say?" Roberto asks me.

"I told them I was going to keep working, and they didn't like it, and Mr. DeMartino took the ring back."

Exodus shrugs. "I told you they were dolts."

"Do you want us to go after him? We could beat him up," Orlando offers.

"Boys," my mother says in her warning tone.

"Well, he made my sister cry."

"No, your sister made *him* cry," Papa says, pouring himself a glass of wine.

"Did they eat?" Roberto wants to know.

"They ate. But there's plenty left." Mama motions for the boys to sit.

My brothers take their seats as though nothing has happened, as though I didn't just return my diamond ring and defy Mrs. DeMartino and change the course of my life. "You're going to *eat*?" I ask.

"What else are we gonna do?" Roberto asks through a mouthful of DeMartino dinner rolls. "Starve because the DeMartinos are idiots?"

I watch in disbelief, as though I am watching a strange family through their front window on Commerce Street. When you come from a big family, it's almost as if you're one person, each brother or sister an aspect of you, like an octopus with tentacles that move in different directions but are always part of the whole. Roberto is the oldest, so he's the leader; Angelo, second, is the peacemaker; Orlando is the middle child, so he is the dreamer; Exodus is the wild card, the free spirit, unpredictable. And then there's me: I'm the baby, I will always be the baby, no matter how much white is in my hair. Because I am a girl, I am my mother's helper and also the maid. Every shirt at this table is pressed by me on my Saturdays off. My brothers work at the market, and until they marry or I marry, I serve them.

Mama pulls plates from the dish server behind her and passes them out to the boys. Orlando loads bracciole onto his plate. "I can't believe you wasted all this good meat on the DeMartinos," he says. He is tall and thin but the biggest eater in the family. His angular face looks like an intellectual's. He has soft, dark eyes, and there is a gentleness to him.

"He'll come back," Roberto says definitively.

"I don't think so," Papa says softly.

"Aw, Pop. It's a lovers' spat. Everybody has those," Angelo adds, winking at me.

"And if he doesn't come back, I wouldn't cry," Exodus says, filling his plate. "Look, men are like fish. You want a husband? You go out where there's lots of them, you throw out a line with some bait, and you reel him in. You check him out, and when he isn't the best, you throw him back. Throw Dante DeMartino back. You can do better."

"He's a good catch," Mama corrects him.

"No, no, *we* are the catches in Greenwich Village," Exodus insists. "Every girl in town wants to marry us. And why do you think we're prizes? I'll tell you why. Pop owns his own business and this building, and we all work in it. People see dollar signs. They see the nice home that Mama makes, and the lightbulb goes off in their heads, and they think, All that could be mine."

"That's not a very trusting way to live in the world," Angelo tells him.

"He's right. And you," Roberto says, shaking his fork at me, "better accept it."

"Sis, don't listen to him. We aren't good judges of what love is all about. None of us is married," Angelo says.

"Because you have it too good at home!" Our mother comes to life. "The problem with this family is that you're all selfish. Nobody bends." She points at me.

"Why should I bend, Mama? Bend to achieve what? To leave your home and go fifteen blocks east and do for Claudia DeMartino what I do for you—only if I go there, I have to quit my job? What would be the point of that?"

"Then don't ever get married. I should've been made out of rubber, the amount of bending I've had to do around here."

"I gave you a hard life?" Papa looks at Mama.

"Not easy," my mother fires back.

"See? You've been spared, Lucia. From a life of . . . well, this!" Angelo smiles.

"It's fine by me if Lucia never marries. I like the way she does laundry." Roberto winks at me. My brothers laugh.

"You know what? You're not funny. Maybe you should do the dishes and my laundry once in a while."

"Whoa, whoa, you're taking things too far. We don't want you to be unhappy, Looch. We're just protecting the family treasure." Exodus pours himself a glass of wine.

"I am not the family treasure! But you, you're a pack of gorillas, the way you act! Everything is funny to you, isn't it?"

"Ma, the Caterina curse has kicked in," Roberto says.

"Shut up!" Mama says to him.

"What are you talking about?" I ask him. I look to our mother, who withers my brother Roberto with a stare. "What's a Caterina curse?"

"Roberto. Your mouth," my father says.

"Papa. What is Roberto talking about?"

"Nothing. Nothing. Nothing." My mother pushes her plate away and leans back in her chair.

Exodus rests his elbows on the table. "Is there a curse on our baby sister? Is it Venetian like Pop, or Barese like Mama?"

"The Barese one would involve some sort of gunplay," Orlando says. Again my brothers laugh.

I look at Papa. "Why didn't you tell me?"

"I wouldn't let him!" Mama interjects. "Sometimes knowing something like that makes it come true."

"That's better than keeping secrets," I say.

"Not necessarily. Secrets do a great deal of good. You take my aunt Nicolette. One of her legs was shorter than the other. There was no need to tell her fiancé before they married. He may have run off. Instead, they were married fifty-seven years."

"Well, Ma, I'm different. I want to know everything."

"What difference does it make? A curse is a curse." Mama takes a sip of Papa's wine.

"It's Venetian," Papa begins. "Long ago, in Godega di Sant'Urbano, on the farm fields above Treviso and Venice, my brother, Enzo, and I were young men, around twenty. And we were farmers. Godega is a fertile valley beneath the Dolomites; you could grow anything there in the spring and summer. But we had a bigger dream. When we would harvest the corn and bring it to market in Treviso, we admired the elegant *mercato* that we saw there. It was a full city block, open, with vendors selling fruit, vegetables, fish, anything. So we saved our money, what little we had, and we came to America in 1907. We wanted to build our own market, exactly like the one we saw in Treviso. Enzo and I were a team. When we got here, the shops were called grocery stores, so we made the English sound Italian and called our place Groceria. Soon after, I met your mother at the home of my cousin. And Enzo met a girl named Caterina in Little Italy."

"Papa, we know about your brother." I don't want to listen to Papa's stories about the old country. "We know you don't speak to him. We know he's a farmer in Pennsylvania, and we've never seen him or met our cousins because you're still angry with each other. What does this have to do with a curse?"

"Mama and your aunt—"

Mama raises her voice. "Don't call her 'aunt.' She is not worthy of any title of affection."

"Mama and Caterina did not get along."

"Pop, that's an understatement. I remember screaming fights," Roberto adds.

Papa continues, "It was very bad. It caused a rift between Enzo and me, one that we could not repair. So we decided that we must end the partnership. We would flip a coin, and the winner would buy out the loser. The winner would keep the Groceria and this building, and the loser would take his money and move out of New York."

Angelo clucks. "We could have been a bunch of hilljacks in Pennsylvania."

"There's a lot of dignity in farming," Exodus corrects him.

"The day of the coin toss came, and your mother was expecting Lucia. This was the summer of 1925. When Enzo lost the coin toss, he wept. Caterina became so enraged that she began to shout. That's when she placed the curse on you." Papa turns to me.

"I don't believe in curses. That's Italian voodoo," I tell him.

"What kind of curse, Pop?" Angelo asks.

"She said that Lucia would die of a broken heart."

"I hate that woman," Mama mumbles.

"So you actually believe that my broken engagement is the result of that curse?"

"It looks that way," Roberto says.

"Hold on! *I* ended my engagement. Nobody made me do it. No witch came to the door with a rotten apple, no strange bird sat in the window, and I've never walked under a ladder, so let's forget about this curse. It's irrelevant." I wave my hand, dismissing the hocus-pocus.

"You do seem to have some bad luck with boys," Orlando says tenderly. "There was the Montini guy. Didn't he go home to Jersey when you turned him away, and threaten to drive his car into the ocean?"

"That wasn't my fault. He was nutty," I say defensively.

"And what ever happened to Roman Talfacci?" Orlando asks.

"I beat him up. He said something untoward about Lucia, so that one was my fault," Exodus explains.

We sit in silence for a few moments. No one knows what to say. Mama's hair has come undone, and strands of white hang down around her face like strings. Papa swishes the last swallow of the wine in his glass over and over again, as if he's looking for an answer inside the faceted crystal. My brothers lean back in their chairs. Maybe they believe the curse, too. Maybe they're wondering how they'll protect me in a world of spells and spirits.

The phone rings. Roberto excuses himself to answer it.

"It's DeMartino for you," he tells me from the doorway.

My mother looks at me pleadingly. "Talk to him. He's such a nice boy."

I go into the kitchen and take the phone from Roberto. "Dante."

"I got the ring back from Papa," Dante says.

I don't say anything.

"Lucia, I still want to marry you. Mama is all mouth. She doesn't mean half of what she says."

I still don't say anything.

"Lucia, what's going on? Have you met someone else?"

"No, no. Nothing like that." Although that's not exactly true. I did meet someone new: Dante DeMartino, the good son, so good he is weak, a man whose happiness comes from pleasing his parents.

"I've waited a long time for you, Lucia," he says softly.

"I know." I'm very aware of how long I have made him wait. Sometimes I've felt guilty, but then I remember that complete surrender is for wives, not for betrothed career girls.

"I want to get married. Don't you feel it's time?" Dante says.

How can I tell him that when I'm at work, time seems unimportant, that I see my life ahead of me, full of exciting things to learn, and a world where the creative possibilities are endless? He wouldn't understand. I remember his face when I told him about my raise. He was pleased for me, but he wasn't proud.

"I'm sorry, Dante."

Dante sighs as though he is going to respond, but he doesn't. He says good night and hangs up. We've gone together for a long time, and usually our spats are over quickly. But somehow, this argument feels like the end of us. I wipe my forehead with the dish towel and go back into the dining room, where my father and mother wait at the table. My brothers have left.

"Lucia, what did you say to him?" My mother looks at me hopefully.

"I can't go through with it."

Mama exhales and looks at Papa with a disappointment I have not seen before. In her eyes, I have failed. I chose a good man from a fine family, and I've ruined it. How can I tell her that love should inspire me, not drain me? How can I tell her that I cannot, no matter how much I love Dante, marry him and live in his family home, where I know I'm not valued beyond the chores I do and the meals I prepare? This is my mother's life, and to say those things would only hurt her. The idea that I have caused unhappiness to so many people in one evening upsets me, and I begin to cry. Instead of making a scene, I climb the stairs two at a time.

When I get to my room, the collar on the dress Mrs. DeMartino gave me feels like it's choking me. I yank it open, tear the buttons all the way down the bodice, and step out of the dress. I pull on my bathrobe, lie down on my bed, and look up through the skylight at the moon hanging overhead like a silver charm, far away with barely a glint of light coming off its surface. Here in my attic room, high off the ground, I am Rapunzel, though I know I am no princess. I sent the prince away, even though I believe that I will not love any man more than I love Dante. I simply don't love him enough. I reach for the phone and call Ruth. The phone rings and rings. I hang up when I remember that she's out with Harvey and her in-laws. I hope she's having a better evening than I did.

"I'm tired," I call out when I hear a knock at the door.

"It's Papa."

He comes in and sits down on the stool of my vanity, as he has done so many times when I've been hurt or disappointed or I've let someone down. No matter what happens to me, my father always knows what to say.

"Your mother is worried," he begins.

"I'm sorry, Pop."

"I am not worried."

Hearing this gives me hope. "You're not?"

"No. You know what you're doing. Why should you marry when you aren't ready? What good would come of that? I don't believe in the old ways when it comes to marriage. When I was a boy, our wives were chosen for us long before we even knew what a wife was. I was engaged to a girl in Godega. I knew I didn't want her, but my father insisted."

I sit up. "I thought you came here to start the market. But you were running away, too?"

"I was."

"So you do understand!"

"Your mother thinks I've put crazy ideas into your head. She thinks you're too independent. But I wish for you the same things I wish for my sons: to work hard and to live a good life. I hope you will always be independent. That means you will always be able to take care of yourself."

"Mama is old-fashioned."

"Her way works for her. It doesn't work for you. I tried to explain that to her, but she doesn't want to hear it. She believes a mother and daughter should be the same."

"But we're not the same, Pop. I can't get along with Mrs. DeMartino just because I'm supposed to. I don't feel any duty toward her! How dare she tell me that I must quit my job as though it's her decision to make. If she decides that, what else will she say and do? I'd be miserable on First Avenue with her. I want so much more. I have so many goals."

"But you're a *woman*, Lucia. Listen to me. A woman is not like a man. She doesn't get to choose. She follows her heart, and that's what makes the map of her life. You love to work, and that's good. But to be a good wife and mother, that's a decision of the heart. If you don't feel it, you must not do it. You will be unhappy, and your children will be worse. The unhappy man finds compensation outside the home. He works, he lives in the world, he can find joy outside of himself. But a woman builds the home, and if she is unhappy there, she suffers, and her children suffer. Your mother wanted a big family. She had a picture of this house, her kitchen, her children, long before she met me. She *knew*, you see. She was happy each time she found out she was having a baby. She wanted twelve! I told her five was plenty. It was in her to be a mother, like it is in you to work. You're a happy girl because you have a happy mother, a mother who wants to be a mother. And I'm a happy husband because she's a good wife. Do you understand what I'm saying?"

"I do, Papa."

"Now, someday you may meet a man who you will give up everything for. And when that happens, you will want to make a home for him. When that man comes along, you will know it. It isn't Dante, because you didn't want to sacrifice everything for him."

"I know, Papa. I didn't."

"And . . ."

"And what?"

"And his mother, Claudia, is a *strega*." Papa says this so nonchalantly, I can't help but laugh.

"You're right, she is a witch. But I could have handled her."

"You say that, but I doubt it. I don't think a lion tamer for the Ringling Brothers could control that woman."

"I know one thing: if I ever find a man who wants me to be happy as much as you do, it will be a miracle," I say.

"Maybe I'm not the best judge of what you should do. You know, an artist should never stand too close to the canvas while he paints, because when he does, he cannot see what he is doing. The same is true of a father. I am too close to you to truly understand what you are. If it were up to me, I would have you stay here with me and Mama forever. But I know that's selfish. You deserve your own life, Lucia."

Papa goes to the door and turns to face me. "Career girls." He closes the door behind him.

I look down at my hand where the white diamond nestled in gold used to rest on my finger. How plain my hand looks without it! These are the hands of a seamstress, not a wife, I think as I study them. Maybe there are times when the curse lands on the right girl.

CHAPTER THREE

*T*he sun is so bright in the Hub, Ruth has thrown clean muslin over the hot-pink bouclé suit she's finishing. "Nothing worse than ordering a bright pink suit and winding up with faded Pepto-Bismol," she tells me.

"Should I close the shades?"

"No, no, I'm almost done. If you need refuge, Delmarr has his shades down."

I haven't seen much of Delmarr this morning, so I knock on his office door. He doesn't answer, but I know he's in there. I can smell the cigarette smoke through the transom. I knock again.

"Go away," he says.

I push the door open. "Are you all right?"

Delmarr sits back in his chair with his feet propped up on the windowsill, staring out at Fifth Avenue. "I've been shafted again."

"What happened?"

"I brought the red gown to Hilda, she met with the McGuire Sisters, they flipped for the dress, ordered three in red and three more in emerald green."

"But that's great news!"

"For Hilda Cramer, the name on the label. For me? I get so little credit for designing the gown, I might as well be the bonded messenger who delivered the thing."

"Someday you'll have your own label." I take a seat opposite Delmarr.

"Not if I stay here."

Delmarr is right. In this business, the designer who does the work never gets the credit. Delmarr takes his orders from Hilda Cramer and follows through with her wishes.

Hilda Cramer looks exactly as I imagine the head of design for a major department store should look. She must be close to sixty years old, and she is long and thin, like a dress model, which she once was. She never made the leap to magazine work because she didn't have the face for photographs. Hilda has a high forehead, a long nose, and thin lips. She wears her hair in a short black bob, streaked with white. Hilda possesses confidence and an aristocratic air that makes her a good front woman for the Custom Department. She fancies herself a Pauline Trigere or a Hattie Carmichael or a Nettie Rosenstein, a designer of refined elegance and Fifth Avenue style, but we all know that Hilda hasn't picked up a sewing needle since the Great Depression. She's a figurehead, and short of having her likeness on the coin of a B. Altman charm bracelet, she rules us like the empress she is. And we obey. We know the rules: this is fashion, so it's about the dress and the name on the label, not the great mind who created it or the team who assembled it.

"She's old, Delmarr."

"Not old enough. I'm looking at twenty more years of indentured servitude with good pay. She'll never retire."

"Did she thank you, at least?"

"You know how her eyes bug out of her head when she's pleased? Well, her eyes bugged. Then she grabbed the gown out of my hands and said, 'I'm late.' Then she was gone, and someone from retail placed the rest of the order."

Delmarr swings his legs off the windowsill and swivels around in his chair. "No matter how hard I try, and what inroads I make, I cannot get to the top. It's a conundrum. How does talent climb to the top? How did Hilda do it?"

"By sheer ambition."

"Not enough. She figured out how to make the big cheeses around here believe she knew something. Or everything. How do you do that?"

"I don't know."

"And that's why I've got the phony title of chief designer when in fact all I am is Hilda Cramer's valet. A talented valet, but still a servant."

"I think you should talk to her."

"And say what? 'Out of my way, old bag'?"

"No, you should tell Hilda that you want to start meeting with clients to get their input, since you're making the adjustments and modifications—" I stop talking because Delmarr's face has turned as white as the bolt of cotton pique propped behind his desk.

"Really, Miss Sartori?" Hilda Cramer's deep voice says from the doorway. "Now a sewing-machine operator is weighing in on how I should run my department? Please!" Miss Cramer holds a pair of red beaded shoes. For a moment I am shocked that she remembers my name, but I feel as though I might throw up, so I grip my stomach with my hand. I look at Delmarr, who is standing but has closed his eyes. "Out, Sartori," Hilda orders. Then she turns toward Delmarr. "I want to speak to you."

I scurry out of the office and back to my desk. Ruth pulls me behind the changing screen. "It was too late to warn you when I saw her coming. She moves like a python! What did she say? Did you see that suit? It's a Schiaparelli."

I can't believe Ruth is thinking about fashion at a moment like this. "She's going to fire Delmarr," I whisper. "And then me."

"No, she won't. Who will do all the work? Do you know how hard it is to find talented people? She's not a fool. She knows we'd pick up our pincushions and head over to Bonwit's before she could say 'whip-stitch.' "

"Sartori. Kaspian. I need to see you," Delmarr announces from his office. Hilda Cramer pushes past him and goes out through the Hub's double doors.

"I'm so sorry," I tell Delmarr. "Did she hear me?"

"Only the last part."

"I'm fired, aren't I?" The thought of losing my job is like death to me.

"No, you're okay. For Godsakes, when you smell Je Reviens, she's in the area, so put a lid on it."

"So what did she say?" Ruth asks.

"Well, we have to make the gowns for the McGuire Sisters. And then . . . we have to build twenty-seven nuns' habits for the novitiates at Sacred Heart in the Bronx."

"No!" Ruth flings herself against the wall melodramatically. "She's trying to torture us."

"That's right. Worsted black wool and white linen."

"She overheard me, and she's punishing us," I say wearily.

"No," Delmarr says, sounding more exhausted than consoling. "Remember, this land is leased to Altman's by the Holy Roman Church, and the least we can do is keep their devoted nuns in costume."

"But she jobbed them out last year." I look at Ruth. "This is all my fault. I'm sorry."

"No, it's much better than that," Delmarr says. "It's *my* fault. The McGuire Sisters know the truth."

"They know you designed the gowns?" I am flabbergasted. No wonder Hilda looked mad enough to rip wool with her bare hands. "Who told them?"

"I was at El Morocco for cocktails after work, and I had the sketch of the gown in my portfolio. I was sitting at the bar, and a cute dish who was there with a couple of friends asked what I did for a living, so I showed her the sketch. Well, the dish turns out to be the hairdresser for Phyllis McGuire. She told Phyllis all about me, so when Hilda walked in for her consultation, Phyllis said, 'I want to see Delmarr's gown.' "

Ruth and I look at each other and squeal. What a coup! What luck that Phyllis McGuire remembered Delmarr's name and repeated it to Hilda.

"Ladies! Please," Delmarr says, though he can't help smiling. "So the nuns' habits are Hilda's little way of keeping me in my place."

Ruth and I go back to our desks. I look at her and know that she is thinking what I'm thinking: Hilda Cramer won't be able to keep Delmarr in his place for long, no matter how many nuns in the Bronx need new habits.

The first rule of life in a large family is that someone is always in the hot seat, but the turnover is frequent, so no one ever stays in trouble for too long. When I broke off my engagement, Mama didn't speak to me for a while, but eventually she warmed up, and now things seem almost back to normal. It helps that the ladies at our church are offering their sons as potential suitors, as if they're sweaters and all I have to do is choose the best cashmere. Mama is anxious for me to find a worthy husband, and when I hear her weeping in the kitchen, I worry that her tears are for me.

"Mama, what's wrong?" I ask, putting my arms around her.

She cracks an egg into a bowl with ricotta cheese and adds a pinch of salt. "I'm a terrible mother." She motions for me to add the flour slowly as she beats the mixture with a fork, forming a dough to make pasta.

"Why do you say that? It's not true." I take the bowl from Mama and finish folding the rest of the flour into the dough. She sprinkles flour across the pastry board on the kitchen table and then throws the dough onto the board with a thud.

"It is true. Your brother Roberto is getting married." Mama kneads the dough, adding handfuls of flour to thicken it.

"What?" Roberto has not brought a girl home for Sunday dinner or announced that he was attending another family's Sunday dinner or made mention of any serious girlfriend. "Mama, are you sure about this?"

"Yes. Tomorrow. At Our Lady of Pompeii. In the back." Mama

shudders. "In the sacristy." She rolls the dough into a large circle, then takes a paring knife and cuts it into long strips.

"Oh my God! You're serious." I sit down. Mama does not have to explain what this means. As they say in the movies, this is a shotgun wedding. A girl does not get the ceremony at the big altar in Our Lady of Pompeii unless she's earned it. "To whom?"

"Rosemary Lancelatti." Mama cuts the strips of dough into small rectangles.

"Who is she?"

"The girl carrying his child. He told your father and me this morning. We're supposed to shut up and accept it." Mama takes two fingers and begins rolling the small rectangles one at a time into tiny tubes. She flicks the finished cavatelli into a pile. I roll the pasta with her. We have spent so many afternoons like this, the two of us, making macaroni. There's something soothing about mixing the dough, rolling it out, and pressing it into shapes. "I don't know, Lucia. I just don't know."

A hundred things go through my mind at once. This is a fine way for the eldest son of the Sartori clan to start his family. What a bad example he sets for his brothers, though they are far from boys. They are men, but they act like teenagers. Not one of them has settled down. Why should they? They work at the market, eat their meals at home, have their laundry done by their sister, come and go as they please, and stay out late without question. Mama takes care of them with the same zeal she did when they were children: she cooks and cleans and makes sure everyone goes to Mass each Sunday. Yet the boys have their freedom; most of their dalliances are never discussed, never mentioned. Occasionally I'd walk in on them talking about a date, but they would clam up when they saw me. Now I wish Roberto had said something. Maybe we could have avoided this. This is awful. It's 1950. Girls know better, at least the girls I know.

"She trapped him," my mother says, reading my thoughts.

"Oh, Mama, maybe not. Maybe it was a onetime—"

My mother bangs the bowl on the table. "Your brother is weak.

How many times have I told him to be careful? The world is full of girls who are looking for a home like ours."

"Let's give her the benefit of the doubt."

"Why? We know what kind of girl she is, Lucia."

"Sometimes things happen out of order." I wish I could explain the world outside 45 Commerce Street, where there are all sorts of new rules and customs, where sophisticated people make their own decisions about their lives without checking with the parish priest, but that's a discussion I will never have with Mama.

"Out of *order*! What do you mean? Your brother knows better. Carrying on like that without being married is a sin! I better never catch you—"

"Don't worry, Mama."

But she is too angry to listen. "I am so ashamed. I was so proud of Roberto! The first Sartori to serve his country. He was such a fine example, Orlando and Angelo followed him into the service. Even Exodus signed up when he was old enough, because he wanted to be just like Roberto. Your brother has ruined everything we built."

"Mama, we aren't ruined. Roberto is going to marry her."

My mother doesn't listen; she cannot hear me as she stays focused in her tirade. "I worked so hard to teach my children to be decent, to have morals, to have standards, to be responsible and . . . aware. Stay awake, I told your brothers. Check the girl's background. What are her parents like? Where are they from? Be careful, Sicilians are different, I said. And what does he do? He finds a Sicilian and makes a baby!"

"I'm sure he didn't intend to do anything *to* us, Mama." I make myself useful, transferring the cavatelli from the board to a tray lined with waxed paper.

"It's too late!" she cries. "The story is all over Brooklyn already. Everyone knows you can't keep bad news secret. It's like trying to hide a dead body!"

"Mama, we'll get through this."

"No, no, never. Where do you go to win back your good reputation,

Lucia? I'll tell you, nowhere. It is gone forever." Mama pulls open the utensil drawer and removes all the spoons, wooden, stainless, and slotted, then rearranges them.

"What did Papa say?" I ask.

"He cried." Mama shakes her head. "Roberto broke your papa's heart. He will never get over it."

"Is she nice, at least?" I ask. I correct myself. " 'Nice' is the wrong word. Is she a good woman?"

"*How* could she be a good woman?"

"I don't know. Maybe she's a nice girl who made a mistake."

"Impossible! You think before you do these things!" Mama slams the utensil drawer shut and sits down at the table.

"Are they going to live here?" I ask.

"Where else?"

The last time the Sartori family processed to Our Lady of Pompeii Church on foot, with Mama in tears, was when our grandmother Angela Sartori died. We seem to have the same grim gait on Roberto's wedding day as we did the day we put Nonna in the ground. It's three o'clock in the afternoon. This kind of wedding gets the least desirable time slot. Mama already pointed out that it's at the exact time Jesus hung from the cross on Good Friday.

Papa wears his good suit, a navy gabardine with a white shirt and a dark blue silk tie. Mama wears her black funeral dress, a simple A-line sheath that buttons down the back. I decided not to put on the shroud, so I'm wearing a light brocade suit with a petal collar. The pattern of the brocade is autumnal, small gold leaves caught in an embroidered mesh of green. My shoes are simple gold satin pumps. In my purse I carry a small orchid for Mama, who refused to pin it to her dress.

The name of our church seems appropriate. Mama is convinced that the Sartori family is doomed and that Roberto's fate is worse than the people of Pompeii buried under the hot lava of Mount Vesuvius.

I love our church, situated on the corner of Carmine and Bleecker in the center of a traditional Italian neighborhood, with its cross high on the dome, and inside, the white marble walls with glittery gold veins, high ceilings, and statues of saints peering out over the glimmer of candles lit for intentions. Father Abruzzi took pity on Papa and offered to do what he could under the circumstances. I've noticed that clergy can be oddly comforting once the deed is done; it's when the sin might happen that they become righteous.

I look around the back of the church for Roberto, but there is no sign of him. Mama, Papa, Angelo, Orlando, Exodus, and I stand in a subdued clump near the holy-water font and wait. Mama keeps looking at the floor, hoping that when she looks up, she will have imagined this scene and we will be at home, playing records and eating fried dough with powdered sugar as we do every Friday night.

The main doors creak open, and Roberto comes in wearing a brown suit, holding the door for his new family. The bride is a tiny thing, all of nineteen years old, with a high jet-black chignon and small features. She is pretty, even though she lacks confidence, as she bites her lip and looks down at the floor. She's wearing a pale yellow suit (where she found it this time of year, I'll never know) and black patent-leather pumps. She has a whimsy net over her eyes on a small hair band. Her mother and father stand behind her, slight and bird-like, looking wounded. There are several small children behind them. Evidently Rosemary is the eldest, like Roberto. The youngest, a girl, seems to be around eight or nine.

"Pop, this is Mrs. Lancelatti and Mr. Lancelatti. And this is Rosemary," Roberto says.

"Nice to meet you," Rosemary says too loudly. I can see that she's scared.

"Hello," my mother mumbles. The most my father can manage is a nod.

Father Abruzzi comes down the main aisle carrying a prayer book. He invites us to the sacristy through a doorway behind the altar. We follow him in a group, and I'm sure every person who genuflects before the altar is having the same thought: Not good enough for the main altar. Though Father Abruzzi tries to be pleasant, you can tell he doesn't like the situation, either. He likes rules, order, and a sense of organization in his parish, and he believes in announcing the banns of marriage in the church bulletin weekly for six Sundays prior to the wedding, another nicety we have not observed in this case.

Father wears his black cassock without the beautiful white and gold wedding vestment (we really are being punished!). I take Mama's hand as he says the opening prayer. This is one of those moments when only a daughter can comfort her mother—sons don't understand piety and virtue, they are ruled by more earthly passions—so when Mama squeezes my hand, I feel useful in a situation that, for her, is hopeless.

Mr. and Mrs. Lancelatti gather the rest of the young children near. I'm sure they won't explain the details to them anytime soon. Angelo shakes his head in judgment. Orlando is trying to avoid getting the church giggles, a problem he's had since he was a boy. And Exodus puts his arm around Papa in a gesture that says, "Don't worry, Pop, this will be the last time this happens." We shall live in hope.

Poor Papa. He can't speak to me about this because it would involve discussing the sexual relations of humankind, a subject he'd never bring up with his daughter. I know he's heartbroken, maybe more so than my mother, who, even angry and disappointed, sees a child coming into the world as the ultimate miracle. With Rosemary's help, the workload around the house will lessen, so something positive will come of this for Mama. But for Papa, this is a personal failure, a violation of his code. How many times has he lectured the boys on respecting women; how often has he taught by his example? How many times has he disciplined them, trying to teach them how to be good men? This is a terrible ending to Roberto's story. Weddings are supposed to be the beginning of new life and love, but I can't see it here. Rosemary is too young to know what she is getting into, and Roberto, with his bad temper and immaturity, will be the worst husband in the world.

I wipe away a tear with my glove, and the advertisement in our store circular comes to mind: "As the day grows long, so do her gloves." I've

always been taught that gloves are a sign of a true lady, but the bride isn't wearing any. She clutches the modest bouquet of yellow roses tightly, as though it's a rope she is swinging from over a giant pit. She has no idea what she's in for. I've lived with Roberto for twenty-five years. He's not easy. A wife with a moody husband never has an easy time of it. I feel someone staring at me, and I follow the gaze to Rosemary's mother. Her eyes are watery, too, but she manages a scant smile for me. Maybe it will bring Mama some consolation to know that she isn't the only disappointed mother in this sacristy.

After the ceremony Papa takes us all out to eat at Marinella, a cozy restaurant on Carmine Street owned by a pal of his. I try to make small talk with the Lancelattis, who are as upset with Rosemary as my parents are with Roberto. Rosemary talks to Roberto, but I can tell that he doesn't really listen to anything she says. He keeps looking over at Papa. He still needs Papa's approval, but he knows it will be a long time before he wins it back.

After the reception I change out of my suit and into a sweater and skirt and loafers. Mama and Papa are still too upset to show Rosemary the house. I was certain the dinner reception would thaw them out, but it only made things worse. It reminded Mama that her oldest son will never have a proper reception in a big hall with a band. I hope Roberto is making his new wife feel at home. When I get down the stairs to the foyer, I see a pile of stuff that must belong to her.

"Rosemary?" I call out.

"I'm in here," she says from the living room. I find her sitting on the edge of the sofa alone. She is still wearing her wedding suit, and her veil is slipping off the back of her head.

"Wouldn't you like to change?" I ask her.

"I would love to, but I don't know where to go."

"Where's Roberto?"

"They have a delivery at the store."

"Oh." I smile, but I'm furious. I can't believe my brother would leave his bride alone so soon after their wedding ceremony. "Are those your things in the hallway?" I ask her. She nods. "Well, come on, let's

take them to your room." I walk Rosemary through the dining room and show her the kitchen and the garden, which she loves. "The living room you know all about. Now follow me." I grab a suitcase and a box and start up the stairs. Rosemary tries to pick up a suitcase, but I stop her. "Don't! No lifting!"

Rosemary smiles at me. "Thank you."

"I'll take care of it. Or Roberto will when he comes home."

I look down at her on the landing. She seems even tinier than she did at the church. "I know this is hard for you," I say softly. "But everything is going to be all right." Rosemary doesn't say anything. She closes her eyes, trying not to cry. "On with the tour!" I say cheerily.

"Can I bring Fazool?"

"What's Fazool?"

"My parakeet." Rosemary lifts a scarf off a small birdcage, and a turquoise and yellow parakeet chirps when he sees her.

"That's Fazool?"

"Say hello to Lucia," Rosemary instructs the bird.

"Pretty girl! Pretty girl!" the bird says.

"Well, that settles it. Fazool, you can stay," I tell the parakeet as he flutters on his trapeze.

Rosemary laughs as she follows me to the next floor. I show her the door to my parents' room at the back of the house. It's closed. Then I push open another door with my elbow. "This is it." Rosemary comes into the room and immediately goes to the windows. She looks out onto Commerce Street. She turns and inspects the room, approving of what she sees. It's spacious, with two twin beds neatly made up in white linens, a large mirror, and an old rocking chair. Mama has cleared the closet for Rosemary. "Roberto and Angelo used to share this room, but we kicked Angelo upstairs with Orlando. Exodus has the room directly overhead."

"Where's your room?"

"My room is at the top. It's the attic, really."

"So far to climb," Rosemary says, sitting down on the corner of one of the beds.

"I don't mind it. Here's your bathroom. Luckily, you have your own." I show Rosemary the bathroom. "It's small but convenient." Mama has placed a stack of fresh white towels on the sink. "Papa intends to make the street level into your apartment, so you'll wind up with the garden. Things happened so fast that there wasn't time to—" I hear what I am saying and stop myself. "Well, they'll get to it soon, I'm sure."

"Thank you."

"I hope you'll be comfortable here."

Rosemary starts to cry. "I hope so, too."

I feel so bad for my new sister-in-law, I put my arms around her. "Don't cry. It was a long day, and you did very well."

"Thank you," Rosemary says again.

"I know it's far to walk, but you can always come upstairs and see me. If you need anything at all, you let me know."

"I will."

"Okay, I'm going to leave you to unpack and settle in. On Friday nights we make fried dough. It's a lot of fun. I'll come and get you if Roberto works late."

"I'd like that." Rosemary blows her nose.

I close the door. Fazool says, "Pretty girl." I turn to go up the stairs but instead go to my parents' bedroom and knock on the door. I push it open without waiting for an answer. Mama is lying on the bed with her arm thrown over her eyes.

"Mama?" I whisper.

"I'm awake," she says without moving.

"I invited Rosemary to make zeppoles with us later." Mama doesn't respond. "Mama?"

"I hope you never have a day like this one. The look on Father Abruzzi's face. I wanted to die," Mama moans.

"Father Abruzzi is not an expert on marriage, and he doesn't have a family."

Mama sits up. "Don't ever say anything against a priest."

"I'm not saying anything against him. But he can't understand what you're going through. He didn't raise four wild boys and a daughter. He doesn't have any idea about your life. And by the way, it isn't very Christ-like to judge our whole family based on one member's moment of weakness. What kind of nonsense is that?"

Mama turns away from me. An argument about the church is one I will never win, but the truth is, I simply want my mother to feel better. I can see this job will take a long time, and I have my own chores to do, so I move to go.

"Lucia? You're right. But don't tell your father I think so."

At B. Altman's, Fridays are Delmarr's "planning days," when he assigns clients and gives us an overview of the latest trends. We tell him what kind of progress we're making, and he adjusts our workloads accordingly. If we're done with most of our everyday duties—hemming, repairs, fittings, and building garments—he takes us on field trips to shop for fabric or trims. Ruth and I love to go with him, because he makes it fun. He buys us lunch, and at the end of the day he always takes us somewhere swell, like the Pierre Hotel, for cocktails.

Friday is also when Maxine Neal from accounting hands out our checks every two weeks. When she walks into the Hub and gives me my envelope, she says, with a big grin, "Congratulations on your raise. You're lucky. You have a good boss behind you."

Maxine's lipstick is the new coral shade the girls are showing on the main floor. Her skin is a deep brown, she is dressed primly in a navy-blue wool skirt and white blouse, and her nails are always done. Whatever difficulties Ruth and I have had pushing ahead in our department, it has been harder for Maxine in hers. She graduated from City College with a degree in business and couldn't find a job at any of the accounting firms in the city. Her uncle is in charge of shipping at Altman's, and he recommended her to our accounting department. She is overqualified, but I know she will prove herself and advance.

"Why don't you come down here and work with us? Get on the gravy train!" I tell her.

"I'm all thumbs when it comes to sewing, and besides that, I'm color-blind. You still want me down here?" Maxine walks over to Delmarr and places his check on the worktable in front of him.

"Not to sew. Never! But you can bean-count," Delmarr tells her as he pours his third cup of coffee for the morning. "And when we blow this joint, you're coming with me, Max. I'm gonna need someone with a head for business when I set off on my own."

"I'll be there!" Maxine says.

"I'm glad to hear I'm not the only career girl who *likes* to work," I tell her.

"Oh, it's not a matter of like," Maxine says. "I *have* to work. When you see the M10 heading downtown at six in the morning full of brown faces, it isn't because we're career girls with a dream." She heads out through the swinging doors to deliver the rest of the paychecks.

Ruth, Violet, Helen, and I usually brown-bag our lunches. When the weather is good, we walk up to the open porticoes at the New York Public Library on Forty-second and Fifth, or head down to Madison Square Park at Twenty-third Street. Today, though, and on every payday, we meet at the Charleston Garden on the sixth floor of B. Altman's for the employee-discount lunch with complimentary pie and coffee. The restaurant has a southern ambience, with floor-to-ceiling murals of rolling green Georgia hills dotted with magnolia trees in bloom.

The four of us are practically a club. We call ourselves the Flappers because we were all born in 1925. We've been devoted to one another since we met seven years ago at Katharine Gibbs Secretarial School, the first stop for any New York girl out of high school who wants to develop her business skills and put something official on her résumé. I knew I would sew for a living, thanks to the careful training of my grandmother, but I didn't know the first thing about business. A few classes that included typing, accounting, and shorthand made me irresistible to B. Altman's, which likes to hire a well-rounded girl. I was hired first, then I put in a good word for Ruth; Ruth recommended Helen, and then Helen recommended Violet.

"How bad was it?" Helen asks, eager for all the details of Roberto and Rosemary's quick wedding.

"Awful. My poor mother. She's still wandering around acting like she's in the middle of the Blitz."

"Can you imagine? Mrs. Sartori is so proud of her family." Ruth shakes her head.

"Not anymore," I tell her. "But I wish my parents could put aside their feelings and be nice to the girl. These things happen." I stab a piece of lettuce.

"I'd kill myself if I ever had to get married like that," Violet says solemnly. "I'm Catholic, and the only girl in my family who *had* to get married was my third cousin Bernadette. They made her live in the basement until the baby was born, and then she was allowed in the yard. But only at certain times."

"How grim." Ruth spoons her pie filling onto the plate, next to the crust. The crust, which will be forgone until Ruth has the final fitting for her wedding gown, looks like an empty beige shoe. "She should have talked to me. There's no reason for a young woman to have a baby out of wedlock. She has to see a doctor and make a plan."

"My mother's plan would be to shoot me," Violet counters. "Aren't your parents mortified?" she asks me.

"Sure. But what can we do? The baby is coming. You can't stop Mother Nature," I say.

"Do you like her?" Violet asks.

"She's very young."

"They always are," Helen says, taking a drag off her cigarette. "The Sartoris have taken two big hits lately. First their only daughter calls off a respectable marriage to the son of the best baker in the Village, and then their eldest son brings home a bride with a baby on the way. What next?"

"If you ask my mother, she'd say locusts. She believes she has failed as a mother. Nobody's doing what she wants us to do. I feel guilty because I started it by ending my engagement."

"Trust me," Ruth says, "you ending your engagement is not what got Rosemary pregnant. Right, Violet?" Violet blushes.

"Your mother thinks Dante is the ultimate catch," Helen says to me. "He's a baker, so you'd never starve. He works in a family business, just like your brothers, which means that you have that in common. He's Italian. If we were to invent someone for you, we couldn't come up with anyone better. Shall I go on?" Helen loves to make lists, and she loves to be right. She's getting to do a lot of both at this lunch.

"Dante is a catch below Fourteenth Street, but Lucia has bigger fish to fry," Ruth says in my defense.

"It's more complicated than that . . ." I begin, but then I stop. Good sense would tell me to go ahead and marry Dante because he'd be nice to me and provide well. But that's not what I'm looking for. Maybe I want to be Edith Head and create costumes for the movies, or Claire McCardell and design sportswear for the masses. But these girls have heard all of that before, and they are as closed-minded about professional dreams as my mother.

"And I can't believe you gave the ring back." Violet sighs. "It was the whitest and hottest stone I ever saw. Not a speck of carbon, just clean, bright white ice."

"I don't care about the diamond," I say, looking down at my hand, which seems downright juvenile with my garnet birthstone ring where a real diamond once was.

"You should," Ruth says with conviction. "When a man buys you a diamond, he's investing in you. It makes no sense that men have all the money, because they have no idea what to do with it. They don't know what's good. The only way they find out what's good is if a woman tells them. They know nothing about how to make life beautiful. They don't decorate homes or make delicious meals or dress up with any level of creativity. Okay, they like their cars. What else is there to spend money on? What better cause for the average man than a wife who likes jewelry?"

"If only men came made to order. It's so hard to find a decent fellow." Violet stuffs her handkerchief into the cuff of her charcoal-gray suit jacket. Then she smooths her unruly eyebrows. "If I ever met a good man and we fell in love, even if he was flawed or, say, had some physical defect like a clubfoot, I wouldn't break it off. I would try to find the best thing about him and hold on to that. I would overlook the negatives. Of course, my mother believes all the truly nice boys died serving our country in World War II."

"Well, now, that makes me feel much better." I dump sugar into my iced tea.

"I don't want to be mean, Lucia. But you made a big mistake," Violet says piously. "There is nothing wrong with Dante DeMartino. I think you're going to regret what you did."

"Oh, please, Violet. I will not. I felt like invisible hands were trying to choke me when we talked about the wedding plans."

"Those hands weren't invisible. They were his mother's." Helen sips her coffee. "Who doesn't feel a little claustrophobic when they get engaged? I did. You give up a lot. Thank God I'm still working. How many times can you scrub the four rooms in your railroad apartment? It takes me all of a half hour on Saturday morning. I need my job."

"You are *not* a romantic," Violet says to Helen.

"Okay, okay, I'm making it all sound like drudgery and boredom, but it's not," Helen says. "Marriage is wonderful. Bill is a terrific husband. But I was nervous right before we got married. I thought, I actually have to live with this man, and it scared me a little. I like to be alone. I used to love to wake up in the middle of the night to read, and I figured that was over. I made a list of the things that I was giving up in exchange for a husband, and the list of what I thought I was losing was longer than the list of what I thought I was getting. But then I got married, and all the things I was worried about never happened. I like him being there when I come home from work. It doesn't disturb me when I'm doing something and he walks into the room. I like sharing my bed. Sorry, Violet, I know that's crude. But I do. He holds me all night like a rag doll. I feel safe. I love that. "

"Yeah, but don't you love Sunday night, knowing the next morning is Monday and you get to come to work?" No one answers me.

After a while, Violet speaks. "I do like working here. The job I had at the carpet company, before Helen got me in here, was horrible.

First of all, I wasn't even *me* when I was working there. I was Ann Brewster, because the last girl who worked at Karastan got married, and all the accounts she handled got mad and went elsewhere when she quit, so the boss decided instead of losing accounts when girls got married, he'd come up with a name, a character, really, who sells the carpet. This way, if I got killed or married, Mr. Zaran would hire a new Ann Brewster in my place. What a racket! I prayed every day that I would meet a man and fall in love and get married so I could go into Mr. Zaran's office and say, 'Find yourself another Ann Brewster!' My wish came true, more or less, when Helen asked me to cut patterns here. So maybe it's not so much that I love my job; I just love it a lot better than the last one." Violet sighs.

"Having a boyfriend doesn't even compare to working," I insist. "When my future in-laws came to dinner and were sitting there looking me over, I'm sure Dante's mother wondered how well I could iron, and his father wondered if I could run the cash register at the bakery on Saturdays. I could see the wheels turning in their heads. That's when that little voice inside me said, 'Don't do it. I don't care how much he looks like Don Ameche. Don't do it! That's not the life for you!'"

Violet looks at me solemnly. "If that little voice was being honest, it would have said, 'Lucia Sartori, you're twenty-five years old, and you should get married, because there will be no men left when you come to your senses and decide you need a husband.'"

"God, Violet, you are such a sad sack." Ruth pats me on the back like a display item. "Just look at Lucia. She won't have any trouble finding a nice man."

"Whatever you do, don't talk to strange men in the street," Violet warns me. "One time my sister Betty talked to a man in the street, and he took her around a corner, clubbed her, and stole her purse."

Whenever we have a few moments after lunch, Ruth and I spend them in the Interior Decoration Department and imagine what our lives would be like if we lived in the designer-showcase rooms with their period furniture and beautiful art. Ruth stops at a Louis XVI dining room table set for an elegant party, with beige linens and pale yellow china that has a pattern of small bluebirds on the rim. "This china is downright posh!" Ruth says excitedly.

"Do you think crystal stemware makes the wine taste better?" I hold up a goblet and twist it in the light of the overhead chandelier. "At eight dollars a glass, it should," I answer my own question. "I love beautiful things." Why do I have to get married to have them?

"Okay, here's what I want." Ruth pulls me over to the display case and points at the place settings. "See there? Spode buttercup china. Royal Crest sterling silverware in wildflower . . ."

"Pure silver. Look at that trim."

"Ma says it will be a bear to polish, but that's okay. And by the way, that is real twenty-four-karat gold in the finish."

"For somebody who isn't too excited about becoming Mrs. Goldfarb, you're pretty excited about your dishes."

"I'm trying to walk on the sunny side." Ruth goes to look at the linen tablecloths and napkins displayed in an étagère in the corner. I become transfixed before a floor-to-ceiling mirror. The top of the frame is a gilt wood flower basket with ribbons that drape the glass. It belongs in the foyer of a Park Avenue town house with black-and-white-checked marble floors. For a moment I see myself in the entryway of one of them, greeting my dinner guests.

"Do you come with the mirror?" a man's voice says with just the right touch of humor.

"No, I come with the china. I'm the best little dishwasher in Greenwich Village."

The man laughs heartily, so I turn to see the owner of the voice. "Oh . . . hello . . ." If I were walking, I'd stumble, but I'm speaking, so I stutter until I find the grace to close my mouth entirely.

"Hello," he says, looking at me as though he can see through to the wheels that spin like the works of a timepiece in my head. "You look familiar. Do you work here?"

I search for a witty comeback, but I'm too busy sizing him up to think of a good line. Ruth comes up behind me and says clearly, "On another floor," answering for me.

My feet feel like they're melting into my shoes. I can't take my eyes off him. He must be six foot two. He's slim, with broad shoulders and big hands. I notice the hands immediately because his shirt cuffs rest on the correct breaking point over the wrist. The suit, a warm gray tweed, is a European cut, so it fits without pulling or creasing the material anywhere, and the pants land precisely at the middle of his polished oxblood lace-ups. I know these shoes, they're a fine Italian leather; I've seen them displayed on the main floor. His shirt is crisp and white, with a wide collar fastened by a gold hook and eye at the top button, and his tie is a bold stripe of black and white. His black hair is parted on the side and neatly combed. His eyes are gray, exactly the color of his suit, and the thick black eyebrows, smooth and neat, taper off, framing his chiseled face. The jaw is square and strong; I'm sure by evening he could use a second shave. But it's his smile that has frozen me like a lump of tundra in the Arctic Circle. His white teeth and ever so slight overbite give him, if I can say the word—even think the word—a seductive smile. I have never seen a man like this, not in person, anyway. And neither has Ruth. I hear her babbling about china and silver, but it all sounds like the low drone of a sewing machine. He nods politely and acts interested in what she's saying.

When I was a girl, Papa took me to a play on Broadway, and an actress stood in the middle of the stage, a street scene jammed with buildings and people, city life in full swing. The music changed, and the city began to pull away piece by piece, wall by wall, person by person, until the girl was alone in a vast expanse of darkness, save the spotlight shining from the rafters. I remember thinking that she looked like a pink pearl on a black evening glove.

This is how I feel. The world has gone away. There are no display cases or dressing rooms or mirrors. Not even Ruth. There is only him and me.

"Lucia? We need to get back to work," Ruth says, yanking my elbow.

"Right, right." I look up at the handsome stranger. "We have to go back to work."

"Don't let me keep you," he says lightly.

Ruth and I lock arms and step onto the escalator. The handsome stranger leans over the half-wall as we descend.

"Lucia di Lammermoor. Like the opera." He grins.

CHAPTER FOUR

*E*ver since I met the handsome stranger, I have found every possible excuse to return to the Interior Decoration Department in the hopes of getting another glimpse of him. Now I can understand criminals returning to the scene of the crime. I need to relive the thrill, no matter how brief. And there's an up side to my curiosity: I'm buying all of my Christmas presents in one place. Linens for Mama, leather cuff-link boxes for my brothers, a satin duvet cover for Rosemary, and a small marble statue of Garibaldi on a horse for Papa.

Christmas is very different this year, with a new family member in the house. If anyone were to ask what makes the Italians from the Veneto different from the Neapolitans like Rosemary (she is, it turns out, only half Sicilian), I would say the difference begins at Christmas. We put up our tree on Christmas Eve; Rosemary's family puts theirs up the day after Thanksgiving. Venetians fast on Christmas Eve and attend a midnight vigil; southern Italians have a banquet, including seven kinds of fish prepared different ways, and attend Mass on Christmas morning. The Venetians like bunches of fresh greens on the door, plain and simple, no glitter, no bows; the Neapolitans like to decorate the outside of the building as lavishly as the inside. Mama's people come from Bari, so they like the ornate as much as the southerners, though in honor of Papa, Mama has always deferred to the traditions of the Veneto.

But Rosemary's presence has changed our household in ways that go far beyond Christmas. We've had to figure out how to include her in our family, and her task has been to try and fit in. Even though she's young, she's a good cook and a fine baker. She taught us how to make tartufo, creamy vanilla-ice-cream truffles with a chopped cherry center that are dipped in hot chocolate syrup that dries to a crust, then rolled in coconut. They're so delicious, Mama and Papa have almost forgotten that she "had to" marry my brother. Rosemary gave me the recipe and told me to put it in a box. "Start collecting recipes, because the day you get married, you'll need them," she said. In beautiful Palmer penmanship she wrote:

ROSEMARY SARTORI'S QUICK TARTUFO
(In America, SNOWBALLS)
Yield: 1 dozen tartufo

3 bags shredded coconut
1 cup heavy cream
1 gallon vanilla ice cream (softened)
12 maraschino cherries

FOR CHOCOLATE DRIZZLE:
¼ box paraffin wax
1 pound dark chocolate

Melt paraffin wax with chocolate in a double boiler
on stove until liquid. Set aside.

Soak coconut in heavy cream. Set aside.

Roll ice cream into baseball-sized balls. Bury maraschino cherry
in center of each. Drizzle chocolate sauce on ice-cream ball,
then roll in coconut until covered. Place on waxed-papered
cookie sheet and freeze.

Papa and Roberto have been working diligently on the downstairs apartment. It will be perfect for a young family, with a new kitchen in the back that leads to the garden, where the baby can take sun and play. They hope to have it done well before the baby's arrival in March, but it seems as if all they do is argue about details, from what kind of faucet to put in the kitchen sink to how many shelves should be in the closet. Roberto hopes to unveil the apartment for Rosemary on Christmas Day, so every spare moment that the men aren't at the Groceria, they are downstairs sanding, pounding, and painting.

Christmas is Papa's least favorite time of year because the Groceria is jammed with tourists and surly customers, with everyone making special orders. Mama, on the other hand, embraces the holidays with gusto. When Papa was a boy, he didn't receive gifts on Christmas. He got a trinket and some fruit on the Epiphany, January 6. In Mama's family everyone received one special gift, and then they cooked a meal for a family who didn't have enough money to make a Christmas dinner. And now, every holiday card that comes into our house is displayed. Mama runs wide red ribbon around the living room door frames and pins the cards to the ribbon. By Christmas Day the archways are covered in cards. I notice that Mama pinned up a card from my ex-fiancé's family. There was no personal note, just a stamp inside that said, "Happy Holidays from the DeMartino Bakery." Dante did send me a card with a handwritten note that said, "I miss you. Love, Dante," which I pinned next to the one from his parents.

Mama stacks holiday records by Bing Crosby and Frank Sinatra on the stereo, and the carols play night and day. The delicious scent of anisette, butter, and coconut fills the house as Mama bakes. The pantry is filled with neatly stacked tins of homemade cookies. We'll tie satin ribbons on the cans and load up the car, delivering them to relatives and friends all over Manhattan and Brooklyn the week of Christmas.

"Lucia, do you think it would be all right if I put lights in the front window?" Rosemary asks as she untangles a string of red, green, and gold Roma lights for the tree. The blue spruce that we have hauled home from the corner touches the ceiling.

"We never have," I say. "But if it would make you happy, we'll ask Papa."

"That's okay. I don't need the lights."

"No, no, you're part of the family, you should have Christmas the way you like it."

Rosemary begins to cry.

"What's the matter?" I climb down the ladder quickly.

"I want to go home," she whispers.

Poor Rosemary. The whole time I was engaged to Dante, I worried about Christmas and how I would have to spend it with Dante's family instead of my own. I will not share this with Rosemary at the moment. Instead, I guide my sister-in-law to the couch and sit down next to her. "But this is your home now." As Rosemary leans back against the cushions, I see how much the baby has grown. Her tummy is high and round.

"No, your father and mother look at me like I'm a *puttana*."

"They don't feel that way at all," I tell her, but she can see through the lie. She and I know the rules, and there's no getting around them.

"My parents raised me the same way your parents raised you," she says. "I knew what they expected of me, and I failed them. Worse, I brought shame upon them. They can't be happy for Roberto and me, because we made a mistake. And they're not wrong. A good daughter doesn't *have* to get married; she waits for her wedding night. I didn't, and now I am paying for it. It's all my fault."

"Wait a second. Roberto is every bit as responsible." I hear Ruth's voice in my head, talking about what sophisticated girls do. But Rosemary is as far from sophisticated as the Christmas lights she wants to string in the front window.

Rosemary cranes her neck to make sure only I can hear what she is about to say. "Roberto is a man, and they always said it and I never believed it, but it's true—a man is forgiven. The girl is always at fault. Forever marked. People say, 'Roberto did the right thing.' But that's not what they say about me. I'll never be able to make this right. Never. But Roberto already has. He married me, so his is debt is cleared."

"Do you love Roberto?" I ask.

"With all my heart."

"In my mind—and maybe tomorrow Saint Ann will see that I am hit by a bus for saying this—love makes the difference." I hope that Rosemary understands that I am talking about making love itself, not just loving a man. "Rules are rules. But I believe if you are going to marry the man, there is nothing wrong with making love to him before the ceremony. One God. One man. What's wrong with that?"

"Everything, if you get pregnant." Rosemary exhales slowly.

"You know that I was engaged—"

"Dante DeMartino. So many girls in Brooklyn are in love with him!" Rosemary turns to me. "All the mothers sent their daughters to pick up the bread when he made deliveries. They poured out of the apartment houses when the DeMartino truck came through!" Speaking about her old neighborhood cheers her up. "Did you and Dante . . ." Rosemary can't say the words.

"Make love? No. I *would* have married him if we had. But I knew that it wasn't meant to be."

"How did you know?"

"I always felt like there was enough time. And I guess what I'm waiting for, when it comes to love, is a man who makes time go by so fast that I can't hold on to it." I prop my feet on the coffee table. I can't believe I'm confiding my deepest feelings to Rosemary. These sorts of revelations are usually reserved for Ruth. But I can tell that Rosemary is a good egg, and I want to her friend, since she's already my sister.

I almost tell her about the mysterious man I saw, the one with the smile and the beautiful hands. Besides my lunch strolls when I look for him, I catch myself thinking about him a lot, too. On the main floor one day, I thought I smelled his cologne, so I followed a man into Custom Shirts. When it wasn't the mystery man, I felt like a fool. I told Ruth about it, and she laughed so hard, I knew what I was doing was crazy. Why can't I let go of the idea of him? And why was I hooked so fast? It was probably something as simple as the low sparkle of chandelier lighting, or the panels of leather on the walls, or the cup of butter-pecan ice cream I had for dessert at lunch that made me feel full and woozy and a little wanton. Maybe the scene itself, the model dining room with the glistening silverware and fine linens and delicate china, made me need a handsome stranger to enter stage left and take my hand and whisk me off into the future. I've been waiting my whole life to feel that magnetic attraction. But I can't tell Rosemary any of this; I'd sound ridiculous.

"We need to finish the tree." I stand and stretch.

"Lucia?"

I turn to her. "Yeah?"

"I thought you were so fancy, but you're just a girl."

"Fancy?" I laugh and look down at what I'm wearing, corduroy pants and Papa's old wool sweater.

"You're so beautiful. Your hair is always shiny. And your clothes, I've never seen anything like them except in *Charm* magazine. You're always going out the door looking smart, on your way to something important. I admire that."

"Rosemary, I'm not fancy. I'm a seamstress. I love clothes. I think they're art. That's all." I extend my hand to Rosemary and help her up.

Papa and Roberto come up from the new apartment, where they've been working all morning. They chat with each other, oblivious to us. I interrupt them. "Papa, Rosemary would like to put some lights in the front window. Is that all right with you?"

"Sure, sure," he says without looking at Rosemary.

"Tell *her*, then," I say quietly.

Papa looks confused, but he knows what I mean. He hasn't had a conversation with Rosemary since the wedding day. I'm sure he doesn't realize it, but he avoids eye contact. Maybe he believes if he doesn't look at her, the whole incident will go away. But deep down, Papa has a dear and tender heart. Despite his hurt, he does right by Rosemary as family; he plasters her walls, grouts tile in her bathroom, and gives Roberto a raise at the Groceria to ensure her and the baby's future. But he doesn't acknowledge her. He's a traditional man, and he cannot accept what has happened.

Now he turns to her. "Rosemary, you may put the lights in the window." He looks at her for the first time since he met her at Our Lady of Pompeii, standing here next to the half-lit Christmas tree. He even manages a smile.

Rosemary faces my father. "Thank you, Mr. Sartori." Her voice breaks, and she looks down at the floor.

Papa turns to go. I grab his arm and raise my eyebrows. He knows the look — my mother gives him the same one, the wordless prompt — and he obeys.

"Rosemary. You may call me Papa." There is a moment of silence, then Papa goes into the kitchen. Roberto looks at me and then at his wife. He goes to Rosemary and holds her tenderly. Even temperamental Roberto has a soft side; maybe he's learning how to be a husband. I can see that my brother truly loves his wife, and that all these weeks of my whispering with Mama and worrying and praying for them were unnecessary. There is a real bond between my brother and his wife, the kind I hope to have someday. Roberto gives Rosemary his handkerchief, and she dries her tears.

I look at Rosemary and think that I could be her. I could be in Claudia DeMartino's living room tonight begging to have some part of Christmas the Sartori way, maybe to put the crèche in the fireplace or the lights on the mantel like we do here, negotiating through Christmas as though it were a maze instead of a holiday. I'm sure she'd make me feel like an outsider. But I'm relieved not to be married, not to have to give this up. I want to be here, with *my* family.

"Where are the lights, Ro?" Roberto asks.

"Over there," she says, pointing to a box near the base of the tree.

"Show me where you want them," he says gently to his wife.

"You sure I look all right?" Mama asks me as she stands before my three-way mirror.

"Okay, how about, 'You look gorgeous'?" She does. My mother has a beautiful shape. She is tall and broad-shouldered, and she has great legs. It's hard to believe that she's over fifty. It's not only her figure, though; it's her face that makes her stunning, her smile and her dark brown eyes, soft as sable.

"Thank you for making this for me," she says. Ruth and I made the dress for Mama between commitments to finish luxurious gowns for the standard round of holiday parties attended by society matrons. I designed the off-the-shoulder blue velvet dress with a trumpet skirt and a long, slim silhouette, very Parisian. To finish the effect, Mama has pulled her hair into a chignon and wears a large cabochon brooch of faux sapphires and glittery Austrian crystals cinched on her waist. "Is this good enough for the McGuire Sisters?" she says as she twirls.

"They may have you come up onstage and model the dress."

"You know, I heard them on the radio. On *Kate Smith*. And they were wonderful."

"Now you'll see them in person." I give my dress a final once-over in the mirror and tell Mama, "Papa and Delmarr are waiting downstairs. Let's go."

Mama puts her arms around me and looks at our reflection in the mirror. "Lucia, thank you for this dress. And for everything. You always seem to know the right thing to say to me when I'm upset. You're a good friend."

"Mama, it's easy. You're my favorite girl."

"When I first saw you, right after you were born, you weren't blue and gray like the boys, and your face wasn't smushed like an old apple. You were beautiful from the moment you breathed. You were a golden pink, and the line of your eyes as you slept curved up like a smile. You were calm and gentle. And I could see even then that you would grow up to be a great beauty."

"Oh, Mama." If I'm such a number, why do I have a platonic date on New Year's Eve?

"No, no, I mean it. I knew you would surpass me in every way, and I wanted that. I prayed for that. And now you have."

I thank Mama, and she picks up her purse to go. As I follow her down the stairs, I can't help but think how deep the ties in my family are. I wonder if outsiders would find it odd that I *like* to socialize with my parents. Maybe there are families in which the laces are loose and there is room to consider your own feelings first. But my brothers and I weren't raised that way. We are bound to one another. Maybe it's an Italian trait, or maybe it's the way things took form in our home, but there's no way around it. This truth defines my life. And I'm not unhappy about it.

Delmarr rises from Papa's easy chair and whistles, which makes Mama blush. "Mr. Sartori, we are the luckiest men in New York City."

Papa takes Mama in his arms and kisses her. "Yes, we are."

"Hey, we haven't even had drinks yet," Delmarr says with a grin. He looks at me. "You and I are chaperones for these two tonight. No funny business in the backseat. Dem are da rules."

"Aye-aye, sir," Papa says.

"I can't believe Lucia Sartori chose me for her escort tonight. Me, over all the suitors who leave notes on her desk and inquiries with the doorman at Altman's! I know how privileged I am."

"Oh, Delmarr, it is I who am honored." I laugh.

"This is why we love you. All that beauty and still a streak of humility." Delmarr takes my hand and opens the door. "Come, Cinderella, we're off the the ball!"

As we drive uptown, the dark, winding streets of Greenwich Village give way to the bright, broad avenues of midtown. As happy as I am to be with my good friend Delmarr on this special night, I wish I were in love. This is the kind of evening I always dreamed of, and I know Dante would not have truly appreciated it. He would be as happy to sit on our stoop and toast the New Year with Papa's grappa from a paper sack. I think about the handsome stranger and wonder where he is and what he's doing. Does he ever think about me? I let myself believe that he might.

They still call the awning over the entrance to the Waldorf-Astoria Hotel "the carriage stop," even though it has been years since Park Avenue has seen a horse and buggy. Delmarr pulls up his black Buick sedan (it's at least nine years old but in mint condition). One of several doormen races to the car and opens the door for me. I step out onto the sparkling sidewalk, which seems to have been poured with chips of diamonds in the cement. Delmarr comes around and takes my arm while the doorman helps Mama out of the backseat.

My parents join us on the sidewalk, and I check Papa's tie, a gift from me, a soft silk in palest blue, cut a bit wider for evening wear. It matches the handkerchief in his pocket. It took me hours to roll the hem of the silk on that handkerchief, but it was worth it. He and Mama look spectacular.

We blend into the crowd. Women in lavish satin gowns of the season's most popular colors—the muted shades of charcoal gray, rose, and chocolate brown—sashay through the doors on the arms of their escorts, handsome men turned out in tuxedos with starched white shirts and sprigs of green in their lapels. The chatter is sprinkled with laughter. As we climb the stairs to the lobby, a string quartet nestled on the landing underscores our entrance. This is what the society pages call uptown glamour: every detail is attended to, including the air itself, which is filled with music.

"Come, revelers. Let us all welcome 1951 with a bang and say good-bye to 1950 with a raspberry," Delmarr says as we go through the gilded doors of the nightclub. The Club Room is packed; as many as eight people circle each small granite-topped table. In the low, smoky light, all I can see are orange cinders from cigarettes and pale shoulders leaning in to conversation. The scent of gardenias, orange blossoms, and rich tobacco lingers in the air as we are led to our table. And what a table! "Ringside," Delmarr calls it. He and Papa hold the chairs for Mama and me. Then as they take their seats, Delmarr leans in and whispers, "Drink up. Tonight is on the house, courtesy of the McGuire Sisters." Delmarr is in such a good mood, he hardly seems to mind that while the McGuire Sisters are onstage in his dresses, the papers will give credit to Hilda Cramer.

A combo takes the stage and begins to play. The percussionist, lanky and with skin the color of toffee, moves wire whisks across the drums so smoothly and quickly that they seem like wings. "These guys are great," Delmarr says. "They usually play at the Village Vanguard."

"Right near Commerce Street?" my father asks.

"You could walk," Delmarr tells him.

Papa puts his arm around Mama. Maybe one of his New Year's resolutions will be to take Mama to a jazz club in our neighborhood. The waiter places flutes of champagne on our table, then, with silver tongs, drops a raspberry into each glass, creating a pink fizz over the sandy bubbles. Papa pulls Mama close and kisses her ear. They are still in love, which seems like a miracle to me. Tonight they are carefree, away from work and bills and children who give them headaches. I get a pang in my stomach, thinking about how sad they were when I broke off with Dante. What good parents don't want their daughter to meet a fine young man and fall in love and get married? They want me to have what they have.

"If you're gonna be my date, you'd better pep up. I don't need a lead anchor on my ankle on New Year's Eve." Delmarr toasts me.

"Is this better?" I sit up straight in my chair.

"You're the only girl in the room in gold lamé."

"That was intentional," I tell him. After Ruth and I cut the material for this dress, I hid the bolt under last year's samples.

"You certainly stand out. I feel like I'm doing the town with Bathsheba. The way this spotlight is hitting you, it looks like you're in Macy's window."

"Excuse me," a familiar voice says behind me. "Delmarr, how are you?"

I look up, but it's hard to see because the gentleman is standing directly in the beam of an overhead stage light. I shade my eyes. My dream man from Interior Decoration! It's him! I can't believe it! I was thinking about him so much today, I must have willed him here.

"Well, if it isn't young Clark Gable." Delmarr stands and shakes his hand. "Mr. John Talbot, I'd like to introduce you to my date this evening, Lucia Sartori. And these are her parents, Mr. and Mrs. Sartori."

"I'm pleased to meet you." John Talbot extends his hand, first to my mother, then to my father, and finally to me. When he touches me, the same woozy feeling I had in Bridal Registry overcomes me. I can't wait to tell Ruth that it wasn't the butter-pecan ice cream after all.

John places his hand on Delmarr's shoulder. "Well, I just wanted to say hello and wish you all a healthy and happy New Year." He smiles and moves back into the crowd.

"My, my, he's handsome," Mama comments.

"How do you know him?" Papa asks Delmarr. Uh-oh, Papa already senses something. When it comes to me, he has radar.

"He's a jack-of-all-trades. I did some business with him on an over-run of fabric out of the Scalamandre Silk Mills. He made me an excellent deal," Delmarr tells Papa matter-of-factly.

Mama and Papa go back to their conversation and drinks. Delmarr leans in to me and raises an eyebrow. "Do you know him?"

"I saw him at the store one day."

"He had the fish eye for you tonight."

"Do you think so?" If only Delmarr knew how much that thrills me. *John Talbot.* At last I know his name. It's beautiful. I can see it engraved on a brass plate or a book binding. It's an important name. It sounds upper-crust, like the names of the girls who order opera coats for every fall debut of the Philharmonic and live in town houses on the Upper East Side.

"Don't get any ideas. He's a man about town. I see him at all the best places with all the best girls."

"But—"

"Lucia, you're not meant to be one in a stable. You're better than that. You're a stand-alone girl."

The lights dim further, and the combo launches into an overture. There is a drum roll. In the pitch black, the McGuire Sisters take their places behind three microphones, the silver staffs shining in the dark. They begin to sing their smooth a cappella harmonies, and the crowd goes wild as the lights come up. Delmarr says that the word is spreading about them; they are destined to be big recording stars. I can see why. Bathed in the stage lights, they are stunning redheads, with fine features and big dark eyes. And those figures!

Mama and Papa watch the show with delight. To think that just last night, they were wearing their reading glasses, poring over bills at the kitchen table, and arguing about which ones to pay first. They never treat themselves. Mama sacrifices everything for her children. If I didn't bring home fashionable shoes and clothes for her, she'd wear the same old oxfords for years on end. She refuses when I offer her money for the family till, though I make a good salary. She always says, "Put it in the bank." I will never be one third the lady my mother is. I close my eyes and take a mental picture. When I'm old, I want to remember the two of them as they are now on December 31, 1950.

Delmarr nudges me when the McGuire Sisters walk offstage one by one after the opening number. The lights and music change, and they reappear in Delmarr's ruby-red gowns. (I wish Ruth were here to see our handiwork.) After a few songs, the sisters go behind an upstage screen and emerge in the emerald-green version of Delmarr's gown, singing, "We're in the money!" Papa raises his hands high in the air and applauds, as do many in the audience. Delmarr leans back in his chair and says, "Damn, I'm talented."

Then Phyllis McGuire, the baby sister of the group, comes forward. A man in a tuxedo hands her a papier-mâché clock, and she shouts, "Countdown to 1951: ten, nine, eight . . ." The crowd joins in, and when we hit "one," the room goes wild. From giant nets along the ceiling, multicolored balloons and silver confetti rain on us. We're all on our feet; Papa kisses Mama, Delmarr kisses me on the cheek and spins me around. The McGuire Sisters applaud as the crowd cheers. As I'm shaking my head and the confetti falls away like snow, Delmarr grabs me again, this time by the waist, dipping me almost to the floor. "Delmarr, put me down!" I laugh. But it isn't Delmarr; this is a cashmere suit, and it isn't deep blue, it's black, and the tie isn't Delmarr's hunter green, it's a silver jacquard. And though I have no intimate knowledge of Delmarr's lips, I know these aren't his, because this person doesn't smell like Delmarr. This man's neck smells like musky amber and spicy cassias and fresh rain. It's John Talbot, and I fit in the crook of his neck like a violin.

"Mr. Talbot . . ." is all I can say to him. Standing nose to nose with him, the sounds in the room fading to a muffle, I feel his warm skin and look into his eyes. He looks at me with such intensity that I have to close my eyes.

"Happy New Year," he whispers. He lets go of me and disappears once more into the crowd.

"What was *that*?" Delmarr asks, looking after him.

I don't answer. I simply sit down in my chair.

Mama and Papa are chatting with the couple at the next table. I'm sure they didn't see the kiss. I put my hand to my lips so I will always remember how I spent the first seconds of this New Year. I look up at the stage where the huge foil numbers sway from the ceiling: 1951. In an instant, they look like lucky numbers to me.

Ruth and I stay after hours in the Hub to finish the buttons on her wedding gown. The cityscape visible from our window is pure black studded with tiny yellow lights, like the combination of my favorite trim: jet beads and canary diamonds. Ruth's Valentine's Day wedding is a week away, and we're feeling the pressure to finish. Delmarr was sweet enough to leave us the key, so we can let ourselves out through the employee entrance on the main floor.

Ruth is built a lot like Elizabeth Taylor, so we took ideas from the actress's gown in *Father of the Bride* and merged them with a design by Vincent Monte-Sano, who recently had a trunk show at Bonwit Teller's. We feel like traitors when we go to trunk shows at other stores, but we can't resist when it's a designer we admire. We're copying Monte Sano's famous beadwork with small pockets in the skirt's layers of white tulle and a small crystal dropped in each. When Ruth walks down the aisle to the *chuppah*, she will literally dazzle.

My January 5 birthday was, as always, lost in the letdown following the holidays, though Rosemary made me a strawberry Napoleon cake and the girls took me to lunch at the Charleston Gardens. Socially,

I'm treading familiar waters. I've had three dates since the New Year: one, a coworker of Helen Gannon's husband from a stockbrokerage (boring); another, arranged by my mother's cousin, with an architect from Florence (my Italian is far from flawless, so we nodded a lot without speaking); and a third with a friend of Delmarr's who served in the army with him (a nice fellow but not for me). I danced with several of Ruth's relatives at her engagement party, but those will never amount to more than a dance, because no good Jewish mother is going to offer her son in marriage to a Roman Catholic girl from Commerce Street. Or vice versa. And it's just as well; I haven't met anyone, Kaspians and Goldfarbs included, that I would set my permanent sights on.

"Why don't you call Dante DeMartino? Tell him you need a date for my wedding," Ruth suggests. "Harvey always thought the world of him. He misses our double dates."

"Sorry to disappoint Harvey, but Dante would think I wanted to get back together."

"Don't you ever want to? Even just a little?"

"I have my moments," I confess.

"I knew it!"

"Of course, Ruth. When I'm sad or lonely or bored to tears on a bad date, I think about Dante. But then I remind myself why we broke up. He'll always work at the bakery, and that's fine, but it also means that he'll always live with his parents."

"So you're right back where you started." Ruth systematically pushes straight pins into her cushion.

"Exactly. You see, Dante's life after our wedding day would not have changed one bit. We'd have a Mass and a dinner dance, and we'd go to his home. I'd move into the room he grew up in, and into his bed, where I'm sure he'd be happy to have me for the next fifty years. But he wouldn't have to give anything up. I, on the other hand, would be giving up *everything*. The day I married Dante, I would no longer work for B. Altman and Company; I would sign on to Claudia DeMartino Enterprises: washing, cooking, cleaning, and mending."

"If John Talbot walked through that door right now, you'd jump at the chance to date him, wouldn't you?"

"It's not going to happen." I should tell Ruth how tired I am of thinking about him. I wish he'd never kissed me. He ruined me for any men who might follow. No one could live up to that kiss. Delmarr is right. Good-looking, sought-after men like John Talbot cause little thrills all over town, only to check their watch one day and decide to settle down, and when they do, it's with a debutante.

I help Ruth into her gown for the final fitting. She stands on the model's box and looks at herself from all angles. She looks like the ballerina in a music box. "You're beautiful!" I tell her.

"I love the dress. Thank you. You've worked so hard."

"I told you the boat neck with the cap sleeve was the ticket."

"Look at those crystals." Ruth turns slowly on the box. "Someday we should open our own shop."

"I would love to." I flounce the tulle until it stands away from her body.

"Why not? There are career girls in my family. My own mother works alongside my dad at the lumber store. When anyone asks my mom if she works, she says, 'No!' But she's there every morning at nine, doing the books and the payroll. She'll tell you she's only helping out for the day."

As I smooth the facing, I ask, "Does Harvey want you to work for him?"

Ruth looks down at me. "A couple days a week. You know, to do the books."

"But you don't do books! You design clothes! You hate math," I remind her. "You always make me split the bill because you can't add."

"I know, I know." Ruth studies her gown in the mirror.

"Oh, Ruth. Can't you see what's happening? Everything is changing."

"That's how it goes, Lucia."

"It doesn't have to be like this! I hate what's happening to us, the way we throw our dreams away as though they're nothing. We're just a bunch of Ann Brewsters, a clique of nameless girls who come to work for a few years and bide their time till they're married. Then we leave, and right behind us is another young, hungry group of girls who come in with the same dreams; then their time comes, and *they* marry and throw their dreams away. It goes on and on. No one ever stays and becomes what they imagined! And I can't believe that you, of all people, don't see it. Ruth, we get married and lose everything."

"You're upsetting me," Ruth says quietly.

"Good! Get mad! Aren't you angry at a world that thinks so little of your talent? You're going to go and do Harvey's books, which anybody can do, and leave a job here that *nobody* else can do like you. Think of all the nights we've worked overtime, not for the money but because our department was the best, better than Bonwit's, Saks, Lord and Taylor's. We weren't just sewing. You were going to be the next Claire McCardell! Come on, Ruth."

"I don't know what to say. You're asking me to choose."

"Yes!" I yell. Ruth looks as though she is about to cry, and there is no sadder sight than a woman in tears in a wedding gown. I breathe deeply. "That's all we have. If you don't choose, believe me, there's a line of people, starting with Harvey and ending with his mother, who will choose for you. Do you want that? Do you want to give away everything you've worked for to make them happy?"

"Well, I can't *not* marry Harvey. I love him."

"That's not what I'm asking you to do. I'm asking you to consider how you really feel. Do you ever think about *why* it's so easy for you to give up your dream?"

I help Ruth step out of her gown and carefully place it back on the dress mannequin. She doesn't answer my question, but why should she? It would only upset her more. I drape clean muslin over the dress, tucking it carefully around the hem so dust can't get in. Ruth puts our supplies away as I lower the window shades and turn out the lights. We walk down the escalators, since they are stationary after hours, to the employee entrance on the main floor.

"I'm sorry, Ruth."

"It's okay."

"No, it's not okay. You don't need more pressure from me."

"It's not pressure. You make a lot of sense. You gave me a lot to think about."

Ruth opens the door. A large gust of wind pins the door back, and it bangs against the building wall. Ruth motions for me to go outside first. She follows me out, then pushes the door shut, making sure it locks behind us. Snow has begun to fall. I bury my hands in my pockets to find my gloves. Ruth knots a scarf around her neck.

"I'm sorry I disappointed you, Lucia."

"You've never disappointed me. I'm just looking out for you."

Ruth looks toward Madison Avenue. "It's hard to keep everybody happy, but I know there must be a way. I have to find it."

"You will." How can I tell my best friend that there is no way to keep everyone happy? I learned that firsthand from the DeMartinos. The thought that I've hurt her makes me sad. I can't leave her tonight feeling sad. "Thank you, Ruth."

"For what?"

"For at least saying you wanted to open a shop with me."

"I meant it."

"I know you did." I give her a hug and turn toward Fifth Avenue.

"Be careful getting home!" Ruth says to me as she heads east to her bus stop.

"I will," I tell her. I look up Fifth Avenue. There's no sign of my bus. The wind is too cold to stand in, and I can pick up the bus a few blocks down, so I start walking. It's better to keep moving.

The tops of the skyscrapers disappear in a dense fog, and the light from the lower floors throws an eerie glow on the full clouds hanging in gray ripples over the city like a ghostly meringue. I pull my black velvet rain hat with the wide brim over my ears and tie it under my chin with a bow. I bury my gloved hands deep in my pockets again and walk quickly downtown.

I wonder what will become of me. Ruth is being kind by offering to open a shop with me, but that's only a dream. Once she's married, she'll work for a while, and then she and Harvey will have a baby, and she'll quit and stay home to raise her family. I could open my own shop, I guess. But how? I'm not a businesswoman; I sew. Maybe it's because I grew up with brothers, but I see the business world as belonging to men. There are women who do it, though, women like Edith Head in Hollywood. I read in *PhotoScreen* magazine that Miss Head has a husband but no children. There aren't many women who work and have children. Motherhood is certainly difficult, but impending motherhood is not easy, either. As Rosemary's due date draws near, I see how she struggles and how nervous she has become. Roberto stands by faithfully but helplessly. I'm sure deep down he's thinking, I'm glad she has to do this and not me. Once again, it seems, women have to do everything.

Of all the men and women I know, the only one whose life I envy is Delmarr. When he's not working, he's out on the town, having fun. He dates interesting women, some intellectuals, some great beauties, some a combination of the two, and he always looks at life like it's a party. He tells fascinating stories of socialites and dances and nightclubs and nefarious characters and artists—the sum total of his experience is so colorful, even he can't believe his life sometimes. What a wonderful thing, to be satisfied and yet full of wonder.

I make the long cross from the corner of Madison Square Park and continue down Fifth Avenue. The temperature seems to be dropping, and the snow is turning to sleet that hits my face like tiny daggers. I decide to hail a taxi. The trucks and cars whiz by me; not a cab in sight. When I spot one, it's taken—no doubt coming from uptown, where, at the first clink of a raindrop, the cabs fill instantly. I'm about to give up and keep walking when a car pulls over and the window rolls down.

"Lucia! It's John Talbot," he says, leaning across the front seat of his 1950 Packard, painted a glossy midnight blue, with beige and cranberry accents on the running board. I remember this very model from Exodus's catalog. My brother longs for one, but they're made to order and expensive. "Do you need a lift?"

I run through the mental checklist of the safety precautions for the unmarried girl alone on the street. I throw out the rules when I remember that it is Delmarr who introduced me to John Talbot. Maybe this fellow has a lot of girlfriends, but he also has a car in the middle of what is turning into a terrible storm. "Do you mind?"

"Not at all."

"Don't get out," I tell him as he attempts to open his door into moving traffic to come around and open mine. I jump into the car.

"I'm going to have a talk with Delmarr. He's got a lot of crust having you work so late."

"It's not his fault. I was helping my friend Ruth with her wedding gown." I smooth my skirt and see that the car seats are made of the finest leather. The interior is clean and neat. This is a man who takes excellent care of his things.

"You make a lot of wedding gowns there, don't you?" John asks, easing back into the flow of cars.

"All the time."

"Is that fun?"

"Well, as you can imagine, a lot of effort goes into a girl's wedding gown, because she wants to present her very best self to the man who's chosen her. But when girls come to us to put together their very best selves, they turn into—well, to be honest, they turn into raging monsters."

John laughs. "But they look so sweet in the newspaper, with their tiaras and veils."

That's interesting. John Talbot reads the society pages just like Ruth and me. I don't think he's looking for the fashion; maybe seeing which names have to be crossed out of his little black book. "Oh yes, we spend a lot of time bringing them back from beastly to demure. Sometimes I wonder if the grooms ever see the side of their fiancées that we do."

"Probably not. You ladies have a way of duping us. We're suckers for you."

"Then I would say you deserve what you get," I tell him.

"Do you have a boyfriend?" John asks in a friendly way.

"Why would it matter to you? You kissed me on New Year's Eve like you knew me my whole life." I can't believe I brought up the kiss. I instantly wish I could take my words back.

"I know. I want to apologize for that," John says sincerely. "I wasn't really behaving like a gentleman, though I can promise you I absolutely am one. I got carried away. That gold dress was something."

"Thank you." Now I'm glad I hid that bolt of lamé in the supply room. We sit in silence for a couple of blocks while I think of a way to get the conversation going again. "Delmarr tells me that you sell fabric."

"It's one of the many things I do."

"How do you have time to do more than one?" I ask.

"I figure I'm young and should try a lot of different things before I settle on one career."

This is a terrible sign, I think to myself. If he's this noncommittal about his work, how could he ever settle on one girl?

"But I will settle on one thing eventually," he says, as though he knows what's on my mind.

I exhale gently. Good. He's not a flibbertigibbet, he's versatile. "Oh, take that right onto Commerce."

John misses the turn and continues down Seventh Avenue South. "Sorry," he says, not meaning it.

"Now you have to go all the way around the block to get me home."

"That was the idea," he says lightly. "I like talking to you. I'm buying time. Is that all right?"

"I spent the day bending over a sewing machine, so you have to spell things out for me."

"Okay. Let me spell it out, then. I want to spend time with you."

"You don't even know me."

"I see who you are."

"Did you know I was born with a curse on me?" I ask. John laughs. "Yes, I was. And my mother, God bless her, thought I dodged it when I was born without a birthmark on my face, because that was her biggest fear. But I think a curse is like a poisonous vapor—when it's released, it may not overtake you all at once, but it will linger. And one day it'll kill you. Do you know any Italians?"

"Sure."

"Did you ever know any with a curse on them?"

"Only you."

"And you're not deterred?"

"Not in the least."

I point to my street. "Okay, over there. This time don't miss it."

John brakes and turns onto Commerce Street. There's one set of footprints on the sidewalk in the newly fallen snow. I point to them. "When it snows, I sit up in my window and watch it come down. And when I see the first set of footprints in the snow, I can't help but think they look like the cardboard feet in the dance kit from the Arthur Murray studio."

"So you dance?" he asks.

"I love to." I won't tell John Talbot that I used to pay my brother Angelo a nickel to dance with me.

"Sometime we'll go dancing."

"I'd like that." I point to my home. "It's number forty-five."

John pulls up in front. "Wait. I'll come around," he says. "I feel bad I didn't get the door the first time." Nice manners, I think, as he rounds the front of the car and opens my door. The snow sticking to his hair reminds me of the New Year's confetti from the night he kissed me.

"Where's your hat?" I want to know.

"In the backseat."

"You ought to get it," I tell him, pulling the brim of my own hat over my eyes. John opens the back door and pulls out his hat. He puts it on, then takes my arm and walks me up the stoop to the front door.

We stand and look at each other for a moment, not long enough to lead to a kiss but long enough to want one. Now that he knows me a little, he knows I'm not the kind of girl you dip in a nightclub and kiss on the lips without asking. But he's not the type of man who dips and kisses a girl in a nightclub without asking first, either.

"Well, good night, Lucia." He tips his hat.

"Good night, John. Thank you for the ride home." I open the front door and, once I'm inside, breathe deeply. John Talbot exhausts me, though in a good way. This isn't a man who makes me feel comfortable. He's a man who keeps me on my toes. I never know what he is going to do.

The house is filled with the familiar scent of simmering tomatoes and basil. I climb the stairs to change into my slacks and one of Papa's old pullover sweaters. I want a nice dish of Mama's penne, and then I will curl up in front of the fire with a glass of Papa's grappa and think about John Talbot.

CHAPTER FIVE

Once Papa finished remodeling the basement apartment for Roberto and Rosemary, he tackled Mama's kitchen. He hung a crisp red-and-white-striped wallpaper and installed pristine white enamel appliances, including the latest gas stove, with four burners and a griddle. It inspired me to give my bedroom a new look.

When I tell Delmarr I want to redecorate, he takes me shopping at the D&D Building on Madison Avenue, where he introduces me to the finest selection of wallpaper in the world: English designs from Colefax & Fowler, French creations from Pierre Frey, and bright American patterns from Rose Cummings. After all our research, we end up going back to Altman's and up to the Interior Decoration floor, where we find a sample from Schumacher of yellow cabbage roses climbing a white trellis against a sky-blue background. Delmarr informs me that Altman's has won the commission to decorate the White House for President and Mrs. Harry Truman. Delmarr's buddy Charles Haight, who started with him in Packaging, will be the chief designer. "What's good enough for old Bess is good enough for you," Delmarr tells me.

Now at home, I've moved all my furniture to the center of the room and opened the windows for a cross breeze. I spent most of the morning measuring out the wallpaper. The adhesive is tricky, so I bought three extra rolls in case of mistakes. As I pour the paste into the tray, there's a knock at my door.

"Be careful," I call out.

Ruth pushes the door open. "Hi. Your mom said you were up here."

"Up to my ears." I put down the roller and sponge.

"Need a hand?"

"What are you doing here? You're getting married next week."

"I'm in good shape. I need to relax a little."

"Then sit over there and watch."

"I'll go nuts sitting. Let me help."

"Are you sure?" Ruth nods. I show her the plans and point to a spot on the wall. "I'm starting right there." I give her a roll of paper to unwind. She lays it across the floor, and like the dressmaker she is, she makes tiny pencil marks on the wall to correspond with the paper measurements.

"You already prepped the walls, I see." Ruth smooths her hand over the wall with approval.

"Yep." And then, as we do in the Hub, we go about our separate chores quietly, like the team we've become. Whether we're wallpapering, conducting a fitting, or setting out the dinner we've ordered in for an overtime job, we know how to complete a task in the most efficient manner. We each seem to know what the other is thinking, and we anticipate each other's needs and assist in reaching the goal. This is probably what a good marriage is like, I think. As we work side by side I feel a pang of guilt. I was too hard on my best friend and I know it.

"Ruth, I'm sorry about what I said last night."

"No, no. Don't apologize. You're honest with me. And I think you're right." Ruth takes the straightedge and cuts the wallpaper to hug the baseboard. I hold it as she tacks the paper to the wall.

"I shouldn't have yelled."

"You're Italian. You yell. It's okay."

I carefully roll the glue on the back of the paper; Ruth helps me lift it from the edges; we walk it to the wall and ease it into position, smoothing it down with the grader. We step back to see the result.

"This is the ticket." Ruth smiles. "Good choice. I like it."

The colors, the mood, and the scale of the pattern suit the room. The overall effect is just right. "I do, too."

"You ever wonder how we know?" With the pencil, Ruth marks the next sheet. "How come we seem to know what works? It's like this wallpaper. You chose the right print for this wall, this room. How did you *know*? The rich girls who come in for fittings, they're always so . . . perplexed. They never know what color is right on them, or what line looks good on their figures. They want to see what another client is having made so they can copy it. They have no original ideas."

"That's what they pay *us* for. To tell them what works. Maybe that's why God gave them all the money and gave us the talent. It's good old-fashioned supply and demand," I tell her.

Ruth helps me hang a second sheet of wallpaper. "Harvey's cousin Jake is coming in from California for the wedding. He's a bachelor, and he doesn't have a date—"

"Ruth, I will absolutely dance with him, but I've already got an escort. I promised Delmarr."

"Oh, right."

"And besides, I have suitors galore. I can't possibly take on another. John Talbot picked me up in his Packard last night."

"*What?*"

"Yep. And he drove me home, and he almost kissed me." I look at Ruth and smile. "And next time it won't be an almost."

Mama has asked Ruth to stay for dinner, since it's only right to feed the volunteer, but she has a date with Harvey. She's missing a delicious meal. Mama has made Papa's favorite Venetian dish, a hearty fish stew from a recipe given to him by his aunt in Godega. Rosemary has helped Mama prepare it and wrote down the recipe for her collection (and mine).

VIOLA PERIN'S FISH BRODETTO
Yield: 8 servings

1 pound shrimp, shelled and deveined
1 pound lobster tail, cut into chunks
1 pound sole, cut into chunks
1 fresh lemon
¼ cup olive oil
1 large sweet onion, sliced
3 cloves garlic, minced
6 fresh tomatoes, chopped
1 cup balsamic vinegar
2 quarts water
3 cups red wine
3 tablespoon fresh parsley, chopped
Salt and pepper

Prepare fish, squeeze lemon over, set aside. In a large pot, lightly sauté onion in olive oil, garlic, tomatoes, and balsamic vinegar. Add water and wine. Stir well. Add fish, parsley. Add salt and pepper to taste. Cook on stovetop over medium heat for 40 minutes or until fish cooks through. To serve, line soup bowls with thin slices of toasted Italian bread. Ladle stew over bread and serve.

Rosemary and I help Mama prepare the bowls of stew. Mama takes her scissors and cuts a bunch of basil from her plant in the window. She rinses it, then cuts it in ribbons to garnish each bowl of stew.

"Maria!" Papa shouts from the living room. "Maria, *presto!*"

Mama throws down her dish towel and goes into the living room. Rosemary and I follow her. Roberto, Orlando, Angelo, and Exodus are smiling mischievously. Mama eyes them. "What is it?" she asks. Papa picks her up and twirls her around. "Antonio, put me down. You'll hurt your back," she says.

"You won't believe it," Papa says, covering her face in kisses.

"What? What won't I believe?"

"Zio Antonio left us the family homestead in Godega. My farm!

The farmhouse where I was born. The barn where I kept our horse, the fields of wheat behind it, all of it. It's ours!"

"Who said so?" Mama demands.

"My cousin Domenic sent me a letter. Here. Look. You can read it yourself." Papa gives Mama the letter, and the boys start talking over one another with plans for our inheritance.

Mama straightens her apron. "What are we going to do with a farm?"

"We're going to visit!"

"When?"

"In August."

"But I already rented a house at the Jersey shore."

"Cancel it. Maria, *viva un po*! I don't want any arguments. We're going to Italy. The whole family is going home."

Rosemary runs her hand over her stomach. "I don't know, Papa. The baby will be very small, and that's a big trip."

"He'll grow! This is my home, and my grandchildren will know it as their own! Besides, it's Italian law, we have to go in person to claim the property in court."

"I am not spending my holiday in Italy feeding chickens and milking goats," Mama says, putting her hands on her hips. "I have enough to do around here."

"You are going to Italy, Maria," Papa says evenly.

"I am not going anywhere," Mama counters.

It is so quiet in the living room, we can hear a taxi horn honking all the way over on Seventh Avenue. Mama and Papa stare each other down. My brothers back away, checking the exits. We all know what will happen next: a big fight that revisits every slight Mama has endured over the course of their long marriage.

"Mama," I plead, trying to defuse the impending bomb. "Can't you be happy for Papa?"

"Lucia, you don't know about farming. My mother's father was a farmer, don't forget. And that is a life of hell, I promise you. You work all day in the field and all night in the barn. It's no fun, and your father and I are too old to take it on. We'll have to sell it," Mama decides.

"I will never sell the farm!" Papa bellows. "Never!"

Mama backs down when she hears the tone in Papa's voice. "All right, all right, Antonio. *Basta!* I'll cancel the Jersey shore so we can see your farm. Wash up for supper. Are you happy now?" She turns and goes back into the kitchen.

Papa watches her go, shaking his head in disbelief. My brothers look at me, and I throw my hands up in the air. We may have been taught that Papa is the head of our household and the leader of the family, but the truth is, Maria Sartori runs the show.

I break the silence. "Pop, I'm sorry. I think it's wonderful."

"Me, too, Pop." Rosemary smiles at him. She squeezes his hand and then goes up the stairs.

During dinner Mama and Papa refused to look at each other. Then Papa grabbed his hat and coat and slammed the front door on his way out for a walk. I told Rosemary to go and lie down, that I'd take care of the dishes. When my brothers and I were little, Mama would tell us that if you eat when you're angry, the food turns to poison.

"Is Papa back yet?" Mama asks, coming into the kitchen as I dry the last of the dishes.

"No."

Mama sits down at the kitchen table. I pour a cup of tea for her and one for myself. "Are you going to sulk all night?" I ask her gently.

"You don't know the whole story," she begins. "I read the letter. Your father got the farm, and his brother got the money."

"Zio Antonio had money?"

"Yes. And he knew of the feud between your father and his brother, so instead of splitting the land and money equally, he did his own division."

"Maybe Zio was afraid that if he gave the farm to both of them, they would end up selling it."

"Of course that's what he thought. Your father's family has never been anything but trouble."

"Well, whose fault is that? You should convince Papa to make peace with his brother." I can tell Mama is surprised by my tone. "This ridiculous feud has gone on long enough."

"We're better off this way," she insists.

"Ma, what is so terrible that Papa and Zio Enzo haven't spoken in twenty-five years?"

"It was a lot of things." Mama squeezes the tea bag against her spoon so hard I'm afraid it will burst open.

"Let me guess. Money."

"Of course it was about money. And it was also about character. Enzo's wife accused your father of making a pass at her."

"*What?*" I can't imagine my father doing such a thing.

"Your father didn't do it, of course. I was there. But Caterina insisted that he did. She was so envious of Enzo and Papa's closeness that she made up a terrible lie to tear them apart. But that was simply the last straw. From the beginning she and I didn't get along."

"Why?"

"She was a prima donna. She never worked. When we all lived in this house, I did all the cooking and cleaning, and she never lifted a finger to help me. I was her maid. I did it because she was older, and I wanted to prove to your father that I could make a nice home and get along with everyone, so in a sense I didn't mind. But Caterina was a very insecure woman. In my mind, the most dangerous people in the world are insecure women. They can do more damage in a day than an army."

"What did she do?"

"She spent a lot of money on things for herself and didn't mind that the rest of us went without. At the end of the month, when we paid the bills, there would always be a royal battle between Papa and Enzo. Those arguments alone would have caused a rift."

"You shared expenses?"

"Papa and Enzo put everything the Groceria made into a pot. Both families ate from that pot. Of course, there was a debt to the bank, and Caterina knew it. I've never been a woman who wanted a lot of fancy things, I'm happy with very little. Caterina, however, needed lots of things to make herself happy. She was furious when she was banished from New York City, but that was the deal: whoever lost the coin toss moved, and the other brother bought him out. It was the only way."

"So Papa chose you over his brother, and that's when Caterina put the curse on me."

"Right. She had to make one final scene. But your father and Enzo were determined to make the deal stick. There is no way one of them would have backed out. A deal is a deal. And I don't think Enzo minded so much. He always missed the country. I think if he could have, he would have gone back to the Veneto and had his own farm."

"Uncle Enzo probably would have liked to get the farm in Godega."

"It's done now, Lucia. I'm sure Caterina will be happy with her pile of lire."

Ruth and I are under deadline to finish a traveling ensemble for a Park Avenue lady who's spending the spring touring Europe. This is Ruth's final big job before her wedding and honeymoon. As we wrap up, Ruth pulls a long sheet of butcher paper off the roll, tears it across the blade, and lays it down on the cutting table. She takes a piece of black chalk from her supply box and writes, "John Talbot," then stands back from it. "Now, that's a distinguished name. Sounds like a scholar or a banker or something grand."

"If he's so grand, why hasn't he called?"

"That, Lucia, is the million-dollar question." Ruth smiles.

"Ladies, for your bulletin board." Delmarr throws a letter down on my worktable. "The Mother Superior of the Poor 'We're Barely Scraping By' Nuns of the Bronx would like to thank you for their habits. They will keep you and yours in their prayers."

"That's nice," I say sincerely.

"Write Mother back, would you, Lucia, and tell her that I would like her entire order to pray that my hair stays in. I saw a touch of scalp in the back this morning. It's small, but it has the potential to spread, and I'm too vain to lose my hair." Delmarr twists to look in the three-way mirror, patting the back of his head. "Is there a saint for the prevention of hair loss?"

"Don't look at me. I don't know from saints," Ruth says.

"I don't think there's a saint, but there are surely novenas for desperate situations," I offer.

"Then include Harvey," Ruth says. "Do they pray for Jews?"

"Why wouldn't they?" I ask.

"Then tell them to pray for the shiny bald spot on the crown of Harvey's head. It's already the size of a postage stamp, but it's okay. I told him I would love him no matter what."

"That's how it is when you get married." Delmarr leans against the wall. "Which is why I never will. What honest person could stand before a group of people and promise that in sickness (yech), poverty (they've got to be kidding), and whatever else comes down the pike that you would *never* leave? The wedding vows are a license to be a complete jerk, with full knowledge that the person you married has agreed, no matter how large a horse's ass you are, to stay by your side until death. A fool could tell you this is a bad deal."

"Could we change the subject, please?" Ruth says pleasantly. "I am almost a bride."

"Lucia, I'm going to lunch with John Talbot. You want to come along?"

Before I can answer, John comes through the doors. He's wearing a black pin-striped suit with subtle stripes in the palest periwinkle. His tie is watermarked Chinese silk in off white against a bright white shirt. Why is he always so well turned out, and therefore irresistible?

"Would you like to come?" Delmarr asks me again.

"I can't. I have plans." I look at Delmarr and smile politely, but I want to wring his neck. I'm not a tagalong on his business lunches, not with John Talbot.

"Okay, no problem," Delmarr says casually.

John looks down and sees his name in chalk. "Someone sending me a message?" he asks, pointing.

Ruth and I look at each other with slight panic. Delmarr picks up on it immediately. "Oh, that was me. I asked Ruth to make a note to remind me about our lunch." Ruth and I are thinking the same thing: Delmarr is a stand-up fellow who can catch a fastball.

"How are you, Lucia?" John says, smiling.

"Just fine. Have you met Ruth Kaspian?"

"Sure, upstairs. Remember? It's a pleasure to see you again."

"Thank you," Ruth says with a smile. "It's a pleasure on my end, too." Delmarr shows John out. Once they are gone, Ruth leans across her drawing table. "He's magnificent," she sighs. "His teeth are whiter than his shirt!"

"That's what they mean when they say 'movie-star looks,' " I tell her.

"You may well end up with him after all. You're a beauty match. My aunt Beryl always says money marries money, and pretty marries pretty. When she's tipsy, she also says poor marries poor, and ugly marries ugly." Ruth pours herself a cup of coffee out of her thermos and refills mine. "Guess what Uncle Milt is?"

"Pretty?"

"Nope. Poor."

The afternoon goes by with no sign of Delmarr. The booking secretary delivers us a message from him around four o'clock that says he'll see us Monday morning, he's gone to an appointment outside the office. There's nothing unusual about this—we spend a lot of time running errands to fabric houses, trim shops, and notions stores. I'm dying to ask Delmarr about John Talbot, but it will have to wait the weekend.

I take the bus home, anxious to start my weekend. Sunday is Ruth's wedding, but I will spend tomorrow admiring the wallpaper in my room. I also have a new book I can't wait to crack open, *Mr. Blandings Builds His Dream House,* and a new shoe shop on East Fifty-eighth Street to wander through. When I get off the bus and make the turn from Seventh Avenue onto Commerce, I feel comforted by the lantern twinkling over our stoop.

"Mama, I'm home," I call out from the vestibule. I'm starting up the stairs to my room when she appears in the doorway.

"You have guests," Mama says, meeting me in the doorway.

"I do?" I try to see around Mama. "Who?"

"Delmarr and that fellow John we met on New Year's Eve."

Mama turns to go back into the kitchen. My heart races. I'm sorry

I didn't apply lipstick before I started home, but I wasn't expecting company. Without taking my coat off, I check my face in the mirror by the door and go into the living room.

"What a surprise," I tell Delmarr and John as they rise to greet me. "So, the longest lunch in history led you to my house?"

"I went by your papa's store for some superior olive oil, and he invited us to dinner," Delmarr explains. "Go take your coat off. Your mother convinced me to make a vat of Manhattans, and they're iced just right."

"Great," I say.

"Pop and the boys are on their way home, honey," Mama calls from the kitchen.

Back in the hallway, I take off my coat and hang it up next to John's. His overcoat carries the spicy scent of amber I remember from New Year's Eve. I hear them chattering inside, so I take a moment to examine the coat. It is tailored with the finest details: a smart black satin lining, leather backing on the collar, chamois lining on the cuffs. The vent in the back is reinforced with silk cording, an old technique that lets the coat fall to the back of the knees without wrinkling. On the shelf over the coatrack is John Talbot's hat. It is a Borsalino; it, too, has a custom touch, a gusset in the crown to fit the owner and no one else. The gloves that rest on the brim are black kid leather with a rollover cuff. John Talbot is particular, and I like that. I pull my lipstick out of my purse and apply it. I look down at my simple camel-wool skirt and wish I had dressed in something more festive, but this will have to do. Plus, I don't want this man to think I'm trying to impress him.

I join them in the living room. Delmarr hands me a glass. Rosemary comes out of the kitchen after Mama. She moves slowly, the weight of the baby, due anytime, evident in her every movement. John asks her lots of questions, how she has prepared for the baby and where she's delivering and all about her doctor. Rosemary asks John why he is so interested in babies. He tells her that it's the only miracle in the world. Mama looks at him with approval.

"We're home!" Roberto calls from the doorway. My brothers are laughing, joking with one another. Papa leads them into the living room, giving Mama the zippered canvas money sack from the store. He kisses her on the cheek.

"I see you got here just fine," Papa says to Delmarr and John.

"Not without a compass," Delmarr said. "These Village streets are as twisty as rolatini."

"Did you meet my brothers?" I ask.

John points. "That's Roberto. That's Angelo. That's Orlando. And the bruiser who looks Irish is Exodus."

"Hey, I'm all Italian," Exodus retorts. "Don't make me prove it."

"Oh, I won't," John jokes back. "I hope that by the end of the evening, you'll have taught me all the Italian curse words I can retain. I'm visiting Capri as a guest of the Mortensons come Easter, and I want to shock them with foul language."

Delmarr laughs. "Believe me, you'll need them after a week with Vivie Mortenson. She's a piece of work."

"Well, these are the boys to teach you," Papa promises. "They know more bad words than me, and I grew up in Italy."

"How do you know the Mortensons?" I ask John.

"They're old friends."

"I made Sally Mortenson's debutante gown," I tell him. John smiles politely. I wonder if he'll be less interested in me now that he knows I make his friends' clothes.

Delmarr reads my mind. "All the girls request Lucia when they come in for a fitting. They know she's the best." He winks at me.

As I watch the men joke and spar, it occurs to me that for most of my life I've been the only girl in the room. When I began my career, I was relieved to be with women. There's an understanding and a language among a group of women that I treasure. As much as I love my brothers, I've never been able to tell them things that I could have told a sister. Mama was sensitive to that and tried to compensate. But some things I would have felt more comfortable saying to a sister instead of Mama. Being the only Sartori girl made me more confident, though. I don't think I would have had the guts to take my sewing samples to Altman's Custom Department had I not had brothers who taught me about competition. And I don't think I would have even tried to get a job had Papa not encouraged me to take care of myself. He told me I would make better decisions if I made them out of want and not need.

I help Mama serve the meal, polenta and roasted Cornish game hens. Delmarr gets a kick out of my brothers and talks to them about working in the Groceria. He asks lots of questions about how the operation is set up. John says he can't imagine what would happen if someone weren't pulling his weight—how do you fire your family? As we eat, John tells funny stories about characters he has met in his extensive travels. Even Delmarr is fascinated. While we clear the dishes, Papa gets down to business.

"So, John, what is your trade?" Papa asks as he pours himself a glass of wine.

"I'm a businessman. I'm interested in starting ventures in several areas. I like importing. Lately I've been working with a textile manufacturer in Spain. I'd like to provide goods to the fabric houses on Fifth Avenue. Among other things."

Papa raises an eyebrow. "Other things?"

"Yes, sir. I like to be useful. I have connections, and I like to use them to do some good. Bishop Walter Sullivan called me to arrange a couple of buses for an upstate retreat—"

"You know the bishop?" Mama says, impressed.

"For many years. Anyway, he needed a hand with transportation, and I helped out."

"I'm sure he appreciated it." Mama smiles, then nods at Papa. "So, you're Catholic?" she asks hopefully.

"I am." John Talbot doesn't know it yet, but he's won my mother over.

"Antonio," my mother says. "The port."

"I'll get Ro's sesame cookies," I offer.

"I make them by the pound, they're my only craving," Rosemary says to Delmarr apologetically. "I hope you like them."

Roberto returns to talk of the Groceria and his dreams of expanding and modernizing it. Papa, in his wise way, lets Roberto go on and on about attracting new customers, opening a second store uptown, and someday having a chain of Grocerias. Rosemary has heard these dreams in detail, so her eyes get a tired look as she nibbles a cookie. Mama likes to hear Roberto's ideas of progress; she takes pride in our ambition. John listens carefully to Roberto as he spins the dream.

"If you have one business going gangbusters, you *should* expand," John tells him. "You can't grow if you don't envision the bigger picture."

"Tell Papa that. He likes the old ways," Roberto says.

"I'm not against the new," Papa says pleasantly. "I just don't understand how to have two stores and meet the quality standards I have set for myself. I'm one man who can inspect one piece of fruit at a time. If the crates come in and I dump them in a bin and stick a price on them without checking, then I'm no better than the store up the street. My customers know they're buying the best because I have chosen it for them. My fish is fresh from Long Island Sound, my meats are from the farmlands of Pennsylvania, and my fruit comes from all over, upstate New York and as far as Italy. I still buy my blood oranges from the same Italian family I met as a boy in the open market in Treviso. The farmer wraps each orange like a jewel, crates them all, and sends them for sale in my shop."

I squeeze Papa's hand. "I used to wait for those crates from Italy. The whole block smelled like sweet oranges!"

"I am not saying that everyone in the world has to be as fussy as me, but my customers trust me, and that is a bond I take seriously."

"Sir, I respect that." Delmarr toasts Papa with his port. "Like you, I believe in quality. But I think we must face the fact that the world is changing. Since the war, in my business, the mandate has been 'How many can we make, and how quickly can we make them?' There was a time when the store told us you could say no to a customer if you knew you wouldn't turn out a quality garment. Now they tell us to take every order. There's a lust for profit, at the expense of quality. They'd like us to work seven days a week, with double the output. I don't know where all of this is headed, but it isn't good."

"Since the boys came home from the war, our customer base has expanded," Mama says. "We used to be a neighborhood market, but now we get more and more people from uptown."

"Two reasons," Roberto explains. "Lots of guys were stationed in Italy and got a taste for fresh basil, the best Parmesan, good olive oil—"

"And where were they going to get it uptown? These bluebloods don't know from authentic Italian. So they began coming to us," Exodus adds.

"But it was more than what we were selling," Papa says. "When I came to this country, the Italians were not embraced. But after we sent our sons over to go up against Hitler, everything changed. We brought honor to our people. It changed the way people in this city looked at us."

"All the Sartoris served?" John asks.

"I'm the only one who didn't make it overseas. I enlisted near the end and got as far as Fort Bragg," Exodus says.

"You still defended your country, Ex." Mama puts her arm around him.

"Did you serve?" Papa asks John.

"Yes, sir. I was stationed in France."

I smile, knowing that this matters to Papa.

By nine o'clock the conversation wanes, since we're all tired from the workweek. The only person with pep is John Talbot, who becomes more animated and engaging as the evening wears on. He's a night person, I think to myself, the opposite of me. I like to be in bed early and wake up before the sun rises, so I have the full benefit of a long morning. I imagine John Talbot at the clubs until all hours. He probably does a lot of entertaining in his business, so late nights are a requirement. It's something for me to consider, though it's a small negative in the sea of delightful qualities I am discovering in John. I'm a girl who hardly shows her feelings (maybe that's another result of living with brothers), but deep within, I feel a quake of falling for Mr. Talbot. I look across the table at him and wonder how I would feel if he were mine.

"You're tired," John says to me.

"It's been a long week. Seems that every custom order these days is a rush. Ruth and I can barely keep up."

"It is definitely the busy season," Delmarr agrees.

"You tell those swankies to wait," my mother instructs us. "There's no sense in killing yourself over a party dress."

"Yes, Mama."

"Yes, ma'am," Delmarr assures her as he and John stand. Delmarr shakes my father's hand and says good night to everyone.

John Talbot turns to my mother. "Thank you for a delicious dinner."

"Come by anytime," Mama says warmly.

"I promise I will."

I show John and Delmarr to the vestibule. While John puts on his coat, I take down his hat and gloves and hand them to him. "Borsalinos are very chic."

"And durable. This hat will last a lifetime."

Delmarr holds out his hat before placing it on his head. "I hope my hat passes inspection."

"Impeccable as always, Monsieur Delmarr. Lilly Dache would approve."

"Ah, thank you, thank you. I'll pick you up around two on Sunday, Lucia. I can't wait to see Ruth in her Elizabeth Taylor gown. She wouldn't let me look, even though I designed it. Evidently men are bad luck in general. Please thank your mother again for dinner."

Delmarr opens the door and steps outside, leaving me and John in a brief moment of silence, which I break. "Good night, John."

"Lucia? Are you busy tomorrow?"

My mind files through my chores. I picture myself curled up with a book.

"Not very," I tell him.

"Would you like to go for a ride?"

"That would be nice."

"I'll pick you up at one."

After I close the door behind him, I watch through the pink panes of glass as he and Delmarr walk up to Barrow and turn.

"He's a looker," Rosemary says from behind me.

"Do you trust lookers, Ro?" I ask her.

"Never."

"Me, neither."

"But I like him. And he likes my sesame cookies, which shows good judgment." Rosemary hands me an index card. She has already written out the recipe for me.

ROSEMARY SARTORI'S SESAME SEED COOKIES
Yield: 3 dozen cookies

3 cups flour, sifted
Dash of salt
1 teaspoon baking powder
2 sticks real butter (warmed to room temperature)
3/4 cup white granulated sugar
3 jumbo-size egg yolks
1 teaspoon vanilla extract
Large handful of sesame seeds
1 tablespoon heavy cream

Take the flour, salt, and baking powder and sift together into a medium-size bowl. In a large bowl blend the butter with a fork into the sugar. Add in the egg yolks one at a time, then add vanilla. Take the dry mixture from the small bowl and pour into the large bowl of wet ingredients. Mix well with hands. Make into a ball; should be doughy. Cover with saran wrap and refrigerate for a couple of hours. After this time has passed, lightly flour cutting board. Roll dough into long strips and cut into 2-inch pieces. Wet sesame seeds in heavy cream. Take each cookie and dip into seeds. Put the cookies on a greased cookie sheet. Bake for 9 minutes at 400°.

I spent the morning pressing my brothers' shirts in the basement laundry room. I never mind the job. The fresh scent of cotton when the steam iron hits the shirt is comforting. I get satisfaction when I look at the freshly starched shirts on hangers arranged in order on the rack, from my oldest brother to my youngest. Between housework and

Ruth's wedding tomorrow, I almost wish I hadn't made a date with John for this afternoon. It's unlike me to accept a last-minute engagement, but there's something about him that makes me want to throw out my rules.

When he comes to the door promptly at one, Mama is waiting with a couple of wrapped turkey sandwiches and a small sack of Rosemary's sesame cookies for us to take on our ride.

"Have you ever been to Huntington?" John asks as he opens the door to help me into his car. I notice a fringe of cloudy white salt on the bumpers, the only sign that the car has been out of a garage since the winter began.

"No," I tell him.

He goes around to the driver's side, gets in, and settles into the seat. "Long Island. It's building up. You know, there are only so many views of the ocean. Finite real estate. That's where the money is." He looks at me and smiles, turning the key over. The Packard engine hums evenly like a church organ. "I have a real estate plan. You know, the entirety of the American economy is built on real estate. I plan to buy a home, then borrow against it to build another, and so on, until there's a development with my name on it. What do you think?"

"I think . . . it sounds great." I don't know what else to say. Real estate is not something I have given much thought to. As we head over to the East Side, cross the Manhattan Bridge into Brooklyn, and sail onto the highway, John Talbot tells me about his big dream to use the real estate money to open an elegant Manhattan hotel with all the trimmings. He sees a nightclub, a restaurant, rooftop views, the works. His enthusiasm is contagious. I imagine the women in their mink coats and pearls. I see the men who accompany them, dapper New York business tycoons, and I see John Talbot in their midst, entertaining them with his wit and charm.

Huntington Bay, Long Island, still has a kiss of the last snowfall on its trees and sloping lawns. The homes are new, dotting the hillsides in a mix of styles: brick colonial, Connecticut farmhouse, and my favorite, English Tudor. There's something about the bricks, casement windows, and castle doors that makes me feel secure.

"You love the Tudor, don't you?" John looks at me and stops the car in front of the house.

"Italians like English design. Mama has family in Forest Hills. They're crazy for the Tudors."

John pulls the car over in front of an empty lot. "Let's go," he says, and jumps out of the car. He comes around and opens the door for me, offering me his hand. "I want to show you something." John leads me up a hill. It's icy, so I slide back and we laugh, but he moves me in front of him and pushes me up the knobby hill until we reach the top. Through the trees I see a silvery expanse hung low with white clouds.

"That's the bay," John says.

A feeling comes over me, one I've never experienced. I connect with this place, deeply and instantly, as if I have been here before. What would it be like to live near the water? To be able to walk to the ocean and hear the waves and smell the sea salt every day? Fancy Upper East Side Manhattan, dressed in black velvet, has always been my idea of sumptuous living, but now I imagine having a view of the ocean. I can see the blue summers and the petal-soft springs when the driftwood bleaches from dull gray to eggshell white in the sun. Papa told me stories of going to Rimini, on the Adriatic coast below the Veneto, where the sand was the color of snow. Against the blue water, it could blind you in the noonday sun.

"You should live on the water someday," John says, as if he knows something about my future that I do not.

My feet get caught in the dry bramble of some old branches. John kneels and helps me out of the twisty mesh. I look down at him and can't help imagining the precise moment he will propose marriage to me. He looks up at me, and I swear he is thinking the same thing. I pull my foot loose and extend my hand to help him up. We go back to the car without saying a word.

Once we're back on the highway, I feel sad about leaving the ocean behind. I look out the window because this isn't something I want to talk about. I need to think about it before I can articulate it. Plus, I want to run all of this by Ruth. She is wise in these matters.

"Would you like to meet my mother?" John Talbot asks.

"Well . . . of course." I'm surprised John wants me to meet his family. After all, this is only a first date.

"We don't have to. We could do it another time," he says, sensing my discomfort.

I change my mind. The more clues I have to understanding John, the better. "No, no. I'd like to. Does she live out here? With your father?"

"No, he died when I was seven. She remarried when I was twelve. My stepfather was a nice man named Edward O'Keefe."

"Do you have any brothers and sisters?" I ask.

"Nope."

"So it's just you taking care of your mother."

John Talbot doesn't reply, and for whatever reason, I don't press him. I'm already beginning to read his signals. He is not direct. When he is uncomfortable or doesn't want to talk, he ignores the question. He doesn't volunteer information. But all interesting men are evasive sometimes, aren't they? He's an enigma. So I'm not terribly surprised when he turns into a circular drive with an arch over the entrance that says CREEDMORE.

If you'd never heard of Creedmore but stumbled upon it, you might think it was a private estate, with its grand driveway lined by hundred-year-old oaks with ivy growing up their trunks like long gloves. But it's not an estate; it's a hospital for the elderly, the infirm, and occasionally, the troubled who need a respite from the noise of the world. This is how it was explained to me when I was a girl.

"Does your mother work here?" I ask John as we walk under the awning that leads to the main doors.

"No, she's lived here for the past three years." John opens the door for me. Beyond the small foyer is an enormous visiting room ringed with the elderly in wheelchairs, some alone, others with weekend visitors. The center of the room is curiously empty, like a circus ring before the show begins.

As we approach the reception desk, I can see that the patients are clean and well cared for, but that doesn't compensate for the sadness

I feel when I look into their eyes. The nurse at the reception desk greets John as he signs in. He shows me through the set of doors leading to the rooms.

"My mother had me late in life. She was nearly forty. Four years ago she had a slight stroke," John explains as we walk. "I took care of her myself for the first year, but then she suffered another stroke, that one massive, and lost her speech. Her doctors suggested a convent hospital on Staten Island, but my mother never liked Staten Island. I asked for other alternatives, and one of the doctors recommended this place."

John opens the door to his mother's room and motions for me to enter. The room is fairly spacious, painted mint green, and sparsely furnished. Its saving grace is a large window on the far wall that overlooks a sculpture garden with a rolling field behind it.

There are two patients in the room. Closest to the door, sleeping in a bed with the pillows propped almost to sitting position, is a small white-haired lady. In the far bed, looking out at the view, another petite white-haired lady is eating her lunch. Her hair is coiffed with marcel waves; her fingernails are short and painted bright red. She wears a pressed pink housecoat with a zippered front.

"I brought a friend today," John says as he kisses her on the cheek.

She smiles and looks up at him, then grabs his arm with her hand. He reaches down and gives her another kiss. "I would like you to meet Lucia Sartori."

"Hello, Mrs. O'Keefe." I smile at her.

She looks me up and down without smiling and goes back to her soup.

"I brought you some chocolate-covered marshmallows." John places the box of candy on her bedside table. "Are they treating you well?"

She can't answer, but she does not seem frustrated by this. Obviously, they are treating her well. Her bed is neat, and the room is spotless.

John pulls up a chair and indicates that I should sit. He sits down on the edge of the bed and takes his mother's hand and chats with her. John has the same strong jawline as his mother, but her eyes are light blue instead of gray. Around her face are touches of faded gold in her white hair, indicating that once upon a time, her hair was red. "Mrs. O'Keefe, were you a redhead?" I ask her.

"Yes, she was. A real Irish girl with a genuine Irish temper," John replies.

Mrs. O'Keefe looks out the window and sighs. She reaches for the candy John brought, unwraps it, and offers John and me each a piece. We sit with her for half an hour as John recaps events happening in the news. She doesn't appear to listen, but he presses on, trying to entertain her.

I have never known anyone who lived in a place like Creedmore. When my mother's mother came to live with us after my grandfather died, we took care of her ourselves. It was unheard of to seek help outside the home. As I look at Mrs. O'Keefe, I wonder if she knew her life would come to this. John is very attentive, checking with the nurses and making sure she is comfortable. My mother always told me to observe how a son treats his mother. What I see today impresses me.

The drive back to Manhattan seems short, except for the theater traffic outside the Midtown Tunnel. It's only six o'clock, but it feels much later. We spent the whole day together, a day so full it seemed to last a month. I am tired from the ride, from all the things I saw and learned, and from John himself. He is intelligent and needs more than an eager listener. He needs a confidante with whom he can share the flurry of ideas that seem to come so easily to him.

John pulls up in front of my house, gets out, and opens my door. He extends his hand and helps me out of the car. Then he lifts me up by my waist. I place my hands on his shoulders because my feet are barely touching the ground. Without a word, he gently kisses me. He holds me so tightly, I feel bound to him. I lean back a little to look into his eyes, but they are closed. I wonder what he's thinking. The cold February twilight sends a chill through me, but his face is warm, and I bury my nose in his cheek.

"Thank you," he says softly.

"Mr. Talbot?"

"Yes?"

"Are you ever going to ask me before you kiss me?"

"Probably not." He laughs.

"Just so I know the rules."

I go up to the stoop and take out my key. John Talbot waits by his car until I am safely inside. I watch him through the windowpanes and can hear the low tweet of his whistling as he climbs back into the Packard. He flips open his cigarette case, pulls out a cigarette, taps the tip on the dashboard, and lights it. Then he drives off down the street. The moment the car turns the corner and is out of sight, I feel sad. There it is, the first sign of falling in love: the great longing that comes from even the slightest separation. When I look at him, I don't feel that I deserve him; rather that I aspire to him. This will be a love I will have to earn, but something tells me John Talbot is worth it.

I sit down and pull off my snow boots, thinking the house is awfully quiet. When I go to the foot of the stairs, I see a note taped to the banister: "Come to Saint Vincent's Hospital! We have a girl!" I rush to put my boots back on and run the fifteen-plus blocks to meet my new niece.

Inside the warm hospital I find the stairs to the third-floor maternity ward and take them two at a time. The waiting area outside the new mothers' rooms looks more like a train station than a hospital. Happy fathers corral the newborns' siblings, not quite sure how to handle the children on their own. I see the occasional grandmother or aunt pitching in to help, but it's mostly the overwhelmed daddies who try to make the children settle down and behave. A nurse, used to the fray, manages the proceedings with patience. I rush to the desk and inquire about the Sartori baby. The nurse smiles and points to the nursery. There is quite a crowd pressing against the large window. Hogging the front are my brothers, my parents, and the Lancelattis.

"Excuse me," I say to the people waiting to get at the window, and squeeze in next to my parents. "Where is she?"

"Oh, Lucia, Rosemary did so well," Mama brags. "She's six pounds, three ounces. She's tiny but strong."

"Which one is she?" I want to know.

Roberto points to an infant swaddled tightly in a white flannel blanket. "Can't you tell? Look at that head of hair." Her face peeks out of the cocoon, a pink rosebud with a head of thick black hair.

"She's an angel!" Papa says proudly. "Not since you were born, Lucia . . ." He gets tears in his eyes.

"That hair reminds me of Mr. Castellini's toupee. A lot of hair on top and nothing on the sides," Exodus comments. The boys laugh.

"That's not funny!" Mama says. It occurs to me that the phrase she utters most often to my brothers is that one.

Papa has his arm around Mama. They look at the baby with such adoration that I can understand why Mama had five children. There's nothing like this moment, nothing as hopeful as the face of a newborn. "Hey, let's give the other families the window," I tell everyone.

"*Andiamo!*" Mama says, giving Papa a gentle nudge to move the boys to the waiting area.

The nurse comes in with a chart and looks at us. "Let me guess. Italians," she says with a half-smile. "You folks really know how to pack a joint."

"Are we being too noisy?" I ask her.

"No, no, I'm teasing. Rosemary would like to see her mother, Mrs. Sartori, and Lucia."

"That's Aunt Lucia," I tell her.

"Boys," Mama instructs, "we'll see you at home in a little while."

"Roberto and I will be in the waiting room," Papa tells her.

In single file, we follow the nurse down a quiet corridor to Rosemary's room, Mama, Mrs. Lancelatti, then me. Mama takes Mrs. Lancelatti's hand as they enter the room. Rosemary is exhausted. She looks even smaller than usual, and the way she's propped up in bed reminds me of Mrs. O'Keefe at Creedmore.

Mrs. Lancelatti goes to the other side of the bed and kisses her daughter. She cradles Rosemary's face in her hands. "I am so proud of you," she says.

"It wasn't bad, Ma. We've decided on her name, and we wanted you to hear it first. She is Maria Grace, in honor of our mothers." Ro smiles. Both Mama and Mrs. Lancelatti begin to cry. "Okay, now you go. I need to sleep."

"Grace, I made a roast," Mama says to Mrs. Lancelatti across the bed. "You must all come to dinner."

"Thank you. That's very kind of you," Mrs. Lancelatti says. They kiss Rosemary and go out into the hallway together.

"Sleep well, Ro," I tell her, and turn toward the door.

"Lu?" Rosemary reaches out for my hand.

I take her hand and sit down next to her. "Are you all right?"

"I just did one of the most important things I'm ever going to do. And it's so strange . . ." Rosemary looks out the window, but there is no view, only the brick airshaft of the next building. "It doesn't feel right to take any credit for it."

"What do you mean?"

"You know, it happened so fast, they couldn't give me anything for the pain."

"No!"

"It's okay, I'm glad they couldn't put me under. I wanted to see her born. My friends who have babies have told me that one moment they were asleep and the next they were mothers. I didn't want that. I wanted to see her come into the world with my own eyes."

"What was it like?"

"She came out, arms in the air, like she was reaching for something. The doctor snipped the cord, and the nurse was about to take her away, and I shouted, 'No! Give me my daughter!' They're supposed to check them out first, but I must have scared the nurse because she handed me Maria Grace. And my baby knew me! She nuzzled me immediately. Then the nurse took her away to clean her up."

"Were you afraid?"

"A little." Rosemary smooths the sheets and smiles. "And then I felt . . . I feel . . . redeemed." If only she had seen the Lancelattis and the Sartoris outside the nursery window, she would know that her wedding day will not be the defining moment of her life. Today is the day that everyone will remember.

"You're so calm," I tell her.

"You know, it wasn't what I thought it would be. Not at all. It was as if I was a parachute and Maria Grace was a diver who made it safely to the ground. I got her here, and my job was done."

"Your job is far from over," I say with a laugh.

"I know. But I also know it's not my world anymore. It belongs to her."

The nurse comes in the door carrying my new niece. "It's time to feed her," she says to Rosemary.

"I'll be right outside," I tell my sister-in-law.

The nurse gives the baby to Rosemary. Maria Grace seems so much smaller than she did in the nursery, her hair much darker and thicker, as if she is wearing a black velvet tam.

"Do you want to hold her?" Ro asks. "That's okay, isn't it?" she says to the nurse.

"Just for a moment," the nurse replies.

Ro leans down and whispers to the bundle, "Meet your aunt Lu," then hands the baby to me. How warm she is! I hold her like a piece of delicate china.

"Nice to meet you, Maria Grace. When you get big, we're going to go to Broadway shows and to get our hair done. We'll buy lots of fancy shoes and purses and paint our nails rose red!" I whisper. "May God bless you all the days of your long and happy life." I kiss her and give her back to her mother.

The smell of the baby's skin, coupled with the look on Rosemary's face, content and at peace, makes me cry. This is a moment so rare and beautiful, I cannot hold it. And yet I want to preserve it, because I know that the birth of the first child of my eldest brother is a once-in-a-lifetime event. We go on, I think to myself. We go on and on and on.

Roberto stays at the hospital with Rosemary. When Mama, Papa, the Lancelattis, and I arrive at home, we can't believe our eyes. My brothers, who have never set a table nor washed a dish in the sum of their collective lives, have the dining room table set with Mama's best china. The long white taper candles are lit, and there's a small center-piece of pink carnations in a glass bowl. I decide not to rib the boys, because this kind of largesse should be encouraged. Angelo has poured champagne into a series of flutes on Mama's best silver tray, and he serves each of us a glass.

"To Maria Grace!" Orlando toasts.

"May she grow healthy and strong!" Mr. Lancelatti adds. *"Cent'-anni!"*

Dinner is good fun, with my brothers teasing and playing with Rosemary's younger brothers. After dessert they go out back in the garden, and Angelo and Exodus toss the younger boys around while Orlando makes up ghost stories to entertain them. Rosemary's little sister stays behind to help clean up. At the end of a lovely evening, Mrs. Lancelatti calls for my brothers to bring in her boys. They're taking the train home to Brooklyn, but first they will stop over at Saint Vincent's and say good night to Rosemary, Roberto, and Maria Grace.

What a day this has been, I think as I climb the stairs to my room. The five flights, which I usually take at a clip, seem like twice the distance. So much to think about: John Talbot, his mother, the ocean, and now my niece. And tomorrow is Ruth's wedding! As I change for bed, I glance at the book I was supposed to begin reading today and figure there will be lots of time for that later.

I climb into bed and turn off the lamp, and the room fills with the streetlight's yellow haze. I think about Sylvia O'Keefe at Creedmore and how happy she was to see her only son. When Ruth and I have a fitting for a young debutante who is plain, with a so-so figure, we notice that the clothes can't make her beautiful; only her inner light can. When people are filled to the brim with love, they are their most beautiful.

Before I go to sleep, I pray for baby Maria Grace, that life will bring her all she desires, that she will grow strong and tall and have big dreams. And then I thank God for sending me a niece. After all these years, it will be nice to have another girl around to help with the dishes.

CHAPTER SIX

*A*fter the most exciting Saturday of my life, I not only managed to stay awake through Ruth's wedding, I threw myself into the hoopla. I was pulled into the inner circle for the hora, a traditional Jewish dance, and I danced with Ruth and Harvey's cousins and Delmarr more times than I could count.

It was a little lonely at work for the next week. I told myself it was because Ruth was away on her honeymoon, but the truth is, I was disappointed that John didn't call.

On Ruth's first day back, she catches me checking the Hub's telephone message board one time too many.

"He hasn't called, Lu. Relax."

"I can't. I miss him."

"Oh, please. What do you miss, exactly? You had one date, a car ride to visit his mother. For Godsakes, why don't you skip the courtship and go directly to marriage? That's how I'll be spending my dreadfully dull Saturday. We just got back from the honeymoon, and we're already 'spending time with Mother.'"

"Lucia, Ruth, come here for a second," Delmarr calls from the fitting room.

When we get there, Ruth lets out a low whistle. For once she is impressed. "Where did you get the loot?" she says as she circles around a rolling rack hung with three gowns, each a confection in white.

"Paris."

"I'll say." Ruth nods in approval.

I gently lift one of the hangers off the rack. The gown is as light as whipped cream but structured as if an architect had a hand in it. Two dainty silk straps hold up a straight sheath of white satin with a subtle pattern of Medici bumblebees. A row of tiny gold and white silk butterflies is daintily sewn up the right seam of the skirt to the waist. Anchoring the left strap is a larger version of the butterfly. I have to know the artist behind this masterpiece. "Who made this?"

"Spies." Delmarr laughs. "Hilda had a sketch artist attending the shows with her, and this is a version of a Pierre Balmain. He's starting a ready-to-wear line, so Hilda didn't feel bad pinching the concept. She also pinched one of Balmain's top seamstresses to make the prototype."

"She's ruthless!" I hold the dress up to my body before the mirror. "Nothing could ever go wrong for a girl wearing this dress."

"You'll find out. Try it on." Delmarr smiles.

"Can I?"

"Come on, I'll help." Ruth takes the dress, and I follow her behind the dressing screen. I unzip my skirt and step out of it.

"No slip," Delmarr says, turning his back on the screen as he lights a cigarette.

"Delmarr," Ruth calls, "I can't believe the construction. The zipper is hidden under the arm, right in the seam. And it's the tiniest zipper I've ever seen!"

Ruth helps me step into the dress, which floats over my hips and falls to my ankles in one smooth drape. I lift my arm as Ruth zips me in. I close my eyes, twisting gently from side to side, and feel the garment on my body. This is a fitting technique taught to us by Hilda Beast, who said once a woman is in her dress, she shouldn't feel it on her body. If a dress is designed and constructed properly, it should either mold to the woman's figure or stand away from it without pulling, binding, or tugging at any seam.

"I can't come out," I shout to Delmarr.

"Why? Doesn't it fit?"

"No, it fits so well, I feel like I'm not wearing anything."

"Love the French!" Delmarr laughs. "That's the idea."

Ruth pushes me out. Delmarr is waiting by the model box and helps me onto it. Ruth grabs a pair of size-seven pumps we keep on hand for fittings and holds the shoes while I step into them.

"I like to think I'm good, but I ain't this good." Delmarr squints at me in the mirror. I look at myself, but I don't see me, I see a girl transformed by the perfect dress. I hold my arms down at my sides and study my reflection.

"Oh, Lucia" is all Ruth can say.

"Hold this moment, Miss Sartori." Delmarr stands on one side of me, and Ruth is on the other. "This is youth. Your star is high in the sky. You may never be this beautiful again. Enjoy it." He winks at me.

"I wish I had somewhere to go in this number," I say to the mirror.

"You do. I'm taking Nancy Smith to the cotillion at the Plaza. Her brother is in town, and he needs a date."

"You want me to go?"

"Gee, I'd come," Ruth says, "but I'm playing canasta with Harvey's parents, and after that we're going for seventeen-cent hamburgers at White Tower. Yippee!"

"Sorry you're busy, Ruth." Delmarr turns to me. "You need shoes, stockings, a clutch. You and Ruth go borrowing."

Ruth and I spend our lunch hour going from department to department, currying favors from Delmarr's connections. The managers are happy to loan to Delmarr because he sends our customers to them for accessories. In the Evening Shoe Department, Ruth picks a white closed-toe mule covered in peau de soie with seed pearls on the vamp. We find an ornate Indian clutch of embroidered tone-on-tone shantung, and over-the-elbow evening gloves with tiny opal buttons from wrist to elbow. I'm so busy, I hardly give a thought to John Talbot, though I do wish he could see me in this dress.

I leave work early to have my hair put up for the gala. On the way home I go to Saint Vincent's to see Maria Grace, but she and her mother are both napping. I stop at the florist and pick up a gardenia for my hair. My escort will probably bring me a flower, but a girl can never have too many.

Christopher Smith picks me up promptly at seven-thirty. I find out his life story between the Village and Fifty-ninth and Fifth. He's an engineer, graduated from Princeton, left college for two years to serve in the navy (even though his father could have procured a deferment, Christopher felt strongly about serving), and now he's working for his father's company, an iron-ore mining firm. Blond, tall, and blue-eyed, Christopher is a typical Upper East Side son of privilege. But he is gracious and warm, with a good sense of humor. This will be a terrific evening. "I'm going to be honest," Christopher begins. "The girls on fix-ups, at least in my experience, never live up to the description beforehand. You're beautiful."

I thank him. In this one instance, I believe the dress is doing all the work. I'm lucky to be wearing it.

The town car pulls up at the main entrance of the Plaza. As we walk up the stairway to the Grand Ballroom, it's as if high society is announcing the coming of spring. The ladies are dressed in pale silks, neutral tones of beige, shell pink, and butter yellow. So far, mine is the only white gown (leave it to Balmain to create a trend instead of following one). Christopher seems to know everyone in the outer reception area. A few girls run up and say hello, warmly to him, politely to me. I'm certain they're wondering what he's doing with me. I may look the part, but they know I am not one of them. Society types are one family, and each member is known. Anyone new sticks out like a red shoe with a green gown.

While the society girls have not changed, the young men have. In the wake of World War II, walls have come down. Customs and rituals normally reserved for the select few of a certain lineage have become more inclusive. The line between uptown and downtown blurred as men returned home from the service with young brides from around the world. Ten years ago, a Catholic girl like me wouldn't have been welcome at the Plaza Hotel, and Christopher would never have agreed to take me. The war changed all that. The uptown boys matured from carefree dandies to sober thinkers. The downtown boys, having fought for their new country, were respected and not treated like second-class citizens. I hold my head high as Christopher leads me into the ballroom. After all, I am the sister of four veterans and the daughter of a successful Manhattan businessman. I belong wherever I want to go and can accept the invitation of anyone who wants to take me.

The superb Vincent Lopez Orchestra is playing as we cross the dance floor to our table. Garlands of daisies and cherry blossoms hang from the ceiling like ribbons. Hand-painted murals of country gardens stand out against the room's ornate gold molding. The tables are set with crisp white linens, and the centerpieces are goldfish bowls with actual fish swimming in them. Ruth won't believe it.

Delmarr waves to me from across the dance floor and makes his way through the crowd. "Christopher, nice to see you again," he says as they shake hands. Then he turns to me. "What do you think?"

"It's a wonderland," I tell him as he gives me a twirl.

"You're the prettiest girl here," Delmarr says as he looks around the dance floor. He leans in to a small cluster of people talking, then takes a girl's hand and turns her toward us. "Nancy, come and meet Lucia." Nancy Smith is the feminine version of her brother, long and lanky, with sky-blue eyes beautifully complemented by her pale gray gown.

"Nice to meet you. Thank you for taking a charity case tonight," she says to me, flashing a dazzling smile at her brother.

"It's my pleasure—" I begin, but Nancy is whisked away by another couple.

"You have fun!" she calls over her shoulder.

Delmarr whispers in my ear, "Her divorce was just made final. This is her first night without the ex. It's like I'm chasing a runaway train."

"Lucia, I'd like you to meet some of my pals from Princeton."

Christopher puts his arm around my waist. Standing behind him is a group of immaculate young gentlemen, the kind I see in group photos on the society pages. Christopher introduces me to each young man, and they pay me compliments on my dress and hair.

"Are you a princess?" one of them asks.

"No, why do you ask?"

"Your dress has the Medici family symbol in the fabric."

"You're sharp," I tell him. "Do you know what the bumblebee means in Italy?" He shakes his head. "Royalty."

"Did you graduate from Vassar?" another of the young men asks me.

"No, I didn't go to college. I went to Katie Gibbs Secretarial School and then got a job as a seamstress at B. Altman's," I say with pride.

"Oh, to find an old-fashioned girl who likes to sew," one of the fellows says kindly.

"Back off. She's mine until midnight," Christopher says as he leads me out onto the dance floor. He's a very smooth dancer. I could get used to a life like this, I think as he pulls me closer. When I look over his shoulder, I am surprised to see John Talbot. In his arms is Amanda Parker, *the* society deb of the moment. As the music changes, John lifts her by the waist, then kisses her as he kissed me outside my house less than one week ago. The picture stings so, I close my eyes. When I open them, she's still draped on him like fox trim on velvet. The monologue in my head begins: he's not really your beau, well, he did take you for a drive; you have met his mother, but you have no stake, no promise from him; you hardly know him. But then I remember his kiss. Isn't a kiss a promise? A show of intent?

"Are you all right?" Christopher asks.

"I'm fine," I lie. Then I decide to turn this buggy around. I am not going to be any man's throwaway girl. John Talbot needs to know I'm not some nobody who's pretty but unconnected. "Christopher? Do you know Amanda Parker?"

"Sure."

"I would love to meet her."

Christopher leads me across the dance floor to Amanda and John. When John sees me coming toward them, he stares at me in disbelief, as though this is a dream and I'm emerging from a Scottish mist with a battalion of poor townsfolk behind me seeking justice. He blanches when he realizes it's really me and I'm really coming to talk to him.

"Amanda, I'd like you to meet my date this evening. This is Lucia Sartori," Christopher says.

Amanda dips her head down and smiles at me, brushing the shiny flip of her curls behind her ear. This pose, the very same one captured on the society pages, is meant to make her dark patrician beauty into something more vulnerable, when it is clear that she is anything but. Amanda introduces John, and then she and Christopher tease each other a bit, but I keep my eyes steadily on John Talbot, who still can't look at me.

"John?"

"Yes?" At last his eyes meet mine, then he looks me up and down, not in a cheap way but in admiration.

"It's good to see you again," I say.

Christopher takes my arm and excuses us, and we go for drinks. I am tempted to turn to see if John Talbot is watching me, but I don't. It wouldn't do any good. He's taken. I should have known that he couldn't possibly be available. As angry as I am, I also understand him. He aspires to be a part of this world, too. But what he doesn't know is that the best he and I can do is pass through it on someone else's arm.

As soon as I'm home, I call Ruth and tell her about the dance. She listens thoughtfully to everything I say and decides that I'm overreacting about the kiss John planted on Amanda Parker. I disagree, and when I hang up, I think about that kiss again and again. Each time I replay it in my mind, it drives me further and further away from the idea of John Talbot. "It's over," I say to myself, aloud, as if the intonation will make it official. I get ready for bed, wishing I hadn't gone to the cotillion at all. I see John's face and wish I had never met him.

"Lucia! Wake up!" Mama shakes me.

"What is it?"

"Get dressed. Hurry!"

I look at the clock. It's a quarter to five in the morning. "What's going on?"

"The baby!"

I hear Mama's footsteps click down the stairs. I jump into my slacks and sweater from the day before, forgetting my socks, and run down the stairs. Papa is waiting by the door. Mama is putting on her coat and sobbing uncontrollably. I pull on the boots that I left near the bench last night, grab my coat, and follow my parents out into the street.

"What happened? Papa? Mama?"

"She's gone. The baby is gone."

"Gone? What do you mean?"

"She died." My mother sobs. "Lucia, she died."

I don't believe it. We find a cab on Hudson Street, and the driver gets us to Saint Vincent's quickly. Mama has not stopped crying. Papa holds on to her, but she is inconsolable. I'm certain there's been a terrible mistake. I held the baby in my arms. She was fine. What could possibly have gone wrong?

Instead of waiting for the elevator, we find the stairwell to the maternity ward. We run down the hallway to Rosemary's room, but it is empty. A nurse directs us to the room where Maria Grace was taken. Through the glass I see my brother and his wife holding each other. A doctor stands close by. We push the door open. Mama is screaming now. Papa tries to calm her down, but nothing he says can make her stop.

The expression on Rosemary's face is so devastating that I have to look away. Roberto is crying, but the tears are of frustration—he doesn't understand. None of us does. I go to the doctor and grab his arm. "What happened to the baby?" I ask him.

The doctor has already been through all this with Rosemary and Roberto, and I'm sure he'll have to go through it again when the Lancelattis get here from Brooklyn, but he explains everything patiently. "The nurse called me to the floor. Maria Grace was having trouble breathing. I checked her thoroughly and found that her heart rhythm had slowed. I ordered oxygen, but she went into cardiac arrest anyway. Her heart failed. We tried to revive her, but nothing worked. I can offer you no reason for something like this. She was a small baby, but that didn't have anything to do with this. I believe she had a congenital condition, a weakened heart from birth, so weak that there was nothing we could have done to save her."

Roberto lunges at the doctor, but my father intercedes and holds Roberto tightly. "My son," he says. "Son." And Papa begins to cry.

"I'm sorry. I'm truly sorry," the doctor says.

Mama holds Rosemary, whose arms are stiff at her sides. She squeezes her eyes shut as if trying to change the picture of what has happened, hoping that this is a dream. Maria Grace Sartori died at 3:32 A.M. on February 23, 1951. She did not live two weeks.

If I live to be an old lady, I will never experience anything worse than the funeral of my niece. Each word Father Abruzzi utters at the altar of Our Lady of Pompeii in the Mass of the Resurrection sounds like a lie. Heaven, the peace that lives in the heart of Christ for those who believe in Him, and the idea that the baby is safe in the loving arms of the Blessed Lady seem like empty promises made to people in a hopeless state. I don't believe any of them. It is so cruel when a child dies, and adding to the horror, the random blame begins. Who is at fault? The doctor? The hospital? The mother and her milk? The circumstances of Maria Grace's conception? Oh, the guessing that goes on, trying to understand the will of God.

At the end of the funeral Mass, our families walk out behind the casket. I can't leave my pew. When Orlando reaches for my hand, I pull it away and shake my head; I want no part of the recessional. I can't bear to look at Rosemary as she walks behind her daughter, knowing that she can never hold her in her arms again. Nor can I stand to see Roberto, who blames himself, certain that some defect in his character made God take away his precious child because he was not worthy of her.

Mama prays, and Papa does, too. I can't. I sit in the pew and wait for everyone to leave. I don't want to listen to words of comfort, and I can't offer any. When the last of the mourners are outside on the sidewalk, I look up at the altar, covered in a haze from the incense.

The past couple of days have been so horrible, I've decided I will never have a baby. I couldn't risk this happening to my little girl. I told Papa, and he said, "You can't do that, Lucia. It's not your decision, it's God's." But it seems to me that if God made the decision to take this baby, He cannot be trusted. I am haunted by how Maria Grace felt in my arms. The newness of her was unlike anything I'd ever experienced. I feel a hand on my shoulder, but I don't turn to see who it is. I can't.

"I'm sorry, Lucia," Dante says in a whisper. I reach up to take his hand. He comes to sit next to me. He puts his arm around me, and I cry. "What a terrible, terrible loss," he says.

"I'm afraid Rosemary and Roberto will do something to themselves. They can't bear to look at each other. We were so happy when she was born. I don't understand why this happened. For what? Why?"

"Maybe the baby came to bring everyone together."

"But why was she taken, when she brought so much joy?"

"I don't know, Lucia."

"Nobody does. That's what makes this so horrible. There isn't any sane reason for it. Dante, can you think of any reason why this should have happened?"

"I can't. There is none." Dante takes out his handkerchief and wipes away my tears. "Your brother and sister-in-law need you. You've got to be strong. I know you can do it," he says. "Come on. I'll walk you to your car."

The church is empty, but the crowd on the sidewalk is still there, comforting Rosemary and Roberto and embracing my parents and brothers. I hold Dante's hand as he walks me through the doors and out into the sunlight. Ruth steps forward and hugs me. Behind her I see Delmarr, Helen, and Violet, who are every bit as devastated as I would be if this terrible thing had happened to one of them.

It is a cold day, with mounds of gray slush from the last snowstorm piled in the gutters. How ugly the Village looks, how rude the horns blaring in the traffic jam, the mess. Where are all the people going, anyway? Don't they know what we have lost?

The wind cuts through me. I sob from the pit of my stomach, not caring who hears my weeping. I lean against Dante and give him all of my grief. I'm only twenty-six years old, and in one moment this exquisite world, with its possibilities and joyous details, went from a lustrous valley to a dark pit. Maria Grace took all the beauty with her.

I look up and see Dante's mother, his father, and his brothers and sisters. They encircle me and hold me without saying a word. I feel their strength, and I am not ashamed to take what I need. Sometimes when the worst happens, the only people who truly understand are the ones who have known you since you were small. The DeMartinos were practically family, and they know what to say and do.

Dante helps me into the hearse to travel with my family to the cemetery in Queens, where the baby will be buried in the Sartori plot. "I'll follow you out there," Dante says. Before he closes the door, he reaches out and takes Roberto's hand. Roberto pulls Dante inside and embraces him, weeping on his shoulder. Dante looks at me and lets my brother cry for a few moments. Finally, Papa puts his arms around Roberto, and Dante goes.

Dante comes and stays with me through the burial at the cemetery, which is worse than the funeral, if that's possible. It is so bitterly cold that we could hardly stand outside. The priest says his final prayers, but Rosemary will not let go of the casket to put it in the ground. We don't know what to do. Roberto kneels and joins her, and for a long time, both of them hold on to Maria Grace. Orlando and Angelo get down on their knees and help Roberto and Rosemary stand. I look around for Exodus, but he is over on the road with his back to us, his shoulders heaving as he weeps.

In the days that follow Maria Grace's death, we are like ghosts in our house. There is no music or conversation. Meals are silent ordeals. Dante has stopped by every day since the funeral, either before work or after. Sometimes he sits with me for a couple of hours; sometimes he comes in for a few minutes. He seems to know exactly what to say and do. His compassion extends beyond me to my brothers, Rosemary, and my parents.

At the one-week anniversary of Maria Grace's funeral, there's a knock at my bedroom door.

"Hi, honey." Dante opens the door. "Can I come in?"

"Sure."

"So, this is your room," Dante says, drinking in the details. He looks at my bed as though he has imagined me there, or imagined himself there with me, then he turns away in embarrassment. "It's exactly as I pictured it."

"Really? I always thought if a man laid eyes on my canopy bed, he'd burst into flames like Saint Lorenzo." I pat the bed next to me, inviting him to sit down.

Dante sits. "So far, so good."

"How do you like it?"

"It looks like a princess who likes to read and sew lives up here." Dante takes my hand. "Honey, I'm worried about you. You need to go outside."

I gaze out the window and think about going outside. Every day I try to go, and every day I stay in my room.

"The longer you wait, the worse it will be. Come on. I'll take you."

Dante sees my suede loafers by the vanity. He brings them to me, then kneels and puts them on my feet. He stands, gently pulls me off of the bed, and gives me a hug. He walks me to the door and puts his arm around me as we descend the stairs. When we get to the entry hall, he helps me into my coat and wraps a scarf around my neck. Then he takes my hand and opens the door. I follow him out onto our stoop.

"See, that wasn't so bad, was it?" he says, putting his arm over my shoulder as we walk.

I look back at my house. "It's so quiet in there."

"I know. It's very strange." Dante takes my hand as we head toward Grove Street. I stop and turn him to me and put my hands on the lapels of his coat.

"Dante, thank you for being there for all of us. I don't know how to repay you. I don't think there is any way."

Dante puts his arms around me. "You're family, Lucia."

"Almost was."

"You'll always be my girl. You were from the first moment I saw you. You were sitting in church with your brothers. You were eight years old, and I was twelve, and I thought, I hope she waits for me. Lucia, I'll wait forever if I have to."

Dante pulls me close. We stand by the wrought-iron gate in front of the McIntyres' brownstone. It's the very spot where he kissed me for the first time when I was fifteen. I wonder if he remembers. He leans in and kisses me softly on each cheek and then finds my mouth. I'm so sad from all that's happened that I fall into this familiar place like the old chenille pillows I've had on my bed since I was a girl. I wonder how many times he kissed me during our time together. A thousand? More? How many times have I buried my face in his neck and breathed in the smell of his skin?

"You must hate me for the way I broke off our engagement," I say.

"How could I hate the girl I used to stare at in church?"

"Well, I was staring back. I thought you were the best-looking older man I ever saw." Dante laughs and takes my hand, and we walk for a long time in silence. The only people in the world who have known me longer than Dante are my own family. "Dante . . ." I say after a while.

"You don't have to say anything, Lucia," he tells me. "I understand."

The only thing that could get me back out into the world is the thought of returning to work. I miss my friends and the comfort of our routine in the Custom Department. I've taken two weeks off, something I was able to do only because Hilda Cramer was in Paris for the runway shows and had no idea who was in the shop and who wasn't. Now Hilda's back, and I'm ready to return to my routine. My room at home was beginning to feel a little like a prison.

By my desk is a rolling rack of debutante gowns to hem. As I flip through them, I see Helen has pinned them up nicely. I take the first white silk shantung gown off the hanger and fit it onto the mannequin. I get out my needle and thread and begin to stitch, following the perfect line of pins.

How can I describe how much I love to sew? It's as though my hands have known what to do from the first moment I held a needle. My left hand pulls the edge of the fabric taut while my right hand pedals in and out with the thread. I'm so good at it, and I've done it for so long, that the tiny stitches are invisible. Hems were the hardest thing for me to learn. It takes precision to keep the hem even as you sew, and a lopsided hem ruins an entire garment. Nonna Sartori used to say to me, "No one has to know how many times you rip out the hem." Sometimes I ripped out a hem fifty times to get it right. Now it's second nature. I get it right the first time.

Ruth bursts in the Hub and makes a beeline for me. "He's here! Talbot. He's on his way in."

"So?" I ask calmly, without taking my eyes off the hem.

"If you want to skedaddle, you've got time."

"If he's coming to see me, I'm ready for him," I tell her.

Ruth sits down at her drawing table and waits, keeping her eyes on the doors. "He's in," she whispers. I don't look up. I keep my eyes on the hem.

"Hello, Lucia. How are you?" John Talbot asks.

"I'm better. Thank you for the lovely flowers you sent. They were beautiful."

"It was a small thing, but I wanted you to know I was thinking of you . . . and your family."

"It was very kind."

"I want to explain something," he begins.

Ruth clears her throat, picks up a sketch, and goes into Delmarr's office.

I sense a big windup for a dissertation about why John chose Amanda Parker over me, but the truth is, I understand it. As much as I may aspire to be a part of the world I make the costumes for, there are certain elements of high society that I find repugnant. I could not live by their code. Everyone knows that marriage has a different meaning above Thirty-fourth Street. Affairs are tolerated, and blue-bloods are loyal to a family crest instead of the bond between a man and a woman. I may like the lifestyle, but I don't approve of the morals. I think more of myself than that. "Please, John, I don't need an explanation. I believe that you should see whomever you like. And good luck to you."

"I broke off with her, Lucia. I don't want Amanda. I want you."

It seems as though Papa and his cousin have written hundreds of let-ters back and forth, planning our August holiday in the Veneto. Cou-sin Domenic and his wife, Bartolomea, sent Rosemary and Roberto a beautiful icon, a silver picture of the Blessed Lady, when Maria Grace died. Ro keeps it on her nightstand and prays her rosary before it, beg-ging for strength.

"I have an idea," Papa says to me as I help him count the change at the store. "I'm going to convince Rosemary and Roberto to come to Italy with us. What do you think?"

"I think it's a great idea."

"A change of scenery might help them." Papa lowers his voice. "How do you think Rosemary is doing?"

"I don't know. She seems a little better sometimes, and then she starts to cry and she can't stop. Mama tries to console her, but it's so hard."

"I'm going to lock up," Papa tells me, and starts his nightly ritual. Since I was a girl, I loved to be in the store at closing time, to watch him put a final mist on the fresh vegetables, feed the "mouser" cat, Moto, and turn out the lights, starting from the back of the store to the front.

"Dante stopped by today," Papa says casually.

"How is he?" Since John Talbot's slow return to my life, Dante has slipped away again.

"He's all right. He wonders why you won't see him."

I can't believe Dante confided in my father! I haven't said a word to Pop about him.

"And don't get mad at him," Papa goes on. "He didn't say anything. I asked him what was happening with you two."

"Why would you ask?"

Papa is spraying the vegetables and doesn't turn around. "Maybe I like him. And maybe I think he's right for you."

"Oh, Pop."

I wish I could tell my father why I've avoided Dante since the night he kissed me. I felt myself fall back into the well of him, and then the same old feeling of being trapped returned.

"Papa, do you like John Talbot?"

"Why do you ask?" Papa walks over to the counter. "You aren't see-ing him again, are you?"

"We go to lunch." I sound vague, but the truth is, John and I see each other most days. We have lunch, go for a drive, or visit his mother. He has been proving to me that I am the only girl in his life.

"He's not for you, Lucia."

"Papa!"

"You asked me! So I tell you the truth. Mr. Talbot is a mystery to me. And I don't understand what he does with his time," he says as he takes off his apron, folds it, and places it under the counter. Then he comes around and stands right in front of me.

"He's a businessman, like you," I assert.

"No, he's a snappy dresser with a fancy car who seems to have big plans and no job."

"I like a man who presents himself well and has polish. It shows a certain confidence. As for his plans, he has big dreams, and you of all people, Papa—someone who came to this country with nothing and built a business—should understand aiming high."

"Lucia, watch what men do, not what they say." Papa places his hands on the counter and leans back against it.

"What am I missing, Papa? What do you see that I don't?"

"All people have blind spots. And you have a blind spot about Mr.

Talbot. You are too enamored of the surface. You like his clothes and his lifestyle, the ease of it. This is a weakness in you, but it is also your talent. You make beautiful garments, and you have an eye for beauty. But you also have a way of covering flaws with skill. You told me about the lady built like an eggplant who needed a new dress. You performed a magic trick: you dropped the waist of the dress and padded the shoulders, giving the illusion of a figure in proportion. When it comes to John Talbot, you cannot see what he is because you admire him too much. And if he does have some defect of character, you are confident you can fix it. This is no good."

"Papa, I know what I want. I do admire him! I don't see anything wrong with that."

"I know that you will overlook his flaws in favor of his strengths. But when you marry someone, you must understand the flaws in order to appreciate the strengths. Lucia," Papa says wearily, "who has known you since the day you were born? Have I ever discouraged you based on my own weaknesses?"

"No, Papa."

"I will never tell you what to do or who to love. I only ask that you stay alert. Stay awake. Don't rush."

"I can promise you, Papa, that I won't rush anything."

I have a sick feeling in my stomach. I want Papa to like John. If I am to continue seeing him, it's important to have my father's support.

"Lucia. Invite the man to Sunday dinner."

"Do you mean it, Pop?"

"Let's see what he's made of." Papa smiles and gives me a stick of cherry candy like he used to when I was a girl. "Let's go home."

After three consecutive Sunday dinners at my house, John Talbot and I are officially a couple. Mama adores him. Papa is unconvinced, but at least he's trying. John and I have begun to see each other exclusively, so Ruth and Harvey have invited us for their first seder in their own home. I usually spend all of Easter week in church, beginning with Holy Thursday, then Good Friday, and the Easter Vigil at midnight on Holy Saturday. Easter morning has always been my favorite holiday, but this year I won't attend any of the festivities. I haven't been back to Our Lady of Pompeii since Maria Grace died. Sometimes I want to pray, but when I try, I can't. I'm still angry at God, and to pray when I feel this way is false. Mama is worried about my faith, but I can't pretend to feel comfort in a place that continues to bring me pain and reminds me how easily God abandoned us when we most needed Him.

I've never been to a seder, but I know that for the last couple of weeks Ruth has been preparing the traditional Passover foods, which symbolize the journey of the Jewish people out of Egypt. The newlywed Goldfarbs (Ruth lost the battle to keep her own name) found a quaint apartment on Gramercy Park, across town from Commerce Street.

"Are you sure you want to walk?" John asks as he takes my hand on the stoop.

"Do you?"

"Sure." John looks handsome in his navy gabardine suit. "Do I look all right for a seder?"

"I'd say so." I find it endearing that John is a little worried about whether my friends will like him. "You look perfectly appropriate. Sharp."

"You look beautiful," he says. "I love you in yellow."

"I made it myself," I tell him. Delmarr picked up some soft wool crepe on a buying trip to Montreal. From it, I built a day suit, with black and white herringbone trim and gold buttons on the jacket. My favorite part is the peplum, which ruffles in a subtle way in the front and then is cut deep in the back to give the jacket movement. I found matching shoes on sample sale at the store, black peau de soie pumps.

"I love a girl who can make her own clothes," John says.

"Just any girl?" I'm instantly embarrassed to be acting so coy. John and I are well beyond this.

"Not just any. You." John stops and pulls me close. He kisses me on the corner of Cornelia Street. A cabbie whistles at us as he goes by.

"Thank you. You make me feel good when you say things like that."

"I love you, Lucia."

I close my eyes to savor the words. John Talbot loves me! "I love you, John," I tell him.

"I was hoping." He smiles.

We walk for a while and stop at the liquor store, where John buys a bottle of wine for Harvey and Ruth. Rosemary made macaroons, which I'm carrying in a pretty tin. John takes my arm as we cross Fifth Avenue.

"Lucia, one thing concerns me."

I feel a pang in my stomach. He told me he loved me, but here comes the bad news. "What's that?" I say as lightly as I can manage.

"Your father doesn't like me."

"He likes you," I lie. Surely John can't see through Papa's excellent manners.

"No, he doesn't. He thinks I'm a phony."

"A phony?" I wave off the idea. "John, listen to me. Papa is old world. He understands things in a basic, simple way. He doesn't understand what you do for a living. He believes that there are only three businesses to be involved in: food, clothing, and shelter. You dabble in other areas, ones he doesn't understand. That's all."

"You understand what I do, don't you?"

"You're an entrepreneur." If I'm honest, I don't think much about what John does for a living. I know he's very busy, he travels a lot, and he makes good money. He dresses well and takes me to the best places. He has a regular table at the Vesuvio on West Forty-eighth Street. What else do I need to know? Papa's apprehension is the reaction of an overprotective father.

"I wish you'd talk to your father and explain that I'm trustworthy."

"Put yourself in his place for a minute. I'm his only daughter. You know he's been protective of me all my life, and as I get older, it gets worse. There seems to be more pressure from him."

"What about the pressure on me? He makes me feel like I'm trying to take advantage of you."

"You know that's not true, so don't worry about it." I tighten my grip on John's arm.

"I'm old-fashioned myself. I'm not looking for his approval. I want his respect."

"Give it time," I say reassuringly.

"I know you're the biggest catch in Greenwich Village."

I laugh. "You're crazy!"

"Don't you see what happens when you walk down the street? Heads turn. Literally, heads turn, because people want to get a look at you. You're not a small person with a small life. You have a big destiny."

I don't know what to say. Nobody has ever seen me this way before. Maybe Delmarr a little, but certainly not Dante, who saw me as the baker's wife. "I never think of myself like that. How far can a career girl go without the right address and surname?"

"You can do anything you want."

I stop John and kiss him. I love that he believes in me and understands what I want. He sees me in the context of a big world, not simply the neighborhood. John sees what I will become.

Ruth and Harvey's apartment is railroad-style, and the rooms are small, but Ruth has decorated boldly, using paint, wallpaper, and draperies made from overstock fabrics at work. She has set a beautiful table; the choices from her bridal registry were the best of the best. Though the fine china and faceted stemware are too grand for the one-bedroom apartment, it doesn't matter. Ruth is happy. She and Harvey, after the world's longest courtship and engagement, belong to each other, and while there were no surprises in what they were getting, they clearly relish the novelty of a life together.

During the meal, John squeezes my hand under the table. It's almost as if we have a secret from the world. We love each other, and we said it aloud. If he is crazy about me, I'm even more crazy about him. I would do whatever is necessary to make John Talbot happy, anything in the world.

When I arrive at work early and see that Hilda Cramer's assistant has left a pile of new work for us to do, it occurs to me that the Custom

Department is like the fairy tale with the shoemaker (Hilda) and the elves (us). A mysterious messenger drops off assignments at night, we make the clothes, and then the messenger whisks them away to see if they pass muster. I imagine Hilda sitting in her sleek Upper East Side penthouse as the messenger holds up each piece and she approves or rejects our efforts.

"What are you doing here so early?" Delmarr asks when he spots me at my desk.

"I'm not sleeping well," I say.

"I could think of a thousand things to do that are more fun than getting to work early."

"Well, I can't think of any. That's why I'm here."

"Fair enough." Delmarr pours himself a cup of coffee and freshens mine.

"Thank you," I say, reaching for the cup. "What are *you* doing here so early?"

"The truth?" Delmarr lights a cigarette. "I'm planning my next move."

"You're not leaving B. Altman's, are you?" My insides go into panic mode. If Delmarr left, what would happen to me, Ruth, and the Flappers? He's our leader. This place would have to close without him.

"Maybe."

"But—"

"Shhh, Lucia, I wouldn't leave you here. You'd come with me."

I feel a sense of relief but also sadness. I love Altman's. How could I ever leave? But how much of my love of this department is about my respect for and awe of Delmarr? In an instant I decide I would follow him.

"So, would you go with me?" he asks.

"Anywhere. Anytime. You just have to name it."

"Really?" Delmarr sits back.

"Yep. And you don't even have to marry me."

"Sorry, can't do that. Not to you. Not to anyone. I love spending my Friday nights at El Morocco, drinking Manhattans and talking with the regulars, getting home around sunrise, and sleeping through most of Saturday. I ain't husband material."

"No, you aren't."

He smiles. "I came here for the bachelor life. If I wanted to be trapped, I would have stayed on the farm in 'Ver-sales,' Indiana. It's spelled like the French palace, but they pronounce it like it rhymes with 'yard sale.' I figured that was reason number one to move. Never live in a town with a name the natives can't pronounce."

"You've never talked about where you're from."

"I didn't think you could handle the excitement." He laughs. "It was rustic. With one movie theater: my salvation. I loved the movies. Especially Park Avenue comedies where the young heiress falls for the butler and you find out he's a prince. The men were swell. They were charming and funny and dressed impeccably and always got the girl. I wanted to be that, not the farmers I saw around me, who worked outside and never said much. I lived for conversation. And then I found my talent. I would draw scenes from the movies, you know, tableaus of characters. A teacher of mine saw the drawings and began to encourage me."

"You were a prodigy."

"Oh, yeah. Nobody could draw like me, at least not in Versailles. But it wasn't my talent that separated me from the folks I grew up with. It was curiosity. I wanted to see the Atlantic Ocean. I know that sounds nuts, but I wanted to know what sand felt like under my feet, and what white waves looked like. I had a list of things I wanted to see. I wanted to find places like that ballroom where Fred Astaire and Ginger Rogers danced in *Top Hat*."

"You're a regular at El Morocco. That's pretty close."

"I worked on the farm and as an illustrator at the local paper. When the war came, I went into the navy with the express purpose of getting to New York City. An old teacher submitted my drawings to the New York School of Design, and I wound up here on the GI Bill. Imagine that. I had to serve in the worst front of the Pacific theater to get my shot at the big town. I wanted to see an ocean, and by God, I got to see one. And when the war was over, I was so happy

I didn't get killed, I promised myself that I would take big risks. So that's when I dropped my last name and invented the suave man you see before you. Delmer Dickinson of Versailles, Indiana, became Delmarr."

"Delmarr definitely sounds more uptown than Delmer."

"Hilda wanted to know if I was French when she interviewed me. I was going to lie and say yes, but then I reconsidered and said, 'Miss Cramer, the only thing French about me is the croissant I had for breakfast.' She laughed, and I got the job."

CHAPTER SEVEN

*M*ost people love autumn in New York City, but to me June is the most beautiful month. Girls' hats change from felt to straw, winter boots go back in the closet and get replaced with breezy sandals, and wool skirts are traded in for glorious billows of crisp cotton pique. Everywhere you turn, women look like bright blooms bursting in a garden.

Weddings are on everyone's mind. The society girls call this June Swoon; Delmarr calls it Bitch Witch Month, since we are deluged by cranky brides and their demanding mothers. We work around the clock to finish gowns in all categories, from the brides, their mothers, the attendants, down to the flower girls. Most brides have their final fittings ten days before the wedding, so the work schedule in the Hub is feverish.

Delmarr ordered up bolts of crisp voile by the ton, in pastel shades of pink, blue, mint green, and butter yellow. By the end of June, we will have used every inch of it. "Stick with the classics," we hear Delmarr say to yet another nervous bride leafing through swatches in his office. After she's made her decision and left, he comes out and ceremoniously declares, "Another wedding party. Pink voile." Delmarr may be a terrific designer, but he is an even better salesman.

Due to the volume of clientele moving through, gossip is rampant. Ruth was doing a fitting for a society bride, and she overheard the girl swapping stories with her maid of honor about Amanda Parker, who was recently betrothed to a lawyer at one of the city's big law firms. Hearing that she is off the market for good makes me smile. I don't need any of John's old flames reigniting and ruining our courtship.

A mere fifty blocks separate my life in Greenwich Village from the grandeur of the Upper East Side, but in truth they are worlds apart. There's a luster and history to uptown life that we first-generation immigrant girls aren't a part of, and we know it. As an Italian girl I'm welcome in the posh private clubs only if I'm on the arm of a member. Ruth is Jewish, so she's out entirely. Helen Gannon's father was a beat cop in Brooklyn, so she's out, too. And poor Violet is the daughter of a widow on public assistance, so she never had an opportunity to secure the right connections and rise above her station. Still, I would choose my friends over any of the daughters of privilege whose clothes I have sewn. My girls have the kind of character that comes from having earned their place in the world.

Helen measures out three and a half yards of white dotted swiss on the cutting table. I'm on my way over to help anchor the fabric when she stands and turns toward us. "All right, I can't keep this secret any longer." Her tone is uncharacteristically chipper. "Girls, I have news. There's going to be a baby Gannon." We gather around and congratulate her.

"Is it okay if I have news, too?" Violet says meekly. "I don't want to take any of the luster away from Helen's."

"You won't," Helen says. "Spill it. I have nine months to regain the luster."

"I'm happy to announce that I have been seeing one Officer Daniel Cassidy. I met him when I reported a lurker at the Fifty-ninth Street subway station. We're on our third date. I think he likes me."

"Are you smitten back?" I ask her.

"I'm hopeful," Violet says with a sigh. Then she beams. "Let's say I have a very Presbyterian view of things, even though I was raised Roman Catholic."

"Let me guess, the cop is a Presbyterian," Ruth says, turning back to her work.

"Yes, he is, but that's not why I'm opening up to new religious ideas," Violet explains. "Instead of believing in the sin ladder, with its steps of venial, mortal, and fry in hell, I have come to embrace the belief of predestination. The stories of our lives have already been written, and we're simply following a divine plan. The good things that happen to us were meant to happen, and the bad things that happen are lessons meant to teach us to be better."

"You're kidding, right?" Ruth says. "I need a drink."

"The only one allowed to drink on the job is Hilda Beast Cramer." Helen leans in. "And I know because I had to fix the facing on her suit jacket, and it smelled of eau de gin at three in the afternoon."

"That's why she never married," Ruth says, sweeping fabric remnants off the cutting table and into a bin. "She's too busy pitching woo with Tom Collins."

"Hey, don't knock the original career girl," I say, feeling a need to defend the old battle-ax. "What's wrong with being a lifer, a career girl first and always? Without her, we wouldn't be working at Altman's."

Violet trims the edges of the waxy pattern paper. "Get you. You're the last person who would wind up like Hilda. You have more beaus than buttons. Has your father thawed toward John at all? Is he going to Italy with your family?" She pins the pattern pieces to the fabric. Helen hands her the shears, and Violet begins to cut the material.

"You know my father would never allow me to bring anyone but a husband on a trip that involves any sort of sleeping, anywhere."

"Don't worry," Helen says. "It may take time, but once you're married, your father will come around."

"First he's going to make it hard on you," Ruth says. "It's all part of Papa Sartori's master plan. He wants to get you out of the country and away from John so he can tempt you with a continental type." She hands me a stack of drawings for filing. I laugh at her comment, but I don't find it funny. Though Papa is cordial to John, he still isn't warm, and no matter what John does or I say, Papa is not budging. Well, I'm as stubborn as Pop. I'll have a whole month in Italy to convince him. When he sees that I love John more after a separation, he will surely accept him.

I sit down at my desk and begin to sort through Delmarr's sketches. We'll build some dresses for the fall; the rest of the sketches, never realized, will be filed. As I lay out his work, I see themes emerge. Delmarr is easing fashion from Dior's New Look, with its tight waists and opulent skirts, into what will surely come next: very feminine, unstructured dresses in fabrics that women can care for with ease. The structure—the pleats, tucks, and padding—is gone, to be replaced with simple lines. Delmarr is offering convenience for the postwar career girl as well as the busy housewife. In the margins he has written words like "easy," "low-maintenance," and "washable." He understands the needs of career girls and homemakers better than we do ourselves. Time is the new luxury, and Delmarr knows it.

Sometimes, if I have a couple of hours before a date, I pull my sewing chair out onto my tiny terrace, put my feet up, and let the fresh air put pink on my cheeks instead of Max Factor. The view is one of my favorite things about my room. When I look across the way at the backyards of our neighbors, separated by fences and the occasional low tree, I see every interpretation and style of garden, from an ornate rococo sculpture garden of marble angels to a rustic country bench under a lone oak tree. Life on Commerce Street is as layered as one of Rosemary's napoleon pastries.

Delmarr says the longest wait in life is when you're waiting for someone to die, but I disagree: it's when you're waiting for a man to ask you to marry him. Since the night of Ruth's seder, when John told me he loved me, I have been waiting for a proposal. What else do we need to know about each other?

With John there's never any talk of me quitting my job, no assumptions like Harvey has about Ruth's career, only ideas about how he and I can work in tandem, partners in all things. I would make him a beautiful home. We could summer in Huntington Bay, and for the rest of the year I picture a penthouse on Fifth Avenue with a wraparound terrace where I can grow roses. I imagine dinner parties by candlelight and long, lazy Sunday afternoons reading on our chaise longues until the sun begins its descent over Central Park. I thought I would never leave Greenwich Village, but now I want to live uptown.

I don't think our future will include children. Maria Grace's passing changed my perspective on that forever, and John doesn't show much interest in child rearing, either. I can see him taking my nieces and nephews for ice-cream sundaes at Rumpelmayer's and carriage rides in Central Park. Our lives will be filled with socializing and careers. Where would children fit in that picture?

While John is attentive and warm and kind, our conversations about the future end abruptly when we get beyond the summer of 1951. Surely John knows that if we were engaged, I would have invited him to Italy. But he hasn't asked me, so he'll stay behind and work while I see the Veneto for the first time. As of tomorrow, June 30, I am still unmarried and unintended. John has business in Chicago during the month of July, and my family and I leave on the first of August, so I won't see him for two whole months. He must realize I'm disappointed, but I am determined not to bring up the subject. There's nothing worse than a woman who has to pry a marriage proposal out of a man.

The aspect of his Italian upbringing that my father holds on to most is the holiday, the month of vacation he takes each August without fail. Every year since Roberto was born, Papa has closed the Groceria and taken our family out of the city. We've rented a lakeside cottage in Maine, a house on the Jersey shore, and a bungalow on Rehoboth Beach in Delaware. Once we arrive at our destination, work is never mentioned. We swim, eat, laugh, and play board games. I've never seen Papa as excited as he is this year, knowing that he'll be returning to his boyhood home with his entire family.

To make our last day together special, John is taking me all the way to the beach on the eastern tip of Long Island. I'm taking extra care in dressing for our date because I want to leave him with the best picture of me until we meet in September. I wear a new white cotton bathing suit, with a vent of illusion netting around the waist. Ruth and I bought suits wholesale when Cole of California came through with their trunk sale.

John is due to pick me up in a few minutes, so I dress quickly. Over my white swimsuit, I button on a full tulip skirt with bold alternating panels of bright white and hot pink. I wear matching pink espadrilles with ballerina ties around the ankles. I load wide gold bangles on one arm. I attach a coral and pearl starfish brooch, the only piece of jewelry John has given me, to the crown of my wide-brimmed straw hat.

When I look into the mirror on my vanity, I see an exhausted girl. A month of working day in and day out does not make for a serene countenance and bright eyes. I hope my bright pink and white ensemble will make up for the gray half-moons under my eyes.

"John's here!" Mama shouts from the bottom of the stairs. I grab my beach bag and go downstairs, where he's waiting for me in a pair of white chinos and a pale blue cotton shirt. He's already tan, and with his black hair, he looks like one of those rich playboys you see in *Life* magazine, on the terrace of a villa on the Isle of Capri.

"You look pretty," he says, and kisses me on the nose.

"So do you," I tell him.

John takes my beach bag from me while resisting Mama's endless pleas to bring some food for the drive. "No, thank you, Mrs. Sartori, we'll get a bite out at the beach."

"All right," Mama acquiesces as she sees us out.

In the car John chats excitedly about a deal he has brewing with a plant nursery in New Jersey. Apparently, the contract for supplying trees to Manhattan's parks has expired, and John wants to get in on it.

"Is there any kind of business you won't do?" I ask him.

"What does that mean?" John shoots me a wounded look, then turns his attention back to the traffic.

Papa still believes that John is frittering away his time in nightclubs and prefers a good party to an honest day's work. Papa told me that John needs to settle on one kind of business instead of dabbling in anything that comes his way. I tried to tell Papa that a hotelier in Manhattan needs connections, and those are made in restaurants and nightclubs frequented by the elite. I say now, "Honey, you're very eclectic in your business dealings. That's all I'm saying."

"Oh. Well, yeah." John's posture relaxes a bit. "It's a big city, and there's a lot to be done. I met one of the mayor's aides in the dining room at the Taft Hotel—that's where all of them have breakfast—and started a conversation over scrambled eggs at the buffet. He mentioned the parks contract, and I made a couple of calls, and here we are. I'm doing a little business with the city."

"That's fantastic," I tell him, giving his arm a bit of a squeeze.

John smiles at me, relieved that I approve. I never tell him what I'm really thinking when it comes to his business life, and he never questions my attitude. I wonder if this is a bad sign. He doesn't instinctively know how I feel, and I'm becoming reluctant to tell him. I'm sure these silly fears will disappear after we marry.

As a girl who's worked since I was twenty, I have a pretty good head for business. I'm no expert, but I agree with Papa: the only way to get results is to focus on one product, make the best item you can, and then sell it to the widest possible audience. Papa taught me the importance of serving the customers and giving them a pleasant experience when they're shopping. The Groceria is artfully laid out, so the customers enjoy the displays as much as the food, and he gives away small samples while people shop. When I told Delmarr, he imitated Papa and made sure that when customers came in for a fitting, we offer coffee or tea with a pastry. It's the personal service that's important.

John drives us all the way out to Montauk Point. We have hot dogs and soda at a roadside stand and take a long walk on the beach. We climb to the top of the lighthouse and stroll through its gardens. As we walk along the streets, admiring the homes with an ocean view, John points out different styles of houses and asks me which one I like best.

I appreciate that he pictures us in homes that I've seen only in magazines. I think of Dante DeMartino, who would have been content to live with me in his parents' home all of his life, with an occasional weekend trip to Coney Island. The life I'll have with John Talbot is beyond anything Dante could have imagined.

As we drive back toward the city, we pass a yard sale in front of an old Victorian house. I see a rocking chair painted pale yellow that would fit nicely before my front window. I crane my neck to survey the goods as we go by. John stops and turns the car around. I start to object, but he cuts me off. "I saw that look. You can't tell me you don't want to have a go at that sale."

We're not the only ones who have taken a detour on the way back from the beach to see what treasures the old house might be hiding. Cars are parked on the lawn, and dozens of people are milling around. The rocking chair has a small SOLD sticker on it. "That was a lure," John says quietly. "Who doesn't love an old rocker?" Then he goes over to a folding table packed with personal items, from handkerchiefs to shoes. He holds up a small turquoise enamel vanity mirror with a matching hairbrush.

"You must have this," John says, pulling out his wallet as he turns to the gentleman overseeing the sale. He hands a bill to the man, who promptly hands it back, explaining, "I don't have that kind of change."

John shuffles through the bills in his wallet; they all seem to be hundred-dollar bills, nothing smaller.

"How much is the set?" I ask.

"Two dollars."

I open my purse and give the man two dollar bills.

John shrugs at the salesman, then kisses me on the forehead and says, "I owe you, honey." I can feel the salesman watching us as we go back to the car. We drive through a series of small seaside towns separated by fields and make our way down quaint main streets, passing an old-fashioned ice-cream parlor and boutiques holding sidewalk sales of clothes, books, and handmade crafts. The twilight sky turns from bright blue to purple as the sun meets the water in an explosion of hot pink clouds. As we near Huntington, John turns off the main road and heads to our spot.

He pulls up in front of the open field where he took me last winter and comes around to open my door. "Here we are," he says, helping me out of the car.

"Look, more houses going up." I point to the field behind us, where two more homes are being built. "Soon we won't be able to park here."

"Why?"

"Because this land will be sold, and somebody will put a house on it."

"You're right," John says. "It has been sold."

"I knew it," I say, sighing and looking out at the bay. "How could land with a view like this sit for long? They're very lucky."

"You are," John says with a grin.

"What do you—"

He pulls me close and kisses me. "This is where I am going to build you a house, Mrs. Talbot."

"*Mrs. Talbot?*" I am thrilled by the sound of it. This moment goes beyond what I imagined it would be.

"You will be, if you say yes. Will you marry me, Lucia Sartori?"

John Talbot gets down on one knee and opens a velvet box. Inside is a ring with an emerald-cut diamond, simple, spare, and white, in a magnificent platinum setting.

"Yes, I will marry you." I rest my hand on John's shoulder.

He stands. "Go ahead, put this ice rink on your finger." He pulls the ring out of the box and places it on my hand. I begin to cry. "Now you're legit, Mrs. Talbot. Two carats' worth of legit."

I laugh. " 'Legit'? What a word!"

John continues holding my hand in both of his. "Well, it's not all that you are. You are everything to me, Lucia. You believe in me, and no one has ever really believed in me before. I'm a successful man, but I've always had to scrape and fight and push to take my place in the sea of men who inherited their wealth, or got lucky on a scheme or a bet. I've traveled the world, and everywhere I went, I looked for the girl who would be mine for life. After all that, I found you right here in New York. I wouldn't have believed it could happen. I'm the luckiest man in the world."

I imagine John traveling without me, and the thought makes me sad. I have such empathy for him; I want to take care of him. And now I'll have a lifetime to love him. He covers my face in small kisses, and then moves to my ear and down my neck.

I know the rules. I am supposed to wait until my wedding night, but I can't. I won't. I would give John Talbot everything I have in this moment, my heart, my mind, my home, all of it, and it would be the right thing to do. John's hands slide under my skirt, and he carries me to the far side of the field, where a hill leads down to a dune. The sky is a veil of orange haze. I look up into John's eyes and see what I have prayed for. This man loves me, and only me. He slowly undoes each button of my skirt and then uses it to make a blanket beneath us on the sand. He gently slides on top of me. "I love you," he says.

All my life I've wondered what this moment would be like, and now that it is here, it's as though I'm not in my body. I'm somehow floating above this romantic scene, savoring details but not feeling as though it is entirely mine. Then John's kiss reminds me why I'm here and why he's chosen *me* out of all the girls in the world. In the rise and fall of his breathing, and his gentle caresses, this feels right. Slowly, all sound and scene fall away, as in the moment I met him. When something is right, there's no need to be afraid, and there is no reason to question it.

I run my hands through his thick hair, and the dazzling stone of the ring catches the last bit of light before the sun buries itself behind the dune. The best day of my twenty-six years turns into night, and if the sun never returned, I wouldn't mind.

John and I don't say a word as he drives me home to Commerce Street. I sit close to him, his arm around me, and every few minutes he leans over and kisses me. The art of conversation isn't an art at all; it's the silence that has meaning. When he pulls up in front of my house, I invite him in.

"They'll be so happy for us. We have to toast our engagement, it's tradition!" I kiss John on the cheek. "You're going to marry an Italian girl. We toast everything, even laundry day!"

John laughs. "Okay, okay, you're the boss."

"And don't you forget it."

As we climb up the stoop, the stairs feel different. I've changed, and the world I live in feels different. These are the steps I played on as a girl, but I get an odd feeling that this is no longer my home. My place is with John.

"Mama?" I call out as we enter the foyer.

"She's in the kitchen," Papa says from the living room. I throw my bag down on the bench and take John's hand and lead him into the living room. "Did you eat?" Papa asks, looking up from his paper. He checks his watch. "It's late. You must have had dinner."

"I'm not hungry, Pop," I tell him.

"How are you, sir?" John asks, leaning down to shake Papa's hand.

"Fine. How are you?" Papa replies.

Mama comes out of the kitchen. "Oh, you're home. Can I get you a sandwich or something?"

"No thanks, Mama. I have something—*we* have something—to tell you."

Mama can sense what I am about to say, but she tries to contain her excitement to let me deliver the news.

"John has asked me to marry him, and I said yes."

Mama shrieks and runs to us, embracing us and kissing me on both cheeks. As she hugs me, I look over her shoulder at Papa, who is staring at the floor. "This is wonderful! Wonderful!" Mama says. "Congratulations! Antonio, get the glasses. We have to toast them!"

"I told you." I wink at John.

Papa stands up and goes to the kitchen for the glasses. He returns with them and a bottle of port. He pours the port and gives each of us a glass. "Lucia, you're my life." He raises his glass.

"Pop?" My father's eyes are wet with tears. "Papa?"

Mama fills in the silence. "Oh, he's fine. He is overwhelmed, his little girl is getting married, that's all." She shoots Papa a look.

"No, Maria, I'm not fine, and I'm not overwhelmed," Papa says. He looks from Mama to John. "I'm disappointed that this young man asked my daughter to marry him without discussing it with me. What kind of a man does such a thing?" He turns to me. "And what kind of daughter accepts under those conditions?"

There is a dreadful pause. Finally, John speaks. "Mr. Sartori, I apologize. I didn't think to ask you because Lucia has already been engaged—"

Mama looks at Papa. John doesn't realize that by making such a statement, he has brought my virtue into question. The implication that I'm used goods, and therefore a separate entity from my family, is not what my father and mother need to hear.

"He doesn't mean it like it sounds, Papa." I move to John's side. "It's just that John is leaving on a business trip tomorrow, and we won't see each other for a couple of months. It slipped his mind to come and seek your permission."

"Yes, yes, that's what happened," John says. Papa regards John with what seems like pity, as though my fiancé is hiding behind my skirts while the gun is aimed at his head.

"You're twenty-six years old, Lucia," Papa says. I wish he wouldn't say my age like that. I sound like the oldest maid on Commerce Street. And I feel like one as I look around this living room, with its faded chintz slipcovers, outdated lace doilies, and ceramic lamps with fringe on the shades. Don't they know that I was looking at mansions today? Estates with an ocean view? I may have been raised here, but I want more. My father came to America for the very same reason. Can't he see that a man cut from the same cloth has walked through the door? John will give me all the things I desire, but he's not enough? "You can do what you want. But don't expect me to be happy for you." Papa puts down his glass and starts to leave the room.

I am furious. I put down my glass and follow him. "Papa, how dare you ruin this moment for me? You say you want me to be happy. *Stai contenta! Stai contenta!* You say it every day, but you don't mean it. Be happy, Lucia, but you can only be happy if I tell you to! You couldn't care less what I want. Nobody is good enough for me, but when I find someone to love, someone I truly love, you humiliate him. He didn't do anything wrong! This is 1951, and your silly peasant traditions belong back on the farm where they came from. I can take care of myself, and I don't need your blessing!"

"Lucia!" Mama is more shocked at the way I'm speaking to my father than angry about what I am saying.

"And I don't want to hear anything else against this man. I don't care what he does for a living, I don't care what kind of family he comes from, and I don't care what you think of him. He's mine, and I want him."

Papa's temper ignites. "You will not speak to me in—"

"Won't speak to you how? Honestly, for once? And Mama, you were more than happy to pass me off to Claudia DeMartino as a scullery maid, so you aren't blameless, either. You just want me married. It could be John Talbot or any man in a suit with the proper hat."

"That is not true!" Mama says indignantly.

I take John's hand and walk him to the door. Mama and Papa do not come after us. "Good night." I kiss John briefly but tenderly on the lips. He seems confused. "I'll handle this. Go."

I go back into the living room. Mama has sunk into her chair, and Papa stands, looking down at the garden with his back to me. "You know something?" I say, talking to Papa's back. "If one of your sons had come home with a girl tonight and she was wearing a new diamond ring, you never would have behaved toward her the way you did toward John. You ruined the most beautiful day of my life. Rot in hell."

I take the stairs up to my room two at a time. I hear my father calling to me angrily from the bottom of the stairs. No matter how old I am, he still is the leader of this household and will not tolerate disrespect. But I can't tolerate his disrespect of me, either. I get into my room and lock the door. I go to my vanity and turn on the small lamp and open the drawer. I remove my savings register from the Chase National Bank and remind myself that I have the means to live my life outside of this house. The long row of deposits written in blue ink soothes me. I'm an independent woman, I tell myself, and when I look in the mirror, I believe it.

Ruth and I take our bag lunches to the garden behind the library for a change of scenery and some much-needed fresh air. Helen took a personal day to rest her swollen feet. Violet spends all her lunches with Officer Cassidy at the White Tower on Thirty-first Street.

It's a beautiful day, so we linger on the lawn after finishing our sandwiches. Ruth has her legs stretched out in front of her and is leaning back on her hands, her face turned up to the sun, eyes closed. "Your father still hasn't spoken to you?" she asks.

"I haven't spoken to him," I tell her, running my hand over the few blades of grass that haven't been matted down. "Mama is so angry that she won't even look at me."

"Do you want to fix it?"

"Either I fix it, or I don't go to Italy."

"You should go to Italy. Once you're married, and I can tell you this from my own experience, a trip to Queens becomes a big deal in a household budget."

"Really?" I want to tell Ruth that may be true of Harvey and her, but I'm marrying an up-and-coming businessman. I don't think travel will be strictly luxury.

"Trust me. Here's what you should do." Ruth sits up straight and pulls her legs alongside her. "Call your priest. Set up a meeting. Bring your parents in and make peace."

"Are you sure *you're* not Italian?"

"When Harvey and I hit the wall with his mother about the wedding plans, she heard me call her a not so nice name to Harvey. She shouldn't have been eavesdropping, but the damage was done. So I had the rabbi come over and settle the dispute. Parents are impressed when you have the maturity to go to the clergy."

"Ruth, how is it you always know what to do?"

"I just got to this marriage thing first. That's all. How's John handling everything?"

"He delayed his trip to Chicago for a week."

"What's he doing out there, anyway?"

I wish I could answer Ruth, but every time I ask John about the business in Chicago, he gets impatient and mumbles something about a potential partnership. There is evidently a wealthy man who wants to do a project with him, and John needs to go out and meet with him. I start to clean up the remnants of our lunch and answer, "Oh, you know, some deal is brewing."

"Have you had the talk yet?" Ruth asks as she screws the tops back on our thermoses.

"What talk?"

"The money talk. About how much you have, and how much he has, and what you're going to do with it." We stand and begin to fold the cotton we brought to sit on.

"No!" I find Ruth's suggestion tacky. There will be plenty of time to set budgets and talk about saving.

"You'd better talk to him now. You don't want any surprises."

"I could never bring up money with John!" He's always flush with cash, he lives at one of the best hotels in the city, he bought me a stunning diamond and takes me to the nicest places. I can't imagine haggling over every dollar the way I've seen my parents do, bills covering the kitchen table, negotiations taking place well into the night.

"What are you going to do when you're married and you need something?"

"I suppose I'll go and buy it, Ruth."

"Nooo. You have to *ask* him if you can go and buy it."

"But I have my own income!"

"Doesn't matter. You're a team, and one half of the team can't be writing checks the other half has no knowledge of." Ruth brings her end of the fabric up to mine, then gives the material a final fold. I don't say anything more as we begin the walk back to Altman's.

I know Ruth means well, but the rules for her marriage don't apply to John and me. I may still have questions about his career, but he doesn't like answering them, and as long as he's happy, I'm happy. That's all that matters.

"Promise me you'll have the talk," Ruth admonishes me as we turn down Fifth Avenue.

"I promise." I don't mean it. Ruth is my best friend, but she has her way of doing things, and I have mine.

Mama, Papa, and I kneel in our living room as Father Abruzzi says a blessing over our heads. We spent an hour and a half discussing our disagreement, and Father Abruzzi sorted it all out, with the conclusion that what's done is done. I am engaged. My parents have to accept it, and I have to accept their concern. Father Abruzzi then calls John in from the street, where he has smoked his way through a pack of Camels. He seems relieved when Papa shakes his hand and Mama kisses him on both cheeks.

"Lucia, when you return from Italy, I want you and John to come for instructions. When you choose a date, we will print the banns of marriage," Father Abruzzi tells me. Personally, I think our priest is obsessed with the banns of marriage. As far as I'm concerned, the only people who need to hear about my marriage are those I will invite to the ceremony. The banns of marriage open up my private life to the entire community of Italian nonnas, who will insist on making a homemade hope chest for me, crocheting everything from blankets to shoe bags to commode seat covers for my future home. All I have to do is give them a color scheme, and the needles will commence clicking from Carmine to King Street.

"We'll be there, Father," John promises. For a non-Italian, my fiancé learns quickly.

I thought the rest of July would drag without John in town, but between work and getting ready for the Italy trip, the time flew. On the morning of our departure, Roberto, Angelo, Orlando, and Exodus leave early to take the heaviest luggage to the airport. Papa is carrying the rest to a taxi waiting at the curb, while Rosemary and I finish getting ready and Mama takes care of the breakfast dishes.

"Lucia!" my father barks from the bottom of the stairs. "How many hatboxes do you need to take to Italy?"

"Three, Papa."

"But you only have one head," Papa says, holding all three boxes up in the air.

"And it needs to be covered in the hot Venetian sun. It wasn't my idea to go in the hottest month of the year to a place warm enough to grow olives." I skip down the stairs and kiss Papa's cheek. "You want me to fry over there?"

"Take them," Papa says, giving in.

Mama pokes her head out of the kitchen. "She can twist you like a *mapeen*," she says, wringing out her dish towel.

"So can you," Papa says.

Rosemary squeezes my hand as we drive through midtown to the Queensboro Bridge, heading to the new international airport. "Look at this as one long shopping trip for the wedding and your new home," my sister-in-law says. "We'll be back in no time."

The first thing I did, at Mama's insistence, was register for my gifts at B. Altman's. She wants my home to be furnished with the finest of everything, from Irish linens for the bed and Egyptian cotton towels for the bath to English china and silver for the dining room. John hasn't had a real home since he sold his family's house on Long Island and put his mother in Creedmore. The Carlyle Hotel is elegant, but I know I can do better.

Mama and I plan to buy furniture and all the fabrics we need for draperies in Italy. I will buy as much Murano glass as I can ship. John has shown me the plans for the house in Huntington, and I want a dazzling multicolored chandelier like I saw in the Milbank mansion when Ruth and I went to give the matriarch a private fitting.

Delmarr's gift is my wedding gown, so he will be sketching while I'm gone. The girls have agreed to help. Helen's last day of work is the week I return. They are saving me a tremendous expense by making my gown, the attendants', and Mama's. That will be money I can save for furniture.

It's hard to believe that I've saved $8,988.78 in the six years I've been working. I never went on vacations, other than the ones with my family, or splurged on jewelry or a car. I made most of my clothes, and the things I couldn't make I bought at Altman's sales with my employee discount. I knew that someday I'd need a nest egg. I plan to spend about a thousand dollars on furnishings in Italy, and I will keep five hundred dollars in the savings account as a little emergency fund. The rest I put into the down payment for the construction of our house in Huntington Bay. My share is a pittance compared to what John is spending, but I gave it to him gladly, knowing that I am half of this partnership. Besides, I got to choose all the tile work, help design the kitchen, and push for an enormous bay window that overlooks the ocean, so my investment is worth every penny.

When we disembark the airplane in Rome, Papa actually drops to his knees, kissing the earth.

"Your father, just like the pope." Mama throws her hands up. Then she helps Papa stand. "You'll ruin your pants," she says, brushing him off.

Papa gathers us around and begins speaking to us in Italian, but he speaks so fast, we have a hard time understanding.

Orlando says, "Papa, please, we're Americans. Give it to us slowly."

Papa explains, more calmly this time, that we will take the train to Treviso and spend the night. "Then we will drive home. Home to Godega di Sant'Urbano."

Delmarr told me that Rome is a lot like New York City, but I don't see it. New York doesn't have parks of ancient ruins or the Coliseum or three-hundred-year-old fountains like the one in the Piazza Navona. Yes, there are thousands of people and the same crazy traffic, but for me that's where the similarities end.

I have no trouble with the flirtatious Italian men because I'm traveling with Papa and four brothers, who guard me like a Brinks truck delivery. When I meander a few feet from the family to look at shoes in a shop window, men seem to gather around like pigeons ready to peck a stale hunk of bagel. Then Papa joins me and gives them the eye, and they scatter instantly. I'm not the only one they're after. Even Mama gets her share of whistles. And when a man made an advance toward delicate-looking Rosemary as we were boarding the train, she barked in her finest Brooklynese, "Buzz off, buster, before I belt ya!"

As the train takes us from Rome to Venice, my first sight of the Adriatic in Rimini makes my heart pound. The roads curl down to the ocean like ribbons, and the white sand is barely visible, every inch covered with people and umbrellas in bold stripes of orange and white and green and pink. The water meets the shore and ripples onto the sand, forming a glittery hem. The houses, painted coral and sky blue, are set into the hills like sequins on silk. The air, though hot, is breezy and clean, leaving an endnote of citrus from the blood oranges growing on the trellis of nearly every home we pass.

Living in the middle of a city, surrounded by bricks and pavement all my life, I never knew that the water would matter so much to me. As I look out over the Adriatic, I think of my home in Huntington. I wonder if John is pushing the workers, whether they have poured the concrete base for the subfloor or mounted the support beams for the walls. John has assured me it will be ready well before we move in on our wedding night.

As the train brakes slowly to a stop in Faenza, children run alongside the train, frantically collecting the coins passengers throw out the window. The war ended six years ago, but you can see that the Italians have not recovered. We look downright opulent in our simple cotton dresses and white gloves, while they, though neatly dressed, wear shoes that are tattered and clothes that are obviously hand-me-downs.

There's a barefoot little girl in an undershirt and white pants, the cuffs rolled to her knees. Her skin is the tawny color of caramel, and her black hair and eyes shine in the sun. Rosemary puts her hand on the window and rests her face against it, studying the girl while the train waits to take on more passengers. I know she is thinking about her daughter, wondering what Maria Grace would be doing, sitting up, eating pastina, cutting her first tooth.

"The candy!" Rosemary sits up and grabs her purse from overhead. "I have a bag of candy! Lu, open the window." I stand and unhook our window. As the train begins to pull out, Rosemary calls out, *"Vieni qua! Vieni qua!"* The children follow her voice and run to our window. Rosemary tosses handfuls of gold-foil hearts filled with hard cherry candy. They jump and catch them like falling stars. The little girl in the white pants reaches for the candy but misses it; another boy grabs the piece that landed closest to her and runs away. I call out to her, *"Corri! Corri!"* As she runs toward our window, Ro throws her the last piece of candy, and she catches it. We look back at her as the train pulls away, her cheeks round with candy as she smiles.

Treviso has always been Papa's dream city, surrounded by a wall and a manmade moat that give it the look of an island. It is softly lit and gauzy; lacy willow trees surround deep canals filled with mossy rocks and gurgling water.

The homes that line the moat are made of brick that has faded to a pale gold sepia. The three-story houses have long windows with simple black shutters. Small footbridges span the moat. The feeling in Treviso is that everyone and everything is connected. There are no freestanding buildings; the city is a fortress.

The streets are cobblestone, but not the typical gray color we see on our Dutch settlement streets in Greenwich Village. These have a smoky blue-green patina that reminds me of turned copper, maybe from the moss that comes from being so near the water. The moss makes Treviso quiet, as though it is lushly carpeted.

When we arrive at the hotel, the manager greets us with such enthusiasm, I wonder if Papa is long-lost Italian royalty.

"Who is Lucia?" he asks, looking at Rosemary, Mama, and me.

"I am," I say.

"You have a telegram, signorina." With great flair, he gives me the yellow envelope.

HAVE A WONDERFUL TIME.
I WAIT. MISSING YOU.
LOVE, JOHN

"How romantic!" Rosemary says wistfully. My brothers laugh. "Oh, you're a bunch of lugs," she tells them.

The manager makes a fuss about giving us rooms with a view of the canal and recommends a nearby restaurant for supper. After we have a nice nap and get dressed for the evening, Papa leads us to the open-air market by the river and explains that at the end of the day, the vendors throw the unsold produce and fish into the curve of the river, and it is carried downstream. Very different from how things are in New York City: Papa spends a fortune to have his garbage hauled from the Groceria by truck.

The maître d' at Lavinia Stella, the best restaurant in Treviso, happens to be the brother of the manager at our hotel. It's clear from our reception that he was expecting us.

"My sons," Papa says once we have taken our seats, "you see how it is in the homeland? Everybody works together. I want you to take a lesson from this."

"Pop, we already work together," Roberto says.

"Yes, but you fight too much." Papa holds out his arms, drawing attention to the mood in the dining room. "See, here you never hear fighting."

I lean in and whisper, "That's because they're duking it out in the kitchen."

Orlando hears this and laughs, but Papa means what he says. His greatest goals in life are to leave a good business to his sons and for his sons to get along. "*Niente litigi!*" he always says. "No fighting!"

Our meal begins with a delicate fish salad of sweet white bream and baby shrimp nestled in greens. Afterward, the waiter brings us orecchiette pasta in a rosy sauce made with basil, tomatoes, sweet cream, and butter. Then we have a platter of grilled lamb chops dusted in bread crumbs and olive oil. For dessert is a small custard for each of us, spilling over with caramel crust.

"If every meal is going to be this good, I'll have to put elastic in the waist of all my skirts," I tell Rosemary, crossing my hands over my stomach and leaning back in my chair.

"I wouldn't worry about it. Today we walked about five miles, on top of the train ride. That's like walking from Commerce Street over the Brooklyn Bridge to my mother's house." Rosemary smiles and takes another spoonful of custard.

Papa raises his glass. *"Mia famiglia."* I smile at him. No matter how much I miss John, I know that one day I will be very glad I had the chance to make this trip with my father.

"Jesus, Pop, could you stop crying? We're gonna get a reputation," Exodus says, playfully looking over his shoulder.

"I'm sorry. I toast you, my family, who I love more than anything in this world. Tomorrow we see Venice, and then to my home. *Salute!*"

We raise our glasses and say, *"Cent'anni,"* a hundred years of health and happiness for all. Now even Exodus has tears in his eyes, but I don't tease him, because I have them too.

CHAPTER EIGHT

*T*here are three ways to get to Godega di Sant'Urbano: by car, by horse, or by foot. Our car resembles a turn-of-the-century model with a rumble seat, like you'd see at the Smithsonian. "Any minute I expect Teddy Roosevelt to crank the engine," Mama says when she sees it. The only member of our group excited by the A-Type Citroën is Exodus, who knows the make of this Swiss nightmare and calls it vintage. The rest of us call it a wreck.

We pile into the car on what has to be the hottest day in Italian history. The trip is so arduous, Mama says her rosary three times, asking God to let the car last long enough to get us there safely. Godega was a small farming town until the community built a new church and convinced Pope Urban XXI to come and bless it. This brought prestige to the town, renamed Godega di Sant'Urbano, and the poor farmers were held up to all of Italy as an example of piety and perseverance.

After passing what seems like the tail end of civilization itself, we see a sign that says GODEGA DI SANT'URBANO. Godega has a very short main street that looks even smaller against the expanse of the farm fields behind it. There is a church, of course, one dry-goods store, one open-air café with tables and grass-green umbrellas, and a war monu-

A very thin chicken rustles under the hay in the corner, startling her. Domenic smiles. "Oh yes, the hen. For some reason, she stays.

"The living quarters are this way," he goes on, and begins climbing a rough-hewn ladder up through a hole in the ceiling. We follow him like ants climbing a branch.

"Not bad!" Roberto, who is ahead of me, says. Papa helps me through the opening, then Mama.

"Zio Antonio lived here until the day he died," Domenic tells us.

There is one enormous room with a long table, simple and home-made, and twelve chairs that have woven seats. The stucco walls are washed in a pale peach that turns to rose around the ceilings and baseboards. A nubby beige sofa and two chairs, low and deep, sit under the windows. The entire far end of the room is taken up by a fireplace made of gray fieldstones, some as large as a hatbox. I have never seen a hearth so large—I could stand in it! A collection of old farm tools hangs over the fireplace. The black tools against the gold background give the effect of tintypes in shadow boxes. There is one floor lamp with a simple rose glass shade. After seeing the stable downstairs, I'm relieved to see they have electricity.

"See, Maria. Simple. No knickknacks," Papa teases her. "My wife has more dishes than a restaurant," he says to Domenic.

Ignoring the joke, Mama asks, "Where do we sleep?"

"Upstairs." Domenic points.

"Another ladder," Mama remarks cheerfully, climbing up to the third floor. I follow her. There are two large bedrooms. Each has two twin beds, which seem like our beds back home until we sit on them. Instead of using box springs and mattresses, the beds are large open wood crates stuffed with straw-filled sacks. With sheets and a blanket over the top, they look like normal beds.

I sit on a bed and smooth the blanket. "It's not too bad."

"Now we know how the chicken feels." Mama rolls her eyes.

Papa and Mama take one room, and Rosemary and I take the other. My brothers will sleep down in the stable. Before Roberto goes downstairs with my brothers, he embraces Rosemary, who buries her face in his neck. Their loss has made them even closer.

The garden is full of ripe tomatoes, yellow peppers, arugula, radishes, and potatoes. Domenic has prosciutto, strips of sweet ham, and bresaola, lean beef in paper-thin slices, both of which he cured in his own smokehouse. He also brought some of his own olive oil in a black flask and plenty of wine, a hearty red Chianti, in ceramic jugs.

Bartolomea takes Mama outside and shows her a hearth made of stone, with a tall chimney. There is a short stone wall next to it (for cooling whatever has been baked, I'm guessing) and another table behind it, longer than the one indoors, with a bench for seating on either side.

"It's too hot inside to cook, you cook here," Bartolomea tells Mama and shows her the utensils stored neatly below the oven, which is open on both ends. Italian ingenuity, I think as I look through. You keep the uncooked dishes on one side and serve the finished product from the other.

"You are hungry now, no?" Bartolomea drapes a bright yellow cotton cloth on the table, anchoring it with small black flasks of olive oil. Orsola puts a plate, a fork, and a small wooden cup at each place setting. Out of a basket brought over from Domenic's truck, Bartolomea unloads trays of delicacies: tiny sandwiches made with crusty bread, anchovies, a platter of blood oranges splashed with olive oil and pepper, fresh figs sliced in half with hunks of hard cheese, succulent smoked sardines, curls of Parmesan cheese, and shiny black olives. There are big, puffy oil biscuits for dessert. Orsola places bunches of fresh grapes beside each plate. It's a feast.

Bartolomea calls us all to lunch. As we take our seats on the benches, time seems to stop; we could be any generation of Sartoris gathering to eat under the Venetian sun.

After a week of sleeping on sweet straw, walking to and from town for an afternoon cappuccino, resting and napping, and reading Goethe's notebook about his Italian travels (my farewell gift from Delmarr), I decide I could get used to the Italian lifestyle—but not without my fiancé. My heart aches for John, and every time I see something wonderful, I wish he were here to share it with.

I receive my first letter from Ruth, who tells me that Helen is getting bigger by the second: Ruth has let out Helen's work skirts twice already. Violet is pressuring the cop and expects a ring by Labor Day. Delmarr seems preoccupied; they are going to lunch, and Ruth will write with the details. She then mentions that John has been to the store a couple of times and came in to say hello to everybody. He told Ruth he was up in Interior Decoration to find the right drawer pulls for a walk-in closet he is designing for our bedroom suite.

"Lucia!" Ro calls, and from the sound of her voice, I can tell that something is terribly wrong. I run around the house to find her kneeling next to Papa, who has fallen to the ground.

"Mama!" I yell. She comes running out of the house with Exodus. I kneel next to Papa and feel his pulse, which seems faint. "Get water," I tell Ro. "We have to take him to town." Exodus and I try to revive Papa. He opens his eyes but doesn't know where he is. "Keep him awake!" I tell Mama as we lift him into the back of the truck Domenic left for us. The rest of the boys are at Domenic's farm this afternoon, helping him fill his silo with hay. It's about a mile away in the opposite direction of town, so we decide to take a chance and find a doctor in Godega.

Exodus drives over the pits of the old road as fast as he can. The movement is okay because it helps Papa stay awake. We pull into town, and I see a group gathered at the café and scream, "*Dottore, dottore!*" The waiter rushes into the restaurant and calls for help. Mama, always calm in a crisis, asks for a cool rag for Papa's face.

The doctor arrives, a man around forty, and directs us to a bench in the shade. He mixes a packet of powder into some water and makes Papa drink it. He explains that the powder contains potassium and other minerals, including some salt. It must taste terrible, because Papa makes a face as he drinks it.

"What happened?" he asks, clearly restored by the bitter concoction.

"Signor, you must stay out of the sun." The doctor smiles. "Every time Americans come here, they faint in the heat."

"It didn't feel hot," Papa defends himself.

"Signor, if a place is hot enough to grow oranges, it's too hot for people."

Exodus helps Papa stand, and we begin to walk back to the truck. Mama stops us. "Oh, no. You're not going anywhere. Not until the sun goes down!"

"Maria," Papa starts to argue.

"No, we are going to sit in the church. Right over there in the back pew of Saint Urbano's. We'll sit in the cool shade and say the rosary and thank God it wasn't anything worse."

Papa throws his hands up. With Mama on one side and Exodus on the other, he enters the church. Rosemary and I exchange a smile.

Papa invites the whole family to the courthouse in Godega to secure the final paperwork on his inheritance. Though the building is very small, it also seems to be the police department: the only *carabiniere* in town stands out front. I sit with Roberto and Rosemary. Orlando and Angelo wait by the door, as if to guard it; from whom or what, I have no idea. Exodus leans against the wall whispering with Orsola. Mama turns and motions for them to be quiet. Orsola gets up and moves away from Exodus so as not to get in any more trouble.

As the officer reads the will aloud, Papa closes his eyes and listens carefully. When Enzo's name is mentioned, Domenic leans over to tell Papa that Enzo signed off on his portion of the estate. Papa nods. I can see that the severed relationship with his brother still bothers him. It's the one thing about my father that I find mysterious. He's a peaceful man. How can he bear to be angry at his brother for all these years? At the end of the proceeding, the officer rises and kisses Papa on both cheeks; it turns out that he is a third cousin to Papa on his mother's side.

After ten days at the farmhouse, we make plans for our side trips. I want to shop in Venice, so Rosemary and I come up with an itinerary. We pack a week's worth of clothing for our trip. It is no small feat to wash clothes in the hot sun, hang them on the line, and press them with an iron that looks like a doorstop. But there's no other choice.

A package from John arrives just before Ro and I are about to leave. It's from Bonwit Teller's, sent one week before we left for Italy.

"I can't believe he spent money at the competition!" Ro says, laughing. I open the box and lift out a small tiara made of white satin roses, with leaves made of pale green velvet on a band of dazzling Austrian crystals. "How delicate!" Ro squeals. The note reads:

> My dearest love,
> For your veil.
> I love you, John

"Boy, you are getting a prince."

"Don't I know it," I tell her. I pack the tiara away.

Most Italians are on holiday in August, so it takes a lot of bartering to get a ride down to the train station in Treviso. Papa negotiates with a car service, commenting that these rides are as expensive as our flight over. But the car trip has an up side for Papa, since the driver is like a built-in chaperone. It's all worth it when Ro and I join the throng walking across the Rialto Bridge into the city of Venice. She points to the gondolas sailing underneath us. We stop on San Marco to look at the Palazzo Dario, its façade inlaid with colors of marble I didn't know existed: red with turquoise veins, gold with white, green with orange, all cut and configured into a wild Byzantine pattern. The guidebook says that Venice was the gateway of trade for the world, from Africa to the Orient, and the influence of many cultures is apparent.

"*Scusi*," a man says to us in Italian. He pronounces each word carefully. "*Puo prendere una fotografia di me con mia moglie? Grazie.*"

"*Prego*," I answer. "Are you American?" I ask as I take the camera from him.

"Yes," he says in English as he stands beside his wife. "You, too?"

"Finally, some of our own!" his wife says from under her wide-brimmed hat as she poses. She is around fifty years old and is lean and tall. Her blond hair is twisted into a long braid. She has patrician beauty, with wide-set blue eyes and a high forehead.

"That's how we feel," I tell them as I snap their picture. "We've been staying up in the country. I'm Lucia Sartori, and this is my sister-in-law, Rosemary."

"I'm Arabel, and this is my husband, Charlie Dresken." Charlie is about Arabel's age, but he is her physical opposite, small and muscular, with red hair and a beard.

Charlie takes the camera from me and asks, "Where are you from?"

"New York City. Greenwich Village."

"Commerce Street!" Ro adds.

"Small world," Charlie says, smiling. "We're from Long Island. Syosset."

"Really?" I ask. "My fiancé and I are building a house in Huntington."

"Oh, Huntington is fabulous!" Arabel says. "They're building some gorgeous homes over there. What does your fiancé do?"

"He's a businessman. Importing," I explain.

"Where are you girls staying?"

"We're at the Pavan Pensione at Campo San Marina," Ro reads off of our itinerary.

"We're at the Giudecca. Actually, we were about to have lunch. Would you like to join us?"

"We would love to!" I say.

"Meet us in the hotel lobby at two," Arabel says as she writes down the address on our itinerary.

Rosemary and I are so excited to dress up and have lunch that we practically run through the streets to find the Pavan Pensione. We are given a room on the second floor, sparsely furnished but clean, with a shared bath down the hall. We don't even mind sharing the bath, as all we have in Godega is an outdoor shower, which is like bathing in a wooden barrel. We put on stockings and gloves and hats, something we haven't done since getting off the plane in Rome. I think we look very Italian; I wear a black cotton circle skirt with a white blouse and a bright red sash, and Ro wears a beige linen skirt and a pink blouse with a pink patent-leather belt. When we reach the Guidecca, we're glad we made an effort. The lobby is marked by an old-world elegance; there are ornate crystal chandeliers and heavy Victorian furniture with velvet cushions.

Arabel greets us and ushers us into the busy dining room, where Charlie has gotten us a table overlooking the garden. We find out that she is an art professor at Marymount Manhattan, and Charlie is a lawyer. They've been married for ten years and have no children.

"Her children are her books and her antiques from our travels." Charlie laughs.

"And so are yours." Arabel pinches his cheek, and he smiles at her. "You see, Charlie and I come to Venice every year, and each time we come, we visit the same churches to look at the same works of art because we find something new every time we look at them."

"Photographs in books don't do the trick," Charlie adds.

"You must join us at Saint Stae. There is a series of paintings there that was commissioned by Andrea Stazio —"

"A very wealthy man," Charlie interjects.

"Very wealthy, who wanted the lives of the twelve apostles interpreted by twelve young artists. So he selected the best around. My favorite in the group is by a young man named Giambattista Tiepolo. He painted *The Martyrdom of Saint Bartholomew.*"

"It will take your breath away," Charlie tells us.

Arabel continues, "The painting always moves me. I think it has to do with the image of this man, Bartholomew, emerging from what looks like a black pool into the light. He is surrounded by evil and doubt, but he persists in his determination to die honorably and see the face of God. It is the best interpretation of suffering I have ever seen. You feel his agony."

Rosemary, who has done her best to listen to a conversation she has no interest in, is in need of a nap. Her eyes have glazed over. All this talk of art is too much for her. But it has the opposite effect on me. I am ravenous for more details, so I ask questions, and Arabel and Charlie are happy to answer.

As I watch the Dreskens interact, I see that they love each other, but there is also a discourse between them, an intellectual connection that I never think about in my relationship with John. When Arabel speaks about the history of Venice and the masterpieces on display, I wonder what I might have missed by not going to college. The only girls from my high school who went were extremely intelligent and wanted to become teachers or librarians. I knew I would work with my hands, but it would have been enhanced by an education in art and literature. Arabel seems to know a little something about every-thing. What I know about the world, I know in detail, but my view is not expansive. It is limited to Greenwich Village and B. Altman's. Per-haps the right connections aren't simply social but a world of deeply layered ideas, shared by people who care about them. Being around Arabel makes me want to be a part of this world. We make plans to join them as they tour Venice. Arabel has lots to show us.

Arabel and Charlie show us as much of Venice as we can take without falling over in exhaustion. What a coup to have an actual art historian explaining things. Today Arabel insisted we see the glassworks of Mu-rano. On the ferry across to the main island, Arabel explains that the glassworks were moved out of Venice because of the smoke and heat produced by the ovens. When we tour the main factory, it re-minds me of the Hub at B. Altman's. Each person completes a spe-cific task, after which he or she passes the work along to the next person, until the garment—or, in this case, the goblet, sconce, bowl, or chandelier—is finished.

"Isn't it hard to pick a chandelier when you haven't seen the house?" Arabel asks me. Maybe because I'm a seamstress, I can envi-sion things as they'll be in their final form. In my mind's eye, a swatch of fabric becomes a full skirt, a handful of beads, a jewel encrusted bodice, a piece of black velvet, a collar. When I walked the acre and a half of our lot with John, I could picture the finished house in de-tail: each room, each doorway, point to the exact spot the bay window should go so the afternoon sun would fill the downstairs with rosy light. What an odd thing, I think, to need to build something so you can visualize it. I couldn't do what Arabel does, but I think perhaps she couldn't do my job, either.

I barter with the salesman when I find a stunning chandelier, one I could never afford in the States. The base is burnished copper, and the arms have leaves of gold. The glass ornaments are fruit in every conceivable color: smoky quartz grapes, peridot pears, garnet apples, pink cherries. He promises that he will wrap each piece of fruit carefully and tells me not to be shocked when the chandelier arrives in a box the size of a room.

"Just so it gets there without breaking," I tell him. What a spectacular vacation! Everything I see feeds my creativity and gives me ideas, from the coral buckle I saw on a lady's shoe to the silk moiré tent we dined in at the hotel. Even the cooking utensils are works of art in Italy, their enamel handles in vivid colors.

The next day Arabel arranges a car for a drive down to Florence to buy silk. I learned about Antico Setificio Fiorentino from Franco Scalamandre, a purveyor of silks on Fifth Avenue. I will be able to repay Arabel's generosity with some of what I know about textiles and fabric. When I bought silk taffeta from Scalamandre to make a gown for a mezzo-soprano at the New York Grand Opera Company, he told me about the factory where the silk was woven. He painted a detailed picture of the place, from the silkworms spinning the thread, to the chuff of the looms operated from morning till night, to the drying room where the freshly dyed fabric is stretched on wooden frames so the color dries evenly. As we go through the factory, I realize that the materials we work with at B. Altman's are only a small sample of what they create here. If I had some of these stripes and plaids, I could design a whole season around the variations of pink.

Arabel points to an off-white taffeta that has a delicate watermark in the design. She says, "I don't know what I could ever do with it, but it's exquisite." She holds it up, and I can see from the way the fabric drapes and from the regal simplicity of the tone-on-tone weave—delicate, with a sheen for dramatic effect—that it could be used for only one thing: my wedding gown. Arabel and Rosemary agree, so I buy ten yards, plenty for whatever Delmarr will create.

When we have to say good-bye to Arabel and Charlie the next morning, I'm sad to see them go. I've never spent time with such an educated woman, and I see what I've missed by not furthering my education. I'm proud of my training and schooling, but I see now that I could have done more. I remember the night at the Plaza when Christopher's friend asked me if I'd gone to Vassar. How I would have loved to go away and live in a dormitory with lots of other smart, ambitious girls. I've done very well with my talents, but I haven't pushed myself. I have ideas and the passion to execute them, but there is a whole world that I haven't experienced, and it would have allowed me to rise to the top.

Mama is thrilled to see us when we return safely from our trip. I give her the strands of Murano glass beads I bought for her. When I watch her try them on in the mirror, I notice that she tilts her head like I do when trying on jewelry. Mama takes her eyes off the beads and looks at me in the mirror. "Are you all right?"

"I'm okay, Mama."

She examines my reflection in the mirror closely, studying me, as she has done all my life. I can see from her expression that she knows something has changed. My mother has always been my closest confidante, so there isn't much I can keep from her.

"Why are you so serious?" Mama asks.

"I don't know," I lie. How can I tell her that this trip has changed me? I met Arabel, who lives in a world of literature and art and infused me with her passion. I saw craftsmanship so exquisite that it made me think about how I could become a better seamstress. Why, though, do my aspirations sadden me? Why do I always feel that I have to give up something I love in order to climb higher?

We spend our last weeks in Godega eating and laughing and enjoying one another's company. This will be my last family holiday as a single daughter. Of all the things I learned and all the places I saw, not one has meant more to me than these precious days here in Papa's family home. These are the moments I will treasure: my mother laughing as she sits in Papa's lap, Roberto walking with Rosemary through the fields, Angelo, twenty years too old to be an altar boy in Saint Urbano Church but serving Mass anyway, Orlando baking pizza in the outdoor oven, Exodus fixing the engine of the old car for the twelfth time, and me digging my bare feet into the grass where my father played as a boy.

As we load up the truck to go down to the Treviso train station, cousin Domenic seems preoccupied. He mashes the tobacco into his pipe as though he's angry at it.

"Are you all right, cousin?" I ask him.

"I will never see you all again," he says.

"Sure you will. You'll come to America, and we'll come back."

"No, you're young, you don't know. You have so much ahead of you that you think you have all the time in the world. I know this time will never come again. You won't come back."

I smile at Domenic and give him a hug. As gay and funny as Italians can be, they can brood and turn dark in an instant. Nothing in life is certain, I want to tell my cousin. This month has been wonderful. Stop complaining! This is easy for me to say, since I've been counting down the moments until I see John.

Roberto loads the last of the bags into the car. Domenic, Bartolomea, Orsola, and Domenica have come to see us off.

"Where's Exodus?" Mama asks, counting our heads as though we are chickens.

"Mama," Exodus says in a tone I barely recognize. His sarcasm and humor have been replaced by a serious timbre.

"Let's go. We have two trains to catch before the plane." Mama moves toward the truck, her purse over one arm and a small satchel in her other hand.

"Mama . . . I'm not going back," Exodus says.

Mama grips the door of the truck with her free hand. "What do you mean, you're not going back?"

"I'm staying here," he says firmly.

"But what about New York?" I ask him. I would almost expect a half-baked idea like this from Orlando or Angelo, but not from Ex, who I've been closest to all my life.

"What about it?" Exodus says evenly.

"It's your home!" I tell him.

"My heart is here." Orsola moves to Exodus's side, and he goes on, "We're going to get married."

"*O Dio.*" Mama plops down on the bench on the truck. "Antonio Giuseppe, you handle this."

We know Mama means business when she calls Pop by both of his names. We back off as Papa and Mama face Exodus, and ready ourselves for the fireworks.

"Ex, what are you doing?" Papa says gently.

"Pop, you know I love the store and working with you. But all my life I wanted to be outdoors. I always wanted a farm. I like working from the minute the sun comes up till it's suppertime. This is what I'm cut out for. I want to grow things in the earth, not just sell them. I like how quiet it is at dawn when I go to milk the cow. I like the way my boots sink into the dirt after I've plowed it. I don't want the noise anymore. I want peace." Ex extends his hand, and we listen to the soft rustle of the breeze moving through the wheat. "That's music to me, that sound. I feel like I've found what I'm supposed to be doing. "

"But I need you back home," Papa says quietly, as he looks past his son to the fields beyond.

"You have three other sons. And you could always hire somebody from the outside."

No one in a family business ever utters the words "hire somebody from the outside." They are considered the highest insult, because the whole point of having a place like the Groceria is to leave your children a profitable enterprise so that the family can stay close and work together.

My mother raises her voice. "We will never hire outside our family. We will close the place down before we hire from the outside!"

"Maria, please." Papa turns to his wife. "There is a tradition here for him."

"And a girl! A beautiful girl! Let's not forget that!" Mama jabs. Orsola looks at the ground. I want to go to her and tell her this isn't her fault, it's just the way our family operates, but once she marries my brother, she will see all of this for herself.

Ex turns to Papa, who is the reasonable one in this fight. "There's nothing that would make me happier than being in charge of my own life. Growing my own food, chopping wood for fire, all of that. That's what I want to do. It's how I want to live."

Mama throws her hands in the air. "Thank God, at last we know what Exodus wants. Well, tell me then, son, who is the imposter I birthed, nursed, raised, and took care of like an angel all these years? Where is he? Maybe *he* can make some sense to me, because you—you're like a drunk right now. Drunk on romantic wheat fields, Italian moons, and Domenic's wine!" she bellows. "You get in this car, and you come home to the United States of America, where you are a citizen! Now!"

Exodus doesn't move. Orsola weeps, and Papa, who isn't supposed to be in the sun, is beginning to fry.

"Maria. Let the boy go."

"Antonio!"

"Let the boy go. If one of my sons has to leave me, this is the place I would want him to go. The Sartoris have been here farming for hundreds of years. I am happy to have a son return to my homestead, where I grew up, and I will be happy to see his children grow up in this house."

The only sound we hear is the thin chicken walking on the straw in the stable. Mama holds her head in her hands and sits down on the bench in the truck; she knows Papa is right. Exodus climbs up into the truck and puts his arms around her. "In my heart I will never leave you, Mama."

After a moment Papa seems to remember that there is another aspect to all of this. He made his mistakes with Rosemary's entrance into the family, and he won't make the same ones twice. He turns to Orsola. "Orsola, welcome to the family," he tells her. She embraces Papa and then each of us, and finally Mama. Papa gives Mama his handkerchief. She blows her nose and says, "Is anybody in this family ever going to have a normal wedding?" Roberto cranks up the truck, Domenic and his family climb aboard with us, and the last thing we see as we take the turn to the road to Godega di Sant'Urbano is Exodus with his arm around Orsola's waist and one very thin chicken peeking out the door of the farmhouse, their new home.

CHAPTER NINE

*J*ohn is waiting at the gate when we get off the plane in New York, holding a dozen red roses tied with a white satin ribbon. He's dressed impeccably, as always, in a beige linen suit, a blue-and-white-striped shirt, and a navy tie. As many times as I took out his picture in Italy, seeing him here, so handsome, makes my heart beat too fast; I can't breathe. I know ladies aren't supposed to run, but I don't care. I run down the gateway and into his arms. I bury my face in his neck and breathe in the smell of his skin, which I have missed desperately.

"How's November fifteenth for a wedding day?" he whispers.

"November! We've got invitations to send, a band to hire, a meal to cater, a dress to make! It's crazy!" I tell him. By now my family has gathered, though they are hanging back like a clump of moss on an old rock.

"I don't want to wait," he says, smiling.

"I don't, either!"

"We can be ready by November fifteenth," Mama says with a hint of panic. I know her well enough to understand that she thinks it's too soon, but since our meeting with Father Abruzzi, she's tried hard not to shoot down every idea John and I have about our wedding. Instead of arguing, she gives John a kiss on the cheek. After my mother has spoken, my brothers become animated once again and greet John with handshakes. Only Papa, dear Papa, has to force a smile. He will never say another word against John, because he promised Father Abruzzi, and he doesn't want to lose me. But why can't he see how happy I am?

Roberto and Rosemary ride in the Packard with me and John and most of the luggage, while Mama, Papa, Orlando, and Angelo follow in a taxi. I tell John about Exodus's decision to stay, and Rosemary regales him with stories of our trip to Venice. When we all reach Commerce Street, John helps my brothers unload the luggage, weighed down with Italian books, candlesticks, leather purses, and silk. The chandelier and all the housewares were to be shipped by boat. John has things he needs to do, so he kisses me and promises to pick me up for dinner.

The first thing I do is take a shower. I stand under the luxurious, pulsating hot water for fifteen minutes, enjoying every second. It feels decadent after a month of washing in tepid water without any pressure. I step out of the shower and throw on my robe. When I go into the hallway, Ro hands me a glass of lemonade. "You didn't have to do that," I say.

"The hell I didn't! I haven't seen an ice cube in thirty-one days. I wanted you to know they really exist." She clinks her glass against mine and goes back downstairs, leaving me to get ready.

I grab a sweater on my way out the door with John that night. New York City is still warm in the evenings, but it feels downright chilly compared to the Veneto. John has made reservations at the Vesuvio.

"How much did you miss me?" I ask once we're settled in our booth.

"Every second. And you?"

"Every half-second." I lean across the table to kiss him.

"I was scared to death you'd meet some Italian count or duke or whatever they have over there and decide not to come home."

"They could have lined up Italian bachelors from the top of the

Alps to the heel of the boot, and I wouldn't have been even mildly tempted. I have the best fiancé in the world. Why would I even look?"

"Beautiful girls can have their pick."

"And I pick you."

"I got you something while you were gone," he says with a grin. "When I saw it, I said, 'There's only one girl in the world who could do this justice.'" John motions to Patsy, a tall, dapper Italian and the owner of the restaurant, who brings a large box to the table.

"What did you do? I—I thought we were saving for the house. . . ."

The box is as big as the table and about a foot deep, fastened with a pink satin ribbon so wide, it takes me a moment to untie it. When I lift off the lid, I am stunned. I pull out a mink coat of the softest, deepest black. It has a stand-up collar, square-cut shoulders, and deep cuffs.

"Check the lining," John says.

I open the coat and see my name embroidered in glittery gold thread. "There's no mistaking who this coat belongs to."

"Lucia is a noble name," Patsy says, looking proud of his role in this whole thing. "It means 'light.' You are such a lovely girl, you don't need a mink coat. Many women, they need the mink coat." He walks back to the bar.

"Honey, can we afford this?" I ask John.

"What do you mean, can we afford it? You get the first fur coat of your life, and you're worried about how much it costs?"

I should tell John that this is not my first fur. Papa bought me a wool coat with a fox collar when I got my job at B. Altman's. But John doesn't need to know that. "It's just that the house is such an investment. It's our dream."

"The house is covered." John takes a sip of his Manhattan and taps the table with the stirrer impatiently.

There's something odd about the way he says that, as though the house is covered but other things are not. I think of Ruth, who made me swear that I would have the money talk with my fiancé. I never did. I never thought money was something we would quibble over.

"Look. I didn't buy you this coat to upset you. I can take it back," he says.

"No, no, I love it."

"You don't act like you love it."

"Of course I do. You gave it to me. I'm sorry if you think I'm ungrateful."

"That's the message I'm getting here. Do you think I ride through midtown and roll down my window and throw a thousand bucks out into the street like it's confetti? Do you think I go out and spend money like a fool to impress people?"

"No, that's not—"

"You don't trust me, do you?"

"What are you talking about? I'm going to marry you."

"But do you *trust* me?"

"I wouldn't be here if I didn't trust you." I can't believe that the wonderful evening, with this extraordinary gift, has escalated into an argument. I take a deep breath. "Oh, John, come on. I'm jet-lagged, I'm not myself. I love this coat, and I'll wear it every day that I can."

John relaxes. "You're my girl. I just want you to have the best."

"I do. I have the best."

"Well, try it on," he says, pulling the coat out of the box and holding it like a towel for a swimmer emerging from the surf.

"Now?"

"Yes, now. I want to see you in it."

I stand up and slip into the coat. It is sumptuous, soft and light. Patsy gives a low whistle.

"Thank you, honey." I lean over and kiss John on the lips. When I open my eyes, I catch my reflection in the serrated mirror behind the booth. In the faceted squares of glass, I see hundreds of me in the mink coat.

"John, are you hungry?" I ask.

"Not really. Are you?"

"Not at all. Why don't you get the car?"

John smiles and leaves the table. I meet him under the awning in front of the restaurant. He tips his hat. "Where to, ma'am?"

"The Carlyle Hotel, please," I answer, playing along. November 15 cannot get here fast enough.

Delmarr and Ruth covered for me during the month of August, since Hilda Cramer never likes anyone to take over two weeks of vacation at a time. But after such a long absence, I'm thrilled to push through the doors of the Custom Department and be back in the Hub. I have the silk for my wedding gown and stories galore for Delmarr and Ruth. I come early to get my desk organized before the gang gets in. I check the calendar on the chalkboard.

Instead of the usual system of fittings in yellow chalk and final delivery in pink, there are symbols I haven't seen before. Ruth's drawing table seems the same, but the storage bins are different. I push open the doors to the supply room and see the fabric all folded flat and stacked from floor to ceiling, rather than standing on end. A feeling of panic goes through me. I go back into the Hub and into Delmarr's office. The signed photo of the McGuire Sisters is still on the wall, and his color wheel is still on the desk. I exhale, relieved.

"Corporate spy?" Delmarr says from behind me.

His voice startles me, and I jump. "Don't do that!" I tell him, and then I throw my arms around his neck.

"What, Talbot withholding the sugar?" Delmarr hugs me back.

"Not at all. What's going on here, Delmarr? Everything looks different."

"Not everything, just a little thing from corporate called inventory. They want to know what we have here: every yard of fabric, every inch of trim, every jet bead in every size. I think Hilda Beast is on the ropes."

"They're going to fire her?"

"Ease her out."

"Then you'll be the name on the label?"

"Noooooo." Delmarr sits down and puts his feet on the desk. "Don't you know anything about the ways of the retail world? The underling of the person they're putting out to pasture never gets the job. No, they'll bring in some hotshot."

"But you're a hotshot."

"Thank you. I could be, but I'm not. Not in their eyes, anyway. And they told me as much."

"Bastards."

"And it doesn't help that Helen quit."

"Quit?"

"She's swelling up so badly that she can't work. Violet is in woo-woo land with that cop she's seeing and can't focus on anything. She sent out three day suits without hemming them last week. We looked like fools. And then Ruth—"

"What's wrong with Ruth?"

"Harvey wants her to quit so they can have a baby. He thinks the job is too stressful. And then there's you. I'll lose you as soon as John Juan puts the ring on your finger."

"No, you won't," I say.

"Come on, Lucia. Be serious for a moment. I get you girls bright-eyed and bushy-tailed out of high school—"

"Katie Gibbs."

"Or Katie Gibbs, and you come in here, guns blazing, ready to take on the world. By the time you hit twenty-five you clear out of here like somebody dropped a bomb. You rush to get married, and when you do, you leave me."

"I won't, Delmarr. I won't."

"Talbot isn't going to let you work. He's going to polish you like the hood ornament on his Packard and set you in a china closet in Huntington. That's your fate, kid." Delmarr fills a mug with coffee and hands it to me.

I was raised with men, so it never occurs to me that there are any limitations on what I can do. But this isn't only about what I want; John has a say. "Why does this have to be so hard?" I know that Delmarr is right. Nobody can be a career woman *and* a housewife. I kept hoping I would figure out a way to do both. But only men get the luxury of a magnificent career and a good home life.

"He loves you, but he loves you if you're there for him every minute. You're allowed your dreams if they're his dreams, too. Trust me. I'm older than you, and I've seen this a hundred times."

I stare down into my coffee cup, which looks like a black pit I'd like to jump into. "It stinks."

"Yeah, it does. But what are you gonna do? That's love." Delmarr swings his legs off his desk and jumps to a standing position. "But for now, in the waning days of the B. Altman Custom Department, I'm going to beg you to finish the Ashfield order. Two evening dresses and a hostess pantset. She's a chub, so keep the flow loose."

"A Madame Rouge." That's one of our code phrases back at the shop. It refers to our larger-lady clientele. Delmarr came up with it when he took a lady's measurements and the numbers went as high as the red mark on the tape measure.

"The rouge-ee-est." Delmarr laughs.

"Welcome back, Lucia," I say aloud.

"Oh yeah, and that, too, kid. Welcome back."

Every year when I leave for vacation, I harbor a secret fear that when I return, my desk will be cleaned out and my job will be gone. The thing I feared most has happened: I left for a month and came back to my gleaming castle on the third floor of the best department store in New York City only to find it in ruins. I go to my desk and pull my handbag from the drawer. From the zippered pocket, I pull out my little red passbook from the Chase National Bank. On July 5, 1951, I wrote a seventy-five-hundred-dollar check to John for the house. My nest egg is gone. If the department closes, I will have to rely on John for money. I don't want to rely on anyone! The thought that I will never work again peels through me like a sudden chill.

"How was Italy?" Ruth booms as she sweeps into the Hub.

I quickly put away my bankbook. "Hi!" I say too brightly.

Ruth gives me a kiss on the cheek. "What's wrong with you?"

"I missed you!"

"No, you look shaky. What happened?"

"We're going to lose our jobs."

"You already spoke with Delmarr? We're too high-end for the new B. Altman's. They want ready-to-wear on every floor. Can you imagine the crap they'll roll in here? The workmanship will be shoddy, the fabrics will be cheap, the kind that never lose the smell of the dye. Yech! New York class is going to take a powder."

"Ruth?" My voice quivers as I say her name, alarming her. She puts down her pencil. "I gave John all my savings."

"You did what?"

"All my money."

"What did he do with it?"

"He's putting it into the house."

"Oh, okay." Ruth breathes a sigh of relief and clasps her hands behind her head. "You scared me."

"Well, he wasn't going to squander it," I say defensively.

"Okay, okay. I believe you. Lucia, honey. I've got something to tell you." Ruth leans in.

"What?" I try not to panic, but my mind instantly goes to Amanda Parker and how the society girls make sport of stealing men from one another.

"You know Harvey goes to the track once in a while for fun. Since the seder, he's invited John a couple of times. Last week Harvey came home and told me that John is a serious gambler. Harvey bets a buck on a horse. He said John puts down fifty, a hundred dollars."

My heart sinks. From the minute I looked at my bankbook and saw that one red withdrawal after pages and pages of deposits, I've been gripped by fear. "You don't think he's gambling *my* money, do you?"

"No, no, I'm sure he would never do something like that. But I know you, and you've been saving every penny since the day we started here."

"Why would he need my money for the house if he has so much of his own?" I wonder aloud. I look at Ruth. She was thinking the same thing.

"Sweetie . . ." I know what she's is going to say before she says it. "You never had the money talk, did you?" I shake my head. She continues, "Hold on. Before we go off half-cocked, let's think this through. You gave him your savings for *your* house."

"Eventually we would combine all our money, anyway," I tell her, justifying my position. "I wanted to be a full partner in everything. Is there anything wrong with that?"

"Of course not. And he's going to be your husband. You have to trust him." Ruth looks at me kindly. "The gambling I wouldn't worry about. You know, sometimes Harvey goes out with the boys and has a few drinks and comes home slightly plowed. I accept it. One guy's cocktails are another guy's horses. What can you do? Everybody has a weakness. You just don't want the weakness to turn into a habit."

On my way home from work that night, as I cross Fifth Avenue, I turn and look back at B. Altman's and burst into tears. The happiest days of my life have been in that building, and now everything is changing.

What will I do without seeing Ruth every day? She knows everything about me, down to such detail that when I confided that I made love to John, she sent me to her uncle, a respected gynecologist on the Upper West Side, so I would be responsible and "use protection." I'll also miss Helen Gannon, who cut fabric so precisely that she seemed to be cutting glass with a diamond. It was never hard to assemble a garment that Helen had cut; she'd look at the measurements and the fabric, then cut to the flow and drape of the customer's figure. Nobody does that anymore, but she did, and now she'll use that talent making drapes or baby clothes. Even though Violet could be annoying, she was always loyal. If you needed help on anything and had to stay late, you could always count on Violet. And Delmarr took me under his wing back when I didn't know a Chanel from a Schiaparelli.

But it's not all about losing my friends. The world itself is losing something. The kind of quality I believe in will no longer be valued. A hand-stitched hem is no longer a study in precision and detail; a garment is slammed through a machine, pulled off the bobbin, and thrown in a bin with dozens of others assembled that day. There's no Delmarr meeting with a client and asking her what she likes, or studying her coloring and shape to create clothes that make her gorgeous. There's no personal service in ready-to-wear. Do women really want to paw through a swinging rack jammed with garments in every size and color? The gentility of my working world will be as woefully out-of-date as a snood come the spring of 1952.

"Why the face?" Papa asks as I'm hanging my coat.

"The store. The Custom Department is getting overhauled." I don't want to get into the details with him, so I go into the kitchen. But he follows me.

"What about your job?" he asks.

"I don't know yet," I tell him in a tone meant to indicate that the discussion is over.

Mama comes downstairs and joins us in the kitchen. "Lu, I think I've decided to wear coral at your wedding. I was sold on the turquoise, but then I thought, I want something brighter, happier. What do you think?"

"Lucia is losing her job," my father tells her.

"Papa," I say.

"So? She's getting married," Mama says lightly. "She doesn't need to work. She'll have more than enough to do at home."

"Now you sound like Claudia DeMartino," Papa says to her.

"Why bring her up?" Mama counters.

"Because she has the same ideas about Lucia that you do." Papa spears a meatball from the pot of sauce simmering on the stove.

Mama gets him a small plate and says, "Antonio, I want you to listen to me. Lucia has chosen a very nice, sophisticated man to marry. They are not going to live like we live. He is a worldly type, he travels, he is part of"—she waves her hand in the air—"uptown. They are going to live in a suburb, okay? With a view of the ocean. In a house with a chandelier from Murano in the entryway. You see what I have? I have the lamp in the hallway that was there when we moved in. This girl is different from us, and you need to accept it." Mama puts her arm around me. "We have one daughter, and I don't want to lose her because you think that no man she brings home is good enough."

"No man *is* good enough," Papa says, "but some are better than others."

"Papa, what is your problem with him?"

"I don't understand him, Lucia."

"Why do you need to understand him?" Mama interjects. "You don't have to live with him, she does."

"You don't want me to marry anybody!" I say.

"That's not true. I accepted Rosemary and have grown to love her. I left my son Exodus in Italy with Orsola because I saw in her many of the things I saw in your mother. They are a good match. If I felt that John Talbot had the qualities of a good husband, I would support you. I don't question that he is in love with you, but I worry, that's all. I worry. I'm sorry. I can't help it."

If only Papa knew how much I needed to talk to him about my fears, today of all days. But he makes it impossible. I constantly feel as though I have to defend my feelings for my fiancé, so I can't be honest. I'm afraid, terribly afraid, that I won't be able to keep up with the pace of John's world, that I'll have to turn a blind eye whenever he wants to invest in another venture or buy something we can't afford. I don't even know how much money he has. I'm afraid to ask and make him angry. I grew up watching my parents share all the responsibilities involving finances, but John acts like those sorts of questions are insignificant, irritating, beneath him. Maybe this is what I'm really scared of: I'm not enough for John Talbot.

"Papa, please don't worry. I need your support. Please." I must look pitiful, because Papa puts his arms around me.

"I will always be here," he says.

"And someday he will love John," Mama promises.

"That would make me very happy," I say. Papa looks so weary in the bright yellow light over the kitchen sink. I'm causing my father to get old before his time.

As I climb the stairs to my room, I wish the floors would never end, that I could keep climbing until I found some kind of peace. I especially miss my brother Exodus tonight. Somehow, when we were all together under one roof, I believed that no harm could ever come to us, curse or no curse.

In the final days before the wedding, I find myself waking up earlier and earlier (today it was three A.M.) and being unable to get back to sleep. I lie in bed and think of John.

This morning I replay a scene from last July in my mind. I'm in John's car, and he's driving me home from work. I ask him to come into the house, but he can't, because he has a business meeting. I'm about to get out of the car, and he says with a big smile, "Do you have the check?" I pull out my checkbook and write out a check to John Talbot. I fold the check at the crease and gently tear it out. "This is all the money I have in the world, honey," I tell him. He takes the check without looking at it, folds it into a small rectangle, then slides it into the handkerchief pocket of his suit jacket. "It ain't much, baby, but it's all you've got," he says, laughing, and then he kisses me. I know it's a joke, but it stings like a slap.

"Lucia!" Mama calls up the stairs.

"Yes, Mama?"

"Can you stop at the Groceria on your way to work?"

I grab my purse. Downstairs, Mama has prepared the bank envelope. "Bring this to Papa and let him go over the figures. The caterer sent a list of hors d'oeuvres you need to look at for the reception. How's Delmarr doing on your dress?"

"Fine, Mama. How many responses have we gotten?"

"We're going to have around three hundred when all's said and done," Mama says. "Where are you having the gifts sent?"

"Out to Huntington."

"How's the house coming?"

"I haven't seen it, Mama. John wants to surprise me. We'll stay there on our wedding night."

"As it should be," Mama says proudly. Thank God she never asks me anything else about my wedding night. Then I'd have two sins on my hands: mortal (making love) and venial (lying about it).

When I arrive at the Groceria, Papa is hanging wheels of Parmesan cheese from the ceiling like a mobile. "Now, that's original," I say.

"Where do you think you get your talent?" He smiles.

"Have you gone to rent your tuxedo yet?"

"Nope." He walks over to the register, and I follow.

"The boys all have their tuxedos. The least you can do—"

"Is show up and give away the most beautiful girl in Greenwich Village." As he methodically places the change in the drawer, he assures me, "I know my role. Your mother goes over it with me every night. She wants the best wedding anyone has ever seen. Finally, one of her children is having a Mariani-style Italian wedding. You know the Barese, they go for the glitz."

"Papa?"

"Yeah?"

"Don't give me any money when I get married. The reception is enough of an expense. Okay?"

"Why do you say that?"

"I want you and Mama to take care of yourselves. I want you to rest."

He closes the register, comes around the counter, and kisses the top of my head. "Sure. Sure."

"I mean it," I tell Papa firmly.

"Go to work," he tells me as he picks up a crate of tomatoes and goes to create his next display.

I walk through the store and wave good-bye to Angelo, who is pouring ice chips on the fresh fish. I'm about halfway up the block when he comes running after me, calling my name.

"Lucia, come back! Something's wrong with Pop."

When I get back to the Groceria, Papa is sitting on a stool. Roberto is trying to give him a cup of water. "Please, Pop. Drink it," Roberto pleads.

"Let me see." I lift Papa's head and look into his eyes. "You're going to Saint Vincent's."

"The hospital? Ba!" he says.

"You're going. And right now," I order him. Papa's color is terrible. He hasn't looked this bad since he fainted in Italy.

"There's nothing wrong with me."

"Hopefully not, but if there is, we're going to make it better."

Roberto goes for the truck while Angelo and I wait with Pop. "I wish you wouldn't make such a big deal out of it," Papa says to me.

"Papa, if anything happened to you, I would die," I say, kneeling beside my father and holding him in my arms.

The worst part of calling home with bad news is that Mama drops the phone, and then you're never sure if she heard it all, and if she did, whether she's all right or in a state of shock. When I tell her Papa is in a room at Saint Vincent's, she drops the phone but picks it back up quickly. She isn't that surprised. She told him his color was poor at breakfast, but he disregarded her completely.

By the time Mama gets to the hospital, she is calm. "Antonio, you've got to take better care of yourself." She stands beside his bed and holds his hand.

Dr. Bobby Goldstein, a heart specialist, joins us in Papa's room. He is lanky and young, with a kind face. "Mr. Sartori, I've been to your market many times." Papa beams. "The best prosciutto in New York City, in my opinion."

"Make my husband better, and you get free prosciutto for the rest of your life," Mama says.

"My wife, always giving away the store," Papa jokes, squeezing Mama's hand. Then he looks at the doctor with a serious expression. "You want to tell us what's wrong with me?"

"The good news is that you didn't have a heart attack," says Dr. Goldstein.

"And what's the bad news?"

"We're not sure exactly what happened to you."

Angelo speaks up. "Doc, Pop was lifting a case of crushed tomatoes when he passed out. Could that have anything to do with it?"

"It could." The doctor smiles. "In the meantime, we want to run some more tests."

"Is there anything Papa can do to make things better?" I ask.

"No lifting. No stress. And in terms of diet—"

"I know all about it: give up butter and eggs and Manhattans."

"Do you smoke?"

"One cigarette after dinner. That's all. Never during the day."

"If you were well, I'd say one won't kill you. But you should stop altogether."

"I'm throwing out those cigarettes!" Mama says.

"Your days of strenuous labor are over. No loading or unloading trucks; no lifting, period. I want you to walk about a half mile a day, but no more. And I'd like you to follow this diet. It may seem bland at first, but in time you won't even miss your old way of eating. We'll need you to stop by for a heart monitor once a month."

"Give up food, work, smoking, and spare time. Anything else, Doc?"

"A good attitude would be helpful. We're going to keep you overnight to do some more tests."

When Dr. Goldstein leaves the room, we try to perk up Papa's spirits. He laughs with us, but I can tell that he's frightened. It's devastating to see the leader of your family full of fear.

"We're going to follow the doctor's instructions exactly," Mama declares.

"Who wants to live like that?" Papa says.

"You do! You want to live, Antonio Sartori, and don't you forget it!" Mama kisses him and lets her cheek rest against his.

"Okay, okay," he tells her. "I'll eat the cottage cheese and lettuce for the rest of my life. Soon I'll grow ears and be a rabbit."

Mama stands up straight and says sternly but tenderly, "I don't care what you turn into as long as you're here and healthy."

Rosemary has thrown herself into my wedding plans like a genuine *comare*. She's put herself in charge of the favors for the guests, traditional Italian *confetti*, tiny net bags of candy almonds. She tied each little bundle with a lace bow; how delicate they look lined up in an open box in the living room. Not to be outdone, Mama's cousins in Brooklyn have made cookie platters for each table. Mama cleared her pantry next to the kitchen and filled every shelf with round platters of baked delicacies—apricot cookies; coconut drops iced in pink buttercream frosting; fig and date bars stacked in pyramids, wrapped in cellophane, and tied with crisp white satin bows. Whenever Mama opens the pantry door, we get a blast of sweet vanilla, cocoa, and lemon sugar through the living room. It reminds me of Christmas. Mama bakes whenever there's something to celebrate.

"I don't know if you'll like this, but it's something we always did in Brooklyn," Ro says, lifting a beautiful bride doll out of a box. The doll is sitting in a pool of lace with a long tulle veil. Her eyes blink when Rosemary moves her; her lips are hot pink, and she has a mole drawn on her chin. "See, we put her on the lead car." I must have a puzzled expression, because Ro sounds a little exasperated as she goes on. "We'll tape her right to the hood ornament of John's Packard."

"It's cute," I tell her, forcing a smile of approval. My Venetian side comes out. I prefer simple adornment. Dolls on cars are pure Neapolitan.

"I knew you'd love it." Rosemary pulls another doll out of the box. This one is dressed in caramel satin, like my bridesmaids, Ruth, Violet, and the doll woman herself, Rosemary. "This is for the attendants' car." Ro looks at me hopefully.

"Did you make those doll dresses?" I ask her.

"Yeah."

"They're pretty. Nice trim work on the lace. Strap her on the second car." Rosemary looks relieved. "And thank you. You've worked so hard on this wedding, and I want you to know that I appreciate it." I give her a big hug.

"Thank you, Lu. You've been so good to me." Rosemary turns away.

"What's the matter?" But there's no need to ask. "It's Maria Grace, isn't it?"

Rosemary fusses with the bride doll, straightening the veil and smoothing the skirts. "I'm having another baby. But keep it a secret. I haven't told Roberto yet. I'm waiting until after your wedding."

I hold her tightly. "Congratulations. Maria Grace will be the baby's guardian angel."

She brushes away a tear. "You know, besides Roberto and our parents, you were the only family who ever held her."

"I know. And I'll never forget what she felt like in my arms." Sometimes I think about the baby, how sweet she smelled and how easily she fit in the crook of my arm.

"What's wrong?" Roberto asks as he comes in and drops the boxes of programs on the front bench.

"Nothing," I tell him. "What's a wedding without a crying jag? Best man, have you picked up the rings?"

"I have it under control."

"Where's the bachelor dinner?"

"The Vesuvio. Where else? That fiancé of yours thinks it's the only restaurant in New York City. Of course, they treat him like a king over there. That's all right. The food is good."

"We're home!" Mama shouts from the hallway. She and Papa are home from his follow-up visit with the doctor. Rosemary, Roberto, and I rush to the entry hall.

"What did the doctor say, Pop?" Roberto asks.

"You're looking at a healthy man. My heart is strong. That caveman diet your mama has me on is working."

"Thank God!" I throw my arms around my parents. "I knew you'd be fine if you listened to the doctors."

"I'm going to put on some tea," Mama says, and smiles.

Papa and Roberto follow her into the kitchen. "Thank God," Rosemary says to me. "Now you'll have a happy wedding day."

"It's the day before your wedding, Mrs. Talbot. Any wish you have, I will grant," John says as I stand on the stoop. He reaches for my hand. It occurs to me that this is the last time he will call for me here at my parents' house. It's the last day that 45 Commerce Street will be my home.

"I know it's against the rules," I begin.

"Doesn't matter."

"I want to go to our house."

"Hmmm." John thinks. "Is that what you really want?"

"Yes! I'm dying to see it!"

"Let's go, then," he says, pulling me close.

John and I don't say much as we speed along the highway to Huntington. As we turn onto the road to the Cascades housing development, I lean over and kiss the man who, this time tomorrow, will be my husband. Suddenly, I don't want to see my house.

"Turn around," I tell him.

"What?" John brakes and pulls over.

"Let's go back to the city."

"I thought you wanted to see the house."

"You've worked so hard on it. Let's stick with our plan." John's intention was for me to see the house for the first time on our wedding night. I want to save something special for tomorrow night. I don't want to ruin the surprise for him, or for myself.

"Are you sure?" John raises his eyebrows.

"Absolutely," I tell him.

John makes a U-turn and gets back on the highway. I look over at his profile, studying every detail as though it were a pattern for a garment. Each feature has beauty and definition: the straight nose, the strong chin, the square jawline, the clear forehead. It's the face of a man without a worry in the world. I catch myself imagining the faces of our children, hoping our daughter will inherit those long black eyelashes and that our son will have that sweet smile. I've almost changed my mind about having a baby. I think I would like to have something only John and I could create together.

"You made the right decision." John seems pleased.

"I did?"

"You need to have some surprises in this lifetime," he says. "Otherwise, what's the point?"

I turn on the radio, and as I search through the static for music, I look up and see Manhattan stretching before us—my home, the city where I was born, the place where I've spent twenty-six happy years. I never thought I'd leave, never thought I'd say good-bye to Commerce Street. But now I have to. I *want* to. I'm going to begin a new life with my husband.

———

Delmarr is surprised when he sees my bedroom. "You *are* an Italian princess. What a room! It's bigger than my apartment. If I were you, I'd just move Talbot in here. What do you want to go all the way out to Hauppauge for?"

"Huntington."

Delmarr makes his way to the back window overlooking the garden. "Whatever. It's still the suburbs. You ever live in the suburbs?" I shake my head. "The 'sub' is in there for a reason. *Sub*tract excitement from your life and replace it with boredom."

"I could never be bored with a view of the ocean."

"You'll see."

Ruth, who's lived in elevator buildings all her life, huffs and puffs through my doorway. "Every time I climb those stairs, I understand why you're so slim." She lays her dress bag over a chair and plops down on my bed. I examine her slacks and sneakers. "Don't worry," she says. "All I have to do is jump into my dress." She sits up. "Your hair is amazing!"

"Mama put it up," I say. She did a beautiful job. We copied a high chignon out of *Vogue*, then Mama anchored John's tiara around it.

"You look stunning," Ruth says.

"Well, homeliness was never this girl's problem," Delmarr says. "The Talbot family won't know what hit them."

"John has no family. There's only his mother, and she's too sick to come. But he'll have my big Italian family soon enough."

"All right, let's get you into your getup." Delmarr removes the muslin balloon from my gown. I have never seen a more beautiful dress. It's a sculptured ball gown, strapless, with a fitted bodice. Delmarr designed a series of tucks under the waist that leads to sweeping flounces attaching over the bustle with a single button.

"My God, it looks like it's made out of cotton candy," Ruth marvels.

"Straight from the runways of Paris," Delmarr says proudly.

"Here are the gloves." Ruth hands me long white satin evening gloves.

"Remember, as the day grows longer—" Delmarr begins.

"So do her gloves!" we all finish in unison.

"Okay, where's my matching bolero for the church? No priest has seen a woman's arms since the Crusades."

"Lu, I didn't make the bolero," Delmarr answers.

"Oh God, no. I don't have anything that will go with this gown, and I can't go sleeveless!" I'm about to cry when Delmarr grins.

"This is my gift." From the muslin sack Delmarr pulls a floor-length white satin evening coat with a portrait collar. The deep sleeves have wide cuffs covered in tiny seed pearls nestled amid beads that shimmer like pavé diamonds. "No girl from B. Altman's Custom Department is going to get married in a tacky bolero."

Like a queen, I put on the dress and Delmarr's coat, this royal robe, and descend the stairs. Papa sees me as I turn the corner of the first landing to greet him in the foyer.

"*Stai contenta*," he says to me, taking my hands.

"Oh, Papa. I am happy." I have never said a truer thing in my life.

I wanted to walk to Our Lady of Pompeii, but Mama wouldn't hear of it. "The hem of your dress will be black in half a block!" So we ride over in Papa's car, with the bridesmaids following in Roberto's car, complete with the doll in the caramel taffeta dress on the hood. Roberto gave John the bride doll for his car last night. The thought of him taping a doll to the hood of his car makes me chuckle.

I peek into the church to see how well it accommodates our three hundred guests. Every pew is practically full. The pew markers, bouquets of white carnations and miniature pink roses tied with caramel-colored satin bows, look lovely. I breathe in the smell of incense, Chanel No. 5 (evidently the perfume of choice for my cousins from Brooklyn), and beeswax from the tall candles surrounding the altar.

Helen Gannon, ready to have baby Gannon at any moment, turns and winks at me from the end of her pew. She is wearing a fuchsia satin swing coat, a glorious contrast with her red hair. It's a wonderful feeling to see everyone you know and love under one roof for the happiest day of your life.

"The priest said to wait in the baptistry," Ruth says. "As if a Jewish girl would have any idea where the baptistry is."

"Don't worry," I say. "We'll go in a second."

I kiss Mama and Papa and wave to Exodus and Orsola. They've been home nearly a week, but I've hardly seen them because I've been so busy tending to last-minute details.

"Come on, Lucia. You're supposed to be in hiding," Ruth chides me.

She and I join Violet and Rosemary in the room off the vestibule. There is a waist-high marble font for baptizing babies under the stained-glass window. A large statue of Saint Michael, patron saint of the angels, carrying a sword and shield, stands in the corner. "Rugged," Ruth comments as she looks him up and down.

She busies herself fussing with my hem while Violet smears on another layer of lipstick. "I'm getting so many good ideas for my wedding," Violet says earnestly. "I wonder if Presbyterians use pew markers."

Rosemary paces back and forth, trying to see out the crack in the window to the street. I stand patiently, holding my bouquet of calla lilies (modeled on Claudette Colbert's *It Happened One Night*). I put the flowers in the font and fluff my skirt. There is an ornate gold cross on the wall, the center of which is a mirror with the sacred heart of Jesus painted on it. I catch the reflection of my eyes in the mirror. Then I lean in and look closely. My eyes are blue, like my father's, and they are clear, since I slept well last night, but something is wrong. I can feel it, and I can see it in my own eyes.

"Ro, what time is it?" I ask.

"It's ten-thirty," she says brightly. "But my watch is always fast."

"At the rehearsal last night, I told John to be here by ten, didn't I?"

"Yes, you did. I heard you," she tells me.

"Is he here yet?"

"I don't see his car. But that doesn't mean anything. You know what? I'm going to go back to the sacristy. I can go outside and around through the side entrance, and I'll see if John is there." Rosemary grabs her coat and goes out the door.

"Men are always late," Violet complains.

"Don't forget. It's a weekend," Ruth says. "Traffic is horrible. John's driving to the Village from the Upper East Side, and it's impossible to get across town on time unless the guy has wings."

We stand in the quiet for what seems like a very long time. I hear the organist pause and begin to play the same tune over again.

Finally, Rosemary pushes the door open and smiles. "He's not here yet, but Roberto did his duty as best man and talked to him around eight o'clock this morning. He was having breakfast, and I'm sure he'll be here any minute."

"What time is it now?" I ask.

"It's exactly a quarter to eleven," Rosemary says as she checks her watch. It's not fast. I made Ruth check the clock in the sacristy a few minutes ago.

"Well, there's nothing to do but wait," I tell them. They don't say anything, but they don't have to. They're worried. And so am I. Where is he? Has something terrible happened? My heart begins to race. I've been dating John Talbot for one year; not once in that entire year was he late. I'm sure Ruth would tell me that there's a first time for everything. But my stomach flips and churns. I feel sick. I need air.

It's funny how a church that's always seemed so ornate and polished can suddenly seem like a hall. When I enter the vestibule, I notice that the collection baskets are stacked off to the side; the bulletin board is tacked with handwritten announcements; and the rubber rain mat, with its series of holes, reveals muddy marble underneath.

"I'm going outside," I tell the girls. I go out to the street. The air is cold, and I inhale slowly to steady myself. I'm amazed that on the most important day of my life, nothing has changed in Greenwich Village. Across the street, a man in overalls pumps oil off his truck through a wide hose down into a valve on the sidewalk. There are three young women at the corner newsstand buying magazines, and in the diner, an old man is being served in his booth by the window. Don't they know what day it is?

"Look, Mommy, the snow queen!" a little girl says to her mother as they pass me. The mother smiles at me, but in her expression, I see who I am. She puts her head down, tightens her grip on her daughter's hand, and keeps walking. The stranger sees it; she knows. And I know, too. She does not want her daughter to see anything so sad.

I wait outside as long as I can, hoping that if I stare at Bleecker

Street long enough, a car carrying my future husband will pull up in front of me. I don't know how many times the cycle of red, yellow, and green is repeated before it becomes clear to me that the car I'm praying for is not coming. I go back into the vestibule. My bridesmaids look at me with forced smiles. Only Ruth looks away. She knows. John Talbot is not going to marry me. Not this morning. Not ever. I've been jilted.

CHAPTER TEN

What happens after a jilting is probably a lot like what happens after a murder. The clues are gathered, the crime scene is cleaned up, all the ugly details are removed, and then life goes on. I don't know what happened in the immediate aftermath, like the seven-course meal at the Isle of Capri restaurant; or who told the band, the Nite Caps, to go home; or where the trays of cookies went. It's been a week, and I haven't asked. My gown is in the closet, and my bouquet is in a shoe box under my bed. I can't find the tiara. It must have gotten lost between the church and home.

The attendants and I waited at the church until three o'clock. I insisted on it. Somehow I convinced myself that three o'clock was the magic time, that John would come to his senses and rush into the church apologetically. The guests, however, left after two hours. My brothers went pew by pew and told them that they could leave, that we would be in touch.

Roberto and Orlando went up to the Carlyle to find that John Talbot was still registered. Orlando cooked up some story about John being ill, and because my brothers were clean-cut and well dressed, the general manager relented and let them into John's room. They found the room clean and the bed made but no sign of John. Not even a toothbrush. The general manager asked my brothers if they were going to take care of the bill. John Talbot owes the Carlyle Hotel $2,566.14. My brothers explained that they weren't family. The general manager didn't believe them.

On the way out, Roberto thought to ask the garage attendant about the Packard. The attendant said he hadn't seen that car in a week or so. Odd. But what isn't odd about a man who disappears?

We called the police, and they issued a missing-person's bulletin after forty-eight hours, mostly as a formality. They had seen this sort of thing before, they told Roberto. It brought me no comfort to know other girls had endured this humiliation. In fact, that made it worse. I provided the police with pictures of John and the tickets for our honeymoon flight to Bermuda. They took everything and promised to return it later.

There's a knock at my bedroom door. I don't answer it. I haven't for a week, why should I now? Mama pushes the door open.

"Lucia?"

I feel guilty for putting my mother through this. It wasn't what she planned for her only daughter. "Hi, Ma."

"I brought you something to eat."

"I don't want it."

"Please, please eat," Mama begs. "Our hearts are broken, seeing what that man did to you. Don't die for him, too! He's not worth it."

Papa's right—Mama is dramatic, Barese down to her soul. "Mama, I'll eat. But I want to come down to the kitchen." I've been lying in bed long enough. The more I stew about John, the angrier I get. I'm not a girl who is content to let things lie. I want to know why he did this to me. And the answers won't come here in my room.

Papa beams when he sees me coming down the stairs. Then he looks up to heaven and thanks God. "I prayed that you would come downstairs, and that you would get angry."

"Well, Papa, both of your prayers have been answered."

———

"Are you sure you want to do this?" Ruth asks as she turns off the expressway to the Cascades housing development.

"Are you getting cold feet?" I ask her. I realize it's an ironic choice of words, but Ruth doesn't let it throw her.

"A little. I lied to Harvey and told him we were going shopping. He was afraid if we drove out here, we might run into John. It's possible he's hiding out here."

"The police checked already," I say.

"Let's have a plan anyway. If he *is* here, we won't get out of the car."

"Fine."

"What do you think happened to him?" Ruth asks tenderly.

"I don't know."

"Lucia, I want to help you, you know that. But I don't understand why you want to see the house. Why would you torture yourself that way? You have to forget about him."

"Ruth, you know how we make clothes?"

Ruth looks confused.

"It's the only thing I know how to do. You make a drawing, I break it down into pieces, those pieces are made into a pattern, the pattern is placed on the fabric, the fabric is cut, we stitch the pieces together, and then we have a garment."

"Okay, but—"

"Listen, Ruth. I sat down in my room with a notebook and made a list of everything that I knew for sure about John Talbot. First I described him: that's the drawing. Then I went through my datebook and wrote down every place we'd ever been, especially the places that we went more than once. Huntington Bay, Creedmore, the Vesuvio, all of them. Those are the pieces."

"Okay, I get it. Now you're sewing it together."

"And when I'm done, maybe I'll have something to look at that will help me understand what's happened to me."

"You haven't been out here since . . ."

"Actually, we drove out here the day before the wedding. But at the last minute I told him I wanted to save the surprise for our wedding night."

"What's the address?"

"It's the last lot on this street." I point to the end of the block. "With a view of the bay."

"What a neighborhood," Ruth says as she passes the new homes with their two-car garages and straw on the ground where the grass will grow. "No wonder you loved it so much."

"There, Ruth!" I point to the hill that would have been my front yard.

Ruth pulls the car over in front of the lot. But there is no house, only a FOR SALE BY OWNER sign on the tree where the driveway was supposed to be. A phone number is printed on the bottom. Farther off in the empty field is a man searching for something in the back of his pickup truck.

"Are you sure this is the right place?" Ruth says, obviously hoping I'm wrong.

"Yes. This is it." I get out of the car and climb up the hill to the man. "Sir?"

"Yes, miss?" He smiles.

"Is this your property?" I ask.

"No, it isn't. I work for the man who owns it."

"John Talbot?" This is the first time I have said his name aloud since I was left at the altar, and my icy tone is not lost on the caretaker.

"No. His name is Jim Laurel. Do you know him?"

"No, I don't."

"Well, if you know Huntington, you know Jim. He owns this entire development."

"So this property wasn't sold to anyone?" I don't even want to know the answer, since it makes John's lies so much worse to know that he *planned* to ruin my life.

"No, it just went on the market. You interested?"

"Maybe." I can barely speak, I'm so upset.

Ruth joins us. "We're looking at, um, lots of lots," she tells him.

"Take my card." The man gives Ruth his card and gets into his truck. As soon as he is gone, I sit down on the ground.

Ruth sits down next to me. "Come on, Lucia. Let's go."

"He lied about *everything*," I say, not so much for Ruth to hear it as for me to believe it.

"I'm so sorry," she says.

I look over the lot, and instead of seeing a sandy hill covered in patches of wild bamboo, low brush, and clumps of old seaweed, I see my home. Each detail is as I imagined it, the Tudor-castle door at the entrance, the glazed brick, the boxwood trimmed low on either side of the slate-and-concrete sidewalk, the rose taffeta draperies blowing in the breeze, and the chandelier, which I took hours to choose in Murano, twinkling in the foyer. The sights and sounds of my home are as real to me as the sand that I dig into with my hands.

"Come on, it's getting late," Ruth says, walking to the very spot where my front door would have been. "You've been through enough for one day."

I start to follow Ruth down the hill but stop and point to the bay. "See that orange haze? It sort of settles over the water like sheer chiffon? The first time I made love to him, that's what the bay looked like. Just exactly like that."

Ruth takes my hand. I turn around as I walk to the car with her. I know that I will never see this place again.

Ruth and I don't say a word as we drive home. We're almost to Commerce Street when she breaks the silence.

"There's one thing I really don't understand. Do you mean to say that John Talbot drove you all the way out to Huntington the day before you got married, and there was *no house*? How did he think he'd get away with this? And what made you change your mind?"

I sit and think about this. Ruth pulls over, puts the car in park, and it idles as I search for an answer. "Somewhere deep within me, I must have known the truth. I knew he wasn't who I thought he was. But I thought I could make him into the man I knew he could be."

"Oh, Lucia," Ruth says sadly.

"And somehow I believed that I was better because he loved me.

You know how it is, Ruth. You think a man can give you what you want, so you surrender. Papa was right. I loved the way John looked, the places he took me, and the life he promised to give me. It was all on the surface."

Ruth nods. She understands, and I surely do, too, what my attraction was to John Talbot. Now I have to figure out the rest of the puzzle so this never happens again.

Papa's Veneto traditions have once again lost the Christmas wars. We won't be fasting on Christmas Eve. Rosemary has prepared the feast of the seven fishes with Mama, and we're all together. Even Exodus and Orsola decided to stay for the holidays. I think Mama had something to do with that. She convinced my brother that I needed him, and Exodus still wants to make up to Mama for staying in Italy.

Mama set a beautiful table: silver candelabras filled with white candles and her best china on a red tablecloth. After we sit down, Rosemary clinks her wineglass with a spoon. "First of all, merry Christmas, everyone!" What a change this is from last Christmas, when Rosemary was the meek new bride who had to ask Papa if she could hang lights in the window. This year she not only put lights in the windows, she also strung them through evergreen garlands down the railings and wove them through the front fence. Orlando calls it Sicily North. "Second," Ro continues, "Roberto and I are expecting a baby in May!"

We leap out of our seats to hug and kiss the ecstatic parents-to-be. In the hubbub we hear the tinkling of a spoon against glass again. Everyone turns to look at Exodus.

"We have news, too!" Exodus announces.

"You're moving home?" Orlando asks.

"No, we're having a baby also! Ours is due in June!"

We cheer the second bit of happy news, but I can't help feeling sad in the midst of all this joy. My brothers seem to know how to pick good partners and create a life. Why can't I?

"Somebody get the door," Mama says when we hear the bell.

"It must be Delmarr. I invited him for dessert," I tell them and go to the hallway to answer the door. Usually I peek through the glass, but Rosemary's garlands obstruct the window. I throw open the door.

"Lucia . . ." John Talbot is standing in the rain on our stoop, wearing his blue cashmere overcoat. I don't move. At the bottom of the stoop are two policemen. I try to close the door, but I'm not fast enough. John pushes it open.

"Please, Lucia. I need to talk to you," he says softly.

"What are you doing here?"

"I came to tell you I'm sorry."

"*Sorry?*" The word sounds so weak and empty, I wish he hadn't said it.

"I have to tell you what happened," John says nervously. "I know you don't have to listen, but please give me a chance to explain."

I look at his face, still possessed of the fine features that I loved so, but there's something in his eyes that frightens me. His shoes are scuffed and unpolished, and even the coat is shabby-looking. He is clean-shaven, but I can smell liquor on him, a first. I look at what a mess he has made of himself, of me, and I can't believe it. Where were the signs that we would come to this?

"Where have you been?" I ask as I let him in and close the door behind him. He'll never be able to explain what he's done, but I might as well learn what I can.

"It doesn't matter."

"Lucia, are you okay out there?" Roberto calls out.

"Sshh. Don't say anything," John whispers. He puts one hand on the doorknob to go back outside.

Roberto comes around the corner. When he sees John Talbot, he becomes enraged. "How dare you come here!"

"I need to talk to Lucia," John says with as much bravado as he can muster.

At the sound of his voice, all my brothers, as well as my father, rush into the hallway. The women stand behind them like a frontline battalion, present and ready to protect me.

"You want to talk to my sister? Are you crazy? After what you did?" Roberto shouts.

"I don't owe you an explanation. I owe your sister."

"You have *that* fucking right," Roberto says. I hear my mother gasp at his language. "Where's her money?"

He pushes past me, grabbing John by the collar and pinning him against the wall. John, clearly weakened and unable to fight back, slumps against the wall. Roberto slams John's head into the plaster. *"Where's her money?"* John doesn't answer. Roberto slams his head again. "You thief!" John still says nothing. Roberto hits his head on the wall a third time. "Where's her fucking money?"

Part of me wants Roberto to keep hurting him, as payback for the humiliation I endured on our wedding day. But I can't bear to watch my strong brother beat this pitiful man.

"Stop it, Roberto!" I say. My brother steps back, and John slumps against the wall. "Please. I want to talk to him."

The policemen, who had been waiting on the stoop, push the door open and put John in handcuffs. "That's all the time you get. I'm sorry, ma'am. He told us you were his wife, and it bein' Christmas, we gave him a gift." One of them gives John a shove. "Don't push it."

I reach for John. "No, Lucia," my father says, holding my arm.

My brothers stand guard, as they have done all my life, until the police car bearing John Talbot disappears around the corner of Barrow Street. I cannot move.

"The bastard even ruined Christmas," Roberto says.

"Yes," I say quietly. He ruined our wedding, our future, and even Christmas. And I would like to know why, even after all of that, I still love him.

The days off between Christmas and New Year's are usually my favorite, because my work is done. Whoever needed a new dress bought it, and by Christmas Eve it has been altered, pressed, and delivered. But this was supposed to be my first Christmas as a married lady. I am full of unanswered questions about what happened with John, and I haven't been able to sleep since he showed up at my door. If only I could understand why he left me, I would be able to press on.

Most of my friends try not to bring up the subject. It could be that they want to spare me the embarrassment, but I suspect that they believe it was due to some flaw in *my* character that I didn't anticipate it. I was asleep at the wheel of my own life, and I deserved what happened to me. I made this bed, and I lie alone in it.

I've been called in for questioning by the police, which, on top of the personal shame of the situation, fills me with fear and dread. What if they think I had knowledge of John's business dealings? I called the only lawyer I know personally, Arabel's husband, Charlie Dresken. He assuaged my fears and told me that he would be there with me, and that I should fully cooperate with the investigation. "You have nothing to hide," he told me. That may be true, but why is it that all I want to do is hide?

The police didn't give Charlie all the details of John's illegal activities, but they did say they were extensive. The police have asked me for a complete list of all the gifts John gave me. They also requested a calendar of our social life, including times and places, as far back as I could remember. It wasn't hard to assemble, since I collected keepsakes from the moment I met him: the McGuire Sisters program from New Year's Eve, menus from restaurants, matchbooks, scribbled poems, even a dried rosebud plucked off a trellis in Montauk from the day we first made love. Putting it all together, though, was almost unbearable.

While the police gather their information, I begin to gather my own. There's one person whose face has haunted me over the last several weeks. I had grown fond of John's mother, Mrs. O'Keefe, and she had begun to look forward to my visits, too. Even though she couldn't speak, she was alert and aware of everything going on around her. I've been worried about her through the holidays. John Talbot is still in jail, and I doubt she knows what happened to him.

As I walk from the train station to the entrance of Creedmore, I wonder what I will say to Mrs. O'Keefe when I get there. The regular receptionist is on duty, but when I greet her, instead of waving me in as usual, she asks, "How can I help you?"

It dawns on me that I've always come here with John, so she might not recognize me on my own. "Could I go inside and see Mrs. O'Keefe?"

Her expression changes from friendliness to concern. "Didn't any-body tell you?"

"No." I get a pain in my stomach.

"She passed away."

"When?"

"Let me check the date." She studies a log behind the desk. "Sylvia O'Keefe died on November sixth."

I don't thank the nurse. I simply turn toward the door. But before I can walk away, I need to know one more thing.

"I'm sorry to bother you again," I say, turning around. "But . . . was she alone?"

The receptionist reaches out and pats my hand. "That nice son of hers was with her when she passed." November sixth? Why didn't John tell me his mother died? What kind of man withholds such in-formation?

On my first day back at work after Christmas vacation, Charlie Dres-ken waits for me during my lunch hour outside the police station on East Sixty-seventh Street. When we go inside, Charlie speaks to an of-ficer at the front desk. Then I follow him to a small office, where we are greeted politely by a nice Italian detective around Papa's age, whose badge identifies him as M. Casella. I begin by telling him that I went to see Sylvia O'Keefe. He was already aware of her passing.

"Miss Sartori, how long did you know John Talbot?"

"One year."

"Was that the only name you knew him by?"

"Are there others?" I ask, my dismay mounting.

"He used five aliases, all with the first name John. The other sur-names are O'Bannon, Harris, Acton, Fielding, and Jackson. Sounds like a law firm, doesn't it?" He smiles, but I don't. "Hmm. He used his real name with you."

I don't respond to the detective's comment. It does not make me feel better to know that John's name was the only true thing he shared with me.

"Did he live with you?" the detective asks matter-of-factly.

"We were engaged to be married. I live with my family. And always have," I tell him in a tone that lets him know my character is not to be disparaged, despite my poor taste in men.

"Did you ever know a woman named Peggy Manney?"

"No."

"She's Sylvia O'Keefe's daughter. She was not on speaking terms with her mother, which created a perfect situation for John Talbot, as you called him, to move in and take control of Mrs. O'Keefe's finances." My mind goes back to the day John told me he was an only child. "Mr. Talbot spent the last several years bilking Mrs. O'Keefe out of her savings, cash, and goods."

"What?"

"John Talbot is a con man, Miss Sartori. He made his living by what we call negotiated theft. He'd build trust with people, and pretty soon he'd be in business with them. They provided the money, and he'd use it to fund whichever scam he had going at the time. When things didn't work out, he'd run. It worked for a long time, because most people are too embarrassed to report when they get taken."

"But you think he stole from his own mother?" I can't believe it. I saw their close relationship. He loved her.

"She wasn't his mother."

"*What?*" Was there anything I knew about John Talbot that was true?

"Talbot found her at church, can you believe it? Went to Saint Anthony's Parish in Woodbury and tagged her. She was a perfect victim—wealthy, lived alone, estranged from her daughter, eager for companionship—so he set about charming her, ingratiated himself into her life. She more or less took him in as her own. In time he convinced her to let him manage all of her finances. When she got sick, he put her in Creedmore. As far as we know, he never physically harmed the old lady, but he certainly brainwashed her. Her home in Woodbury became his base of operations."

"But he lived at the Carlyle Hotel."

"Sure, he had a suite there off and on, depending on what he was up to in the city. Guess whose money was bankrolling it? Sylvia O'Keefe's. That's why we need an accounting of whatever he gave you, in case any of it technically belongs to her rightful heir. Peggy Manney has made a list of her mother's jewelry that's missing." Detective Casella hands me the list, and I pass it to Charlie. My head begins to pound, and I rest my face in my hands.

"I know, it's unbelievable." The detective shrugs. "And if Mrs. O'Keefe hadn't died and the money hadn't run out, he'd still be fat and happy."

"And married to me," I say softly.

"You're lucky. So are a string of other girls he almost victimized. Amanda Parker, for example."

"What's she got to do with this?"

"Talbot tagged her, too. He wanted her father to bankroll some construction scheme he had going. We tracked this story down through a developer out on Long Island—"

"Jim Laurel?" I ask weakly.

"How do you know Jim Laurel?"

"John had supposedly purchased land in the Cascades development from him. He said he was building our house on it."

"That was never going to happen. Jim Laurel is a smart businessman. Talbot told him that he was in business with Daniel Parker, and Laurel wanted in. But it turned out to be all smoke and mirrors. Did Talbot ever get any goods or cash from you?"

"Almost all of my life's savings. Seven thousand five hundred dollars."

The detective makes a note of my loss. "Do you know that John Talbot was with Mrs. O'Keefe when she died?" I ask him.

"That was the least he could do."

"I think he genuinely cared about her."

The detective shakes his head as though I'm an idiot. "We found a storage unit filled with stuff. Boxes and boxes of stuff from B. Altman's. You work there, correct?"

"Yes. Our bridal registry was there, too."

"So this stuff, you think . . ." He hands me another list, which I scan quickly.

"These were for our wedding. I had all the registry gifts sent to a post office box in Huntington. John said he was picking them up and taking them to our house."

"These goods aren't stolen, then. They should be returned to you."

"I don't want any of it."

"You can decide that when we return them. By law we can't keep this property if it belongs to you. You're not the one under arrest here." He jots down some notes and then looks at me. For the first time, Mr. Casella softens. "Take the stuff back. He owes you."

Then he goes on to ask me more questions, mostly about places John and I had been.

"There's one more item Mrs. O'Keefe's daughter asked about. Did Talbot ever give you a two-carat emerald-cut diamond in a platinum setting?"

"For our engagement."

I can tell the detective doesn't want to say what he has to say next. "You need to return that. It was stolen from Mrs. O'Keefe and right-fully belongs to her daughter. You understand, I'm sure."

Charlie nods at me. "It's okay," he says, and pats my hand.

I open my purse and give the detective the ring, which I have kept in a ring box. I get up to leave.

"If we need to get in touch with you . . ." the detective begins.

"Call my office." Charlie gives Mr. Casella his card.

Out in the street, I become so angry that I can't think. "I'm such a fool!"

"No, you're not a fool. John Talbot was an excellent con man," Charlie insists. We hail a cab, and we ride in silence until Charlie drops me off at work. "Lucia?" he says. "Forget him. You're a young girl, and dwelling on this won't do you any good."

"Thank you for coming with me today, Charlie."

As I enter the store, even the smell of exotic perfumes can't revive my spirits. Ruth is waiting for me in the Hub, ready with a cup of hot coffee and a cinnamon bun from Zabar's. "So, what happened?"

Delmarr comes out of his office and motions to me.

"Come on, Ruth," I say. "I might as well tell the story once."

"Jesus, I heard the whole story down in the islands," Delmarr begins.

"What?"

"John Talbot went after Daniel Parker's dough. Tried to get a loan, then tried to get a job in his brokerage firm. But Parker had someone run a background check on him, and they found a lot of holes in his stories. They also wanted a complete report on what he had in the bank. Before things went too far, Talbot ditched the whole plan, even if that meant ditching Amanda, too. To mess with a guy like Dan Parker . . . I don't know if that makes Talbot courageous or an idiot."

"Did Amanda Parker talk to the police?" I ask, knowing the answer. "Of course not. Girls on the Upper East Side don't get dragged into police stations to have their integrity called into question. No need to make it worse for *her*."

"It is worse for her," Ruth says. "It made the paper." She hands me an article from the morning *Herald*. The headline reads, SOCIETY POSER NABBED. I close my eyes, not reading another word. I give the article back to Ruth.

After returning all of the gifts on the police list, including the starfish brooch (another of Sylvia O'Keefe's pieces), there's only one other bit of business to tend to before I am finished with John Talbot for good. I must talk to Patsy Marotta at the Vesuvio.

The cabbie gives me a roguish grin as I climb into his cab with an enormous muslin sack. "For me?" he asks.

"Nope," I say flatly.

"It ain't a dead body, is it?"

"No, sir," I say, a touch of impatience creeping into my tone.

"You got enough room back there?"

"Yes, sir." I give him the directions to the Vesuvio. I'm not feeling very chatty.

The restaurant doesn't get busy until about eight o'clock, so I've planned to arrive around six. As I push through the polished brass door, I can't stop myself from thinking that this is the first time it wasn't opened for me by John Talbot.

I stand in the doorway and look around the dark restaurant, which smells of fine tobacco, sweet wine, and prime rib roasting in rosemary, which must be the special tonight. Patsy is where he always is, at the bar, half propped on the stool, one foot resting on the brass rail and the other extended out, as if he's always ready to jump up and run to the kitchen. The bartender gives Patsy a look when he catches sight of me. Patsy puts out a cigarette, then turns to face me. "I thought you'd come see me eventually."

"I won't take too much of your time," I say.

"Would you like something to drink?" he asks.

"No, thank you." I glance at the empty tables. "Could we talk there, maybe?"

Patsy rises and shows me to a table.

"Did you know about John?" I ask him. "Do you know he's in jail?"

"The police spoke to me." He shrugs.

"Well, Mr. Marotta, since John Talbot gave me this mink coat in your restaurant, I'm returning it to you. I figure you would know where it came from."

"I do know where it came from."

"Where?"

"From Antoine Furriers of New York City and Toronto. It's totally on the up-and-up."

"Antoine Furriers may be on the up-and-up, but I'm sure this particular coat was stolen."

"It wasn't. He earned it."

"I doubt that."

"No, really. From time to time I would hear of jobs and pass along the information to John, because I knew he had his finger in several pots. Or so I thought. The owners of Antoine Furriers have lunch here a few times a week. They told me they were looking for someone to transport furs between New York and Toronto. They had a driver

and a truck, but they needed a more experienced businessman to accompany the goods over the border and make the transaction. John
did it for several months, and he asked for the coat in lieu of cash. It
was entirely legit."

There's that word "legit" again. It makes my skin crawl.

Patsy continues, "You keep the coat. It's yours."

I stand and pick up the unwieldy bundle. "You know, everybody
keeps telling me to keep this stuff, as though it's the stuff that matters.
Like a coat or a ring or a chafing dish can make up for all that's happened to me. I can tell you, Mr. Marotta, that they don't make up for
anything. I get no comfort from these *things*."

Patsy doesn't answer me. He just gazes toward the kitchen before
taking a puff of his cigarette.

I thank him, and knowing that I won't come to his restaurant again,
I say good-bye.

"You're a good kid" is the last thing he says to me.

The official closing of the Custom Department at B. Altman & Company is set for November 1, 1952. They graciously informed us this
morning by a mimeographed letter on each of our desks, signed by
someone whose name we've never seen before. The letter said we have
exactly seven months to wrap up any outstanding work; but first, dear
employees, kill yourselves through another June Swoon so that you're
too exhausted to find yourselves a new job outside the company.

Ruth swears that closing the Custom Department is a step toward
luring us all into retail, where we will sell from the floor and oversee
alterations from time to time. The rats are jumping off the sinking
ship on a regular basis. Every day someone else comes in and announces his or her resignation. Violet left to become a housewife.
Only Delmarr, Ruth, and I hold out. When we have lunch with
Helen, we tell her that baby David came at the right moment. She
is spared the painful details of disassembling our shop. It started
with the high-end fabric stock, for which no further orders were to be
placed. Then they began to take our best machines and send them
God knows where. And we're actually supposed to refer our private

customers to a new department called In-Store Consultation, where girls right out of high school run around the store gathering garments they think the customer will like. This is what B. Altman's now calls "personal service." We hear it was the brainchild of Hilda Cramer, who wasn't fired but was given a sweet deal that moved her out of Altman's and into her own private salon in White Plains. Occasionally we hear her on the radio with the style maven Ilke Chase, talking fashion for the working woman. Ruth and I joke that we may call and make an appointment with her, since we're unemployed career girls who could use some good advice.

I turn in my seat and look out the window. This morning I felt okay; not better, but on my way to better. It's been a month since I was questioned by the detective. I know I have to stop dwelling on the past year and start thinking about my future. Last night I made a list of the designers I most admire, and even went so far as to look up their addresses and phone numbers. I intend to call every one of them, even Claire McCardell, and see who's in need of an experienced seamstress with a specialty in the application of beadings and trim.

Ruth calls to me from the front desk. Even our receptionist is gone, so whoever is walking by picks up the phone. "It's for you, Lu." I answer.

"Lu? It's Roberto. It's Pop again. He fell."

"Is he at Saint Vincent's?" I ask.

"No, come home."

I jump in a cab and rush home. I run up the stoop and find Rosemary waiting at the door. She looks miserable, six months pregnant, standing in the door with tears streaming down her face. "It's not good, Lucia," she tells me.

The boys have carried Papa up one flight and into his bedroom. When I enter, I blurt out, "Has anyone called Exodus?" It must be the sight of my papa in his bed in the middle of the day, something I've never seen before, that makes me want all of us together again. Maybe having one of us missing weakens Papa's resolve. Maybe all of us together could pull him through.

The bell rings downstairs. Rosemary and Roberto go to let Dr. Goldstein in. Mama is sitting on a footstool at the head of Papa's bed.

I take my father's hand and sit down on the bed next to him. "Papa, are you okay?" I ask him, knowing he is not. "I love you, you know. With all my heart."

"*Grazie*," he murmurs weakly.

The doctor asks us to wait outside, but Mama stays put. After a few minutes the doctor joins us in the hallway.

"I'm sorry to have to tell you this, but your father is very sick. We've known it for some time now."

"But his heart . . ." I can barely speak.

"It's not his heart. He has cancer. We believe it began in his pancreas, and it has spread to his liver."

"Cancer?" I say softly because I don't believe it.

"It was diagnosed in November. We've known for some time that we'll be able to do something for his pain, but that's all."

I turn to my brothers in disbelief. "Did any of you know?" They are as shocked as I am.

My mind goes back to the month of November, to the night that Papa came home from the doctor while we were preparing *confetti* for the wedding. He and Mama gave us a good report. They said he was healthy. They must have lied so I would have a happy wedding. I begin to cry. Orlando puts his arms around me.

"Is he in pain?" Roberto asks.

"Soon we can give him morphine, which we administer through an IV drip. I've spoken with your mother, and she'll arrange for a nurse to come and take care of that."

"How long does he have?" Angelo asks.

"It could be days. Maybe less."

We hear a muffled cry from the bottom of the stairs. We look down at Rosemary, who weeps into her hands, feeling the loss as keenly as we do.

"What can we do?" Orlando asks.

"Stay with him, be strong for him. That's all you can do. And I'll come back and see him whenever I'm needed."

I say, "Angelo, call Exodus right away. Roberto, take care of Rosemary. Orlando, go back to the Groceria, keep it open, and make sure everything's running smoothly. Papa would want that. Okay?" Orlando nods and goes. I stand on the landing for a moment, say a quick prayer pleading with God to save my father, and then go back to my parents' bedroom.

I tiptoe in. Mama has not moved. She holds Papa's hand and looks at him as though the intensity of her gaze could cure him. Papa has gone to sleep. I put my hands on his face and kiss his cheek. I whisper to him, "We're here, Papa."

The boys, Mama, and I take turns sitting with him day and night. I don't know how many days; we have stopped counting. Sometimes I look at Roberto's face and know that he feels guilty about his fights with Pop. I'm so ashamed of the night that I told my parents to rot in hell that I beg God to wake Papa up so I can apologize for my terrible behavior. If I could have that moment back, I never would have said those things. I didn't mean them. And now I know Papa was right about everything. He was right about John Talbot.

Taking care of Papa becomes the focus of life in our home. It's been two days since the doctor visited. Papa takes broth and weak tea, and while the morphine dosages are small, they help him sleep. He knows that he is dying, but he is determined to wait until Exodus arrives. We tell him repeatedly that Exodus is on his way, though Orsola will have to stay behind due to her pregnancy. When I talk to Papa, I try to lift his spirits: "Papa, you will have two grandchildren by summertime!" This makes him smile. When he naps, I cry, knowing that he will never see his grandchildren.

Exodus should be here by tomorrow morning. Papa is weakening; his fight to stay alive is really the fight to see Exodus one last time. Mama is amazing. She doesn't cry, and at night she still climbs into their bed, and he sleeps in her arms.

The boys alternate working at the Groceria and being here with Papa. There is none of the usual squabbling or bickering, so I'm surprised when I hear the low tones of a tense conversation at the bottom of the stairs. I look at Mama, who motions for me to see who it is.

"Maybe Ex made it sooner!" I tell her. Papa's eyes open, and he smiles.

Roberto comes up the stairs, followed by an older man whom I've never seen before. "Lucia, this is our uncle Enzo."

Roberto steps aside. At first I extend my hands as one would to a stranger, but when I look into his eyes and see my father, I throw myself into his arms. The two men are so alike. The broad shoulders and delicate hands, the large head and curly salt-and-pepper hair, the paunch, not enough to require a diet but enough to consider one from time to time. "I'm so happy to meet you. Thank you for coming to see Papa," I tell him.

"I came as soon as I heard." Even his voice reminds me of my father, when he was healthy and strong.

I take Uncle Enzo into my parents' room. Mama stands when she sees him, and for the first time in three days, she begins to cry. Her sobs awaken Papa. I don't think he initially believes that his brother is here. Not until Uncle Enzo kneels next to the bed and takes him into his arms. Papa looks so small. He makes a sound, a deep moan, as if he has finally released a sadness that he has been carrying since before I was born.

I motion to Mama that we should give them some privacy. I put my arm around her and lead her out of the room. Before I close the door, I look at the two of them, two boys who came such a long way to fulfill a dream. Years of estrangement and hard feelings fall away as my uncle holds my father.

Angelo gives up his room for Uncle Enzo. The nurse comes and tells us Papa's system is starting to shut down but that he has a strong heart. She wants to increase the morphine dosage. Mama explains to Papa that more morphine will ease his pain. Papa shakes his head decisively. Mama assumes he doesn't want to go to sleep until Exodus arrives, so she tells the nurse to keep the medication level where it is.

None of us can sleep. We stay in Papa's room, and when we need a break, we go down into the living room, where Rosemary has made sandwiches and cookies and there is always a fresh pot of coffee. What a Sartori she has turned out to be. My brother Roberto is a lucky man to have such a splendid wife.

We're all relieved when the front door opens and Exodus bolts in. "Where is he?" Exodus drops his bags and runs up the stairs. We follow behind him and pile into Mama and Papa's room, as we used to do every Sunday morning before church. Mama would make us come to their room to see if there were shoes to be polished or hair to be slicked down with a touch of pomade. Uncle Enzo is on one side of Papa, and Mama is on the other. Exodus hesitates when he sees Uncle Enzo, trying to make sense of the situation. Uncle Enzo gets up and steps away. Exodus puts his hand on our uncle's back and then moves in and kneels next to Papa. "Pop, I'm here. Can you hear me?" Papa hasn't opened his eyes since last night. "Squeeze my hand, Pop. It's Ex. I'm here. I made it. I made it." Papa must squeeze my brother's hand, because Exodus yells, "That's it, Pop! Squeeze my hand! Good!"

Mama runs her hand through Papa's thick, curly hair. Then she pulls her handkerchief from her pocket. Papa's eyes are closed, and a tear rolls down his nose and off his cheek. As Mama gently wipes it away, I hear her say, "He's gone." Her eyes never leave his face. "My love is gone."

When the funeral home comes to take Papa away, the boys insist that Mama, Rosemary, and I stay in the living room until he's in the hearse. Uncle Enzo stays with the boys. It's as if he has been a part of our lives all along.

"Mama, when did you call Uncle Enzo?" I ask.

"I didn't call him."

"I called him," Rosemary says softly. "I couldn't bear for Papa to go without saying good-bye to his only brother. I hope it was all right."

Mama embraces Rosemary. "It was exactly right."

In the weeks after Papa's death, our family came together as never before, and we found out what Antonio Sartori meant to people in

Greenwich Village. Over the years Papa would come home with funny stories about customers; sad stories about families who needed food, which he'd send over; or poignant stories about what it was like to be an old-fashioned grocer in a modern world. The only frozen item Papa allowed in the store was the ice to lay the fresh fish on.

I always thought I was like my mother's people, but when Papa died, I saw how much I am like him. He was a perfectionist. "To you, they are a crate of oranges; to me, they are a sculpture!" he'd say as he stacked oranges into a glorious pyramid with waxy leaves in the spaces between. He made topiaries out of pasta boxes and ceiling treatments out of dried herbs. The ropes around the casings of salamis were works of art, knotted a certain way and at a certain length so the customers could see what a delicacy they were buying. I have the same feeling about sewing. Perfection was my problem and the customer's right—after all, she was paying. Papa felt the same way.

We had one strange request during Papa's funeral. When we called Domenic to tell him of Papa's passing, he was devastated, but then he asked us a favor. He wanted us to take a photograph of Papa in the casket. When Mama heard, she said absolutely not. But I told the funeral director, who agreed to take the picture, and I sent it off to Cousin Domenic without telling Mama.

Uncle Enzo comes back to the city to visit and to see if there's anything we need. We put on a big dinner for him. Rosemary is hoping that someday the families can reunite. She's working on it. Mama is happy to see Uncle Enzo, but she hasn't quite warmed up to the idea of seeing Zia Caterina. We're not going to push her. Mama will let us know when she's ready, and then we'll go for the full-blown reunion.

After the dishes are cleared, I ask Uncle Enzo to come into the kitchen. I say, "Do you remember the curse Zia Caterina put on me before I was born?"

"Oh, she didn't mean it!"

"I'm sure she didn't," I say. Clearly, he is as upset by the memory as Mama was when Roberto confessed the family secret last fall. "Still, what exactly did she say?"

"She said she wanted you to be beautiful but unlucky in love."

"Well, Zio, you can tell her that the curse worked out fine."

"Lucia, she didn't mean it. Caterina has a temper. I've lived with it for forty years. She curses everything: the priests, you, me, the cow. Everything."

"It's okay. Really, it's okay." I embrace him. "Once a curse comes true, it's over." I look my uncle in the eye. "It's *over*. Right?"

"*Sì, sì, finito, finito.*"

CHAPTER ELEVEN

*A*ntonio Giuseppe Sartori II was born on June 1, 1952. Mama wept when Rosemary told her the baby's name. And there's nothing like a new baby in the house to alleviate grief. He's a good baby, with a sweet temperament.

About a month later Delmarr invites me to lunch as a thank-you for getting him through the final bridal season of the Custom Department. He takes me to the cafeteria at Saks Fifth Avenue, partly as a joke but mostly because the food is delicious.

"Kid, you've had one helluva year."

"Don't I know it." I shake my head slowly. "The worst was losing Papa."

"The Talbot fiasco was terrible, too. I still blame myself a bit for that. I'm sorry I introduced you. I'm sorry I couldn't see him for what he was. I should have done a better job of protecting you," Delmarr says sadly.

"It's not your fault. Let me tell you how I *know* it's not your fault."

"Okay."

"And after all that happened . . . I still love him." Delmarr is the only person in the world I could admit this to, and I am relieved to finally say it out loud.

"Why, Lucia? Why do you still love him?" Delmarr says tenderly.

"Why does anybody love anybody who has hurt them? Because there's always hope. Papa didn't talk to his brother for thirty years. At the end of his life, his brother came to see him, and they forgave each other. All my life, there was this impossible family burden we were hauling around, and then in the final moments, Papa got the best gift of all: his brother's forgiveness. I know that's why he went like an angel."

"I don't think Talbot's going like an angel."

"Probably not."

"I have a proposition for you," Delmarr says.

"You know I'm a nice girl," I halfheartedly tease.

"Yeah, my loss, kid. Anyhow, I got a new job, and I want you to come with me."

"I knew Claire McCardell would hire you!" This news is a huge relief. I won't have to leave behind everything familiar if I can continue to work with Delmarr.

"No, I'm out of retail, custom, all of that. I'm going to Hollywood to work for Helen Rose."

I'm flabbergasted. "Helen Rose who made Elizabeth Taylor's wedding gown when she married Nicky Hilton?"

"The very one."

"Delmarr, how on earth did you meet up with Helen Rose?"

"Her second in command went to the competition. And she heard about me, get this, from Hilda Cramer, who was out there on radio assignment to interview the great costume designers of film."

"*Hilda* got you a job?" I thought I had already heard the most amazing news, but this is even better.

"Oh, she told Helen Rose I was the cat's pajamas, socks, and nightcap."

"Well, you are, and it's about time everybody important knows it!" I'm so happy for Delmarr. He belongs in Hollywood, where glamour and elegance still matter.

"She asked if I had any talented staff I'd like to bring along, and I told her all about you."

"You did?"

"Absolutely. Come with me, Lucia. You'll go right on staff, making a salary."

"Are you serious?"

"Yep. Pack your bags, kid. We're going to California. If ever there were two New Yorkers who needed a fresh start, it's us. There's one thing, though. I want your personal guarantee that when I tell you to drop a guy, you'll drop him *pronto*. That's Italian for fast, you know."

"I'll do whatever you say." I throw my arms around Delmarr's neck. "Thank you, thank you!"

"One more thing. I'm thirty-six, if anyone asks. We're going to the land of youth and beauty, and forty isn't a number anyone wants to hear. It's like the failing grade that puts you out of school. Forty and you're out."

"No problem. But Delmarr . . ."

"What?"

"I thought you were thirty-four."

"Even better."

"Who's gonna take care of Ma?" Roberto whines.

"I can take care of myself!" Mama counters. "I'm not some old lady."

"You're not old, but you are a lady. And there are some things that a mother needs her daughter around for, okay?" Roberto smacks the table lightly with his fist, just like Papa used to do.

The change in Roberto since Papa's death is noticeable. Though he's assumed the unelected position of patriarch, life was so much easier when Papa was the leader. Despite Papa's being from the old country, he had a progressive way of looking at things. Roberto acts like God has personally selected him to keep traditional family roles, established in medieval Italy, thriving and intact in America. I'm sorry that I announced my job opportunity to the family during Sunday dinner. I should have known better.

"I think Lu should go," Rosemary says as baby Antonio, wrapped in a soft blue blanket, sucks on the tip of her pinky. "You boys might not know this, but she's very talented. She doesn't take in mending or make curtains. She's an artist in a custom shop."

"We know where's she gone every Monday through Friday for the last eight years, Ro," Roberto tells her.

"Hollywood is so far away," Orlando says sadly.

"There's always the *Super Chief*, the fastest train in America, and it runs both ways," I remind him.

"Last fall was horrible. We don't want anybody to hurt you ever again. Okay?" Roberto says as he tears off a piece of bread. "You're too good, Lu. It's always been your problem. You get sucked in by bad elements. It's not your fault. But it happens, and we gotta stop it."

"I'm getting older. If I'm going to make a new start, I need to do it *now*." I wish I could explain to my family what it's been like since John Talbot left me. The changes are subtle, but I feel them deeply. I used to be pursued by young men from good families, but no more. The kind of suitors who have approached me lately aren't men my family or I ever would have considered. The other morning, when I passed the school yard on my way to the Groceria, the young men didn't even call my name. When I smiled, they didn't acknowledge me. I need to go somewhere I can begin anew.

"We'd like it if you'd find a nice guy in the neighborhood and start a home. Now, if you don't find a nice guy, we love having you here. You're a big help to Mama and Ro and the new baby." Roberto beams with paternal pride.

I'm grateful when Mama changes the subject. Roberto may believe that he has the final say over my life, but he doesn't. I'm a modern woman, and I'm going to do what I want to do. I haven't worked this hard for so long to stay home and be the maiden aunt to my nieces and nephews, no matter how much I love them. It's time for me think about how *I* want to live, and if giving up my glorious room and life in New York City is part of the package, then that's how it must be.

After dinner I help Rosemary wash the dishes and put them away.

"Thanks for speaking up at dinner," I say.

"Listen, Lu, there's enough help around here. I know you feel a duty to your mother, but this is the good thing about being in a big family: many hands make light work."

I laugh. "I noticed that. Since you moved in, taking care of the house has been so much easier."

"I love it here."

"You don't miss Brooklyn?" I ask, wondering if I'll be homesick in Hollywood.

"Only the Promenade. There's something about water. I used to walk along the river every night after dinner. It's very soothing."

I never got to show Rosemary the spot that would have been my home on the water, but I remember the feeling of peace I'd have whenever I looked out on Huntington Bay. "I wonder if I'll like the Pacific Ocean."

Mama yells, "Telephone for you, Lucia!"

I dry my hands and go into the living room to take the phone from Mama. "Hello?"

"Lucia, it's Dante." I haven't seen him since Papa's funeral. We didn't get to talk much, but once again, when we needed them, the DeMartinos were there. My heart melts a little at the sound of his voice.

"Dante, how are you?" I ask warmly.

"I'm fine. How have you been?"

"We're muddling through around here. It's not the same without Papa. Thank you again for the beautiful flowers you sent to the funeral home. And to your whole family for coming to be with us."

"I'd do anything for you, you know that."

"I know." I've been asking myself since November why I couldn't be content with a nice fellow who loved me. Why did I have to go for heat and danger, the slick John Talbot? What was I thinking, going above Fourteenth Street for love?

"Would you like to go out for dinner on Saturday?" he asks. His voice breaks, exactly like it did the very first time he asked me out on a date.

"I'd love to," I tell him.

The last gown we build in the Custom Shop is Violet Peters's lace fantasia wedding gown, rows of lace and ruffles over a full skirt with a bodice of illusion netting and long sleeves that come to a point. The gown is too silly for Delmarr's taste, but he designs it to please Violet, who's ecstatic when she sees the final result. It's appropriate for a girl who will recess out of the church under the honor guard of the New York City Police Department, their swords forming a silver canopy in the air.

I have to say, I can't wait to get to California and make movie costumes. I'm tired of wedding gowns and all that comes with them. If I ever marry, I'll wear a suit, like they did in my mother's day. The world has gone too crazy for big weddings. Maybe it's still the postwar glow, a glorification of true love and men coming home to devoted women, but enough is enough.

Ruth, Helen, and I throw Violet a bridal shower at the Plaza Hotel, just the four of us over high tea. The place is posh, with its flower arrangements of long-stemmed roses and pink lilies spilling over their tall pedestals like fountains. Everything comes to the table on polished silver, cookies and tea sandwiches served on a three-tiered tray by a waiter wearing white gloves.

Violet cries when she opens the three-piece leather luggage set we bought her and finds her new initials embossed in gold on the handles: v.p.c. "I'm gonna be Wallis Simpson on my honeymoon!"

"And then there was one!" I toast myself with champagne and say loudly, "What's to become of the old maid?" I'm feeling a little tipsy.

"Come on, you've got plenty of time," Ruth says kindly.

"Girls, let's face it. I'm a very poor planner. I chose a career that's becoming obsolete and a man who, last time I heard, was in jail. And now I've agreed to go out on a date with my ex-fiancé."

"The closing of the Custom Shop is not your fault," Ruth begins.

"And how could you have known that John Talbot was a con artist?" Violet adds.

"Grab Dante DeMartino. We all loved him, and you should get it over with and marry the man," Helen says.

"I want to go to Hollywood more than I want a husband," I announce with such conviction that the ladies at the next table look at me.

The girls stare at me. I realize too late how rude I've been. Three career girls making jobs of being wives don't need to hear about my big plans in movie land. What do they care about palm trees, convertibles, and sunsets on the beach, and worse, enjoying all these things alone? But it's clear to me: I'm the left shoe, the oddball, the sideshow. I want to work like a man. No one puts it that way, but that's the truth. That's my dream. When I look back on all I've been through, my working life is the one thing that has never let me down.

None of the fancy things I have been given in my life, from Papa's gift of a coral necklace on my sixteenth birthday to John Talbot's mink coat, meant nearly as much to me as the things I bought myself with the $48.50 a week I made at B. Altman & Company. There isn't a man who can come along and buy me anything that I cannot earn myself. "Never let the man know that," Mama used to say to me, but the lesson didn't take. I've spent wisely and never splurged. I remember the radio, the hair dryer with the deluxe bonnet, and the canopy bed from Interior Decoration that I bought with my own money. I calculated how many hours I had to work against the value of the purchase. I could practically tell you how many stitches I'd need to sew to walk out of B. Altman's with whatever item my heart desired.

My biggest problem with the opposite sex is that I know how to be happy on my own. It's in my nature to make the best of a bad situation. Even now, with the department closing, there are opportunities to pursue for a worker of my caliber and experience. I may have to travel across the country to seize an opportunity, but still, it's mine for the taking.

"Who says everybody has to get married?" Ruth says.

Violet takes a bite of her cookie. "It's the building block of society."

"Well, you girls may have to be the blocks," I tell them.

"You don't sound sad about it." Violet looks sad enough for all of us.

"I'm not," I say.

"Violet, Lucia has her happiness coming. In fact, she's owed it," Ruth says to me, and smiles. How I will miss her when I move to California. Her friendship has shaped me, made me feel safe, and given me a confidante I could laugh with. I am so lucky that I met her when I most needed a partner. "I hope you're never sad again," she tells me. "You've had enough of that for a lifetime."

It's that funny time of year in New York City, the week in September when it's neither hot nor cold, and there's a mugginess in the air that ruins the best hairstyles. I leave the curlers in an extra hour to keep the humidity at bay. Dante has invited me to the San Gennaro Festival. I haven't seen him in a couple of months, and I'm looking forward to catching up with him.

Dante picks me up promptly at seven (men who are late have never been my problem). He whistles when I come down the stairs. "Do I have a date with Ava Gardner?" he asks.

"I'm her stand-in," I say.

Little does Dante know, I copied this outfit right out of *Photoplay* magazine. Ava Gardner, during one of her brawls with Frank Sinatra, was wearing black capri pants, a white blouse, and a wide waist-cinching red belt with matching flat sandals. I copied it down to the smallest detail, including the delicate gold hoop earrings, nestled against her dark hair.

Commerce Street is jammed with cars, every parking spot taken, which is rare. The festival brings families from all the boroughs, and even though we're twenty blocks from Little Italy, cars have overflowed into the Village. As we walk over, Dante doesn't take my hand, but he guides me when we cross the street by placing his hand on the small of my back.

"How's work at the bakery?" I ask.

"Good. Papa's cranky, but he's always cranky. And Mama's taking care of the house, as usual."

I look at Dante and envision how close I came to living with his family on First Avenue and East Third Street, with bleached white diapers hanging on the line in the backyard and his mother making homemade pasta on the farm table in the kitchen. For one moment I reconsider what life with Dante DeMartino might have been. He's handsome, and so mannerly and sweet. He has deep roots, like mine, and Papa thought we were a good match. Dante is not a shallow man who flits through the world having a good time at the expense of others. Ruth would call him the genuine article. As we walk through the crowd, men tip their hats to him, and women smile and ask about his family. John Talbot might have elbowed his way into society, but Dante has a common touch. I wonder why I never appreciated it before.

As we walk under the glittery white arches over Mulberry Street, I wonder how I can bear to leave Greenwich Village. It has been my home all of my life. I know my people well, and they know me. For every gentleman who tips his hat to Dante, there's one who throws me a kiss. We're not only welcome here but celebrated. Will the Hollywood movie stars treat me with this kind of affection and respect? This is where I belong, in the heart of Little Italy with people just like me. All around us window boxes are stuffed with small red, white, and green Italian flags, and I wonder if I'll ever see anything like this again. Will it be enough to stick flags in the urns outside my Hollywood bungalow?

This morning I ate only a banana for breakfast because I want a sausage and pepper sandwich and then a sack of zeppoles, fried dough rolled in sugar, which I am not sharing. Dante waits in line for our sandwiches while I watch the Italian men from Faicco's flip the sausage on the grill and shovel the steaming peppers and glistening onions onto the soft white bread and into a waxed-paper sleeve. Papa and I would eat these sandwiches every year at the festival, and holding on to this tradition makes me feel like he's still with me.

After we've covered every inch of the festival, I watch as Dante gambles at the roulette wheel, which unfortunately reminds me of Ruth's story about John Talbot losing a bundle at the track. With each spin of the wheel, I recall more clues that should have steered me away from John. Why didn't I listen to my father? Poor Papa, who gave in to the idea of John Talbot so he wouldn't lose me altogether.

What a silly girl I was. If Dante DeMartino loved me before, he'd really love the new Lucia Sartori, sadder but wiser. Dante quits the wheel after losing five dollars and buys me my sack of zeppoles before he runs out of cash. "Good thing I can walk you home," he says with a smile. "Because the cab fare went to San Gennaro Church." As we walk out of Little Italy and head back toward home, I suggest we sit on the post office steps and eat our zeppoles.

We sit quietly, watching people leave the festival, carrying balloons on strings and stuffed animals won at games. Then Dante brushes the powdered sugar off his hands and says, "Lu, there's something I want to tell you."

I sit with Dante, the drone of the crowd behind us, lights spilling out windows and down onto the street, and the taste of sugar on my lips reminds me of all the feasts I have gone to with him. Suddenly I want to lean over and kiss him. Instead, I sit back. "So, what do you want to tell me?"

"I'm getting married, Lucia." Dante stares down at his hands.

I'm glad he's not looking at me, because I need a moment to compose myself. Then I say warmly, trying to sound upbeat, "Oh, Dante, congratulations. Who is she?"

"Juliana Fabrizi."

"I don't think I know her. Is she from the neighborhood?"

"Yeah, they live near us on First Avenue. Her father has a deli on East Tenth Street."

"Oh. Well, maybe if I saw her, I'd know her."

"I don't think so. She didn't go to school with us or anything. She's younger."

"Younger?"

"She's eighteen."

"Eighteen." I whistle low in disbelief. I can't believe this day has come so soon—I am not the youngest girl on the dance floor anymore. Who would have thought that Dante DeMartino would be the man to point it out to me? "What's she like? I mean, besides the fact that she's eighteen," I say pleasantly.

"She's very easygoing. Pretty. Sweet."

"Does your mama like her?" I ask.

"Very much."

"Then she must be a great girl."

"You think so?" Dante still seeks my approval.

"You know, Juliana is very lucky. You're the best. They don't make 'em any better than you."

"That's exactly what I say about you. You have just one flaw."

"Only one? This I've got to hear." I put a big smile on my face, but what I want to do is cry. I liked it better when I controlled the situation, when I knew that Dante loved me, and no matter where I went or what I did, he was there in the bakery pining for me. He was my security as much as Papa was, a man who would love me and wait for me no matter what. But all of that has changed because he has fallen in love with someone new. "So, what is my one flaw?"

"You're not the marrying kind."

Dante looks at me at last, but he can't hold the gaze. He seems to be trying not to cry. I can't cry about the truth. If I did, the person I would betray is me. I stand and brush the sugar off my capris. I extend my hand to Dante, and he takes it and stands up. We look at each other.

"I'm sorry, Dante," I tell him. And I know that if I told him I wanted him, he would probably drop Juliana Fabrizi instantly and return to my arms. He's waiting for me to say the word, but I'm not going to. I will not hurt him again.

"I know you are," Dante says sadly. And on this, my last date with Dante DeMartino, he holds my hand all the way home.

Closing down the Custom Department should be a simple operation since we've been dismantling it since last February, but there's still a ton of paperwork to finish. The most difficult chore is the final inventory of the fabric supply room. Each remnant represents a memory of some dress we made, suit we built, or coat we tailored.

"Look, Lu. Nuns' wool!" Delmarr lifts the flat board over his head. "How do those girls live in this material? I wouldn't cover a car seat with it."

"They take a vow of poverty, you know. It wouldn't be the same if their habits were made of silk chamois."

"Here. You should have this." Delmarr brings me a yard of gold lamé.

"New Year's Eve!"

"You know, we did a lot of work in here. I'm surprised we still have fingers."

"Do you ever wonder what it will be like when we walk out those doors for the last time?" I point to the Hub's swinging doors, which have marked every coming and going for seven years.

"You don't have to worry about that."

"What do you mean?"

"They're taking the doors off tomorrow."

"Taking them off?"

"Oh, yes. They're reconfiguring the floor, so the doors are going, and then these walls, and soon the third floor will be one big open space full of racks and racks and racks of machine-made crap. Won't that be pretty?"

"Horrible."

"Lucia, observe this closely. This is the day elegance took a powder."

I look at Delmarr, expecting him to laugh, but he doesn't. Instead, he looks as though his heart is breaking.

I'm so happy that Mama has a new grandson to coo over on our first Christmas without Papa. Sometimes I see her cry, and then she pulls herself together and throws herself back into holiday preparation, but I know it's not easy for her. And it doesn't ease her mind to see me packing for California while she grieves.

Delmarr is astonished at our Christmas Eve feast and is moved (spiritually, I'm not sure, but definitely aesthetically) during Midnight Mass at Our Lady of Pompeii. "Do you realize all the things that have happened to you in this church?" he whispers. "And you still come back? I can't believe it!"

"It's called faith," I whisper back.

"It's called fear of hell," Delmarr says as he looks up at the stained-glass window behind the altar. "My own father, a dyed-in-the-wool agnostic, used to call any donation to the church fire insurance."

Mama nudges us to stop whispering. When I look at the poinsettia-covered altar and the pew markers, white carnations with red ribbons, I close my eyes and imagine how I must have looked on my wedding day. It's been a year, but it seems like a lifetime has passed; and then there are those moments so painful and raw it feels like yesterday. I have the same feeling about Papa's passing. Sometimes it feels like he's been gone for a long time, and other times I half expect him to pull up in the truck and yell from the street for Mama to come with him for ice cream.

Delmarr kisses me on the cheek after Mass and gives Mama a big hug. As he turns to cross Cornelia Street on his way home, he looks back and shouts, "Monday morning, six A.M., Grand Central Station. Connection to Chi-town. Then the *Super Chief* to Hollywood!"

I wave. "See you there!"

I have one week to finish my packing. It's the hats that are causing me agita. How many to take and where to put them. The California sun is bright, and I don't want it to ruin my New York complexion.

I'm in the basement doing my final load of laundry before leaving for California. I can't believe I'm feeling sentimental about this old May-tag, the ironing board, and the drying rack, but for so many years I was the Sartori family laundress, and I took my role very seriously. I hear a loud thump. At first I think it's the machine, but I realize the sound came from another room. I sprint into the next room, afraid the baby fell, but Antonio is napping quietly in his crib. I run upstairs to the kitchen and find Mama on the floor. She has collapsed, and there is a pool of blood next to her face from a gash in her forehead. I grab the phone and call for an ambulance. I get down on the floor next to Mama and try to listen for her heart. Soon the paramedics arrive and load her into the ambulance. I pray aloud to God, "Please don't take her."

Here we are again, I think as we wait for a report from the doctor at Saint Vincent's. The boys were bereft when Papa got sick, but this is even worse. This is Mama, and I don't think her sons can picture the world without her. Neither can I.

After a while the doctor comes out to talk to us.

"Is she all right?" Roberto asks him.

"Your mother had a small seizure. At first we assumed it was a stroke, but it's more like the precursor to a stroke. We're going to have to spend some time figuring out what happened to her, but hopefully we can prescribe some medication that will prevent any such episodes."

My brothers are silent and every bit as bewildered as I am. As she herself has pointed out, our mother is young. "How bad is it, Doctor?" I ask.

"We won't know anything for twenty-four hours. She's responding to stimuli, which is a positive sign. I'm sorry. We have to wait and see."

Angelo fights back tears. I gather my brothers in a circle and reassure them like Mama did with us when Papa got sick. "We're going to stick together, and we're going to wait and see what the tests tell us. And then we'll figure out what to do."

The boys stay in the hospital most of the afternoon, until I send them home. I remain by Mama's side. Sometimes I sit on the bed and wipe her face gently with a cool washcloth. When I cry, I try not to make any noise to wake her.

When the morning comes, my body feels like a bent wire. I slept sitting up in the chair and woke up whenever Mama moaned or a nurse came in. But I'm seized with panic when I open my eyes to find her bed empty. I run out into the hallway and grab the first nurse I see.

"My mother, Maria Sartori, where is she? Is she okay?"

The nurse answers in a soothing voice, "She's been taken down for tests."

"Thank you," I tell her. Please, God, don't let me lose my mother.

I go back to Mama's room to wait. As soon as my brothers arrive, the doctor gathers us together.

"I have hopeful news. It definitely wasn't a stroke. She's sustained some damage to her heart, but it's minimal. Basically, your mother has a rapid heartbeat, which has probably been there all of her life and which caused her to short-circuit. The blood supply to her brain was affected. Luckily, you found her almost immediately." Roberto puts his arm around me as if to thank me. "But she'll need physical therapy and a lot of help at home." The doctor leaves us, and we embrace one another, feeling relieved. We are very lucky.

Mama is able to communicate by suppertime. She speaks slowly, and sometimes she has to stop and search for a word, but she understands everything we're saying. She's hungry, and in our family that's always been a sign of good health. Rosemary sneaks a first-class dinner of spaghetti al burro and chopped greens into Saint Vincent's.

Roberto insists that I go home. The long, hot shower feels fantastic, but all my clothes are in suitcases, so I have to unpack to get dressed. I pull the stool from my vanity out onto the terrace, yank the long telephone cord out the door, and sit down to make a call. "Delmarr?"

"How's your mother?" Delmarr says with concern. "Rosemary called me."

"Mama almost had a stroke."

"Jesus. But Rosemary said she'd be okay."

"Eventually." And then I bite my lip, because I'm starting to cry. "I can't go to California."

"That's okay, honey, you can join up later. Helen Rose isn't going anywhere. She'll understand. I'll explain the circumstances."

"Could you?"

"Of course. She's a human being, not a cold cookie like Hilda Beast."

"Thank you." I wipe away my tears and exhale, knowing that Delmarr will always look out for me.

"No problem, honey. You take care of yourself. And Mama Sartori. I'll call you when I get there, and we'll make your plans then."

I hang up the phone. It was sweet of Delmarr to say we'd make our plans at a later date, but we both know the truth. I'm never going to California, I'm never going to work for Helen Rose, and I am never going to sew the costumes of the stars. I'm going to stay here at 45 Commerce Street and take care of my mother for as long as she needs me. When that duty is done, and I hope it won't be for many years, I'll think about my life and what I want. For now I am the daughter my parents raised, and I will put my family before anything and anybody else, including Delmarr, Helen Rose, and a glamorous life in Hollywood. I must find a way to be here, to take comfort in doing my duty. Zia Caterina's curse has real teeth. Yes, I am brokenhearted, but not by the loss of a man. It's the closing of the Custom Department that broke my heart, and the loss of quality, style, and service that went with it.

CHAPTER TWELVE

*L*ucia and Kit's tea party has lasted past suppertime and blended into evening seamlessly. The silvery afternoon rain clouds have gone and left behind a sky the color of indigo ink. I've been sitting here for hours, Kit thinks to herself, but what a story. She shivers. The rear apartments on 45 Commerce Street are evidently cooler because they aren't over the boiler. Kit looks over at Aunt Lu's mink coat and considers asking if she can try it on, just to warm up.

"Aunt Lu, if the Custom Department closed in the early fifties, what did you do at B. Altman's until 1989?"

"I took a position in Evening Wear. The hours worked well with taking care of Mama. Look at this." Lucia shows Kit a framed article from *New York* magazine featuring the B. Altman bridal shop. The headline reads, LUCIA SARTORI, MOTHER TO THE BRIDES. How ironic that a jilted bride-to-be became a mother of sorts to hundreds of New York girls seeking the perfect wedding gown.

"When did your mother pass away?"

"Not until my forty-seventh birthday."

"That's why you never made it to Hollywood?" Kit asks.

"No, I didn't."

Kit leans back in the chair and looks at the wall. "Aunt Lu . . . this wallpaper, it's the wallpaper you put up with Ruth, isn't it?"

"It's the very same." Lucia smiles.

"*This* was your room?" Lucia nods. Kit asks, "Where's the sewing alcove and the bay window?"

"I lost them when they divided the floor in half," Lucia says quietly.

"They chopped your room in half? That's criminal! Who did it?" Kit realizes she has raised her voice and takes a deep breath.

"My nephew Tony."

"Oh, that's rich. You mean to tell me that *my* Tony Sartori, Duct Tape Tony, is the sweet little baby who came after Maria Grace? He hacked your room in half?"

"He's the one. Each floor was divided, if it wasn't already, into two apartments. More rentals, more income, you see."

"What a sleazebag! I'm sorry, Lucia, but there's no excuse for such a thing."

"The worst part was that he did it as soon as my brother died. Roberto hadn't been gone a month before Tony took over the building and changed everything."

"Lucia, I don't mean to be rude, but shouldn't you own this building? If all your brothers are gone, how come you didn't end up with the building?"

Lucia shakes her head slowly. Clearly, this is something she's still struggling to understand. "When Papa died, he left everything to my mother. When Mama got sick, she turned everything over to Roberto. Roberto had four sons. He was very traditional, much more so than Papa, and he believed the family property should always remain in the hands of the men. That's how I got cut out. Of course, Roberto insisted his sons take care of me, and they believe they do take care of me. And I suppose this apartment would be expensive today. If I ever have a real problem with them, I pick up the phone and call Rosemary, and she straightens her boys out. It could be worse."

"But that's not fair! You took care of your mother! The family should have thanked you or repaid you somehow."

"Roberto didn't look at it that way. A daughter's duty in those days was always to her family."

"What about Rosemary?"

"She wasn't in the immediate family. And she's a woman, too. I don't believe my brother left anything to her—just the order that their children take excellent care of her. Besides, she had her own mother to look after."

Kit stands and paces, fuming at the injustice. "Did they cut you out of the sale of the Groceria, too?"

"I never worked there like my brothers, but when they sold it, they split the sale among themselves. That was fine, it was their company," Lucia says evenly.

"I think it's terrible! You're as much a Sartori as they are."

"You're of a different generation. These were the rules my generation followed. I don't like them, but I understand them. It all goes back to Italy and the way property is passed down in a family. It's not a good deal for the women, but that's the way it is."

"Well, it's a raw deal." As Kit sits down again, she notices the stacks of B. Altman's gift boxes. "Lucia, what's in all the boxes?"

"Dishes and things." Lucia pauses. "They're my wedding presents."

"Oh my God." Kit wonders how Lucia has lived with a daily reminder of John Talbot in her home all these years. "Why did you keep them?"

"The police kept them as evidence after they apprehended John. They convinced me to take them back. And then I tried to return them to my guests, but they wouldn't take them. Bad luck, they told me."

"So the Caterina curse, it was for real?" Kit shudders.

"Maybe I believed it, and that made it real. We'll never know." Lucia puts the empty teacups on the tray and stands. "I'm exhausted. Are you?"

"Totally."

"I hope I didn't bore you," Lucia says.

"*Bore* me? Are you kidding? It was riveting. Every morsel of it. Thank you."

"Come back another day, and we'll go through the boxes. There are some lovely things in there that I think you'd like. A hand-painted urn. Some crystal vases. Enameled teaspoons."

"Thank you, Lucia. I'd love that."

As Kit descends the stairs back to her own apartment, the deep compassion she feels for Lucia gives way to a hunger for the truth. She goes into her apartment with a plan. Although she would like to know what happened to Delmarr and Ruth and Violet and Helen, she has to find out what became of John Talbot. She stays up late into the night making a list of as many dates, places, and names as she can remember from Lucia's story. Perhaps tomorrow, before getting back to the play she is writing, she can make a trip down to the New York Department of Records.

John Talbot's aliases were all common names, so searching through the records of 1951 and 1952 brings up hundreds of documents. It would take Kit a lifetime to sift through them. She goes to the information desk in the outer office and waits in line.

Kit follows the research assistant back into the main library, where he makes copies of all the police records from the Greenwich Village and Upper East Side precincts. There are several pages with references to a John Talbot. Kit takes the voluminous material home to read.

A few phone calls, a long session on Google.com, and three reading sessions at Starbucks later, Kit has the John Talbot dossier.

Lucia Sartori's old flame is alive. The problem is, he's in prison again. After a twelve-year stint for various theft charges, he seemed to go straight. When he got out, he looked up his buddies who'd found him work before, including Patsy Marotta at the Vesuvio, who got him a job out on Long Island with a restaurant-supply company. Talbot stayed clean for a while, but about twenty years ago he slipped back into his old ways. He got involved in a stolen-car operation, shipping parts from Germany to the United States. Kit figures this most recent conviction will probably keep him in prison for the rest of his life.

Once Kit has uncovered all the facts, she knows that she must share them with Aunt Lu. She's pretty pleased with herself for the successful detective work and excited by the prospect of helping Aunt Lu find a resolution, but she's also dreading having to deliver such monumental—and potentially upsetting—news. In the end she decides that Lucia has been living with the aftermath of John Talbot for fifty years, and she deserves to see how he turned out.

The walls of propriety have come down after Lu and Kit's tea. Kit feels absolutely at ease charging up the stairs to the fifth floor and banging on Aunt Lu's door. "Lucia?" she calls out.

"How are you, Kit?" Lucia says, opening the door in her bathrobe. Lucia must also feel that their long afternoon has put them on familiar footing.

"I'm great, thanks. But busy. Really busy. Let's see. First I wanted to know if you'd like to go out to dinner with my friend Michael and me tonight. Just Chinese. At Ma Ma Buddha."

"I'd like that, dear. Thank you." Lucia beams.

"Okay, I'll come get you around seven." Kit turns to go.

"Kit? You said 'first.' "

"Oh, yeah, that means there's a second. I also wanted to mention that I've found John Talbot."

Aunt Lu looks at Kit. Then she steps back into her room and sits down in the nearest chair.

"Lucia, are you okay? Are you upset with me? I just had to know, and I wanted to share what I found, but if it makes you unhappy, I won't . . ."

Lucia doesn't answer.

"Lucia?" Kit says nervously.

At last Lucia breathes deeply and closes her eyes. "Where is he?" she says.

"Oh, Lucia. I'm so sorry. I didn't mean to—"

"Where is he?"

"He's in the slammer," Kit says honestly.

The way Kit says "slammer" makes Lucia smile. "Well, he always had a difficult time with the up-and-up."

"No kidding. I Googled him—I mean, I went online and found all sorts of articles about him. And I got some of his police records, too. He's at Sing Sing. The state prison in Ossining, right up the Hudson."

"Kit, I hope you won't be offended if I ask you to leave. I'd like to be alone. I need to think."

"Absolutely," Kit tells her. She pulls Lucia's door closed and goes down the stairs with a heavy heart. What possessed her to go digging in the graveyard of Lucia's lost loves? She should have known that Lucia was not the kind of woman who goes looking for closure. If she was, she would have looked for John Talbot herself.

As Kit is settling down with her laptop to try and make some headway on her play, there's a knock at the door. She is surprised to find Aunt Lu standing there, still in her bathrobe.

"Come on in." Kit ushers her in and closes the door, knowing that under normal circumstances Lucia would be far too proper and modest to wear her robe outside her own apartment. She's not herself, Kit thinks, and it's all my fault.

Lucia looks at Kit. "I want to see him. But I can't make the trip alone. Will you come with me?"

"Of course," Kit tells her. "I'll take care of all the arrangements, and we can go this weekend."

"This weekend?" Aunt Lu touches her hair.

"Yeah, Saturday is visitors' day. But we can leave around lunchtime, so you can get your hair done as usual." Kit knows Aunt Lu's Saturday rituals as well as her own. The smell of Aqua Net lingers in the hallway every weekend after Lucia's visit to Village Coiffures.

"That would be nice," Lucia tells Kit. "I would like to look my best."

Kit waits for Lucia in the vestibule before they leave to take the subway to the train. She looks at the old bench, imagining Lucia and

John Talbot saying good night. She looks at the panes of pink glass in the door, and she pictures young Lucia peering out, waiting for her date to arrive. Kit has never paid attention to the building in such detail before. She looks up at the ceiling and sees an ornate chandelier; studying it more closely, she sees that the multicolored crystals on it are glass fruit.

Lucia calls from the landing, "I'm coming, Kit."

"Take your time!" Kit calls out pleasantly. She continues to look around the vestibule with a new awareness until Lucia joins her.

"Lucia?" Kit points. "Is that your chandelier?"

"Yes, it is," she answers simply. "No sense storing that in a box. It's to be enjoyed." She shrugs.

The view from the train to Ossining is so tranquil that Kit isn't surprised when Lucia tells her that there was an entire movement in painting called the Hudson River School. It turns out that Lucia took courses in art at the New School for Social Research with the encouragement of Arabel Dresken. The clefts of the hills, the wide pewter-colored river, and the Victorian homes make Kit feel as though she's speeding through another era. She needs all the soothing visuals she can get. Her stomach is churning with the fear that Lucia and John Talbot's reunion will be a disaster.

"Why are *you* so jittery?" Lucia asks Kit.

"I'm scared to death that John Talbot will be a creep."

"He won't be a creep. He'll be what he always was, slick and confident and full of vinegar."

"How do you know?" Kit wonders.

"I'm an old girl, and I've been around a long time. There's one rule that applies to everyone, from the time they're born until they die. People don't change. Maybe slightly, but never deeply. We are what we are, I guess. And I'm glad about that, because I have a lot of things I want to ask John."

"I have more questions, too. But not for him. For you," Kit says, seizing an appropriate opening.

"Well, then. Ask me." Lucia sits up and smooths her skirt.

"What happened to the other girls at Altman's, like Helen Gannon?"

"Dear Helen. She had another son, Albert. And her husband did very well on Wall Street. They moved to Scarsdale. I used to take the train out to see her and spend the weekend with them. We still chat on the phone quite often."

"How about Violet?"

"Violet died two years ago. She was married to Officer Cassidy up until the end. He has since remarried," she says skeptically.

"Boy, that was fast."

"That's what we thought."

"Did they ever have kids?"

"No."

"And how about Ruth?"

"Ruth Kaspian Goldfarb," Lucia says tenderly. "She and Harvey moved to Florida. They have three girls, all of them quite accomplished. One teaches fashion design at FIT. I see Ruth once a year, when she comes up to celebrate Rosh Hashanah with her sister. And I still talk to her at least once a week."

"Oh . . . and Delmarr! What happened to him?"

"He made it big in Hollywood. He did costumes for television. All the big song-and-dance specials. Every time he was in New York, he would come to see me and say, 'Kid, when are you coming out west to make it big?' It wasn't meant to be. He never married, and he always had a grand time. He left a string of brokenhearted women coast to coast. I never knew anyone who refused to be pinned down like Delmarr. To the end he was a solitary man in a very social business. He died last year. I took his passing very hard."

"And how about your brothers?"

"You know about Roberto. Angelo became a brother in the Maryknoll order. Orlando married a nice Jewish girl, Rachel, and they had a daughter, Rafaella. And then my dear Exodus, he and Orsola had seven children, four girls and three boys, all of whom are still in Italy, doing well. I made many trips to the Veneto to stay with them. The kids loved it when Zia Lucia brought them Yankee baseball gloves and Hershey's chocolate. Sadly, the men in my family didn't have very long lifelines. None of the boys lived much past Papa's age."

"Aunt Lu, did you ever marry?"

"No. But there was a man in my life for a long time. He was already a widower when I met him, even though he was only in his forties. He and his wife never had any children. I wasn't the love of his life, and he wasn't mine, but we had a lovely, uncomplicated relationship. We did love each other in our own way. He was a wonderful companion."

As the train pulls into the station, Kit watches the wives and children of prisoners, dressed in their Sunday best, disembark and walk toward the visitors' entrance. The mood is surprisingly happy, even though the travelers are on their way into a depressing place.

Lucia pulls her compact out of her purse and goes over her face with a round powder puff, never lifting it off the surface but pressing the color against her skin. Then she freshens her lipstick. She offers Kit a mint, then puts one in her mouth. "How do I look?" she asks.

"Beautiful," Kit tells her. Lucia is wearing a black skirt and a white blouse with a long mint-green scarf. She wears her mink coat. Her hair is done.

"Let's see what John Talbot has to say for himself," Lucia says.

The women follow their fellow passengers down a sidewalk marked with bold arrows and the word VISITOR showing the way. Kit's nervousness returns tenfold. Horrible scenarios race through her mind. What if John Talbot is a lunatic? What if they get caught in a prison riot? What if something terrible happens to Aunt Lu and Kit has to explain it to Duct Tape Tony?

Kit and Lucia are patted down and put through metal detectors (not too different from going to a Knicks game at the Garden, Kit thinks). Unfortunately, a guard confiscates Lucia's tin of cookies. They are then asked to wait. After almost half an hour, they are shown into a large room filled with visitors and surrounded by guards.

"How will we know him?" Kit asks as they find a place to sit.

"I'll know him," Lucia says.

Metal doors extending from ceiling to floor swing open, bringing to mind the Trojan horse going through the castle gates in all those B-movies. As the metal scrapes the concrete, there is a low rumble followed by the entrance of a sea of prisoners in orange jumpsuits entering the vast meeting area. Lucia scans the crowd for a few moments.

"There he is." She points.

Kit sees a tall man with thick white hair standing near the doors, away from the rest of the men. "Wait here," she tells Lucia. She walks quickly through the crowd and approaches him. "Are you John Talbot?"

"Yes. Are you Miss Zanetti?"

"Yes, sir." Kit blushes. No one ever calls her Miss Zanetti, and she finds it a little bit provocative.

"Where is Miss Sartori?" His voice breaks. He clears his throat and leans on his cane.

"She's right over there." Kit motions over the crowd to Lucia. "I'll take you to her." She turns and begins to walk, then realizes she's moving too fast. She slows down and takes his arm. He walks fine on his own, but he's slow.

"I see her," John says.

Lucia stands. Kit can tell that Aunt Lu is trying not to reveal any emotion. As Lucia and John exchange greetings, she seems to warm up. John takes Lucia's hands into his own. They look at each other with the wise knowing only old lovers can share. For a moment the years seem to melt off them, almost as if a vapor has lifted off the present and left behind their youth, when men were gents and women were girls, and as the day grew longer, so did a lady's gloves. "Lucia, as beautiful as ever," John says grandly.

"Thank you, John."

"I'm going to leave you two to chat," Kit says.

"No, no, sit right there." Lucia points to a chair nearby. Kit slides down into it, embarrassed to be as eager to hear what John Talbot says as Lucia is. John helps Lucia into a chair and then takes a seat across from her. Lucia sits up straight, her spine like a steel rod, and John leans toward her, resting his hand on the top of his cane as they talk.

John asks, "How is your family?" While Lucia tells him, Kit can't help but smile. The last time he saw them, Roberto beat him up.

"Did you ever marry, Lucia?" John asks.

"No." She takes a deep breath. "Did you?"

"Four times," he answers. Lucia smiles as John puts his hand to his head as though he is pounding a message to his brain. "Twice to the same woman, but four total."

"Any children?" Lucia asks.

"No children." Kit notices that the look on Lucia's face is almost perplexed, as if she's trying to connect this old man to the dashing fiancé of her youth. He's probably thinking the same thing.

"John, I came to thank you," Lucia says, to John's obvious astonishment. "Back in 1979, you sent me a letter. It was a lovely letter, and you enclosed a check for seventy-five hundred dollars." John nods slowly. "I thought it was very brave of you to get in touch with me and honor your debt after all that time. I wanted to thank you in person for that."

"It disturbed me that I took your money. I know that's funny, isn't it, coming from a man whose current address is the state penitentiary." John laughs. "But I knew what that money meant to you. I always knew what I had done was terribly wrong. A good woman can make a man do the right thing. And in my lifetime, you were that woman."

Lucia bows her head. "Thank you," she says. They sit in silence, then Lucia looks up again. "John, we have a few things to clear up. I always wondered why you came to my house that Christmas. What did you come to tell me?"

John stares out the window while he considers her question. "It was simple, Lucia. I came to tell you that I loved you." He straightens the collar of his prison uniform. "I know you probably won't believe it, but I didn't set out to hurt you."

"Oh, John, you had me marked from the minute you saw me," Lucia says. "Didn't you?"

"Sure, in the beginning I thought you could help me. I suppose my initial thought was always about advancing myself in some way. But you were so lovely and accomplished that I really fell in love with you. That's how things got as complicated as they did. I'd never been in that boat before, believe me. I even tried to convince your father, who was dead set against me, to see the light. He offered me ten grand to leave, and I turned him down."

"My papa offered you money?" Lucia is stunned.

"He was surprised when I turned him down. But, see, I wanted to marry you. You wanted the same things I did. But then I had a bad run. The worst of my life."

"A bad run?" Lucia says the words slowly, apparently not quite sure what to make of a man who has dismissed the happiest year of her life as a bad run.

"See, one thing after another went wrong when I was with you. Everything I touched went south. Jim Laurel backed out of our Huntington deal. And Daniel Parker ruined me all over the Upper East Side. He got it in his head that my business wasn't legit. And your father was never going to trust me. I saw that he'd never make me a part of your family or allow me to help expand the Groceria. The last straw was Sylvia dying a week before our wedding. No matter what the police told you, Lucia, she was like a mother to me. She wanted me to have that money. I took good care of her. I deserved it. We deserved it. But that rotten daughter of hers took everything."

Lucia watches as John spins this fable, this strange version of the truth. Kit can tell that she'd like to stop him, but he has a certain look in his eye. He must have had a similar look in 1951, painting the dazzling picture of their future together. It's a manic look, one of daring and wild intent, but it's also the face of a salesman. John is so convincing, he is almost irresistible. But Kit sees that Lucia is right: John Talbot hasn't changed. He can justify every crime that landed him in this prison. The only thing he's guilty of, in his mind, was trying to better himself, to become an important businessman.

"To be perfectly honest, I was overwhelmed. And then there was you, and the wedding, and the life with your family, and I couldn't face it. I couldn't pretend for one more minute that I could pull off a traditional life with the mother-in-law and the father-in-law and the kids running all around. I needed a good streak, and it wasn't happening. It was as though I was cursed; I couldn't catch a break. So I took the coward's way out. I left."

Kit watches Lucia's eyes reveal the pain from so long ago. The excuses must seem weak, much like the character of the man she was to marry. Lucia holds up her hand to stop his story. "John. I've heard enough." He looks surprised. Evidently there aren't a lot of people who stop John Talbot in his tracks. "There's just one more thing I need to know." Lucia takes a deep breath. "The day before the wedding, when we drove out to Huntington to see the house, how on earth were you planning to get out of that? *There was no house.*"

John shakes his head slightly. "That was my one piece of good luck in a long while. You gave me an out, Lucia. I think you knew you gave me an out, too. You made it easy for me to walk away. If you'd pushed me to show you that house, I would have had to tell you the truth. But you gave me an extra twenty-four hours to figure out what I was going to do. And I couldn't see a solution, so I walked away."

Lucia thinks for a moment. "And to think I would have followed you to the ends of the earth."

John fishes in his uniform for cigarettes and offers one to Lucia, but she declines. "But you see, I didn't have to worry about you, Lucia. You didn't need me."

"What are you talking about?" Lucia leans forward in her chair.

"You had a life without me. You loved your job. You had a home. A family. You were an independent career girl. You were going to be just fine. Believe me, I've known women who need a man to take care of them. You can't leave those girls at the altar."

The din from the conversation in the room escalates. Since there isn't much time for the prisoners and their visitors, people talk loudly, as if what they're saying to one another will matter more. A loud and frightening buzzer goes off, signaling the end of visitation.

Lucia, John Talbot, and Kit rise to their feet. He whispers something in Lucia's ear, kisses each of her cheeks, and then lightly kisses her lips. He holds her, his eyes squeezed shut as if he's trying to see the picture in his memory more vividly. John goes back through the huge metal doors without turning back.

"Are you okay?" Kit asks.

"That was just fine," Lucia says softly.

As they join the herd going back to the train, Lucia stops to take in the view of the prison, set beside the Hudson River.

"What is it?" Kit asks.

"He told me that every night before he goes to sleep, he pictures me in a white cotton dress standing in a doorway. We're alone, and he takes my hand and says to me, 'Come out and see the ocean, Lucia. It's all I have to give you.' And you know what's funny about that?"

"What?"

"I'm seventy-eight years old, and I never did have a home near the water, but John does. He's in a cell with no window, but he's still on the water."

Kit helps Lucia into the window seat and takes the aisle. They ride in silence for a while, each thinking about the distinguished white-haired man, once the most dashing man at the spring cotillion at the Plaza Hotel in New York City. Kit turns to Lucia. "Do you regret anything? You know, with all that's happened to you, the turns of your life, do you wish things had been different?"

"You can't keep bad things from happening," Lucia says. "And the good things—I don't think you can take any credit for them. They're luck."

"So it's a no. No regrets," Kit says, leaning back in her seat.

"I don't regret anything that's happened to me, because somehow those things were meant to happen. The one thing I wish is that I had reacted differently to some of the events. I let things get me down and keep me there, sometimes for too long. And I believed I could some-how control the bad things, and that was a big mistake. Things turn around when they're meant to. You can't force it."

When they arrive back on Commerce Street, Lucia invites Kit up-stairs to her apartment. "It will only take a minute," she promises as she opens her door. "I want you to have something."

She crosses the room and comes back with a dress bag. Kit opens it and takes out the gold lamé dress Lucia wore at the Waldorf on New Year's Eve.

"Of all the things I ever wore, this was my favorite."

"Oh, Lucia," Kit says, and embraces her. "I will cherish this all my life." She holds the dress up against her body. "And if anything will keep me at my goal weight in this lifetime, it will be *this* dress."

After visiting John Talbot, Lucia and Kit fall back into their routines, with one difference: Kit now checks on Lucia frequently and takes her out to eat once a week. It's been a rough Monday. The cuts on Wall Street mean that the temp pool has been reduced by half, so Kit is doing the work of two people. No playwriting these days, only com-pany business. Kit climbs the stairs slowly. By the time she reaches her apartment, she has opened all of her mail.

There's a letter from the Cherry Lane Theatre. How ironic, Kit thinks, theaters soliciting poor playwrights for donations. Can things get any worse? She opens the letter anyway, because it might contain good news for some lucky playwright, word of upcoming productions and workshops. But as Kit reads the letter, she sees that they don't want money. And there's no mention of another playwright or an-other play. It's from the artistic director, Angelina Fiordellisi, and it's about Kit's play *Things Said While Dancing*. The artistic director loves the play and wants Kit to come and work on it at the Cherry Lane. She asks if Kit would be willing, and if she is, to please call her at her office at her earliest possible convenience.

Kit opens her door and tosses the rest of the mail onto her sofa, and without stopping even to take a sip of water, she shoots straight up the stairs and raps on Lucia's door urgently, knowing that this news will thrill her to bits.

"Lucia! It's me. Kit!"

"Coming," she hears from inside the apartment.

"Hurry, I've got good news!"

Lucia opens the door. She looks fabulous in a pink suit with a big brooch, an enameled yellow rose.

Kit says, "You look amazing! I have news. Finally, somebody in the American theater wants to work with me. The Cherry Lane wants to develop one of my plays!"

"That's fantastic!" Lucia beams, but she doesn't invite Kit into the apartment. In fact, she is barricading the door with her body.

"Sorry. Do you have company?"

"I do," Lucia says, trying to communicate with her eyes.

"Oh. Who?" Kit whispers. "A guy?" Lucia nods. "Oh, wow!"

"No, no, come in," Lucia says, and opens the door wide.

A suave older gentleman in a classic navy sportcoat and charcoal slacks is sitting on one of her chintz chairs. His gray hair is neatly combed, and his pencil thin moustache recalls another era.

"Kit, this is Mr. Dante DeMartino."

"Oh my God! I've heard all about you." As he rises to greet her, Kit notices that he's holding the picture of Lucia on New Year's Eve. "She was stunning, wasn't she?"

Dante looks directly at Lucia, and Kit can't help but compare this to the way John Talbot closed his eyes and seemed to prefer an image from memory. "As beautiful as she is in this photograph, she was even more so on the inside," Dante says. "Still is."

Kit decides to lighten the moment. "And you *do* look like Don Ameche. I have the DVD of *Midnight* downstairs."

"Besides my striking resemblance to Mr. Ameche, what else did Lucia tell you about me?"

"Just wonderful stories about what life was like when you were my age. What the Village was like. How you lived. She told me that you didn't have to carry a gun in your purse to the San Gennaro Festival, and girls wore gloves and men worked in the family business, and everybody was happy."

"She told you the truth, then." Dante smiles.

"At least for Italians, right? So, what are you two doing tonight?"

"I'm taking Lucia to dinner."

"A date?" Kit grins.

"I hope so." Dante winks at Lucia. The way he winks is sexy, Kit decides, and it's a small revelation to her. How could men her grandfather's age be sexy?

"Well, I'll leave you two alone," Kit says. "Have a wonderful time."

Lucia walks Kit to the door and steps out into the hallway with her. Kit gives her a silent thumbs-up.

"Congratulations on the play, Kit. I'm proud of you." Then Lucia lowers her voice. "And thank you. Dante has been widowed for three years, but I never had the guts to call him. The trip to Sing Sing put everything in the past, where it belongs. And I have you to thank for it."

Kit goes back down to her apartment and grabs a Diet Coke. She takes the letter from Miss Fiordellisi and reads it over until she has committed it to memory. She leaves an identical message for every one of her friends on speed dial, giving them the details. Then she sits in the window and looks at Commerce Street, leaning out to see the bright red barn doors of the Cherry Lane Theatre, a place she dreamed would produce one of her plays someday. Kit looks at her street, with its stoops and window boxes and beat-up trash cans, and remembers why she moved to New York. Her passion for storytelling brought her here; the desire to live the artist's life in a place that inspires it keeps her here. She takes a moment to be grateful and to remember that talent may be a gift, but persistence is its own reward.

She hears the downstairs door slam shut and leans out the window to see who's leaving the building. Lately, she has a little bet with herself about Tony Sartori's bald spot, which from the fourth floor looks worse by the month. With his ego, she predicts a toupee by Christmas. But it isn't him.

Dante DeMartino and Lucia Sartori walk down Commerce Street hand in hand, on their way to dinner. When the sidewalk narrows, he puts his hand on the small of her back to guide her. She turns to him and smiles. Another couple, around Kit's age, comes around the corner. Once they have passed Dante and Lucia, the young woman nudges her boyfriend as if to say, See, that could be us someday. Kit wants to shout out her window, Only if you're lucky! That's not just any single girl out on a date, that's the most beautiful woman in Greenwich Village. And someday I'm going to write a play about her.

ACKNOWLEDGMENTS

How lucky I am to have been born one of the seven Trigiani kids! I have learned so much from my sisters and brothers, each one a magnificent person, each of whom I would be proud to call my friend if we were not related. Each one has given me a particular gift by their example, and it is a wonderful thing to finally be able to thank them; so, my gratitude to Mary Yolanda for your elegance, Lucia Anna "Pia" for your compassion, Antonia "Toni" for your strength, Michael for your humor and artistry, Carlo for your tenacity, and Francesca for your joy. I will be grateful to you all forever for your loyalty and big hearts.

    At Random House, I thank my editor, the brilliant Lee Boudreaux; Todd Doughty, whose professionalism and good nature inspires me; Laura Ford, Anna McDonald, Vicki Wong, Dan Rembert, Beth Thomas, Allison Saltzman, Libby McGuire, Janet Cook, Tom Nevins, Allyson Pearl, Carol Schneider, Tom Perry, Sherry Huber, Ed Brazos, Eileen Becker, Ivan Held, Steve Wallace, Stacy Rockwood-Chen, Maureen O'Neal, Allison Heilborn, Kim Hovey, Allison Dickens, Candice Chaplin, Cindy Murray, and Beth Pearson. Gina Centrello, thank you for your support, energy, and Italian moxie.

    To Suzanne Gluck, the best agent on earth and an even better friend, my love and gratitude. More of the same to WMA's brilliant beauties, Emily Nurkin, Karen Gerwin, Jennifer Rudolph Walsh, Tracy Fisher, Alicia Gordon, and Cara Stein. At ICM, more still to my champion, the great Nancy Josephson, and the fabulous Jill Holwager. In movieland, thank you Lou Pitt, Jim Powers, Todd Steiner, and Michael Pitt.

I don't know what I would do without the amazing Lorie Stoopack, who works hard and makes it fun; and the astute "Manuscript book club," Mary Trigiani, Jean Morrissey, and Mary Testa. I would be lost without you.

For their sparkling and vivid memories of Manhattan in 1950, thank you Helen McNeill, Ralph Stampone, and June Lawton. To the librarians of the New York Public Library system, thank you for your guidance. The recipes are from the files of my late friend and beloved grandmother Viola Trigiani. My grandmother Lucia Bonicelli, a craftsman in sewing and design, inspired the fashions throughout the story. To B. Atman expert David Manning, director of media relations for the Graduate Center, City University of New York, thank you for your excellent research. To gorgeous Elena Nachmanoff and Dianne Festa, I am devoted to you and Saul and Stewart for life.

Thank you with heaps of love to: Nancy Bolmeier Fisher, Kate Crowley, Eydie Collins, Elaine Martinelli, Elizabeth Dawson, Tom Dyja, Ruth Pomerance, Pam McCarthy, Nigel Stoneman, Ian Chapman, Suzanne Baboneau, Carmen Elena Carrion, Melissa Weatherhill, Rosanne Cash, Charles Randolph Wright, Bill Persky, Joanna Patton, Larry Sanitsky, Debra McGuire, John Melfi, Father Tony Rodrigues, Grace Naughton, Dee Emmerson, Gina Casella, Sharon Hall, Constance Marks, James Miller, Wendy Luck, Sharon Watroba Burns, Nancy Ringham, John Searles, Helen and Bill Testa, Cynthia Rutledge Olson, Jasmine Guy, Jim Horvath, Craig Fissé, Kate Benton, Jim Doughan, Ann Godoff, Joanne Curley Kerner, Max Westler, Dana and Richard Kirshenbaum, Sister Jean Klene, Daphne and Tim Reid, Caroline Rhea, Kathleen Maccio Holman, Rosemary and Anthony Casciole, Susan and Sam Franzeskos, Jake Morrissey, Beáta and Steven Baker, Eleanor Jones, Brownie and Connie Polly, Aaron Hill and

Susan Fales-Hill, Karol Jackowski, Christina Avis Krauss and Sonny Grosso, Susan Paolercio, Greg Cantrell, Rachel and Vito Desario, Mary Murphy, and Matt Williams and Angelina Fiordellisi.

Michael Patrick King, I adore you. If there is an afterlife, I hope I live downstairs from you there too.

To the Trigiani and Stephenson families, our Italian relatives, the Spada, Maj, and Bonicellis, thank you. To Ida Trigiani, the best mother on earth, my love always. To the people of Big Stone Gap, Virginia, my everlasting gratitude. To the great Jim Burns, please keep an eye on us from heaven. To my dear papa, Anthony, I miss you as much as I loved you, which is immeasurable.

And to my husband, Tim Stephenson, who puts up with more agita than ten men, your character and goodness still thrill me. As you lead me by the hand through parenthood, I am glad it is you who chose me. Thank you for our baby girl, who is lucky to have such a splendid papa.

ABOUT THE AUTHOR

ADRIANA TRIGIANI grew up in Virginia and now lives in New York City with her husband and daughter. She is an award-winning playwright, television writer, and documentary filmmaker. Trigiani is the author of the bestselling novels *Big Stone Gap, Big Cherry Holler,* and *Milk Glass Moon,* and has written the screenplay for the movie *Big Stone Gap,* which she will also direct.